I0731205

NEW WORLD ORDER

BOOK ONE

LOST AGE PRODUCTIONS

New World Order
Book One

Copyright © 2020 by Lost Age Productions.

Edited By David Seaman

https://www.ebonfall.com/

Paperback ISBN: 978-1-952982-03-3
Ebook ISBN: 978-1-952982-04-0

Published by Green Sage Agency   07/10/2020

Green Sage Agency
1-888-366-9989
inquiry@greensageagency.com

TABLE OF CONTENTS

CHAPTER

1

"Activate stealth mode," commanded the dark-haired Tristan Hart, Pilot of the Otis 52, the latest gunship model designed by Institute VI, an elite mercenary fighting unit.

Erik Gabrio, his co-pilot, nudged several black-tabbed levers. The yellow indicator lamps above them flickered and changed to a pulsating, sparkling green.

Tristan leveled his gaze through a forward row of six narrow, glass portals, awaiting the shimmering glow of the stealth transformation. "Now wouldn't be the time for the USC to dole out the usual delays," he muttered. The corners of his lips turned up slightly when a dull, pinkish glimmer reflected into the cockpit, signaling that stealth mode had been acquired.

"Hang on. We'll know shortly if those idiots can think of anyone but themselves," retorted Erik.

The Otis 52 settled slightly in its descent into Gaustead, Vuton's northernmost port city. Dawn had not yet broken, and with the powerful sleek craft now rigged to run silently, they descended in relative safety. The Otis 52 airship had already earned a sterling reputation from its' first three beta flights, successfully destroying much larger Federation warships.

As the Atomian Embassy Building came into view, Tristan adjusted the controls and reduced the forward momentum to an appropriate glide speed. He distinguished the Federation's embassy from the clutter of other similar buildings by its' imposing rooftop gun turret, an ominous sight by any soldier's standard. Its' overreaching barrel loomed in the twilight. Rooftop activity was nonexistent—no men, no lights, no movement; the weapon's warning system, with a life of its' own, continually scanned for any possibility of attack—it hummed quietly, flashing only a bright blue indicator lamp.

Tristan bent his will to quell a chill of sweat forming on his brow. It almost worked. While he scanned the skyline, a brilliantly-lit kaleidoscope of red, green and yellow beacons, streaming from buildings with rounded walls, climbed skyward. Below, flashy vehicles glittered along corridor slots that comprised an endless maze of roads, bridges, and heavily fortified edifices. More gun turrets protruded atop many of the buildings, but none as substantial as the one defending the embassy. Gaustead was a heavily armed city.

Erik poured over a schematic of the embassy's interior, having been supplied with their mission directives before departing Institute VI. Tristan had worked with him for several years and considered him a trusted partner. Erik was known for his cockiness, an attitude that bespoke a fearless demeanor. He wore his short, blond hair tightly slicked back, appearing more renegade than he was. Erik's suave appearance hid the fact that he could fight, and that he could be relied on to cover Tristan's back.

Institute VI had trained him well. The organization had hired Tristan nearly five years prior and was comfortable allowing him to select his team amidst background checks and compatibility validations for each recommendation. Tristan kept the organization updated regarding Federation dealings in Eshen and various other countries. His past employers had lower hiring standards, but supposedly this was far more critical than any previous mission. The urgency convinced Tristan to volunteer his piloting skills and again risk his life. He craved adventure, and this mission was extremely appealing. Erik wasn't as passionate about adventure, more concerned with less substantive rewards, like promotions and renown. In the past, neither had placed much emphasis on their employers. They enjoyed their work along with the associated perks.

"Looks like they disabled the turrets. Not bad," claimed Tristan, brushing his unkempt hair away, still exercising extreme caution as he brought the craft around, knowing full well that an arming mechanism could engage in an instant and knock them out of the sky.

Erik replied nervously as he leaned forward to catch a glimpse of the enormous rooftop cannon. "Just land the damn ship. Our USC people should be waiting for us on the roof."

The dark gray barrel took on a more menacing appearance as the Marne approached. Tristan steadily dropped altitude, sliding in over a landing port adjacent the gun's swivel housing. Throttling back, it settled onto the landing pad. As the ship transferred its' weight from the wings to the landing gear, he reflected on his dislike for missions that knowingly pitted him and his team against Atomia. The Federation's technology was superior to theirs, and Federation soldiers were better outfitted than United Separatist Coalition soldiers. Keyed by the thought, he hastily ran through the shutdown checklist, only calming after the steady whine of the twin turbines finished their spin-down. A flashing red light—the intrusion alert sensor on the instrument panel—was activated by movement on the outer deck. He expected company and wasn't overly concerned, but still glanced out the side ports. Their entrance and exit strategy had been completely prepared, and Tristan expected them to execute without incident—they usually did. Nothing could be allowed to alter their primary objective: to destroy the building on which they had just landed.

Tristan, the first to disembark, zipped his waist-length, black jacket partway and quickly covered the short distance to the aft door. His clothing had been stitched with unique fibers to provide a reasonable degree of protection from flying projectiles, Droth rounds included. He guided his bladed Droth 4.5 from its' sheath along his thigh and gave it a quick flip. *Droth* was the manufacturer that created this hi-tech marvel. The weapon hummed, and its' jagged, multi-purpose blade extended. Above and below the barrel, two smaller blades clicked into place. He visually interrogated the action with dark, scrutinizing eyes and pressed a small button. The blades quickly retracted, transforming the Droth into a formidable, hand-held weapon. Many nicknamed the 4.5 the "hand cannon"; its' penetrating power was akin to shoulder mounted guns two or three times its' size. Tristan felt comfortable with it strapped to his side, enjoying pride associated with carrying something provided only to Institute VI mercenaries.

Erik just finished his own bladed Droth inspection.

Alerted by boots shuffling on the metal grating, Tristan looked past the turret and identified the reason for the instrument panel alarm as a stout, burly soldier-type approached. His tan short sleeves, straining at the seams, had been shoved to the top of protruding triceps, allowing him the unrestrained freedom to wield two military-issue firearms. He shot several glances over his shoulder as he passed under the weighty turret barrel. "Your tardiness is intolerable. We have to make up for lost time!" Out of breath, the newcomer was clearly displeased.

Tristan, irritated by the unexpected drama, ignored the insinuations. "We're here now."

The bearded, dark-haired man waved one of his weapons toward the walkway. "Follow me! Security has been disabled, but there are still guards in the embassy!" He abruptly turned back toward a set of gaping blast doors.

"Amateurs," muttered Erik, peeved.

Tristan glanced one last time over his shoulder at the looming turret. Once more, he inspected his Droth, making sure it was securely strapped in its' holster, and then sprinted after the burly man.

He burst through the doors, skidding to a stop in front of another uniformed man with short, dark cropped hair, widow's peak, and a red-headed woman standing at his side. The woman showed her impatience while she tapped her fingers against her tightly crossed arms, eyeing Tristan suspiciously. She appeared formidable and especially critical due to a wrinkle across her brow. No matter; a woman, complete with petite, oval face and full lips, was a pleasant change.

She ran her hand along the barrel of her older model Droth and let it fall back to her side. "Don't pin your hopes on those two, Hardie," she said, sounding frustrated. "Don't forget that they're mercenaries. They could very well be fighting us next time we meet them, unless the Federation has already paid you off, too?"

Hardie frowned. "Hold it, Voleta. No need to be looking over our shoulders now. We have too many other things to worry about!" He scowled as he greeted Tristan. "Didn't catch your names?" His slow drawl spilled out defiantly.

Tristan's initial perception was that Voleta was an angry person, sounding nastier than she appeared. "Tristan Hart," he replied. "And he's Erik Gabrio." Growing anxious to commence the mission, he kept his eyes on her and cut short the awkward introductions.

"Tristan, eh?" said Hardie boorishly. "Pleased to meet you. I'm . . ."

"We don't give a damn who you are," scowled Erik. "After this job's over, you won't see us again."

The dark-haired, burly man behind Hardie and Voleta checked the magazine in his pistols and began laying out the mission objectives. "Our target is the zyn repository beneath this embassy building. Voleta . . ." he said, pointing to the red-headed woman, ". . . will open these blast doors and escort us down to the basement. She'll return here and ensure an uncluttered escape route. Oh, in case you weren't briefed, we intend to hitch a ride with you before we blow this place."

"That wasn't our agreement," snapped Erik, his tone rife with hostility.

"You're damn right it wasn't. But if we get croaked, you don't get paid. So, the way I see it, you don't have a choice."

Metal support rollers beneath the heavy door panels strained noisily, a blast of compressed air released and the double doors slid closed. "We're ready to go!" declared Voleta.

Tristan shrugged and turned to the burly man. "We won't leave you behind, but this should have been arranged through the USC." Vuton's Unified Separatist Coalition, USC for short, had offered him jobs on three different occasions, but he turned them down. Contending against Federation troops was self-elected suicide, something he had no desire for.

The burly man released a smug half grin and turned toward the hallway, his tight waist shifting his muscular frame with ease, halting momentarily to allow Hardie the lead. While waiting, he turned back. "Don't trust either of ya! I'm Cole Asbury, Mr. Edde's right-hand man and I'm in charge of this operation. In case you didn't know, Mr. Edde is acting director of the USC. So, I suggest you follow my lead, or I'll make sure your asses are blown up along with this worthless hunk of concrete, metal and zyn!"

Tristan shrugged complacently and followed Erik, Cole and Hardie down a long hallway fitted with dim light bulbs along the ceiling. The group double-timed it down the length of the corridor, the squeaking leather of their boots echoing off the walls, emptying into the central commons area of the embassy. Tristan eyed another elevator on the far wall guarded by a thin man with short, red hair, and a wispy mustache. His upper teeth protruded, outfitting him with a permanent grin.

Once across the empty lobby, Cole whispered. "Lance! Is everything ready? Did you override the system?"

"Yes, sir," replied Lance. "I hacked into their internal security network and, just as planned, the 5th-floor alarms were de-activated. Science Department's on that floor, along with most of the building's guards. Androids are controlled by a pretty tight program though; it's buried in a secure server somewhere, and I'm still hunting it down. I'm doing my best; but be ready to take them down if I can't kill their controller."

Tristan's last encounter with Federation androids was a miserable experience; one he didn't care to repeat. He had underestimated their stealth and nearly got snuffed; but that shouldn't happen again. Disabling the AC was vital; androids were formidable and unpredictable, and their outer shielding was difficult to penetrate. Those reasons alone prompted Institute VI to procure such expensive weaponry—close range; non-human attacks were on the rise across Vuton. Their presence was yet another indication of the Federation's technical talons.

"We'll take care of the androids! Just keep those guards sequestered on five! Secure all the factory doors once we reach the basement! Give Voleta access to return to the roof. I'll contact you when the bomb is set and cue you for egress," commanded Cole, gripping both raised firearms.

Lance smartly replied. "Yes, sir! The elevator is cleared and ready to transport you to the zyn repository."

The mission rationale dawned on Tristan. "So that's the reason? . . . I should have known zyn was at the heart of this." Disgusted, he glanced around at the crew, wondering their take on his most recent realization. This was about as useless an excuse for a mission as he had seen, yet it was too late to back out.

"You got a problem with that?" snapped Cole.

"Should I?" questioned Tristan. "The mission—destruction of a zyn repository—the fuel powering our cities and even our gunship. Don't you find that rather paradoxical?"

". . . Ironic that you're about to blow this place to oblivion" confronted Cole, ". . . All too willing to turn around to do the Federation's dirty work! That's the lowest of the lows, switching sides like that!"

Erik grasped his Droth. "Can we please dispense with the preaching and concentrate on the mission?"

Air hissed as the elevator doors slid open.

Cole scowled and hastily stepped out.

"I can't wait to blow this place into the great black void. It'll be an unforgettable experience! Best of luck to you!" said Lance, eyeing Tristan and stepping away from closing elevator doors.

Tristan, Erik, Hardie and Cole were confined to the plunging room; it lurched as it launched into a near-freefall, giving Tristan a sickening rush in the pit of his stomach. It was one of the fastest elevators he'd ever been in. The first view of the expansive repository came less than a minute later, filled with noisy machinery clanking alongside labyrinths of far-reaching ladders, scaffolds, and swaying walkways. The schematics that Cole had been provided didn't delve nearly as deeply as they should have.

No sooner had they stepped onto the grated metal floor did a loud whir of gears from adjacent walls begin, parting and exposing lifeless androids neatly nestled within. They snapped to life in a blaze of flashing red indicator lights on their handheld guns, their stoic pale-gray faces, and their armored chests. Block feet clunked out of hiding, stepped forward, and methodically advanced. Tristan and Erik crouched, scanned for cover, firing their Droths as they hustled. Hardie and Cole dove behind a waist-high metal partition and blasted into the foray of metallic men. The first android onslaught went down quickly; in unison, five heads rotated upward and then fell forward as their collapsing metallic bodies spewed fountains of sparks. Behind them, more androids kicked against the fallen machines' useless remains, teetering as they ascended the blockade. Several side doors hissed, introducing another surge of robots.

"Hardie! We'll hold them off while you open the main repository door! *Go!*" shouted Cole.

Hardie leaped over the wall and crouched under a long, narrow shelf containing several keyboards. He yanked one down while eyeing a nearby monitor and began pounding away.

Erik reloaded his weapon and unleashed rapid triple bursts into the metallic assault. Two androids stumbled, teetered and collided with each other.

Cole shouted across to Tristan. "When he gets that door open, you and I are going! No one else!"

"What?" exclaimed Tristan.

Cole replied, panting. "Your friend can stay with Hardie. Plus, someone needs to fire up your ship if you're gonna get us outta here in one piece!"

"You could have told us before!" Tristan was disturbed, not only because of the time constraints, but because Cole's decisions seemed so erratic. He was obviously making decisions on the fly, dangerous at best.

Cole turned ghostly white. "Sorry! Mr. Edde likes me to improvise. It keeps us safe."

Tristan didn't want to hear it, but needed to stay focused; the androids were struggling to rise above the clutter and were closing in. He fired; each triple round connected, halting several more androids. But more kept spilling out of the wall cavities. At this rate, they'd run out of ammo.

Erik shouted above the deafening din of attacking androids and bursts of fire. "Don't take too long."

Hardie formed a sly grin as he pounded his fist on a square, green switch. Beeping followed, and a hidden partition beside the console hissed open.

Cole shouted. "Hurry!" Fire flashed overhead from the closest android when Cole leaped through the opening. The android released a triple blast. Bullets streaked through the opening and nicked Cole's sleeve.

Tristan threw himself forward, pulling his legs in just before the wall slid shut. While the ringing in his ears slowly subsided, he steadied himself against the wall and rose to his feet, only to find himself standing on top of an enormous, rectangular structure between a double row of yellow and black stripes marking a walkway stretching out before him. It led to a rounded glass partition this side of a raised room protruding over an abyss of emptiness falling off below; his heart pounded when he glanced over the side and stared down nearly 50 stories. Until now, he had been unaware that he was afraid of heights; this view tore at his nerves like no other. A long set of narrow steps stretched downward, four or five floors, and then turned out of sight—he couldn't follow them after that.

After one look at Tristan, Cole began to laugh. "First time in a zyn repository?"

Tristan clung tightly to the railing; he was so caught up in the moment that he felt numb, overwhelmed by the sheer volume of machinery and dazzling technology surrounding him. "No. I've been in one before, just not this massive."

"Zyn is not the only reason we're wiping this place out," lectured Cole. His voice had a distinct tone of pride. "The embassy's presence represents Atomia's far-reaching efforts to gain Eshen influence. You're aware that Vuton is now Atomia's ally. Feria, Oxium and Amstye, in a feeble effort to present a unified front, have resisted, but they can't hold out forever. Zyn assures victory; whoever controls this stuff will rule others. Eshen relies heavily on zyn for military and civilian purposes alike. Without zyn, housing, business, and military infrastructures crumble."

"And you're accusing Atomia of having too much power?" queried Tristan contentiously.

"It's not that simple. At the current extraction rate, they're bleeding the planet dry! Our scientists have proven that there's only enough zyn within the planet's substructure to provide fuel for just over 100 years! Even though it's regenerating under the planet's crust, our latest research has determined that we're still running out. Why would one country be so compelled to control this natural resource, something that benefits all of humankind? Whatever the reason—it can't be good."

"Look. It's not my problem," replied Tristan. "You're welcome to continue this discussion with Mr. Edde."

"You boys from Institute VI are something else. I suppose that's why you're such good mercenaries. Could the Federation be harnessing all the resources for them only to strip power from every other nation? Where are you from, Amstye?"

Tristan hesitated. "Feria," he answered.

Cole shook his head. "Ultimately, Feria will suffer just like the rest! If the Federation achieves world domination, Feria will drop like a bag of dirt. What's wrong with you?" Cole's pitch turned higher when Tristan scoffed.

"Finishing the mission is the only thing that matters right now," said Tristan, pushing hair out of his eyes. "In fact, I'd reload if I were you. It's too quiet."

Cole checked over the side rail, poised to jump. "We're almost there." He leaped over the bright, yellow rail, landing one floor below. Tristan chose not to jump and used the grated, cascading metal treads. After descending five levels, ladders replaced stairs and, together, they descended, sliding down one tall ladder after another. Tristan's once-sweaty palms burned from the friction, but he kept going; the further down, the more rattled his nerves. It seemed that the bottom would never come, forging on, glancing down to gauge his progress. Below, Cole hadn't slowed his rate of descent, now two floors below.

After what seemed an eternity, they finally reached a yellow and black striped platform, barely wide enough for the two men. A phosphorous, green hue enveloped the entire area through which Tristan recognized the largest vat of zyn he'd ever seen—a thick, green liquid contained in an enormous, transparent tank as large as five Otis 52s laid end to end.

"The Mainframe computer's across that bridge. We'll set the bomb there." Cole pointed across an arched, dark green metal bridge.

"Right behind you." Tristan glanced up through the dizzying, man-made cavern, musing that they had descended so very far. The sight of it made his head swim.

The men's long strides landed them on the bridge in short fashion. A recorded woman's voice began blurting out as soon as Cole's boots slammed onto the metal flooring. *Intruder alert! Lower level mainframe computer. Intruder alert!*

A deep frown settled onto Cole's forehead; his eyebrows nearly becoming one. "Dammit! What's Lance doing? That shouldn't have happened!"

Tristan's hope of a quick turnaround dwindled as Cole's realization sunk in. He scanned the far wall. "Androids will soon be all over us!"

Cole chuckled. "I brought you this far; the rest is up to you. Show me how good you *really* are, and arm that bomb!"

CHAPTER

2

The closed-loop recording kept blaring—*Intruder alert! Lower level mainframe computer. Intruder alert!* It would only be a matter of time before embassy guards appeared. Tristan scoped out the walls the next level down, worried that more metal warriors would materialize. A horrible-smelling, green mist from the enormous vat of zyn, hung like a low-level fog above every surface. It would be bad enough if it only distorted his vision, but it also nauseated him. The grated surface beneath his feet undermined his sense of safety—if he could see down, someone else could see up through the triangular grooves. The mainframe computer at the end of the bridge hummed along with a mind of its' own, lights flashing and drives spinning.

"Damn! Lance has some explaining to do!" muttered Cole.

Tristan pushed past Cole, eyeing the level below as he dashed to the computer. A dark silhouette, at least a head taller than he, was molded into the pillar alongside the mainframe—a deactivated android.

Cole followed closely, keyed, whispering, and sounding like a bundle of wracked nerves. "When we blow this place, the Federation will be in some deep doodoo!" His voice quivered with excitement. He yanked his pack around. "Tristan! Set the bomb!" he barked, tossing him a cylinder about the size of his forearm, wrapped in black tape.

"Shouldn't you be doing this?" Tristan caught it with one hand, eyeing Cole warily.

"You've worked for the Federation before," Cole replied, his tone settling somewhat. "I'd hate to be stabbed in the back while planting that bomb; so, if you don't mind, I'm going to watch your every move."

"Then sit back and enjoy the show," Tristan pulled a black keyboard toward him. On the vertical panel behind the shelf, small lights flashed, triggering a memory that whispered to him from years ago—*'Help us! He's killing everyone!'* Instantly catapulted back in time, he was forced to re-live the horrible act that followed. He shook his head, his best attempt at rejuvenation, desperately wanting to reset his focus. He stared at the annoyingly timed message scrolling across the panel's central screen; the shrill mechanical voice continued an unwelcome clamor—*Intruder alert! Lower level mainframe computer. Intruder alert!*

Cole depressed his pistol's safety and goaded Tristan again. "You plan on backing out?"

"What?" Tristan still caught up in the haunting memory, ignored the leveled firearm.

Cole dropped a round in the chamber and armed the weapon. "I said, you planning on backing out?" His eyes pierced Tristan's disgruntled glare.

"Keep your gun in your pants. I'm fine," said Tristan as he cautiously rotated the bomb, eyeing it guardedly. Cole's advance didn't shake him; neither man would leave the facility without completing the mission—they needed each other. Painfully, he slipped back in time, rehashing the events from that fateful day. Might this be his only chance to right the wrongs that plagued him? Tristan delicately peeled a layer of black tape from the cylinder's flat-sided bottom and slid a shiny portable drive into a USB port. A toggle switch protected by a soft clear plastic cover was featured prominently on the body of the bomb, labeled *"Disarm"*.

"Don't touch that," from Cole." It's for dumbasses who think they're heroes. If someone gets down here before it blows, they'll probably flip the switch.

"So? What's the point of that?"

"It doesn't disarm; it blows them to shit ahead of schedule.

"What if someone gets down here before we get off?

"Then *we* get blown to shit ahead of schedule...... Guess we should hurry."

A flashing image on a small, orange screen hesitated; moments later, green dot matrix lettering began scrolling across. "I've uploaded the scanner and identified the zyn modules. How many minutes for the timer?" asked Tristan.

"Ten." Cole's hushed voice was tinged with tension.

"Ten? You're cutting it way too close."

"Nah. That's just the way I like it. Next best thing to flipping the switch."

Tristan shrugged, apprehensive, but punched in the sequence code anyway. The digital display flashed 10:00 and began counting down. "These people are crazier than shithouse rats," he said himself.

The robotic-voiced loop discontinued, ushering in a welcomed silence; but started up again, synchronized with an updated message spilling across the screen—*Unknown device. Cannot process. Intruder Alert.*

A din of whirring motors and mechanical joints resonated from a nearby pillar. A towering, dark silhouette's flashing red eyes sprang to life as it separated from its' polished charging station. It was almost twice the size of the other androids, with chunky arms and legs, and wide, platformed feet. Each arm had a massive weapon attached—a long barreled protrusion of some sort, and a rapid-fire machine gun. Tristan threw himself around the far end of the computer panel, shouting at Cole, who had dropped for cover beneath the keyboard shelf. Both men, pressed against the flimsy cubicle wall, crouched; gripping their guns and waiting for the robot's next move. Tristan barely took his eyes from it, angry that he didn't have more time. He glanced at Cole, nodding toward the robot. "Damn! Not another one!"

Cole eyed the door across the room and pointed. "To the exit! *Go! Now!*"

Cole lunged, and Tristan followed, trying to detect movement from the robot; its' power cells still charging. Usually, it took longer for the larger ones to fully activate, but with the machine gun already leveled, its' circular magazine rotating into position, the threat was indeed imminent.

Cole holstered his pistol and reached for another, an ion blaster with a longer muzzle and thicker grip. He slid the cover over the arming switch and released it, allowing it to click into place and arm; a bright blue flare jumped between two metal stanchions on top of the barrel. They sparked again and then glowed brightly while awaiting Cole's command. He aimed and depressed the trigger twice, sending two sizzling blue orbs streaking across the room, colliding with the android's chest. The recoil jerked Cole's arm upward. The metallic being stumbled, giving them the time they needed to dive through the open doorway. Tristan spun around and slammed his hand against the "Close Door" switch. They heaved a sigh of relief when the doors slid shut, shielding them from the double blasts from the robot's weapons array. As the doors came to, bullets grazed the opening and sprayed the back wall of the elevator, ripping it into shredded metal fragments.

"You should have taken that damn thing into account. I know you saw it!" shouted Tristan above the sound of exploding projectiles. He remained crouched in the corner, arm wrapped over his head while the elevator began its' ascent, breathing shallowly to avoid a plume of thick, gray smoke from the shattered wall. His hands still burned from the handrail friction.

"We're not out of this shit mess yet!" shouted Cole, his voice high-pitched and nervous.

Tristan retrieved a magazine from his belt and slammed it into his Droth. "This'll be tricky. Let's hope that the elevator still works and Erik's prepped the Otis 52." He wiped his forehead, eyeing the green hue now leaking through the wall's perforations. He couldn't help imagining little skinny-tailed rodents scurrying around an occupied outhouse.

"He better, or he's not getting paid!" mumbled Cole absently; checking his magazine.

The elevator shuddered to a stop, the doors shaking unevenly as they jerked open. The panels stopped halfway—just enough to squeeze through—while the motors hummed loudly and ground to a stop. Mounds of twisted metal were scattered throughout the lobby where they had last seen Lance—no dead bodies, just piles of smoldering, motionless androids. Erik and Hardie probably made it out alive. At least Tristan hoped for that, while he and Cole jumped over the debris and raced across to the other elevator. It would be great if its' ascent was as fast as its' descent had been. Jumping inside, Tristan spotted a lone android; thankfully, one of the smaller ones, lumbering through a set of doors down the wall and firing a volley of tracer rounds directly at them. Tristan quickly engaged the button marked "Roof". Fortunately, the bullets didn't penetrate; nothing stopped the rising room's movement. Moments later, the doors glided apart, hissing loudly, exposing Lance.

The man's worry lines deepened above his idyllic grin. "Finally! Move it! The guards are on their way! Hurry!"

"What happened? I thought the alarm wasn't going to be activated until *after* we detonated the bomb! That harebrained screw-up just gave them more time to get here! They're gonna be all over us!" snapped Cole.

Lance replied nervously. "Somebody else hacked into the alarm system, sir! They were cloaked completely, and I couldn't monitor their code!"

"Damn!" shouted Cole. "Shut this elevator down. There's a big fuck'n robot chasing us and . ."

The elevator's floor split apart and heaved upward, creaking and groaning like a raging animal, sending jagged metal shards into the false ceiling above.

Tristan glanced at the demolished floor, thinking by the eruption's sound that their bomb had detonated early. He was only a little relieved when a hulking android began climbing through the mangled flooring, working itself up from the elevator shaft. Its' head and broad shoulders scraped against sharp, serrated flanges as it pulled itself up and studied its' surroundings.

Lance screamed. *"Run!"*

The three men leaped behind a waist-high blast wall leading to the stairwell entrance on the embassy roof; Cole and Lance crouched just across from Tristan. Unmistakable aqua blue stripes on shale gray uniforms heralded a mass of Vutonian soldiers pouring onto the roof from a stairwell on the far side of the emerging robot. More soldiers streamed out of another stairwell on the opposite side. Their faces, shielded by gray metal reflectors, serving as protection and digital eyesight, gave them a mechanical appearance. Tristan zipped up his jacket at the sight of their twin rifles poised to fire.

Cole frantically studied the advancing soldiers. "We're nearly surrounded!"

"What do we do?" demanded Lance.

"Get the bastards out of our way," shouted Cole. "If that oversized android reaches us, we're screwed!"

Still crouched, Cole popped his Droth above the wall and raked an adjacent armored wall, shattering a buttress of painted mortar. Three soldiers, now running toward them, fired back, their bullets zinging over Tristan.

Tristan fired several short bursts. His volley sprayed into the nearest soldier's chest, throwing him back against his two companions. "Cover me!" yelled Tristan.

Cole fired, forcing the dazed soldiers behind a blast wall; Tristan bolted forward and activated his Droth's blades. He leapt over the wall, pushing the blades into the first soldier's chest. Then with a rearward kick, booted the other in the groin, and raked his blades across the screaming man's throat. He stopped screaming; just gurgled and fell backward.

Cole joined Tristan, panting. "Took you long enough!"

Tristan managed a half smile and bolted for the sealed blast doors.

Cole pressed his finger to his ear and activated his transceiver while he and Lance trailed Tristan. "Voleta! Get the blast doors open *now*! We're clear!" His urgent tone echoed along the walkway through more tracer fire.

Tristan's earpiece crackled with Voleta's voice, "Affirmative!" He thought of her oval face, hoping that she was as good as she had earlier tried to impress.

Like clockwork, grinding loudly, the heavy armored doors slid open, revealing Voleta crouching low and waving them in. "This way!" she shouted, lunging out of sight behind a mound of black barrels emblazoned with bright yellow skulls and crossbones.

Tristan dove, not looking back. Another explosive discharge just missed the barrels, but impacted the concrete wall above Cole and Lance, spewing dust and flying mortar chips. The robot adjusted its' gait and bore down with five guards lined up behind it, poking their weapons out randomly and blasting away. Tristan fired over Cole's head, covering him and Lance effectively enough to enter the hallway. The launch pad was just on the other side of the doors at the far end.

Hardie crouched behind a fuel tank beside the Marne's bulkhead. "Go! Go!" he shouted to his approaching companions, motioning feverishly. "They're right behind you!"

Tristan caught a glimpse of Erik's face through the narrow, cockpit windows. Thankfully, he had already begun the start-up sequence. The loud whine offered a glimmer of hope, but didn't relieve the adrenaline rush from being chased and shot at. Voleta reached the Marne's short aft ramp first, stopping to return fire; Lance and Cole joined her, sending their bullets flying, while Tristan edged backward, firing into the lumbering robot's torso. Just steps from the ramp, Tristan leaped onto it, yelling frantically. "Get us out of here!"

Erik eased the miniature joystick back; the ship obediently responded, lurching off the roof. Erik swiveled the control and maneuvered the sleek vessel as if it were hung by a single cable. He pitched the nose down just enough to angle the Marne's dual muzzles directly at the Android and cowering soldiers. Several muffled bursts pulsed through the ship; a moment later, the soldiers' ruptured bodies and body parts spilled onto the ground. One of the robot's arms shattered against the elevator's wall. Bullets ricocheted off the Marne's tough skin as the Android continued to fire its' only remaining weapon.

Erik gritted his teeth and shouted. "Die, you sonofabitch!" He pressed the arming mechanism, a red trigger on the back side of the stick, and fired two more triple blasts. The robot's chest ignited into a blaze of flames and gaped, exposing the walkway behind it. Erik tilted the joystick port and was sucked into the captain's chair; the ship effortlessly cleared the roof and shot into the darkness.

Lance was frantic. "The turret is back online!" he shouted.

Tristan leaned, trying to catch a view through the side window, a small, triangular opening fitted with ultra-thick, bulletproof glass. He watched the turret begin a slow rotation toward them, its' nose rising while it came about.

"Move! Get us out of here!" Tristan thumped Erik's shoulder. If they were going down, he wanted to be responsible, not Erik.

Erik tightened his safety restraints and refused to budge. "It's under control! Sit down!" He nudged the joystick to starboard just as the turret released its' first barrage. Searing blasts of ion tracers whizzed by, shaking the ship and forcing Erik to port, nearly knocking Tristan off his feet.

"You're gonna get us killed!" Tristan thumped Erik's arm, harder this time.

"I know what I'm doing!" He reached over and pounded his closed fist on an oversized red button. "Almost there . . ." The ship shuddered in response to the release of two pulsating blasts of pure, white energy. Moments later, the embassy's roof shattered in a violent display of fire and glowing incendiary projectiles, unmasking the massive underlying level; comprised now of twisted steel beams and smoldering carcasses. A wavy mist filled the cavernous opening followed by a rippled discharge of bright orange and red flames.

10 minutes! Tick tick.

The turret teetered, wobbling back and forth as if tethered on a spring from below. It teetered again, the invisible tether released, and the massive hi-power cannon seemed to float, downward, its' barrel tipping slowly, finally plunging down the side of the decapitated structure.

Hardie, gripping a suspended hand strap, thrust a closed fist high. "Yea! Whoohoo! That should keep them off our butts awhile."

"That was way too close," said Lance, nervously forcing a smile.

Voleta snapped seat restraints across her trim torso and cinched them tightly. "The Federation will issue a Seizure Warrant for your ship and force airship ports to deny us entry. If they locate us, we're toast. To be safe, our best option is to shuttle to the subterranean rail system rendezvous point where we can meet up later in *Lathe*," (Lathe being an underground base of operations). She took a breath and glanced at the others.

Erik quipped, "This ship will outrun anything but the speed of light. I can dump you people where you need to be. Less weight for the ship to haul. As far as ports are concerned, I don't need no stinking ports. If I fly low and slow in *stealth*, I'll get where I need to be, a tavern at Institute VI, yeah."

"OK, then. Tristan. I'll help you reach Mr. Edde. In case you forgot, you get paid once you sign the mission completion forms. After that, you'll be ordered to return to Institute VI."

Tristan nodded. "I'll go with you." He tried to catch another glimpse of the fiery plumes of smoke rising out of the building's belly, but the ship had already angled away, cutting off his view. Flashing red lights dotted the darkened cityscape below. Traffic was just beginning to stream in the public flight corridors above the city, signaling that the enormous metropolis was starting to emerge from its' slumber. Satisfied that Erik could handle the ship, he sank back into his chair, rubbing his arm that had been bruised from the hard port turn. "Have Mawson upload a new registration number. We'll need it if we're ever going to land this bird safely."

"Don't keep Headmaster Mawson waiting too long," cautioned Erik.

"I won't," said Tristan. Hearing Mawson's name reminded him of how he came down when a mission ended. The humdrum of civilian life was a bore; he preferred a mercenary's.

Cole pointed. "There's a good spot!"

Tristan quickly located an area near the city center surrounded by skyscrapers. The ground traffic lanes were just beginning to congest with early morning traffic; not a bad choice since it afforded a decent amount of cover. Briefly, he realized he didn't pay any attention to the precise elapsed time before the blast. He imagined some bespectacled lab assistant finding the downward-counting device and, with a toothy grin, thinking of getting awarded the *Order of the Hall of Heroes Medallion*, flicking that switch.

Hah. He will never know.

"You want to set down here?" asked Erik.

"Trust me. Once on the ground, we'll be lost in the crowd. Suit up into your civvies, people," ordered Cole.

The group methodically stripped off outer layers and packed them away in their bags, solemnly exchanging fighting outfits for casual street garb.

Hardie removed his vest and handed it to Tristan. "This should keep you, just in case."

Erik gently slipped the Marne from the darkened sky and over an open spot adjacent to a deserted walkway.

"Follow me!" ordered Cole.

The airship hovered while the five passengers jumped from the aft ramp. Several onlookers saw the activity, mumbling to themselves, then moved away. "Gunship? What Gunship?"

Apathy was Tristan's friend.

The group melted into the crowd and followed Cole into an underground train station. Cole motioned for them to wait while he talked to a man in a dark blue uniform and wearing a hat that shielded his eyes. Cole turned back, giving them thumbs up. He was probably USC. Who else would Cole be confiding in? They walked over to a deserted platform and into an awaiting train. Moments later, a hiss of compressed air released from somewhere outside, just before the doors closed and the train began its' heavy trek out of the station.

With extra time on his hands, Tristan took a moment to study what few passengers there were; most appearing destitute. They seemed so poor that they shouldn't have been able to afford the train fare. When the train broke out of the tunnel, the landscape was scattered with poverty, homelessness and destitution as far as he could see. Flimsy enclosures made of sheet metal or cardboard sheeting, dusted rubbish-strewn hills bordering the tracks, wispy fires sending thin trails of smoke into the dawning sky; the entire countryside seemed surreal, yet somehow comforting to these strange people. As the train sped on, there was no end to the panoramic visage of economic duress. Who would have believed that such a dire state existed?

Hardie's voice roused Tristan from his musings. "You and Erik were fantastic! I hope we get the chance to work together again." Hardie's comments seemed out of touch; hadn't he noticed the abounding human detritus just beyond the train's picture windows? Tristan glanced stoically, unable to muster a favorable expression.

"Thanks," nodded Voleta. "I'm afraid I judged you too soon. We couldn't have done this job without both of you. I'm certain Mr. Edde will be pleased with our results."

An unpleasant odor from some derelict slouching near him made Tristan gag. He eyed some open seats further down and rose to his feet, pausing to listen to a recorded announcement blaring through the car. "This is a public alert issued by the Vutonian government. A terrorist group known as the USC has been identified as responsible for the destruction of the Atomian Embassy in Gaustead. Remain vigilant in all crowded public areas. Rescue efforts are underway to locate survivors and secure the embassy and other strategic government buildings. President Drakkar has issued a message for the Vutonian populace. 'The USC will pay for this heinous act, and Atomia will fully support Vutonian search efforts. Together, we will bring an end to these cowardly acts of terror. Senator Lathe Xander of Atomia also spoke out. 'These terrorist acts are the USC's effort to enslave us and hold dominion over the freedoms we hold so dear. They want nothing less than all-out war; we will do everything in our power to protect Vuton and its' citizens. Our thoughts are with the people of Gaustead.' Remain alert and report any suspicious activities to Vutonian or Atomian Police immediately!" The intercom buzzed as if someone had double-clicked the microphone, and then went silent.

"You ever been on a train?" Cole asked, eyeing Tristan. "Sit down. Quit acting so damn suspicious."

Lance chuckled. "Don't let him fool you. He's uptight on every mission. He's just as nervous as you are."

"Shuddup!" barked Cole.

Lance smiled to himself. "You're familiar with Vutonian geography, right?"

"Of course . . . ," replied Tristan, curious to uncover the real reason for Lance's probing. As the train sped along, he remained distracted by the many homeless people crammed in makeshift housing along the tracks. The clickety-clack beneath him and the gentle swaying with an occasional lurch numbed Tristan's senses.

"Just in case, let me fill you in. Vuton has thirteen primary urban centers. Eight of them form an outer ring; four comprise an inner ring. That design provides protection for large urban centers. The four center rings were designed to provide protection for the inner, centralized capital. Transportation into the ring system, outer or inner, is restricted to either train or air. However, the capital has no train service due to surrounding mountainous terrain." Lance seemed excited to expound on his geographical expertise. His voice tapered to a whisper as he leaned into Tristan. "We believe that the Federation controls most of Vuton's cities. Destroying zyn repositories and creating as much chaos as possible, hopefully will nullify the alliance between Vuton and Atomia. Our latest Intel supports rumors that the two countries are in discussion to merge and become a combined single nation-state. Vuton's proposed Federation alliance would enhance its' control, and solidify its' power structure. Mr. Edde's plan is to expose the fact that Atomia has more enemies than previously suspected. We must fight to keep Senator Xander from becoming Atomia's next Sovereign; he's responsible for creating and promoting this dark threat. Senator Galik, the nominee runner-up—his greatest opposition—is not eager to sign off on an expansion of Atomia's influence. He campaigns on a more peaceful platform. You can imagine that the destruction of zyn repositories is a powerful countermeasure we can leverage against Xander. The embassy is our first successful strike. I can just see our names splattered across all Eshen news channels!" Lance's eyes gleamed.

Now brought up to speed, Tristan allowed the new information to sink in. Rain had started falling, sending large droplets of water smearing sideways on the windows. This weather would only make people outside the train more miserable.

Lance continued. "We'll soon arrive at our headquarters between Gaustead and Lathe, and, as you've probably noticed, is in the middle of Vuton's slums. I'm sure you know Vutonian cities are double-layered; the upper class's luxuries and conveniences are confined to the skyward platforms; the slums to the lower. Most USC facilities are located in the slums, hidden from scrutiny. The lower tiers harbor a nasty existence for those folks, but there's nothing we can do about it…yet. The Azdahri populace has long since accepted this part of Vutonian culture and, years ago, when they merged, did nothing to change it. It seems that the only thing they care about is their white hair. We're going to stand out like sore thumbs; maybe we should buy some wigs?" Lance chuckled quietly.

"Where are you from?" Tristan asked, now wanting to know more about the Azdahri.

"I was born in Reyna and spent most of my life in Feria, a fact I keep to myself when around Azdahri. They hate Reynans. What about you?"

"Feria. In Eshen, Azdahri has been for centuries a mostly unused term. Why the emphasis now?"

Lance glanced questioningly. "The Azdahri's are those with white or platinum hair; as I said before, all Vutonians and Atomians are Azdahri. Until recently, the word wasn't in their vocabulary. Now that it's resurfaced, it's quickly become in vogue. Word has it that a literal translation means, 'Exalted Ones.'"

Tristan continued to muse, still watching the storm race by. The train had just traversed under Lathe's upper platform shadows, protected from the rain in the resulting darkness.

"Are you really helping us just because you're paid?" asked Lance candidly.

"Yeah. What other reason would I have?" Tristan shrugged, feeling uncomfortable from the man's probing.

"I live in the slums and, whenever possible, I help out the USC. I do what I can to stop Vuton's corruption, because if I don't, the entire continent of Eshen will eventually be one big slum."

"Tristan . . . . Come here!" ordered Cole.

"Thanks for the info," he said to Lance and worked his way through the swaying car.

"We're almost to Mr. Edde's. I wanted to touch base with you about your pay."

"Good. We want to be paid in Trade Federation Credits. 30,000 TFCs."

Cole nodded. "I understand. However, we may have to change the agreed amount."

"I wouldn't go against the Headmaster's agreement," argued Tristan solemnly. "That'll land you in nothing but trouble. A deal's a deal. 30,000 TFCs; no questions asked."

"Dammit! I didn't sign the contract!" Cole's chest began to rise and fall more quickly. "Mr. Edde did. Look, we asked for one of you, but we got two. We weren't aware of Erik's participation."

"So what? 30,000 is 30,000, even if I brought an army!" Tristan knew he was lying. He had been very clear with Mr. Edde that they worked in pairs. Mr. Edde had agreed, and personally sanctioned Erik.

"I'll let Mr. Edde handle it," Cole replied, and then promptly changed the subject. "You ever think of leaving Institute VI?"

"Why would I? It keeps me off the street; better than working in civilian sectors."

"Yea, but you can't do it forever."

"Maybe not, but I'm not one to dwell on the future. I live in the here-and-now."

"So, you're a robot—submitting to someone else's control?"

Tristan was riled, but chose to accept the prodding, "No one controls me!"

"*Someone* does! You really don't think about the future, do you? Someone has to!"

Brakes squealed. The train rapidly lost its' momentum. Within minutes, the swaying ceased. It had halted alongside a crowded, dimly lit platform.

"Here we are," said Cole, rising to leave. "Let's go chat with Mr. Edde."

CHAPTER

3

In Vuton, aircraft, radios, firearms, and long-range artillery were nearly as ubiquitous as in Atomia. Atomian New World Order protagonists made sure of that. Even with such technical advances, neighboring countries' travel agencies rarely promoted Vuton due to its' rampant poverty. Vagrants lined the thoroughfares or hid away in makeshift shelters barely able to withstand the elements. Traveling by ground was difficult; the city streets were lousy with trash, perhaps deliberately thrown out of upper windows of the towering buildings occupied by the elite. It was strange to think that Vuton's southern neighbor, Atomia, was one of the most prosperous countries in the world. The contrast was stark.

Cole led the way to Mr. Edde's location, his sudden stoicism prompting Tristan's curiosity. Cole's nonchalant demeanor made him seem complacent. Lance, Voleta and Hardie followed quietly, tension running strong. The stench of human refuse bombarded their senses. Why would Mr. Edde, a man of apparent influence, endure these hardships? Then Tristan remembered what Lance had said about the slums being as good a place as any to hide.

The group hurried after Cole's quickening pace and crossed the street. He chose to cut diagonally toward the far side in an attempt to avoid a small gathering. A woman with thick, ratty white hair stood guarding two children warming themselves near a barrel fire. Dark smoke blew randomly. She didn't seem to mind, standing nearly motionless with hollow eyes fixated on the heat source. Tristan spotted a man arguing with a lone female. He shouted and waved his hands in her face while she cringed and stared at the ground.

"No use helping her," muttered Cole blandly, "It's better not to get involved. Things are pretty bad down here. Most of Vuton's slums are like this. Jus' ain't right."

Cole's callous observation provided Tristan more insight into the man's outlook, "It's their own fault. They can leave whenever they like," speculated Tristan, reflecting on something his mother had taught him—people chose their own course through life.

"Not that simple," returned Cole. "They don't have enough credits to leave. There's no law here, which is why so many women are raped and beaten daily by jobless men; they have no credits, nothing. To make matters worse, the rape victims are further forced into poverty, caring for those children without any means of support. Shit. It's bad down here, Tristan. Hunger is so prevalent that rogue gangs have been known to cannibalize corpses." Cole's voice quieted as he continued.

"It's none of my concern," said Tristan, not wanting to involve himself any further. Mr. Edde's office had to be close. Then they'd finally be out of this squalor and closing the business deal. It couldn't come soon enough. The stench was awful.

Cole turned with an empty stare. "Damn . . . . You boys from the Institute are all screwed up!"

Tristan didn't know what to say. Cole hadn't stopped to defend that helpless woman, and now he was confronting him. The fresh memory of her slumped shoulders troubled him greatly. This unexpectedly harsh environment was unnerving.

"We're hoping to change things down here," said Lance. "Atomia has more of a grasp on Vuton than you might think. Make the rich richer, and the poor poorer, is what it seems. We struggle to encourage self-respect, hoping these sorry souls will someday lead decent lives."

"It's Mr. Edde's dream," added Hardie, "If we don't end Vuton's shit cycle, all of Eshen will eventually stink as well."

Drawing closer to Tristan, Voleta kicked a label-less bottle off the curb. "In an effort to align you with USC's point of view, Mr. Edde will probably offer you a permanent position."

"If the credits are good," stipulated Tristan, "and Headmaster Mawson agrees it benefits Institute VI, then I'll get on board."

"Mr. Edde controls a fortune; if that's your concern, credits won't be an issue," affirmed Voleta, sounding stuffy.

"Enough . . . . We're here," said Cole, pointing toward a cluster of dilapidated structures.

Tristan glanced up. Collectively, the buildings were no-name, definitely not offices. They looked more like a rundown factory. The main structure was encircled by a handful of buildings connected to each other's second floors through a web of tangled walkways covered in black fungus or mold. A burnt stench from a bygone era permeated the air. The gloomy surroundings had no perceivable activity; broken pavement and puddles of runny sewage abounded. Cole skirted a pooled depression and jumped onto the entryway steps.

And then it dawned on Tristan—"An old zyn factory. Classic!" Faint reminders drifted through broken glass: a familiar, green hue, the same that he'd experienced at the embassy. It was clear that the poisonous remnants had been left to nature's undoing—not a safe choice.

"It's been shuttered for almost a decade," said Cole as if reading Tristan's mind. "No one would dare nose around here. Exposure to zyn isn't usually at the top of a vacation list. Come on. Mr. Edde will be in his office waiting."

Once they had entered through the blast doors, the disparity was night-and-day. A spacious entry appeared newly constructed—floors, walls and ceilings gleaming from recent installation, elegant crown molding, baseboards, carpeting and the like. Throughout, blossoming foliage was neatly arranged around thickly-cushioned couches and chairs. It was a world apart from what lay on the other side of those stout, metal doors; Tristan had a difficult time accepting the stark contrast. Quite a few USC employees milled about the cavernous space, most not taking notice of their arrival except for several who nodded as Cole made his way toward the staircase on the far side of the room.

The group proceeded up carpeted stairs. Tristan felt padded layers depress with each step, feeling guilty for soiling plush surfaces with grimy boots. He glanced up at the landing; a tantalizing aroma of frying bacon suddenly lured him. On the second floor, they were welcomed by a neatly arranged cafeteria with enough seating for 20 or so patrons. A couple, deep in conversation, occupied one of the small, circular tables, sipping from white porcelain mugs. A cook behind the food line, smiling broadly and wearing a tall, white hat, cracked open two eggs with one hand and let them drop onto a sizzling grill.

"You all get something to eat. Mr. Edde is expecting Tristan and me," said Cole, motioning toward the food line. Tristan, his stomach growling, hesitantly followed Cole.

Centered above the door, Mr. Edde's office entrance was monitored by a black box with a flashing red sensor. When Cole was a few steps away, the doors automatically swung inward.

At first, Tristan felt remarkably at ease. Then he was caught off guard by opulent, albeit subdued, luxury occupying every corner of the spacious office. It was warmly colored with brown, lacquered woodwork, and fitted with meticulously carved inlays mounted on wood trim throughout. A fireplace across the room roared, its' flames reflected off the shiny surfaces. A single light fixture hung over the conference table, not centered with the room. Its' hard, white glow contrasted the warmer lighting, seeming to illuminate the walls and bouncing off the art deco ceiling tiles above. Tristan had seen this decor many years ago in old, government offices. Green-painted trim outlining white ceiling tiles seemed outdated compared to the rest of the decor. Mr. Edde, slight of frame, stood with his back to them, staring into dancing embers.

"Mr. Edde," Cole said, clearing his throat in an attempt to gain the man's attention. "The mission was a success."

Impressed by the ambience, Tristan scrutinized row upon row of hardbound books lining shelves on either side of the fireplace.

Mr. Edde quietly replied, "I know. The news channels have been inundating us with the story," The flames continued to hold his attention. "Disabling one repository will not cripple Atomia, but it'll make them hurt for a while, because we hit them where they are vulnerable. Expect far more vigilance from them. Because of our actions, they now understand that retaliation is an ever-present threat. Congratulations, Mr. Asbury." He smiled at Cole. "You performed quite well. I expect that you will only build upon this grand success."

"Thank you." Cole's apathetic business demeanor relaxed into a broad smile.

"Now." The slender man turned toward Tristan, his medium length, dark-brown hair highlighted with subdued streaks of silver-gray, catching the firelight. "You must be Mr. Hart."

His rounded, blue eyes caught Tristan's attention at once. "Yes, I am."

"Very glad to make your acquaintance . . . . Mr. Mawson afforded you the highest recommendation—said that your piloting skills were exemplary."

"I can hold my own," replied Tristan reservedly.

"Of course." Mr. Edde smiled warmly and faced Cole. "Mr. Asbury. If you don't mind, I'd enjoy a private moment with Mr. Hart."

Cole nodded. "Of course."

Tristan couldn't help but notice Mr. Edde's commanding presence. His silver highlights took on a polished sheen under the overhead lamp. He hoped his own hair was tamed, but knowing that probability was next to nil, he hastily patted down wispy ends. Mr. Edde's request sparked a touch of anxiety; he hadn't expected to feel so awkwardly exposed and intimidated.

"The USC needs your caliber of pilot. Don't get me wrong; we have good pilots, but none have received combat training. Their backgrounds are in cargo and troop transport; most have never seen another man die. With this in mind, I created a special requisition and maintain the highest confidence that you will accept my offer."

"You'll need to discuss that with Headmaster Mawson," replied Tristan, fully appreciating the request, although apprehensive.

"Already done. I've transferred the required credits for your next mission to Mr. Mawson."

Tristan was caught off-guard. ". . . That's impressive. Usually, the Headmaster takes more time to review these offers."

Mr. Edde nodded, quietly studying Tristan. "Mr. Mawson and I have maintained a long and profitable relationship."

"You have a personal rapport with the Headmaster?" asked Tristan. The fact that they knew each other intrigued him.

"I have many relationships with powerful people," said Mr. Edde. "They've helped elevate me into my current position. When you run with the right crowd, you gain information that, when used correctly, creates influence, which leads to control—where true power resides."

"Information is merely an *initiator* of power. Information creates *knowledge*. Knowledge is required for *wisdom*. And wisdom is the cornerstone of victory—and *influence*, and *power*, and *control*. You'll do well to remember that. And for what it's worth, here's some free advice. Don't be afraid to question—expand your knowledge."

"Thank you," said Tristan, surprised that Mr. Edde was pulling him under his wing so quickly.

"Mr. Mawson signed your contract. You may review it." He pulled open a drawer and lifted out a short stack of papers.

Tristan leafed through the documents, noting the Institute VI insignia and Mawson's signature.

"Your next mission is twofold," continued Mr. Edde, "Return to Institute VI post-haste. Headmaster Mawson will provide you with a state-of-the-art aerial gunship. From there, you'll travel directly to Ascalon as the Institute's ambassador, where the Annual Castalia Ball is taking place. You'll be expected to rub shoulders with top politicians, including well-placed governmental officials. There, you'll rendezvous with our informant, to obtain critical zyn repository schematics, floor plans, and updated weaponry information. It will be stored in a coded memory device. The source prefers to remain anonymous; our only clue to the person's identity is that he or she is referred to as 'Liberty.' I've done my best to confirm this person's loyalty; you'll have to trust me on this. Once supplied, protect the information with your life! It must be delivered to the World Council to provide them with vital intelligence; allowing their intervention into Federation affairs. We'll remain here, awaiting your return with both the storage device and the informant. Expect to begin the next phase of our campaign immediately upon returning. Any questions?"

"Can I catch a shuttle back to the Institute?" asked Tristan as he mentally processed the orders. The ball sounded interesting, even fun; but he was concerned about the informant's anonymity. If Mr. Edde didn't know who to expect, how could *he* possibly find out?

"I'll have one of my men transport you to Istrus, where someone from Institute VI can meet you and shuttle you the rest of the way. Mr. Mawson will arrange that."

Tristan calculated the large credit transfer funding this arrangement. "Gunships aren't cheap."

"Neither is success," replied Mr. Edde.

"Is the Headmaster covertly working with the USC?" asked Tristan in a clumsy attempt to mask his curiosity.

"If you don't mind, I'd rather discuss that later, when we're not so pressed by these gravely urgent matters."

"Yes, sir," replied Tristan. His new mission had greater inherent importance than he had previously realized.

The man's tone remained friendly, "I'm expecting good things from you, Mr. Hart. Pleasant travels. The doors are controlled by sensors and will let you out, and close automatically."

Tristan's thoughts whirled with anticipation. So many people were putting so many variables into motion—just for him, it seemed. He felt privileged as the doors opened to a new journey with Cole and the others.

CHAPTER

4

CRESCENT 16, 1870 O.C.
LOCATION: INSTITUTE VI
CITY: SOUTHEAST OF ISTRUS

On final approach and ten minutes out, the view of Istrus heightened Tristan's zeal to assume command of his promised gunship. With a trusted colleague piloting the ten-man shuttle, Tristan casually perused the desert landscape, rippling sand as far as the eye could see. He was pleased to be in familiar territory. The short flight was more a nuisance than anything—hustle onboard, quickly gain altitude, level out and then start the descent; they sped toward a marvel of a structure: Institute VI. Along the horizon, the complex gradually emerged out of the heat waves, filling his rounded portal with a towering, circular configuration comprised of two clamshell-like buildings pancaked atop each other. Four antenna arrays, pointing each north, east, south and west, were centrally mounted onto the upper convex surface. The roof was dotted with other antennas— whips, modules and wands of varying heights. Sunlight bleached the structure—making it appear as desolate as the adjacent mountain range, one of Tristan's favorite apartment views. One couldn't help but sense extreme isolation. Institute VI, a self-contained base supporting approximately 3,500 personnel, lay between two of Vuton's cities— Istrus, an outer city, and Castra Nova, an inner city. Vuton boasted eight outer cities and four inner, with the capital centered directly in the country's formidable Zocust Heights Mountains.

The boxish craft slowed drastically, the roar of its' engines dwindling, now hovering as it settled into a docking bay between the upper and lower modules. The sun's glare gave way to the landing bay's artificial lighting; Tristan felt welcome relief when he no longer had to squint.

Undeniably, he was glad to have arrived at his home of nearly six years. It wasn't necessarily homey; but it was comfortable, furnished with the most modern conveniences one would expect from a technologically advanced culture. Once he stepped off the mobile gangway, he began to unwind. Several of his buddies greeted him with usual male camaraderie, handshakes and slaps on the back. He was cautioned to expect a debriefing session with Mawson. The men recognized him as one of their most proficient pilots; he was quite proud of it, but kept his feelings to himself.

Matt, a scheduler, checked an electronic tablet strapped to his forearm, scrolling down through the pages. "Hart! Headmaster Mawson expects you to be at a meeting in two hours." Just then, a loud buzz sounded throughout the landing zone. Another flight was arriving. Matt paused and shouted over the engine's roar. "It's in the Sky Bright Conference Room, the newly remodeled one in the Second Tier Eastern Quadrant."

"He doesn't waste time, does he?" exclaimed Tristan, fighting the temptation to complain. He was tired, and the incessant din fatigued him even more.

"Never has!" The man turned and disappeared between two smaller shuttles undergoing repairs. A waist-high droid chattered while it connected a communications link to one of the vessels. It moved back, knocking a dome-shaped head against a protruding landing gear panel. The impact was immediately followed by garbled electronic frustration, not much more than high-pitched multi-tonal beeping.

Tristan passed through thick sliding glass partitions, both sound barriers and insulation from the harsh environment, glad to leave the noise and heat behind. Along the way to his apartment, he glanced out an extended row of plate glass windows. He could feel the deck's vibration with each step. The entire floor in the circular structure's second layer rotated 360 degrees in an hour, giving the occupants a constantly changing display of their surroundings. Even more impressive, it was powered by incredibly efficient but stunningly expensive Microbray solar panels, which were supposedly the best in the market. As formidable as the engineering was, it couldn't possibly distract from the natural grandeur that technology was designed to obviate – the adjacent mountain range. Tristan relished the view; in the evenings when the orange sun settled, they glowed like bricks in a giant kiln.

Fresh, dark gray paint on his apartment door caught his attention; the smell was faint, but the new sheen was noticeable. He opened the door carefully, picked up a stack of mail and tossed his duffle bags to the side. He flopped into his favorite recliner, the one thing he missed when traveling, and shuffled through the daunting collection of advertisements and bills—nothing personal. He pressed the power button on the universal remote; an entire wall bristled to life with a news broadcast. He wasn't interested, and punched in his favorite movie channel, wincing at the out-of-date selection: something about survival in the Vutonian slums. Not wanting to be reminded, he pressed the *Mode* button. A pleasant videoscape colored the wall with changing displays of Reynan rivers and waterfalls. That's what he needed. Two hours would pass quickly, and he'd be back in the thick of it again. He set his alarm and settled back to soft music playing from the scenic displays, and dropped into a carefree slumber.

✕✕✕✕✕✕✕

Four others milled about the medium-sized conference room large enough for a ten-seat table with several more chairs against the end walls. A polished credenza butted up along the wall opposite the window. On it sat a full water pitcher and a dozen glasses. Tristan glanced out toward the mountains, guessing that by the time the meeting ended, thanks to the rotating building, he'd be viewing rolling expanses of sandy, sun-soaked, desert terrain.

One participant caught his attention; as always—Headmaster Mawson. This man didn't need to speak in order to be noticed; thanks mainly to a scar running diagonally from the corner of his right forehead down over his left eye. Deep worry lines cut into his skin just beneath the dull, puffy fault. His droopy, padded cheeks were obscured by thick white chops, framing an oversized nose and permanently downturned smile. He was a perfect choice to interface with world leaders; the scar was intimidating. He had been Headmaster for nearly two decades and was usually in full uniform; decorative shoulder boards and wrist gauntlets included. Out of habit, he rested his hand on the haft of his ornamental sword. Holstered on his belt was an outdated semiautomatic pistol, fitted with a hand-carved wooden handle, a relic to even the most elderly. Mawson's piercing gaze made him seem all too ready to use them if needed.

Erik had already arrived; standing by the window, quiet and unassuming except for a restless stance, shifting nervous glances between Mawson and the mountains. When he looked out the window, his eyes turned a shimmering silver-blue.

Zeddicus Sangray, Institute VI's best semblance of a bionic man, stood at the far end of the room, the sun's glare through the window rendering him foreboding. He was clad in the most intimidating gear in the room—black armor, smooth and reflective, flexible and rigid, right down to his fingers and head covering. Tristan had never seen the man's skin. He had been severely burned during a previous mission and, after nearly a full year of many reconstructive surgeries, and fitted with the latest bio-mechanical 'black skin,' had gained enhanced physical prowess. He had the strength of four men. The transformation had been striking, both visually and functionally. Several tiny lamps flashed randomly across his shoulders, and a pair of contiguous red stripes starting at the top of his helmet ran down the middle of his faceguard, neck gear, torso and left leg. With an impeccable track record of no failed assignments, he was contracted for only the most crucial missions.

Loci Talbot, Mawson's trusted second, stood next to her boss. Her wavy, brunette hair, dark eyeliner and fair complexion were a pleasant visual respite from the predominately male staff. Mawson insisted that she be battle-ready at all times—shoulder guards, wrist gauntlets, and flexible torso armor. Her knee-length dress, bound by thick, leather straps wrapping her body in three different swaths, seemed slightly oversized.

"Tristan. Welcome. Sit where you like," Mawson's greeting sounded grave as he motioned toward the table.

Tristan heard the door's air-seal hiss behind him as he selected a chair two places down from Mawson, facing the window. If the meeting turned too boring, he could subtly divert his attention between the outside scenery and the speaker.

"Congratulations are in order, my friend . . . ," said Mawson, beaming and turning toward Tristan, ". . . for your success in the destruction of Gaustead's embassy. Your and Erik's performance were exceptional."

"Thank you." Tristan wondered at the depth of detail Mawson really shared and grew edgy. "Is it true that you retained Mr. Edde as a long term client?" This was a topic far more interesting than their last job. But would he answer?

"That's correct. The man was most pleased and has already signed a long-term contract. Expect future deployments."

Erik slammed his fist down on the table and rose to his feet. "I don't get it," he barked. "I had just as much to play in that mission as Hart. Why wasn't I offered a contract?"

Zeddicus' flashing LEDs flickered with increased intensity. The room turned deathly quiet except for the whirr of motors in Zeddicus's shoulder joints as he repositioned his arms.

"Tristan's resume, including overall hours flown, far exceeds yours. That seems to be what Mr. Edde wanted." Seemingly undaunted, Mawson's stern tone cut through the developing drama.

"Bastard!" Erik slammed his fist down again. "I'm the one who flew us out of that shithole!"

His manner jarred Loci. "Erik. I have another mission for you, equal in scope to your last one," she said. "Calm yourself. No need to act like a child."

Mawson continued. "Erik, your next undertaking will bring you to Amstye. You'll lead a detail extracting an ambassador's son and removing him to safety."

"Dammit," he raged. "You've got to be kidding me! That kind of job is for rookies! I don't have time to babysit."

"They're easy credits. Report to the Yeoman's office and you'll receive your orders. And Erik . . . this is the highest priority. I expect your full cooperation," warned Mawson.

Erik shoved back his chair, allowing it to clatter against the credenza. Two glasses fell against each other and toppled over. The water in the pitcher rippled, lapping over the side. He leaned over Tristan as he passed. "There's no victory here for you! What you did isn't as big a deal as Mawson thinks; my time's coming and I *will* be shoulder to shoulder with Zeddicus!" He glared once more at Mawson and stomped out of the room.

Loci smiled reassuringly. "His outbreaks are reprehensible and don't go unnoticed. Ignore his crap."

"Right . . . ," said Tristan, taken aback by Erik's behavior. He glanced through the glass door and watched Erik stomp out of sight like a child throwing a tantrum, and then took in the mountains.

Mawson twirled a bright, silver pen between his fingers like a miniature baton. He stopped abruptly, causing it to point toward the armored man shrouded in polished, black coverings. "Zeddicus. You've been given your Lathe assignment. Impress us as usual. Report to the 4th-floor atrium office for the specifics. You know the drill."

Zeddicus' helmet tilted toward Mawson, its' shiny, angled dome coming into view. "It will be done," quite formally. His lights flashed again as he turned to go. The emotionless and even sonorous bionic tone was short and clipped.

Mawson scooted his chair closer, "Good. Let's focus on our business, Tristan. I wanted to keep this between us. Mr. Edde has requested your presence at the famed Castalia Ball held in Vuton's southernmost inner city Ascalon," He sat on the edge of his seat.

"Do you have any details?" asked Tristan.

"Yes, indeed. I was invited to represent Institute VI. It wasn't for sale, but Atomia offered an unexpectedly generous price. We'd be foolish to ignore this new development. They view our military operations as capable of 'supporting' other reticent factions, and potentially capable of helping them with their new global initiative."

Tristan chilled at the thought. Was he talking about selling out Institute VI? That came out of nowhere.

Before he could respond, Loci interjected. "All the bigwigs will be at the ball, including Senator Leith Xander, accompanied by a collection of his top military brass. That's not to mention representation from Amstye, Feria, and Oxium. Vuton is hosting the event, and President Drakkar accepted an invitation."

Speaking up now seemed inappropriate, but Tristan was unable to dismiss an unmistakable, internal conflict. Sell Institute VI? Accompany Mawson? A new global movement? His heart raced as he tried to comprehend new developments. Had Mawson truly arranged this with Mr. Edde?

"Good," continued Mawson, "We depart tomorrow at 1300. I suggest you get a good night's rest."

"A question, Headmaster," said Tristan.

"Yes, of course." Mawson twirled the silver pen again, this time in the opposite direction, and continued eyeing it cautiously.

"What are your ultimate intentions if and when these new arrangements mature?"

"Let me put it this way, Tristan. Atomia has offered enough credits to purchase a small country; it would be foolish to ignore their proposition."

He said it like he didn't care. "Don't you find it odd that I'll be working with their main antagonist, the USC?" asked Tristan.

Mawson chuckled. "We're an independent faction. If this purchase materializes, we'll extract you. Their business will be conducted directly with the Federation. Placement is everything. We'll have only one opportunity to make it right. I'm sure you'll agree with the importance of being on the right side of this beast."

That's not what Tristan was worried about. He could land mercenary assignments practically anywhere. Pilots were in tremendous demand worldwide, and he was one of the best. "Of all the work we have, it seems odd to limit our options. Atomia is only one country."

"Your curiosity is surprising, Tristan. That could be a problem, you know. Killed the cat, you know. Atomia is the planet's wealthiest nation. United with Vuton, Atomia will be the strongest force this world has ever known. Prudence demands attention. Institute VI can be a key player in these unfolding events, and should be. Consequently, I make decisions for its' benefit." Mawson's pen fell, clattering onto the polished wood surface.

"Yes, sir." He could sense a chill in the air; Mawson's scar swelled as his worry lines deepened.

Loci pushed back from the table. "Good. If there are no more questions, I suggest we end this little gathering." Leaning with her hands on the table, she started to rise out of her chair.

"I have one more question," Tristan ignored the woman, leveling his focus at Mawson. This might be his only opportunity to satisfy his curiosity.

"Yes?" said Mawson warily.

"Mr. Edde said that you and he go way back. Will this decision have a negative impact on your friendship?"

"Mr. Edde will handle these and other situations quite well. I wouldn't be solicitous. He's more resourceful than you credit him. Remember, Tristan. Our number-one rule is never to become personally involved with our clientele."

Generally choosing a more reserved approach, Tristan immediately felt out of his element. He did his best to address his concerns, frustrated by Mawson's lack of empathy. He wanted to draw out another question, but his mind went blank.

Mawson rose from his chair. "Enjoy your evening. It'll be awhile before you return. Prepare yourself, Tristan. Wear your Institute VI uniform tomorrow. We must look sharp. Many eyes will be upon us. Until we separate in Vuton, you will serve as my bodyguard. Unfortunately, Ms. Talbot won't be able to attend."

"I'm looking forward to it."

"I'm sure you are. The Vutonians know how to throw a party."

CHAPTER

5

CRESCENT 17, 1870 O.C.
CITY: ASCALON

Ascalon, by any man's standards, a sprawling metropolis and city on the rise, was not only Vuton's fastest-growing metropolis, but a popular tourist destination as well. Tristan had passed through once before, but hadn't taken the time to explore. Today, he was focused on the Marne, the USC's latest gunship acquisition. So far, so good.

The Marne flew well, and for its' size and complexity, was highly responsive. Buffeted by rising heat currents, the vessel yawed to port, quickly self-righting. A slice of the unfolding cityscape sped past the forward viewing ports. In classic children's book style—red clay roofs on all sizes of buildings, their walls gaily decorated with pinks, light greens, and pale blues—the urban medley spreading out below was like a dream, and it resurrected a favorite childhood jaunt to an amusement park. He could still summon the excitement from his favorite, high-speed ride. It was a brightly painted, boxy container with wings, attached to a cable and slung round and round, high off the ground. The faster it went, the louder the wind whistled against the cable and the more his stomach tightened. His mother would buy him three or four tickets so he could ride forever—at least that's what it seemed.

Below, a canal, crossed by a handful of bridges, connected the inner and outer cities. A construction site arose from Ascalon's heart, surrounded by urban sprawl, which seemed to flow downward from the central complex's sloping sides. The top of this behemoth looked like a misshapen capsule—jutting, unfinished sides, the entire structure as wide as it was tall, a colossus of metal and glass—ascending through the clouds. Several triple-decked airships drifted lazily by, creating an illusion that both the present and future glories of the city had consented to meet in mutual admiration.

Mawson gazed serenely out a starboard window; pensive, perhaps preoccupied with thoughts of the upcoming black-tie gala. "You're soon to mingle with some of the world's most influential leaders. Not many from the ranks are afforded such promising opportunities. Are you nervous?"

"No," Tristan lied, his thoughts instantly redirected. *Of course, he was nervous*, what with being thrown into a virtual lion's den—a mix of wealth, leadership, nobility and politicians. With his luck, the informant probably had just that kind of power, some VIP, impossible to manage. He was having difficulty taking this trip seriously, especially since he was tethered to Mawson as a bodyguard. The man didn't need any such thing, no matter how important he thought he was. That scar would scare anyone. Tristan was anticipating some free time; the ball could be a good place to unwind.

"Remember. The Atomians view Senator Xander as something akin to a god; similar accolades have already surfaced in Vuton. Be sure to greet him with the Federation salute—right arm forward, palm up."

"I've seen it before." Distracted by nervousness and the approaching convention complex, he shuffled through mental images. Video clips could only take him so far. A disdainful reminder of what that salute represented, he wished they could just shake hands. He was thinking Xander would be very successful as an escaped fugitive, "*The dogs wouldn't catch him 'cause his ass doesn't stink*".

"Excellent," replied Mawson, turning back to the window.

The Marne listed to port. At the lower altitude, the effects of the rising heat waves had diminished significantly. Nonetheless, the crosswind was unnerving. The gunship was tracking to the auditorium's docking stations to the left of a grand circular drive spanning the pedestrian side of the enormous structure. The boulevard was lined with Atomian flags—a black sun with flaming red tips curving outward and clockwise. Interspersed were Vuton's "seeing eye" ensigns—fiercely depicted by a large black pupil topped by a curved, jutting eyebrow, and supported by an upside-down rendition of the same. The fluttering flags appeared fierce and powerful under the intermittent shadows of air vehicles ferrying in other "distinguished" guests, *"If they escaped, no one would find them,"* he quietly muttered, smiling.

Mawson raised his finger. "When you rendezvous with the informant, get back to the Marne and leave immediately! Mr. Edde's financial commitment to the mission demands this."

"Affirmative, understood." Tristan wouldn't take his eyes off the landing zone entrance, a half-circle opening, situated in the center of the structure's vaulted roof. By comparison, the entire Institute VI could fit inside the massive domed complex. Preparing for a go-around, he'd set the ship's configuration to allow for the unconventional approach. The image of an immense wheel had taken shape; the auditorium was the hub. Tubular, glass walkways from the lobby radiated outward like spokes on a wheel. The Marne shuddered abruptly, forcing Tristan to scan the radar screen. A green wand of light rotated around the circular detector. Fast-moving blips appeared and disappeared with each rotation. He eyed the display's left side, trying to determine the source of the discharge while he re-positioned himself and cinched his restraining harness. Out the port window, a bright image flashed in the periphery—a Gryphon. Seldom seen, the vessel was constructed of five, baton-like appendages that radiated out of a small, central hub. This one quickly slipped past the Marne through the portal. Angered by the pilot's careless maneuver, Tristan strained to calm himself. "Asshole," quietly to himself.

Mawson tightened his belts. "I know. But we're playing both sides here—working for the USC and integrating into the politics of the Federation. Rumor has it this is the final push to merge Atomia and Vuton. Atomia is supposedly financing the construction of that huge building bulging out of the center of Ascalon, and plans exclusivity of usage rights." He glanced out the window. "This is the most precarious political situation in which we've ever meddled; there's no room for mistakes." Mawson shifted forward into the navigator's chair and clipped his harnesses securely.

Tristan reduced airspeed, let the nose drop, and listened to cockpit sounds; the air traffic controller cleared them to land. A number of aircraft had already arrived and were parked in three long, straight lines adjacent the landing zone; red lights bordered the rectangular platform, glistening off the crafts' polished surfaces, with a row of steadily glowing green lights down the runway's middle. The Marne groaned when he lowered the landing gear and set the thrusters to neutral, as if complaining of the extremely slow speed. The Marne was a thoroughbred, not a workhorse. Rear blasters ignited, tilting the ship slightly. It shuddered just above the surface and gently settled onto its high-pressure tires.

Mawson hastily unbuckled and jumped to his feet, wiping his brow with the back of his hand. The two men made their way down the Marne's ramp, and proceeded toward the large doors at the end of the platform. The line was long at the security checkpoint. Tristan felt proud in his Institute VI uniform, a smartly designed black suit edged with gold piping and belted by a gold buckle. It provided him with a strong sense of belonging. This was his most distinguished ensemble, one which he seldom wore. He especially favored the wide shoulder pads—heavy with gold trim, jutting out over his broad shoulders. He could sense the crowd's excitement while they chattered like a coup full of hungry hens. Women in sparkling formal gowns eyed him coyly, but Tristan ignored them. He was more concerned about getting past the checkpoint and four Vutonian soldiers, examining paperwork and herding guests through metal detectors.

The ballroom was the largest dance hall Tristan had ever seen. The ceiling was decorated like a night sky animated with twinkling stars. It was set against tall, golden columns lining an arching wall. The entire area was an enormous theater decked with an unending dance floor, including over-reaching, second-level balconies.

A podium had been installed at center stage, directly behind a long table covered with a deep crimson material. The table was lined with several dozen chairs. Many more circular tables dotted the area. A string orchestra strummed popular tunes, struggling against the endless chatter of well-dressed attendees. Caught up in the moment, Tristan found himself enjoying the immense sense of wealth and influence projected by Atomian and Vutonian aristocracy. The setting and atmosphere of affluence were far removed from his comfort zone, yet he found it compelling. He scrutinized unfamiliar faces, hoping to uncover some indication of who his informant was; someone appearing as out of place as he felt—moving too quickly, not dressed so well—something notable. But in the dazzle, anyone could be "*Liberty*".

"Well, here we are!" quipped Mawson. "What a sight to behold. This ballroom was built centuries ago. It's where many past Vutonian Sovereigns delivered eloquent speeches; truly a place of renown!"

Starlight sparkles and melodic euphony displaced Tristan enough to make him wish Mawson wasn't there.

"Do you see the royals?" Mawson discretely tipped his forehead.

Tristan cast his gaze toward the long, crimson table. "Yes, sir."

"Let me give you a quick rundown. Most would consider it blasphemous if you didn't recognize any one of them. In fact, you'd probably be escorted back to the ship, so pay attention. At your far left, the man with the long white hair—that's Salvador Dukes Seryth, the Lord Commander and the senator's right-hand man. He commands Xander's military faction otherwise known as The Valkyries, the coalition responsible for security and protecting the senator. Many have tried to abscond with this power, without success. Seryth is known for taking care of the senator's dirty work. Avoid his bad side at all costs."

Except for a few, the throng of revelers was a veritable sea of white hair—everywhere he turned—an impossible reality. But, Seryth was easily identifiable. His silver-white hair was long, down to his chest; out-of-place with the conservative short-cropped hairstyles currently in vogue. His dress uniform, brightly polished armor, was obviously more for show than everyday use. Like a dry lamp wick, the man was intensely compelling. Even though infamous for pernicious chicanery, his public demeanor was imposing—unabashed and unafraid.

Mawson muttered, barely intelligible. "And the gentleman speaking with Seryth is General Nyvala, an avid Xander supporter, idolized by Atomia's military. In my opinion, Xander displayed great wisdom in accommodating the general. The man has influence over the Atomian armed forces more than most realize."

Tristan perceived Seryth's respect for Nyvala. The general's strong features *drew* respect: medium length, gray handlebar mustache and goatee; thick, white eyebrows and gray hair tightly pulled back. His great coat, deep teal in color and distended in the back, appeared to have wings. He projected power and savvy.

"And the two women sitting next to him . . . ," continued Mawson, ". . . On the left is his daughter, Eliza, the one with the dark hair. She's half Atomian and half Oxium. This, of course, conflicts with Atomian marriage custom. Xander's views are well known— Oxium women are considered lowly and inferior. Her presence here could create some strained discussions."

Tristan paused. Eliza's dark eyes matched her hair. She held his gaze for as long as he could stare without looking conspicuous. Her skin glowed. Her floor-length dress and long, flowing hair, bouncing freely with each movement, struck a deep inner chord in him, resulting in a pleasurable, yet restrained smile.

"And the other young lady is the daughter of the great Xander. Her name is Rose."

Rose's style—short-cropped white hair and thin white eyebrows—was the antithesis of Eliza's. Her alluring smile turned up softly at the corners, pushing her cheeks into perfect, small mounds of cheerfulness. Her dress sparkled with flashes of silver.

More business-like than ever and suddenly frowning, Mawson continued. "Sovereign Drakkar is on the far right, speaking to that group of military officials and ambassadors."

Tristan's first impression of Drakkar: ghost-white hair, white eyebrows, flaccid expression, gaunt cheeks, and a near-lifeless stare; sent chills down his spine. His pure white suit, a ghastly choice, stood him invisible in a blizzard in the dead of winter. Behind him, six armed guards in jet black uniforms formed a chilling backdrop.

A silver flash—long, platinum hair—seized Tristan's attention. Seryth was making his way across the dance floor.

"Oh! It looks like the LC wants to chat," said Mawson. "I think you can handle it alone from here, Tristan. Improvise if you have to; but please, lose those worry lines. Maybe you should have a drink? Your forehead makes you look like you just destroyed a Federation zyn repository." He grinned and made his way toward Seryth.

Relieved that Mawson's efforts might delay the meeting, Tristan's discomfort couldn't have come at a more inconvenient time. The hordes of contented guests, mingling, drinking, and snacking on pâté-smeared crackers, no longer interested him. He glanced again at Eliza and Rose, still engaged in conversation. Eliza, perhaps not even twenty, was the most mesmerizing woman he'd seen so far. Rose seemed more mature, too much so for his liking. The ladies were probably bored with the political repartee on every side. Their glamour, their beauty, merged perfectly into this spate of wealth. The two looked as if they hadn't worked a day in their lives. Where was this great Xander? Tristan wanted to uncover his informant, looking for anything that didn't belong. He paused on an impressive display of Atomian flags, decadently unfurled from high columns. Their flaming black suns scorched the onlookers, as if silently inspecting them from above.

"Quite a party, isn't it?"

Tristan jumped. The voice sounded familiar, but totally unexpected. He turned and faced Mr. Edde. "What are you doing here?"

Mr. Edde swirled a long-stemmed wine glass, peering into its red depth. "I'm enjoying the party. Watching all the wealthy nobles flaunt their fancy outfits. Blatant disregard for the people suffering beneath them. Surreal, isn't it?"

Tristan couldn't suppress a swell of apprehension. "What if someone discovers you?" That would mean their entire team had been compromised.

"Nonsense. I fit right in. I'm not Mr. Edde tonight." He smiled and finessed his fake, handlebar mustache. "No. Tonight, I'm Randolph Croxton, a Ferian businessman who supports the divine Federation!"

His response caught Tristan off guard. Edde's assumed identity started to seem like him weaving threads in a spider's web, expanding ever outward. Tristan wasn't used to such antics, nor was he enthusiastic about playing along. "Sorry, but you were the last person I expected to see here."

Mr. Edde's tone was complacent. "I'm everywhere, an arrangement that I find propitious. It allows me to experience a wealth of different perspectives."

"Have you uncovered our informant, *Liberty*?" asked Tristan as he mused over the man's choice of words.

"No. Not yet. Before leaving Lathe, I tried; I didn't want to depart without that vital information, but I ran out of time. You've probably already discovered that I'm the impatient type. I'm quite anxious to meet this one who could redirect our future."

"You're crazy," said Tristan. "You're smack in the middle of a scorpions' nest, yet your composure is astounding. You've got serious balls."

Mr. Edde coated the insides of his glass with a swirl of wine before taking another sip. "Fear only hinders you."

"Are you going to hitch a ride with me and our mysterious snitch?"

"No. I have my own flight to catch. I have important business to attend to in Aurelia."

"Aurelia?" exclaimed Tristan, doing nothing to mask his surprise. "Why would you have any business in that backwater? Don't they still use mules to get around?"

"Don't underestimate them. The Collector religion and belief in their sun god has considerably delayed needed technological advances, but they're a resilient people. Atomia has already initiated an alignment strategy. When they are unified with Vuton, Aurelia will become one of the Federation's vassal nations. That will position the Federation to expand its New World Order into the northern hemisphere. That's bad, I might add, for the rest of us. I'm going to launch propaganda efforts immediately. I leave tonight and have charged Mr. Asbury to act in my stead. As soon as you return to Lathe, he'll provide you with your marching orders."

"Yes, sir," acknowledged Tristan, instantly provoked. It wasn't that he wanted Cole's responsibilities; he wanted recognition for his abilities. This announcement proved to be bittersweet.

Mr. Edde tipped his nod toward Seryth. "Looks like someone has his eyes on you."

Seryth's gaze was unexpectedly leveled directly at Tristan. "What are they talking about?" he asked, glancing through a barrier of scattered nobles.

"I don't know. But, no worries. Mr. Mawson knows what he's doing. You can trust him not to betray our cause. Couldn't stand the thought of losing his income." He chuckled and sipped again.

Mawson slid quietly into the crowd, leaving Seryth in Tristan's direct line of sight.

"Damn," mumbled Tristan, straightening his waistcoat and forcing a smile.

Mr. Edde lowered his glass and smiled, "How about that, eh? Show your best manners. I'll keep in touch. You won't find me, but I'll be aware of your every move. Good luck, Mr. Hart." He turned and walked off quickly.

"Tristan Hart?" More of an exclamation than a question.

The man's deep voice caught Tristan off guard. He expected his voice to be higher pitched. "Yes, sir." He stiffened and continued. "Lord Commander Seryth! It's a pleasure to make your acquaintance personally." He lowered his head and positioned his arm into the Atomian salute, trying to will away a flutter of gut-wrenching queasiness. This had to be the most awkward moment of his day.

"Pleasure is all mine. I hear that you're a decent mercenary and a damn good pilot."

Another surprise. How did he learn of his flying abilities? Maybe Mawson told him? "Thank you, sir." One edge of Tristan's lips curled upward. "I've always been captivated by flying machines."

The man's eyes intensified. "Indeed. Who was that man with whom you were speaking?"

Tristan felt like he had been hit by the *Marne*. He couldn't remember Mr. Edde's fake name. "Who was it? "Oh! Yes, him. A Ferian businessman." He tried to prolong the moment; his thoughts froze.

His mind shouted, "Come on! Remember his name!"

"Randolph. Yes! Randolph, er, Crockhead. He was quite congenial. Just walked up and started chatting." Tristan released a nervous laugh.

"Never seen him." Seryth's tone was flat.

Tristan felt his life unravel. Had Seryth made him? How far to the door, and the *Marne*? Oh, shit.

"You've never met Senator Xander, have you?" asked Seryth.

"No, Sir. I've dreamed of that moment." His response made him feel even worse. First, he stumbled over Mr. Edde's fake name, and now, he sounded like a complete and utter suckup. Surely he had aroused the man's suspicions.

"He's a magnificent man. Words couldn't describe the inspiration that flows from his every word. His presence is divine." Seryth's gleam sparkled.

"Yes, sir. I've heard that."

"He'll begin his speech once everyone calms down." Seryth brushed back his long, white locks and leaned in.

Tristan's heart raced.

"I heard you were the one who destroyed our Gaustead Embassy, including the underground repository."

Wine from his breath wafted over. "Sir . . . ?" He didn't know what to say. "I . . ." His heart felt like it was rolling down a hill. Androids, the bomb, the descent, the narrow escape—flooded his thoughts and stopped his ears. He was less frightened then than at this very moment.

Seryth slapped him on the arm, "Damn good work. Keep it up."

Tristan was flabbergasted. His thoughts went blank. Was Commander Seryth the informant? Should he try to establish a connection? Death if he was wrong. He hated not knowing. "Thank you, sir. Just following orders."

"That's the attitude! A soldier doesn't question; he just does!" Seryth chuckled. "We need men like you. Perhaps someday we can talk about your joining the *Valkyries*. With us, you'd have an incredibly promising future!"

Tristan still hadn't collected his thoughts. If he didn't ask, he'd never forgive himself. ". . . I don't understand . . . I thought you'd be upset?"

Seryth nodded and tossed back his head, the action intensified by his flowing hair. "Politics and war are nothing but a game. Only a select few are good at it. But Xander is the game master. Just make sure you're on the winning side when the dust settles, okay?" He reached out his hand. His fingernails were perfectly manicured, almost feminine. "Enjoy the show." After shaking hands, he removed a white handkerchief and wiped his hands. A moment later, he was gone, smiling and edging through the crowd toward the long crimson table.

Tristan studied the jumble of regally-clad spectators in the ballroom, hoping for any indication pointing him to his contact. Men in dark suits and colorful ties, and women in glittering evening gowns were the norm, but there were plenty of exceptions. The more he thought about it, the more remote it seemed that he'd ever identify the person. Better to wait than to appear overly concerned. Movement at the podium drew his attention to several high-ranking military officials seating themselves next to Lord Commander Seryth directly across from Sovereign Drakkar. All the white hair was still stunning. The time for the senator's speech was approaching, prompting Tristan to join Mawson at the edge of the dance floor. From there, he could better observe the famous speaker sitting stiffly and engaging in small talk; he seemed more interested in the swelling audience.

"What were you thinking, telling the damn Lord Commander, of all people, that I helped in the embassy attack?" demanded Tristan. "Are you nuts? I thought you had my back!" His hoarse whisper strained over the music.

"I'd settle down if I were you, Tristan," cautioned Mawson. "Believe it or not, I happen to know what I'm doing, so don't question my motives. Perhaps you'd be better served to locate our informant rather than wasting precious time confronting me. That's your assignment! Now, please, if you will. The senator is about to deliver his speech."

"Next time you rat me out to a bigwig, how about a heads-up? I think I pissed these trousers. Good thing they're black," he quietly remarked through gritted teeth.

He couldn't locate the elusive spy any more than he could find a needle in a haystack, an impossible task, so he ignored the request. "Perhaps you also told the "glorious" Lord Commander that I'm undercover here in hopes of meeting a secret operative who is gonna help us blow him to shit?" fumed Tristan, again through gritted teeth.

"I'm growing tired of your insinuations, Hart. Trust me. You're in good hands, but that could soon change if you don't redirect your energy!" demanded Mawson. A deepening frown fell back in submission. Tristan considered "redirecting his energy" by placing a *Size 12* up Mawson's self-righteous ass. His pointy-toed boot would widen that self-righteous sphincter considerably.

The throng's deafening applause made it impossible to converse. Tristan squelched his frustration and refocused on the podium, worrying if the man *really* had his best interests in mind. Straining to see beyond the sea of heads and hats, Tristan discovered Xander was all but invisible. The room overflowed with an unexpected fervor of chanting, "Xander, Xander, Xander!" Arms extended, his swarm of worshippers proclaimed their obeisance. That was, everyone except a small group of ambassadors off to the side—three Ferian ambassadors capped in maroon fedora hats trimmed with short silver feathers and wearing fur shoulder wraps over billowing blouses; four Amstynian ambassadors dressed in royal blue jackets and straight black trousers; and three Oxium ambassadors easily recognizable in distinguished black leather coats and knee-high boots. The wary men stood gaping, unable to conceal their discontent.

Mass adoration and hysteria collided, prompting Tristan to scan for exits. Thanks to the distractions, the doors along the back wall wouldn't be much of a stretch, if he sprinted. The crowd, shifting like jelly on a stunt ship, parted just enough to allow him a view of the despot-to-be dressed in stiff black. The jacket sported a maroon Nehru collar against his long neck, emphasizing gaunt cheeks, a tight smile and flowing white hair. His stride emanated confidence and ended with the sovereign's handshake. He quickly moved on, offering a smile to the Lord Commander and General Nyvala, but not his hand. Upon reaching the lectern, the moment's intensity enveloped him. He stood, absorbing the energy of the crowd, closing his eyes momentarily and then casually inspecting his closest observers. He scanned the ballroom, not appearing rushed, eventually motioning, palms down, sending a blanketed hush throughout.

Through the intense calm, Xander's quiet, low tone was quite unassuming. "My respected Atomian and Vutonian comrades, my fellow Azdahri! I say to you, first and foremost, and then to all others united in our cause—welcome!" A banner behind him fluttered; his long white hair, somewhat disheveled, stirred. He tucked stray ends behind his ears.

"Eight years of personal effort to unite the Azdahri people have come and gone. Yet, when set against so many historically divisive decades, those eight years now seem miniscule. Let us never forget what these few years have spawned—the rebirth of our nation, one formerly threatened by those intent on our subjugation! Their vision of our defeat has, for us, generated an incendiary and unquenchable resolve for strength, success, and regeneration."

"As they were centuries ago, Atomia and Vuton will soon once again become united! Ours was the most powerful nation in existence; past global unification attempts nearly destroyed our great race.

That unspeakable alliance shattered our military might, decimated our economy and fractured into two, our once great land............... We must try again!"

The audience exploded, and then quickly subsided under his raised hand.

"We fell from being the greatest empire the world had ever seen, into utter despair; becoming worldly vagabonds, facing early extermination. But now, centuries later, our dreams, our hopes, have been rekindled! We are alive, rising out of the ashes of our suffering!"

"New dreams and possibilities have been forged from the same dwindling freedom fires that the rest of the world maliciously labored to extinguish. I say to you today, my comrades, the fetid water thrown upon us, intended to extinguish the remaining glowing embers of our freedom...........will become a fading wisp of stinking vapor,...... floating from the rotting carcasses... of our enemies!"

The remarkable explosion of the audience's previous applause was now dwarfed by what could only be described as adulation's deafening roar that lasted at least five minutes.

"Representing evolution's pinnacle, Atomia has become this age's most technologically advanced nation. Our prolific scientific and technical expertise has launched us decades, if not centuries, into the future. Vuton's sophisticated military strength supersedes any other, and is now positioned as the world's greatest military might! While we seethe with unspent power, we remain silent and motionless among the unsuspecting nations. Why? Because our bureaucrats spend their time placating our enemies, motivated only by their desire to prevent our growth, our destiny."

Amidst the rousing bouts of applause, Tristan listened in shock. Xander's words were deeply stirring. Even so, the man was working up to something, something grandiose in scale but sinister in intent. It left Tristan with an impression of a verdant tree rooted in corpses along a river of blood. Glancing across the spellbound audience; he was reminded of the latent power resident in credulous individuals. He had no desire to be counted with them. Seryth, with his wry smile, was especially disturbing. Even Mawson, supporting his chin with his thumb and forefinger, seemed enthralled.

"We've all heard from our noble Reynan "counterparts". Their lofty peace lectures continue to infest our airwaves. Yes, Reyna has undoubtedly forged ahead, expecting and promoting dubious peaceful triumphs founded on their naïve ideologies and earning them the title of world peace promoters. The world that they envision is fantastic, or better said, fictitious—they would herald a new, Reynan world, purportedly irenic and harmonious. Their heraldry would be reasonable if one could suppose that worldwide disarmament could be achieved." Xander paused, enduring an explosion of booing and hissing.

"The essence of their drivel lies in one primary fixation–free trade! Out of disarmament, they expect explosive economic growth. Their idealistic endeavors would then be launched into all cultures, exposing them to Reynan corruption. Since their Atomian conquest, they've never ceased striving for a new world. But what *is* the state of our world?" Xander questioned the people. They stood waiting to be fed while he sharpened his tone.

"War! The world is at war! Able nations rise to consume the weak, but none have truly risen against Reynan aggression. Nations claiming neutrality exist with the persistent fear of being devoured by these raging conflicts. And, I ask you . . . Where is Reyna on the swinging pendulum of conflict between Thracia and Aurelia? Where has Reyna been during the ongoing Vudria and Tholiad hostilities? After a century—this war still rages! What about their neighbors, victims at best? Need I remind you of Jador, a country consumed by internal strife? Our own great Atomian nation quakes in fear of the ever-present threats of Oxium, Amstye, and Feria! Why? These three threaten war in order to stifle our unification efforts! Even Antegonia's vile warriors threaten Reyna's peace-keeping efforts and fragile borders. This is the 'peace' that they promote!"

Tristan kept the ambassadors in his field of vision while he contemplated the not-so-veiled threats of aggression Xander proposed. The gaily dressed men were growing more and more uncomfortable— their heads were shaking while they hid their lips behind cupped hands. He sensed anger as they paced back and forth. One of the men, tall and rotund under a flat maroon hat, seemed the most taken aback. The skin on his face and neck nearly matched his hat. How could Xander, knowing of the ambassadors' presence, speak like this? One of the Ferian ambassadors met his eyes. He saw the furrow of the man's brow—very upset. Tristan couldn't place the comment about Reynan aggression. He was well aware of Thracia's pending attack on Aurelia. Hearing about Oxium, Amstye and Feria raised submerged concerns that rang bell after bell. Would his homeland become engulfed in war? He hadn't even considered Jador, a land so far out of reach, both by distance and by culture. The world was swiftly bowing to bedlam, what with so much fighting and conflict. Was this Xander's doing too?

The sound system boomed. "In Reyna's so-called *new world model,* the Azdahri people looked to them for hope: hope for a new and prosperous economy, international trade, and religious freedom. Some hoped for international solidarity and unification. All in all, we placed our hopes in the world council seated in Reyna. Still, others pined for global respect as a form of enlightenment."

Scattered throughout, many downward thumbs obviated rejection of Reyna.

"All this hope was in vain. We listened to false promises; at best, placebos to sooth our infirmities. There is only one form of hope that could ever stand the true test of time—hope through our own supremacy. Your faith in Atomian values, eternal and innermost in your heart, will be the impetus for change. I want to recruit you! Together, we shall forge ahead, with *genuine* hope, in our truly powerful and worthy principles. Elect me as leader of the Azdahri people, and I will initiate the Ebonfall Manifesto; finally ensuring the world will breathe the rarified air of peace *through strength* it both needs and deserves! I will restore the glory of the Azdahri and avenge its honor! We are a just and fair people and have mercifully provided Reyna with more than enough time to create *anything* positive out of their empty ideologies! They have failed! Now,....... it is our time!"

It was as if the high ceiling constellations thundered, each star releasing a mass of unquenchable energy into the night sky. Xander stopped, stood statuesquely, and beamed before the deafening roar of worshipful sycophants.

"We will chart the New World Order our way! The Reynans have refused to recognize that radical change is necessary! I say to Reyna and all of Eshen, prepare to face the wrath of our great nation! To all who dare impede Azdahri ideals; let this be your warning! We will avenge ourselves by introducing to you your own punishing fears! Let us merge Vuton and Atomia's power! Allow me the privileged opportunity to lead you according to the Ebonfall Manifesto!"

He stepped back from the chorus of ecstatic voices. His forehead twitched, laboring to conceal his reaction. The thunderous adulation continued. He raised his hands. No response. He waved his open palms. Reluctantly, the audience submitted.

"Look upon our flag! Look at it with pride! Together, we can remove all obstacles to victory! Our flag beckons to you. 'Salute us." He motioned to the black sun ringed with flames on the banner behind him.

Hundreds of craned necks extended right arms and upward palms.

Not wanting to, Tristan followed suit. Instinct told him to reject what he had just heard. Was he reading a fairy tale? Had Reyna truly caused the world's problems? As far as he knew, the answer was a resounding *"no."* It sounded like Xander and his men were responsible, but that had yet to be proven. He glanced at the ambassadors' section, now empty. Where had they gone? Euphoric excitement animated the ballroom. He strained on his tiptoes, scanning for Eliza. There she was, clapping excitedly. She seemed to take all of this a little too seriously. If Xander was to become sovereign of the merged nations, could his quest for more power and authority be stopped? Soothing musical strains drifted idly by while Xander embraced Sovereign Drakkar. Tristan eyed them through the melting crowd.

"He's quite a performer, isn't he?" asked Mawson. "Change is coming, Tristan," he said, just before disappearing again.

Tristan, growing desperate to be approached by the informant, assayed the faces of passersby, hoping for that elusive clue. Would the operative ever show himself—or should he expect a woman?

CHAPTER 7

String instruments played on Tristan's nerves as he nervously eyed the Ballroom deluge of stylish coiffures ebbing and flowing like graceful currents in a lazy river. The dancing and excited chatter of the guests heightened his senses. It wasn't long before he found himself longing for solitude. The smell of roasted game and fried potatoes caught his attention. Against the back wall, a buffet line cast an orange hue from heat lamps. A row of busy chefs and servers doled out meats, vegetables, and baked goods. His stomach groaned. All he'd had to eat since departing was an energy bar, bland and dry. A spry couple passed close by, dancing; the man wore a blue velvet suit too snug for Tristan's liking, and the woman a frilly white dress, long and bouncy and flowing with each step. He swung her around, bringing her within arm's reach of Tristan, before he deftly retrieved her to his side. Tristan's defense mechanisms blossomed. Unexpectedly, he felt overcome in the midst of the war-thirsty crowd. He was an outsider, and he feared that he looked it more than ever. Had it not been for the prestige implied by his gold-piped uniform, he probably would have left.

His personal communicator indicated two hours had already passed. He needed to locate the informant. The flood of attendees made it seem impossible. Tempered-smiling dancers twirled around him, sharpening his edginess. To make matters worse, the festivities triggered childhood dance recollections. He didn't want to go through that again. The passionate melody soothed over the prickles from Xander's words, allowing the seeds of discord to seep into the hearts of the listeners without obstruction. If the sower secured the political power to water them, they would be sure to take root and bear the fruit of discord and conflict. An Atomian war would be a war to end all wars, one far greater in severity and conflagration than any in the past 200 years. If the Federation succeeded, they would be gifted a vassal world, a dawning realization for Tristan he was certain others present didn't understand, or simply ignored.

Tristan glanced at his communicator—silence accompanied by a flashing message indicator. With nothing to distract him, anxiety took root, fueled as it was by the impending conflict. He had to find Liberty or Liberty had to find him; either were acceptable, but fleeting time was ushering in a personal crisis. He discovered two Amstynian ambassadors against the far wall—they stood silently, rigid and isolated; the others had left. Mr. Edde had been true to his word and disappeared; even the Head Master wasn't to be seen.

Unexpectedly, a youthfully vibrant female appeared before him. "Hello! Would you join me for a dance?" she asked, eyes sparkling as if floating in a sea of stars, as she pushed long dark brown hair from her shoulders, exposing a full bosom. Tristan's instincts allowed him the view. He quickly shifted, but it was too late. He feigned composure, fairly certain that his awkward manner had already been detected. She was more woman than he had first thought. It was Eliza Nyvala, the general's daughter; her figure, a teenage form, tight and fit, was an unexpected pleasure.

Nervously, he pressed at his thick mop of dark, flyaway hair. Unable to slow a quickening pulse, his tongue knotted. She greeted him as if they were old friends, making the moment even more difficult. "Maybe some other time? I need to focus on a most pressing matter." Tristan looked past her as if searching for someone, but she rose onto her tiptoes, blocking his view; her bright hazel eyes proving an irresistible distraction. His senses were flooded—his growling stomach, the music, the unending babble—all around him. Considering his mission, his responsibilities, initiated a swell of anxiety. If he entertained her, the informant would never come.

"Really? You're attending the annual Castalia Ball! I would hate to wait an entire year for another chance to dance……with me."

She, an impatient teenager, wasn't buying his explanation.

"Look. Isn't there someone else you could ask?" He watched her expression, trying to discern any hint of acceptance. There was none.

She planted her feet and wedged her hands on her hips. "Like who? There's no one here but old gas bags and pompous politicians. You're the only one even *close* to my age."

Was she complimenting him? Dancing with a carefree teenager would be like robbing the cradle. He was certainly at least five years older. "I . . ."

"You don't have to be shy. Honestly, you're the cutest one in the room," she said, glancing back at the orchestra pit, "which isn't saying much. But, hey. When the moment presents itself, I really should seize it, right? So, how about it? Dance with me!" She extended her hand and let it fall limply at the wrist.

She was playing coy and wasn't going away. Cute, and she was or not, the girl spelled trouble. The general's daughter. Talk about career-ending. Feeling a nervous sweat coming on, he glanced around. If anyone was watching, he couldn't tell; most seemed lost in the moment, including him. He was trapped by his own embarrassment—a child asking him to dance. "It's not that I don't want to . . . . It's just . . ."

"Oh . . . . . you can't dance? What a shame. Most people from Eshen are taught early on to dance. For crying out loud, it's practically a religious experience. Surely you can manage something? Tell me you don't have two left feet."

She had no idea. His feet felt like concrete blocks. He couldn't even feel his feet. "I'm waiting to meet someone. You seem like a nice girl, but . . ." He wanted her to go away. Enough was enough.

"So, who're you meeting?"

The girl knew no bounds. Feeling truly harassed now, his tongue was no more than a fat lump of dysfunctional flesh. ". . . a . . . someone really important."

Eliza pouted, causing her smooth lips to wrinkle abruptly.

Tristan swallowed hard. There was no way out. He could suggest that they get something from the buffet.

"I'm not stupid. You're making up excuses. If you really don't want to dance, just say so." She dropped her hand and took a step toward the orchestra, barely clearing a twirling pair behind her.

He was convicted. He had lied to a girl young enough to be his little sister and guilt set in. "No, wait! It's not that. Honest. I don't know how to dance. I'm sorry." He half expected a laugh.

She spun around, stunned. "At all?"

"Well, I know a Ferian dance, but that's not saying much." His voice became lost in the melody drifting across the battleground like morning fog.

"Really? Let me guess. The Billiard Four Step? No, wait! The Septin Bango? Still nothing?"

This can't be happening. "Yeah, . . . sorry." Tristan's tone followed his downcast eyes.

"The Waltz of the Butterfly?"

He thought about it for a moment—the name triggered a fleeting image of him and his mother waltzing across the rough oak planks of their living room.

"That's it, isn't it?"

Oddly nodding, he wanted to beg her to slow down. "It's an old dance, and I'm sure the musicians don't know . . ."

Her eyes glistened with glee as she turned and disappeared into the crowd.

"Wait just a second!" he shouted, throwing up his hand in an attempt to stop her. He had no idea what had just happened. What a strange girl. He glanced around; dancers twisted and turned on every side. Where was his informant? Alone and hoping for a miracle, he paced nervously. Xander, haphazardly scanning the audience, was busy befriending other Atomian politicians. The clinking of metal against glass drew Tristan out of his slump, causing him to face the source of the racket.

One of the musicians grabbed a microphone. "Excuse me, ladies and gentleman. We have a special request from the lovely Eliza Nyvala and will be playing *The Waltz of the Butterfly*. She has dedicated this song to her dance partner. Please, do enjoy."

What? Dedicated this song? Tristan was horrified. No. That couldn't be! What was she thinking? "Shit!" He had barely been five and couldn't remember the dance. The revelers, many with mouths agape, parted. If he could have disappeared, he would be gone already. His heart sank even further when Eliza reappeared.

"All right! Excited? Everyone will love it!"

He could barely hear her above the ringing in his ears. She truly had no idea what she just put into motion. "What're you doing? I can't dance!" He couldn't conceal his demeanor – of a man losing control.

"But you said . . ."

"I never got to finish. My mother taught me a long time ago, but I was only a child, and now, I can't remember any of that! That's what I was explaining when you ran off."

The musician's voice again boomed from the speakers. "A one, and two, and one, two, three!"

The waltz began.

"I wish you would have told me sooner!"

"You didn't let me!" He clenched his fists just as they entered the human circle. He turned clammy with sweat seeping from every pore. He dreaded each step forward.

"Oh, well. Too late now, huh? Here, follow my lead. We'll get it down."

He wanted to scream.

She led; he stumbled, afraid to mimic her movements. As far as he was concerned, he looked like a doofus before nobles. He tried to remember; but kept drawing blanks.

She pressed her mouth up against his ear. "As soon as you get the hang of it, take the lead!"

"The lead? The lead!" he glared, and immediately wanted to lead her over a cliff. But the unexpected warmth of her closeness felt soothing, yet did nothing to relieve his awareness of the multitude of piercing eyes. There was no escape, yet his train of thought went off the tracks, when he stepped on her foot.

"Ow! Dammit!"

Her hoarse whisper stung his ear. "Sorry!" Still trying to keep his wits, he thought about Xander's movements—his interest seemed centered on General Nyvala. What was he doing now? He needed to pay closer attention to those men; they moved quickly. Eliza's movements came without warning. She pulled him to the left and then swung him hard right. He felt cursed as he fought to maintain his balance. His skin crawled as gasps from the onlookers shattered his confidence. He was desperate to remember those steps!

"Spin me!" Her voice sharpened.

"I can't!"

"Then I'll spin you!"

"No! I'm the man!"

"Then act like one!"

He lifted her hand and spun her once. Success! His confidence blossomed, but was it too late? She gripped his hand and threw her arm over his head and onto his shoulder. His body didn't respond, causing her to smack his nose. Instantly, his eyes pooled. Breathe! "Why didn't you let me know?"

"You said you knew the dance! Consider it payback for stepping on me!"

In disdain, Tristan shook his head.

"The song is halfway over, and this isn't going very well."

He glanced up just in time to see a woman place her hand over her gaping mouth. Was his performance that wretched? Gradually, the movements his mother had taught him returned. Hopeful, he drew Eliza closer. More couples joined.

Wide-eyed, his youthful partner gazed up at him.

He spun her twice, and then gracefully shuttled her back and forth between outstretched arms. He felt like he was gaining control, and guided her between two couples. He did his best to swoop her gracefully along as they made their way.

Exuberance radiated from her smile.

He was actually enjoying himself, spinning her to either side and causing the crowd to cheer. Now, they looked as if *they* were the ones who had practiced for weeks. The music gradually faded as it neared the end of the song. Back and forth they went; another twirl and then a dip. He held her in place, allowing their new fans time to mount yet another burst of cheer. A quick glance showed Xander and Seryth, both clapping. Her father, General Nyvala, stared stoically; his hands hung limply. Tristan lifted her into a tight embrace.

"That was swell," she said, smiling. "I guess you can dance after all."

"Thanks."

She leaned into his ear again, struggling to speak above the applause. "Meet me just outside the main entrance."

"What?" Her warmth caused an unexpected tingle in a part of his anatomy he had thought dormant, from disuse.

"Will you remember me?" A coy look formed.

What? Will I remember you? What is this about? She was the most unpredictable person he had ever met.

Waiting, she stared into his dark brown eyes and smiled, "After all, I did take the *liberty* of asking you to dance!"

No, this can't be. She's the informant? No! But he had to be sure.

"Well? Will you remember me?"

Her impatience bothered him. "Yes. I'll remember you." He thought about her soft voice in his ear.

"Perfect. I'll be waiting! I loved dancing with you." Tossing her hair back, she hurriedly turned toward an arched doorway.

His eyes trailed her vanishing figure.

Mawson appeared out of nowhere. "Quite a performance, Tristan. At first I was concerned, but you finally caught on."

Where'd *he* come from? "Thanks. She surprised me." The man's presence brought him crashing back to reality.

"Yeah. Heard she's a little spoiled rotten horror, and challenges her father quite often. More importantly, any news on the informant?"

He no longer trusted him. Would he tell Seryth? Mawson had established his lack of discernment, and created in Tristan a fear of his big mouth. "No, sir. Still looking."

Mawson's questioning gaze deepened. His penetrating stare bore right through Tristan. "That's too bad. I hope he or she makes contact soon. Maybe they're waiting for everyone to get drunk?" He chuckled to himself. "Good show, lad." In another moment, he was gone.

The crowd closed in; Tristan pushed himself through the commotion and between the arches.

CHAPTER

His eagerness to leave the ballroom hubbub stemmed from wanting another taste of intrigue that their engaging conversation had offered. As he exited, Tristan felt excitement he hadn't experienced for years. He paced himself with deserved saunter, not wanting to draw undue attention. Once in the foyer, a gaily decorated area—more Atomian flag-banners draping tall, brown-marbled walls, an information booth with a line of people waiting in front of three weary attendants, and a busy bar—he stood near some potted plants and scanned for Eliza. She had gotten his interest in more ways than one: a button nose, a figure of fitness usually reserved for a sports enthusiast, and a seductive, carefree attitude. He had to keep in mind that she was a mere child, too young for peril or risk, but there she was. He was a caretaker at heart, and it often inhibited him. He'd spent too much time worrying instead of working. This sense of responsibility welled up for Eliza. During the dance, had he been too callous? The mission was his priority, but he could already sense that he was sidetracked. He felt vulnerable.

He could see Eliza down the hall, standing inconspicuously alongside one of the dozens of large trees planted in bright brass pots. Several Atomian elites milled about, taking no notice of either of them. Barely noticeable under the tree's shadow, she was completely lost in a brochure.

"Wasn't that fun?" she asked. The sparkle was still there. "Thanks for dancing with me. It felt great being in the spotlight again."

Spotlight. He cringed. "You do that often—suck men into embarrassing situations and watch them choke?" asked Tristan, unnerved. He had to credit her for her feminine guile. Maybe that was what was attracting him?

"It wasn't that bad, now, was it? I thought you were absolutely splendid." She reached up to tame his hair. As soon as she pulled back, it immediately went awry. "Dancing was one of my mother's greatest passions, and she was insistent on teaching me. When I was younger, I spent a lot of time in expensive dance schools and learned some of Eshen's more popular dances. Hey, it paid off!"

"So . . . You wanted to talk?" asked Tristan, lukewarm to her choice of topics, more concerned with how their sleuthing would pan out. It was then that he wondered if her father was aware of her involvement. He didn't seem particularly amused by their dance.

"Impatient now, are we?" She paused, coyly eyeing him. "I have information for Mr. Edde!"

"I see." He wanted to press the issue but held back—at least for now.

"Come. We can't talk here." She grabbed his hand and pulled him through the tree-lined atrium.

Its high ceilings passively implied power, and along with her grip, made Tristan feel just the opposite. She squeezed his fingers so tightly that he winced from his Institute VI graduation ring biting into his flesh. They slipped down another hall, eventually landing them on a balcony overlooking the Ascalon skyline. In the city's center, the construction site was brightly lit. Too many to count, cranes were busy hoisting shadowed pallets, the noise from their grinding motors and whirling cables drifting across the urban sprawl. He caught a whiff of zyn exhaust, generated from a low-speed air shuttle humming by.

Twinkling lights spread an iridescent enchantment across the cityscape, not visible from the Marne. Their glow against the star-encrusted sky was comforting, especially accompanied by faint orchestral melodies. He dropped her hand, tried to shake off the pain as discretely as he could, and leaned cautiously over the balcony's railing, pulling back rather quickly. He thought of the zyn factory and that 50 story drop he and Erik descended before reaching the vats. A wave of dizziness came and went; his skin turned clammy.

"I have the data Mr. Edde requested," repeated Eliza insistently. "It not only identifies a covert zyn repository—quite a significant find

I might add--but also Federation weapon's data, including strategic deployment plans for the upcoming war." She cupped a small chip in her hand.

Finally, he was getting somewhere. A secret zyn repository was one thing, but information about the Federation's weaponry made his blood rush. "Thanks," he said as discreetly as he could, eyeing a man over Eliza's shoulder. He reached out his hand. "May I have it?" He wanted to take it.

"No," she said defiantly. She balled up her fist and put it behind her back. "It stays with me until I personally deliver it to Mr. Edde."

"Don't think that's possible. He's leaving the country tonight. Someone else is going to assume his responsibilities." Tristan wanted to be the first responder.

Not intimidated, she became insistent. "Really? How strange, since this is the intelligence he has craved for so long. Either way, I'm going with you, and I'll be the one who turns it over."

Tristan eyed her warily. "What's with you?"

"Excuse me?"

"You're the general's daughter, and he's one of the most influential men in Atomia. He's also a key Xander supporter. I'm baffled that you're lending support to a group whose primary intent is to cripple the Federation."

"Humm. Why do *you* fight the Federation?"

"Because it's what I'm paid to do."

"Right. So you're questioning *my* motives? You're as directionless as aimless icebergs floating in Declegon's waters. Don't you hold anything dear? Or are you a stupid cyberbot? Have you considered how many lives are at risk, or are you only interested in your precious paycheck? You're free to question my motives, no matter you having no dog in any fight!"

She was spoiled, just like Mawson had said. Even worse, she was treating him more like a brother than a colleague. "And what of your father?" asked Tristan. Another wave of zyn exhaust descended from a passing craft. The engine noise interrupted their conversation, forcing him to wait until it had moved on. "Won't he notice you're missing?"

Her gaze was glued to his. "I have an alibi. I'm supposed to be going to study at the Gaustead Science Academy. Plus, I need to earn more university credits. My father preaches, 'the better the education, the better the politician'; he encourages sound instruction. Every day, my tutor, by lying to my father, risks his life. There are those of us who see the flaws in Senator Xander's vision. Most, the senator included, have recognized that with Vuton's support, Xander could achieve his goals. The opposing candidate, Senator Galik, promotes global peace via greater Reynan involvement. It's more than clear Xander wants war, and iron-fisted control."

Tristan shrugged nonchalantly. "But there's nothing we can do about it. Let the politicians handle the politics."

"And stand by while millions are slaughtered?" Her expression pleaded for sensitivity.

She had an arsenal of rebuttals, and clearly more resolve than the average teenager.

"I'm privileged to be a general's daughter and to be intimate with military secrets, like single-strike weapons capable of destroying entire cities. Did you know they have a mobile weapon the size of a skyscraper that can level any major target—a gigantic cyborg that can level a city! No one stands a chance against Vuton's military. Galik knows this and *could* render those weapons useless, but not without our support. Senator Galik hates that Xander's rhetoric is intended to inflame the military—he wants *all* the power! Once Xander is elected, the populace will absolutely support him. He'll conquer Eshen entirely and gain a most coveted Aurelian foothold. That's why the USC is key. By striking fear in the Vutonians, they'll see that Xander is unable to control the rebellion, and then they'll vote for Galik. We have to make this happen!"

"It's a losing battle." Only the one in power maintains control. Tristan couldn't imagine Xander losing the election. He already had majority support. Mawson was more than willing to sell out Institute VI, leading him to believe that the entire conflict was only about the credits. "If we do as you say, and strike fear into the populace, Xander will strike harder against the USC. It would be a massacre; Xander has a resource monopoly."

"Don't you believe in hope?" Her face became drawn, exposing a deeply rooted sadness.

"What?"

"When everything looks like a solid wall designed to block your every move, and you have naysayers constantly telling you, 'No, you can't do this or that,' you begin to accept your limitations. But don't you see that struggle instills hope, because, deep down, you believe that there is *still* a chance? We can turn back the swollen tides and avoid destruction!" Her voice strengthened as she continued.

Tristan chuckled to himself, barely catching it in his throat. She was intelligent, but her words weren't grounded in reality. "You haven't seen the real world. It's not what you think. That food chain demands obedience. You thinking you deserve better doesn't change the food chain, on the top of which you currently reside, with the rest of the hierarchy. I love your optimism. It's cute. It really is, but it's not reality."

"And *that's* why you'll never be a leader."

That stung. Who did she think she was? His moppish, dark hair fell into his eyes as he lowered his head.

"Let's get going. I'm ready."

"You don't want to pack anything?" asked Tristan.

"They'll have clothing for me in Lathe."

"My ship's that way." As he led her toward an adjacent balcony, turned left at the hallway and approached the docking bay entrance, he enjoyed a sense of confidence filling his thoughts—it felt powerful to have a stealth vessel at his disposal—he could come and go as he pleased; that was real power. The corridor's outer reaches weren't well lit, and it was quiet. Most people were still in the grand ballroom.

Up ahead, the shadows hung low and bathed three men leaning against a wall; they began sauntering toward them. One man had a green mohawk, quite disturbing to Tristan. Another was bald and masked, and the third had two ponytails protruding from the top of his otherwise shaven head. Their unexpected approach was menacing. The two unmasked men were darker than the third and had black makeup streaked around their eyes. The closer they came, the more their manner seemed inappropriate—no formal attire and roughshod. Instinct kicked in; Tristan reached for his sidearm; smarting when he discovered an empty holster. No weapons had been allowed past security.

The Mohawk stepped forward. "Well, well. Look what we have here. Some stragglers from the ball. Not such a good idea to walk alone in the dark now, is it?"

The masked man's black eyes scoured Tristan.

The man with the ponytails broke out in a hoarse cackle.

Tristan raised his hands. "We don't want any trouble. If you'd allow us to pass." He remembered Xander doing the same thing, trying to quiet the masses.

Mohawk quickly retorted. "And what if we don't?"

Eliza slid behind Tristan, nervously squeezing his arms and peeking out from his side. "Come any closer, and I'll scream!"

The man in the mask raised a pistol.

"You scream, you die," growled Mohawk.

Tristan studied the three, angered by their incessant laughter. Digging his fingers into his empty holster, he grimaced. Maybe negotiating would help? A fool's dream. "What do you want?" Malicious intent was obvious; political retoric would be completely absurd, but what else could he do?

"Your slut's been naughty, and I've come to punish her," snickered Mohawk.

Tristan glared at the pervert, extending his arms. "Out of the question. She's the general's daughter. If you touch her, you'll have the entire Federation on your ass."

"They won't catch us." He leaned closer.

Tristan coughed at the smell of a foul odor.

"I have no problem slitting your throat right here and now and dumping your sorry ass in one of them there airships. You get my drift? You can either move outta the way, or I'm going to have Wally here do my dirty work."

The masked man grunted loudly.

"Wally?" Tristan thought to himself, "Wally is a chess club president!"

Tristan's pulse accelerated. No weapons. No words. No strategy. His stomach knotted. How could he get Eliza onto the Marne? That was their only safety.

"What do you want with me?" Eliza's tone was terse.

"You put a target on your back, bitch! You pissed off the wrong man, and now you must pay."

"Who?" Prolonging the conversation was Tristan's only recourse. He needed more time to devise a plan.

Eliza fumbled in her pocket and then pressed a cold cylinder into Tristan's hand.

He turned the object in his fingers until he realized what it was. A spray canister with a trigger meant only one thing—Meka Spray! He'd seen it used before; once it made contact with the mucous membranes, the burning sensation drove its victims mad. His fingers tightened; Eliza stepped back.

Mohawk wavered slightly, "You don't get to ask the questions, bitch! Now get outta my . . ."

Tristan whipped his hand around and squeezed the trigger. Foam spewed out of the canister and blanketed the man's unshaven face. He threw his hands to his eyes, gasping, and screaming for help. Tristan dropped the device. It clattered onto black marble, giving him time to snatch Mohawk's bone-handled knife out of its sheath. He spun him around and pressed the blade against Mohawk's throat. A trickle of blood immediately ran down his neck.

"You sonofabitch! What did you do? My fuckin' eyes!" Tears poured; his face glistening with burn blisters from the bubbling foam.

Wally peered through one of the eye holes of his uneven mask. He hastily tried to reposition it while he raised his pistol. Click... click.......nothing; testimony not so much to the 3.3's reputation, as to the probability that "Wally" probably didn't clean the weapon any more often than he did himself.

Tristan held the knife in place, only a hair's width from ending the man's life. "Who do you work for?" shouted Tristan.

"Yaaaah! Fuck you!"

"Who the hell do you work for?" shouted Tristan, moving the blade along his throat, opening the skin a few inches

"The Enlightened One! The Enlightened one! He hired us!"

"Why does he want Eliza?" Blood continued to flow down the man's white-whiskered skin; a growing red stain moving down his stinking T-shirt.

"I don't know! Hell, I didn't ask!"

Tristan eyed Wally and Ponytails, both with semiautomatics aimed his way. "Drop them now! Or I'll slice off his head" shouted Tristan, pressing a little harder, puncturing the man's windpipe.

The man spat through dripping foam and tears. "Drop them! Drop them! Dammit, drop them!"

An awful stench rose from the mix of perfumed foam, sweat and blood. Tristan longed to push the stinking Mohawk man away.

They dropped their weapons.

Tristan shouted. "Back up! Now!"

With their hands in the air, as if he was going to shoot them with his knife, Wally and Ponytail inched backward.

Tristan whispered hoarsely. "Grab the guns!"

Eliza bolted for the weapons, scooping them up, and, struggling under their weight, lugged them back.

"*Your name?*" Tristan's tone was harsh.

"Tye! Tye!"

"Last name!"

"Martus!"

"Good choice." He released him, kicking him in the back and sending him sprawling on all fours. He would search Institute VI's database to uncover more info on these thugs. Maybe he'd discover just who this Enlightened One was. "Follow me!" he ordered. He and Eliza ran past the men, a vacant security checkpoint, along the zone and onto the Marne's extended ramp. A couple of lone mechanics eyed them warily from beneath a wide-winged, silver and red ship. Tristan, breathing heavily, flipped open the security pad's cover landing and pressed his thumb against the glass. Motors whined, allowing the smooth, gleaming surface of the Marne to separate as the ramp retracted. He could still hear Tye's shouts while they entered. Eliza dropped the weapons in a netted hold, and Tristan ran to the cockpit. "Strap in," his voice echoed. He pointed at the chair behind the pilot console.

Her voice shook. "Okay!"

On the main console, Tristan flipped several switches forward, instantly bringing sleeping thrusters to life. The overhead panels blazed in a maze of flashing lights and beeps. Seconds later, the Marne leaped from the landing pad. He slid the control stick forward, aiming for the exit port high above, and the safety it promised, a sparkling nightscape luring them to freedom. The Marne replied with a high-pitched whine and shot into the sky. Moments later, moonlit sand rippled beneath as they sped to Lathe.

9

Traveling at cruising speed, the *Marne*'s engines hummed softly, their gentle timbre as deft as the fingers of an expert masseuse. The sense lessened with every flight except for the shrill roar during ascent. It was so very loud. Eliza's jaws ached from the change in cabin pressure. The overhead clock's square orange numbers read a few minutes before midnight. She yawned, glancing around for a more comfortable seat. They were all the same; black, thinly padded, and rigidly upright. The curved instrument panels encircling Tristan flashed a hundred different lights; gauges read out measurements and data she couldn't understand, and there were beeps and blips that must have been important—she wondered how long it had taken Tristan to become such an accomplished pilot. She'd never want to fly such a machine. She still felt riled after the attempt on her life, but the ordeal was losing its effect. Tristan had been so strong, so fearless. His presence gave her strength. Tall and handsome, his hair sprang from his head in a hundred different directions—unruly and untamable— fitting his personality. He kept his distance, yet seemed to care, and he seemed to be a respectable person. She wanted to better understand him. He'd asked if she'd been hurt, but that was the last they had spoken.

Tristan gave her a concerned glance. Maybe he was concerned about her wellbeing? Down deep, she wanted him to care. It felt good to think of him like that. His deep brown eyes fixed on her for the briefest moment.

The engines' din shifted, increasing slightly, causing her to strain when she spoke. "I'm so glad you were with me. I don't know what they would have done."

"You put yourself in that situation—a general's daughter turned traitor. No doubt, whatever people you pissed off are more formidable than you realize. Those bandits snuck through security and were waiting for you. You really need to pay more attention to what's going on around you. Someone is tracking your every move. Even the last 20 minutes with you has made me uncomfortable. I hope that you covered your tracks."

Her annoyance flared at his indifference, but she shouldn't have been so surprised. What could an 18-year-old girl possibly understand? The only men who truly listened to her were her father, her brother, and, of course, Lord Commander Seryth. She loathed the latter, now that she grasped his intentions in her father's political organization. "Of course I covered my tracks! I shredded every document my hands ever touched, and I have an alibi for every situation. I'm not stupid! I've never seen those thugs, and don't know how they found me." She tried to sound complacent.

"What about the *Enlightened One?*"

"No . . . I've never heard of him . . . Come to think of it, that name does sound familiar, but no . . . it couldn't be the same one . . ."

"What do you mean?"

"The name sounds familiar. That's all." She probed her memory; only a faint recollection surfaced. Possibly she had heard of him in Aurelia or somewhere else during her travels. "I'm pleasantly surprised you didn't end their miserable lives. Most in your shoes would have shot them."

"If you *did* help Mr. Edde, enemies tracking you will be coming out of the woodwork. That's why any connection to the *Enlightened One* has to remain intact. Their deaths would have eliminated any leads to the man behind the scenes. Once back at Institute VI, I'll search Tye Martus' background. He shouldn't be hard to find. Then we'll launch an investigation into the *Enlightened One*. In case you didn't notice, I was unarmed."

"I'm glad it didn't come to that. I know so many who would have. The Azdahri have become a bunch of savages, and Xander's exploits are only making things worse. They crave blood; an easy means of executing revenge."

"Sounds like every other nation to me. People hate. Everyone thinks they have the right to judge, and when others don't agree, they're shot, or whatever. You familiar with the history of Vudria and Tholiad? What about the Jadori? Even the Aurelians and the Darshani slaves? Entire races have "whipping posts", to cast off self-manufactured guilt and shame on someone else. They want to unburden their afflictions on others."

"I suppose you're right. But there are those who think it doesn't have to be like that. Like the USC, Reyna, and Declegon--all passionate peace advocates." She derived a certain pleasure from the mental sparring. It reminded her of time spent with her brother; sitting for hours, discussing the pros and cons of the Xander Youth League. They never solved anything; but, in the end, she was pleased that she better appreciated his feelings and beliefs.

Tristan chuckled. "Without a doubt, the USC wants peace. But, consider the cost. They're willing to wage a pricey war only because they hold "Xanderism" as infallible. Don't pretend your motivation is so far removed from anyone else. It's not. It's just what you believe. So be it. Live with your choices."

"You throw crap on my beliefs. Not everyone is lost in relativism, caring nothing about right and wrong. I don't live like that, and never will."

He shrugged. "That's the way it is, and your saying otherwise doesn't change anything." Her righteous speech was beginning to irritate him.

"And what's "right" for you? Should Xander control the Azdahri people? Should he go ahead and start a world war, killing millions under his fine-feathered auspices?" Tristan's grayscale reasoning was too apathetic for her liking.

She was far more of a political activist than he cared for, "Should Mr. Edde have his way?" questioned Tristan, "Destroying zyn repositories, and in the process, killing soldiers, fathers and sons, as well as innocent citizens? Allow me to answer: 'It's all about the credits.' That's what makes things happen, isn't it? It's what makes the world go 'round'. Whoever has the money, has the power, and these movers and shakers are gonna make the world into whatever their credits can buy."

She could sense his frustration, but wanted to continue pressing him. How could a man be so narrow-minded, especially one who had exhibited such sterling character a few moments ago? "Do you talk to everyone like this?"

Tristan raised an eyebrow. "What do you mean?"

"Do you speak to everyone like you're speaking to me?"

"No. I usually don't have an audience that gives a rip about any of this."

"Well . . . . I'm glad you share it with me. You need someone to whom you can vent your frustrations." She smugly replied, nurturing her debating success.

Tristan quickly replied. "I'm not frustrated! You asked a question, and I answered it."

She had risked damaging his ego, knowing full well it often supported a man's passion. "Anyone who acts so shallowly has never been able to dig deeply enough to discover true purpose. That's what I believe. So, keep telling me what you believe in. I think you'll find the error of your ways, and maybe find something you can actually believe in, something you're not yet aware of." She drew a smug grin.

"I'm done with this conversation."

Her grin broadened. "When you're ready to continue, I'll be available."

The zyn-powered ATV that Tristan and his companions rode from the landing pad to USC headquarters seemed deathly quiet compared to the *Marne*'s turbines. The train ride he'd previously taken had kept him at a safe distance, but now he was in closer proximity to the homeless than ever before. These vagrants had made their fragile abodes in mangled bushes and against broken down walls along roadsides. Makeshift tents, made from dirt-smattered cloth, provided barely enough room for one person lying down. Fires smoldered; the air thick with smoke. Occasionally, they seemed to see him, their eyes seemingly locking onto his. They must be the lowest caste in the land. What codes of conduct retained any semblance of civility? What would it be like to speak with one of them? One day, he hoped to find out.

The ATV's knobby tires lurched to a stop, forcing Tristan to steady himself on the facing seat back. He breathed deeply as calm settled in, only then realizing the ringing in his ears. The ride had lasted barely 30 minutes, but it felt like hours. He was tired from the long flight and longed for a decent night's sleep. It took only a single, hasty glance to acquaint himself with his surroundings, filled with the stench of smoky fires dotting the desolate thoroughfare; and the strong, burnt aroma of bygone years of activity, emanating from the desolate factory. The large puddles of liquid sewage surrounding the entrance plaza had somewhat abated since his last visit. What a shame that a once-productive zyn factory had been allowed to crumble into a depressing array of black, twisted metal and waste.

Tristan approached a lone guard who was nodding off from boredom. He straightened to attention when asked permission to speak with Cole Ashbury. The man led them through the reinforced entrance and into another place and time. The filtered air instantly refreshed him; an abundance of green plants reminded him of a better life. How could such a place exist in the midst of those slums? The guard led them up the carpeted stairs and past the cafeteria. It was more crowded than his last visit; the air was thick with the heavy aroma of fried meat and freshly baked loaves of bread. His stomach growled, again, reminding him how long it had been since he'd had a substantial meal. He glanced at Eliza and wondered if she needed something to eat. Neither had eaten since the ball.

The guard deposited Tristan and Eliza in Mr. Edde's office. It was just as before: in a word, comfortable. Had there been a fire in the large stone fireplace, he was sorely tempted to stretch out and rest his eyes. They sat across from each other on thickly padded sofas.

"Tristan," greeted Cole as he barged into the room.

Tristan tensed, throwing a glance over his shoulder. He was surprised that Cole had let himself go, unshaven and his hair unkempt.

"Glad you made it. I wasn't expecting you until later," continued Cole, raising a mug of beer in salute.

"Surprise." The word fell out of Tristan's glum expression. He glanced at his personal communicator—sunrise was just about to arrive.

"Smart Ass." He sipped from his mug. "And you must be Liberty? Allow me to introduce myself. I'm Cole Ashbury, and we at the USC are honored by your presence. It's great to work alongside an Atomian putting herself on the line to spill the guts of the Federation, especially one so young. Why you must . . ."

Tristan's blood rushed. "This is Eliza Nyvala," interjected Tristan, "General Nyvala's daughter." He knew exactly what Cole was up to.

Cole coughed, a dribble of beer running down his chin. "What? What the hell did you say?"

"Thanks, Tristan. I can introduce myself," said Eliza, obviously perturbed.

"She's the bloody fucking daughter of . . ."

"Cole! Language!" Tristan's voice rose with his temper. Why was Cole drinking beer at this time of day?

"I know. I know. But damn. This is crazy. I had no idea . . ."

"I know. No one did. Not even Mr. Edde."

"Is this a good idea?"

Tristan shrugged. "I don't know. Can you contact Edde?"choosing not to dignify him with a "Mister".

"Yeah. Was planning to anyways. Wants to talk to the snitch himself. But first . . . ." Cole sauntered over to Mr. Edde's desk and flipped a switch, turning on a wall-mounted monitor. "I believe, Ms. Nyvala . . ."

"Please. You may call me Eliza."

"Right . . . . You have some important information for us?"

She didn't seem at all uneasy talking to Cole as she pushed herself up out of the deep cushions and dug under her narrow waistband. "Yes, I do." She handed him a small chip, which he quickly examined under the desk lamp.

Cole plugged the device into a port in Mr. Edde's computer. "Let's see if we can connect." He reached for another switch, bringing a wall-mounted monitor to life.

Mr. Edde's blank stare appeared, faded in and out, and then stabilized.

Cole admired his "hi-tech" effort for a moment, before adjusting the volume. "Perfect. Mr. Edde. How's the audio?"

"Loud and clear, Mr. Ashbury. Ah, and this must be our much-anticipated informant, Eliza Nyvala. I would never have expected you to be the heroine of the hour. When I saw you and Tristan leave the ball, I found it nearly impossible to accept—but here you are. I must say, your audacity is most impressive. I've never met anyone your age with such passionate determination and courage. You'll be remembered throughout history."

"Thank you for your kind words, Mr. Edde, but I didn't do this to be remembered. I did this because it's the right thing to do." She stared at the monitor. "Feel free to call me Eliza."

Cole interrupted, sounding sarcastic. "Don't count on it."

The speakers boomed. "I believe in titles, Ms. Nyvala. Consider it a holdover from the past. Old habits die hard. Trust me. Your selflessness will be rewarded. Time is precious, so let's focus on more pressing matters. I've pulled up the documents . . . ." He motioned to a screen before him.

They shifted their gaze to an adjacent monitor.

"Incredible," he continued. "What you have provided is an unprecedented geopolitical leap!" The excitement in the man's voice was unmistakable. "A hidden zyn repository, the third largest . . . , right there in Lathe. Are you seeing this, Mr. Ashbury?"

Cole leaned closer, wobbling slightly. "Yes, sir. It's larger than anything we've seen so far. I can't believe it. It's been sitting under our damn noses!"

Tristan edged closer and began scrutinizing the diagram; outlining a labyrinth of underground passageways. The facility was enormous—at least twice the size of any previously encountered. "Where is it located?" he asked, turning back to the camera.

Eliza stood beside him, wide-eyed.

"Under Lathe's principal power plant. It provides half of Lathe's power." Mr. Edde shook his head. "If we miscalculate, the bomb will throw the entire city into chaos. It's a risk we must take. No mistakes."

"Right!" exclaimed Cole. "I hope Lance learned from his prior screwups. I'll show Voleta the drawings, so she can plug in an escape route. Hardie and I will assemble the bomb. Don't worry, Mr. Edde. It'll go according to plan. If I'm right, the Fed won't have a clue we're coming. This repository is so hush-hush, we'll catch them with their pants completely down around their ankles."

Mr. Edde hesitated, an air of reservation in his tone. "Don't underestimate them! I have Intel that security was increased at all repository locations after our last attack. Can you put something together in 48 hours?"

"You bet. Won't be a problem. Shit . . . . Voleta could have it done in 24!"

Mr. Edde shifted to his lower screen, eyeing it keenly. "Good . . . . And what do we have here? Requiem 377 Bomb. Also known as the 'Supernova.' Interesting. Immense knockdown, can level ultra-fortified defenses, cities, *mountains!* The results will be...epic, historic! The 'Supernova' has got to be the most powerful of their weapons; one that will alter not only our planet's topography, but its' *destiny*. Testing is scheduled to begin within the next three months." Mr. Edde leveled his gaze at Eliza. "It seems you bring us more than I expected, Ms. Nyvala. This is something I won't let slip through the cracks."

"There's more . . . ," she said timidly.

Mr. Edde shifted his focus to the other screen, and began reading. "The Iomega Android—the size of a super dreadnaught carrier— with immense speed, armaments and firepower. Appears humanoid. Can be controlled by one pilot. Has been tested. Can destroy airships and ground units with ease. Underwater still has challenges. Scientists are working on it. Soon, the Iomega will be master of sky, land and sea." His eyes lifted. "Grand weapons of war. I believe Xander will use everything in this arsenal to subdue the totality of Eshen, and he won't stop there! Thank you, Ms. Nyvala. You've gone far beyond the call of duty. This Intelligence has shed abundant light on the surmounting crisis. I'll provide a more thorough review later, but I must say 'congratulations!' These documents paint a bleak picture, but this is a USC victory. We now know what our enemy's capabilities; and have what we need to present to the Reynan World Council. They'll be able to convict Xander of conspiracy. Mr. Ashbury, not a moment to lose. Have your plans ready in two days. I will contact you in 48 hours, and we'll review what you have. Mr. Hart. I hope you'll be ready."

The three stood in silent anticipation. The room was quiet, except for a hum coming from the speakers. Mr. Edde glanced at them, one by one, shuffled papers and then eyed his wrist chronometer.

"Yes, sir," said Tristan, his mind flooded with unspeakable images of destruction. The Iomega, an astonishing weapon, was their greatest advantage. He wanted to see it in real life. He sensed that the meeting was about to close and wondered if he had asked everything necessary. Mr. Edde seemed rushed. He didn't want to hold him up, but he had more to discuss.

"Good. I must take my leave."

"Mr. Edde," said Tristan, his voice hurried. "If I may, we encountered a problem."

"Oh?"

The screen flickered.

"Eliza and I were ambushed when leaving the ball. A group of men tried to jump us, claiming that they worked for the *Enlightened One*. I got one name and was hoping to find what I can about him. I'm concerned that this might happen again."

Mr. Edde stroked his chin. "The *Enlightened One*? But that's impossible. Could it be?" A deep frown settled across his brow.

"Could it be *what*? You familiar with that name?" asked Tristan.

"Vaguely. By many, he's considered a criminal mastermind. Some say he's organized crime's global puppeteer, and single-handedly responsible for triggering a less-than-golden age of corruption. Of course, some consider him mythical; some theorize the name refers to an entire group of criminals. Regardless, we can't ignore this development." Still stroking his chin, he continued. "While traveling, I'm afraid that my hands will be tied. I plan to be in Aurelia sometime during the next eight hours. That's the only opportunity I'll have to decipher these documents. When the opportunity presents itself, I promise my full attention. In the meantime, Mr. Hart, I expect you to keep your eye on Ms. Nyvala. We have many enemies, and the more allies we acquire, the more enemies we will face. But take heart! We will prevail. Make haste, Mr. Ashbury. Take care." The screen flickered and then went to black.

Cole turned to Tristan. "You heard the man. Take Eliza to the cafeteria. I'm sure she's hungry. I'll summon the rest of our crew; we'll start work immediately."

"I know. I heard him too," Tristan replied. His stomach growled loudly.

Cole centered Eliza's hands in his. "We're in your debt. What you've accomplished hasn't been without great risk. It's inspiring to see how you've put everything before the greater good."

Tristan rolled his eyes. He was stuck with the carefree informant longer than he had planned and realized that his highest priority had suddenly become keeping her as far from Cole as he possibly could.

CHAPTER

'10

Muted music played in the background, so quiet she had to strain to hear it. She pictured the dilapidated buildings just beyond the walls, miserably shabby in every way possible, and realized that she was on edge. It was impossible to ignore. Light seeped in through the crack beneath the door. She should have rolled a towel to block it. Too many distractions and she wasn't as tired as she thought she would be. The firm mattress lent little comfort; Eliza tossed and turned and finally gave up, sighing heavily, throwing off the blanket and sitting up. She searched for her shower thongs. Somehow they ended up under the desk chair, still damp. A chill was in the air, better than the mugginess she'd felt when they arrived. She tucked her arms and shivered, then jumped out of bed. Exploring the USC headquarters seemed like the thing to do. Surely her tired mind eventually would give in. She brushed her hair and pinched her cheeks, and was soon bathed in a flood of bluish-white light. Gray, lightly textured walls had a steel tint from the stark lighting. Every so often, pictures of waterfalls, forests, and beaches had been hung. Two pajama-clad personnel sprawled on couches in an entertainment room; a movie about a flying dragon played on the big screen. She might stop in later.

Down the hall in a secluded office, she found Tristan hunched over his tablet. She was surprised to see him still up. The room seemed smaller than before. She probably hadn't paid enough attention. With the USC's resources, she expected the workspaces to be larger and better appointed. He sat at a plain metal desk on a thinly padded chair, no more comfortable than the *Marne*'s seating. He didn't notice her, so she walked over to an elevator and took it down to the second floor. It deposited her in front of Mr. Edde's office. The black box above his door hummed and slowly panned. The cafeteria was bustling with unfamiliar faces, night owls. The same orchestra music played from ceiling speakers, louder and clearer on this floor. She suddenly felt homesick. She was hungry, but not starving, and didn't fancy eating alone, even though the aroma of baked fruit cobbler hung thickly. She found herself longing for familiar food, and especially wanted some wolfberry tort dessert, her favorite. The bland USC offerings–chicken and potatoes–matched her mood.

Tristan had introduced her to the team. Hardie and Lance were nice, but Voleta was conspicuously standoffish. She didn't trust her. The two men jumped at any opportunity to praise Eliza for her courageous, as they put it, anti-Federation efforts. They seemed intent on impressing her. If she were to successfully sabotage Xander's world domination efforts, she needed these people—the awareness of imminent risk had escalated, once she relinquished the USB drive. Their compliments delighted her, though, and gave her a sense of belonging. She had craved her father's attention, which he seldom offered. Not much angered her. Self-composure was a matter of discipline; his lack of loving expression wore on her in a way she found difficult to express. If she tried harder, he might change. Deep inside though, she was convinced her actions would change the world.

The gray walls of the long hallway were dull, yet their sullen ambience was not enough to make her try that mattress again. Past the cafeteria, a man dressed in green coveralls pushed a smudged, yellow cart full of cleaning supplies. Several partially open doors beckoned, and her curiosity took over. She pushed against a black lacquered door and greeted Cole and Hardie, deep in thought, pouring over chrome cylinders and bundles of colored wiring. They had to be working on the bomb. Could those small devices truly neutralize an entire zyn facility? Wasn't it too dangerous to have them in the building? She had to credit them for electing to preserve the power plant; saving millions the pain of living without much-needed energy; but being in the room spooked her. Cole glanced over and smiled, beckoning and quickly launching into a technical explanation of green and yellow fluids and their chemical properties. Listening to him was better than counting sheep, but after a while it made her nervous. Cole probably noticed a glaze settling over her eyes. He stopped his dissertation, smiled, and returned to his work.

She slipped back into the hall and peeked into the next room. Voleta was scanning a large repository blueprint. She noticed Eliza right away and waved her over as she continued putting X marks on bright blue paper. After a brief discussion of entry and exit points, Eliza left her to her work. Further down the hall, Lance, the resident computer whiz, was typing something. His fingers flew while he verbally described a mainframe hacking program to her. Except for Tristan, of the three team members she had just visited, Lance proved the most intellectual. She did like computer geeks and adored his wavy, red hair. He seemed a thousand times smarter than she could ever imagine herself, but was more interested in his computer than her, "Typical". She continued her self-guided tour, ending back in front of Mr. Edde's office. Last time past, the door had been closed. Tristan had moved in, and was paging through a heavy, worn book.

She knocked softly. "May I come in?"

He lowered the book and casually glanced over. "Yeah, sure." His heavy eyes drooped back to the printed pages.

"What're you reading?" They were alone, and her racing pulse was unexpected.

"*Life of a Slave,* about an old Darshan who escaped Aurelian rule. It's intriguing. The Aurelians treated him and his kind brutally. Reading this shows me what slavery is really like."

"Yes. It's heartbreaking that one race would deem itself superior over another." She eyed the book pensively, reflecting on her brother's whereabouts, and began nursing a curiosity of the Darshani plight. "Have you ever visited Aurelia?"

"No . . . . Never really wanted to, either. They use mounts for transportation, don't have indoor plumbing, and, worst of all, have no aircraft. From what I can tell, it's because of their stupid religion. I know Mr. Edde is working to have the Aurelian government remonstrate Xander and his Ebonfall Manifesto, if not to actually gain them as an ally. Honestly, I commend him for trying, but I don't think there's any real possibility of success. The country is so poor. I suppose it offers the Federation a foothold; nothing more. It couldn't be anything more."

Eliza chuckled. He had no idea of Xander's real ploy. "It's not that bad, you know. It's a beautiful country, sparsely populated, and the palace in Antion is stunning. There's more—the coastal city of Tarrant is called the city of the sunset. The sun falls beautifully over the buildings and beaches, causing small rainbows to dance through the evening skies. Or the Aurelian Frostbacks? Or the Temple of the Adunai? Or the . . ."

"All right, I get it. It's not as bad as I might think."

"No, it's not! You need to see the good in things, Tristan. An attitude like that will greatly enhance your understanding, and enrich your life. My mother taught me— a positive mindset, a positive influence on the world. Even a small improvement is worth the effort."

Tristan cracked a smile and sat back on the leather sofa. "Wise Woman." thinking to himself about the boy who saw a stall full of horseshit and thought he was getting a pony for his birthday. The kid got a shovel.

"She was so wise and the best mother." Eliza sensed the earlier melancholy slipping away and found herself captured by his gentle demeanor. She'd never forget his first smile. If only she could preserve it. She etched his chiseled face, upturned lips, and tossed hair into her memory, glad that he was finally showing some emotion. He was one in a million, and she was falling for him. That could be a huge mistake.

"Did she take you to Aurelia?"

"No. My mother passed long before I went there." She paused and listened to a sad refrain of string music drifting in from the hallway, causing an ache from the memory of her mother's loss, as if it had happened yesterday. "I was in the Xander Youth League, as are most Atomian teenagers. We were allowed to discover the world, all at Federation expense, to understand its' cultures, and to learn how we can effect positive change. We uncovered unique forms of government, currencies, lost cultures, and even bygone religions. We encouraged and initiated new members from Atomia, and they could even train as Federation leadership. It was truly exciting to relate to people my age."

"Did you recruit many?"

She chuckled, pleased with Tristan's interest. "No. But, I did recruit this one very engaging, Reynan boy. He was a year older than I and so cute, with long, auburn hair and a great body. At the time, that was all I needed to decide he would be a great leader." She chuckled and coyly rolled her eyes.

Tristan nodded. "What happened to him?"

Her laughter subsided. "He remained with the League; and fell for one of my friends instead of me. That just about killed me. After that, I dropped my romantic dream of visiting the Reynan Crystal Palace in Antassus, got political, and took a hard stand against Xander's efforts."

Mr. Edde's fish tank suddenly sprang to life. The blue-hued lamps in the cover pleasantly illuminated the water, causing a pair of gold-speckled fish to glitter as they flitted together through their watery world. Bubbles rose from a quiet wake, eventually breaking the surface with delicate pops.

"Don't give up. I'm sure your dreams will come true."

"Really? You think so?" She tried to play down her response, not wanting to appear uncertain.

He eyed her quizzically. "Yeah . . . . I don't see why not."

Her racing heart flushed her skin. "Thank you, I needed that." She hoped that he was right.

"Well, I do respect you. It seems like you're giving up a good life in order to help the USC. Most people would think you're crazy. You're quite good at playing the Atomian "Princess", traveling the world, sitting at banquets, and has more than any heart could wish."

She shook her head, eager to continue. "It's not as good as it sounds. I wish I were a real princess, though. I envy Reyna's Princess Kiahna. A magnificent crystal palace is her home. She has access to the world's most expansive jungles, splendid mountain ranges and rivers so clear you'd think you were dreaming when you gaze into their depths. She often travels her country; and is well known for aiding those in need. She's a living legend. I only wish I could follow in her steps."

"You've done your share of global exploration. You've seen the need for global change, right? Isn't that better than impacting a single country?"

"It's more than that. I've never really had the opportunity to express my opinions. The Azdahri are conceited, refusing any suggestions from a half-breed."

"A what?"

"I'm considered a half-breed. My dark hair is a major disadvantage. I can only imagine how the Darshani are treated. Xander believes that the Azdahri are *the* master race and that snow white features belong to the elite. He and his race despise others, whether they admit it or not. Xander is a champion of a hateful caste system. He promises other races Azdahri membership. That's a line of you-know-what, but convincing. Never forget, he'll settle for nothing less than Azdahri supremacy. That's the reason my brother is favored so much, and I'm not. Ever since we were young . . ."

"Your brother?"

"Yes. Leomaris, or Little Leo as I call him. I wish he was still the little boy I remember. His beliefs and rhetoric anger me, even though I know he will always be family."

"Do you envy him?"

She was concerned how Tristan might think of her. She'd been challenged most of her life; that was the way of a half-breed. She often sought approval and recognition, probably in the wrong places from the wrong people, and was aware of the pitfalls. She stared into his deeply set eyes, sensing acceptance, and decided to continue. "Yes. I mean . . . , I love him. He's my brother, but he always got more attention than me. In most peoples' eyes, he's a Prince, and, like my father, a future Federation leader. *I* was considered an oddball. I inherited my mother's features along with her carefree attitude. My father never failed to let me know I was atypical of children my age. He said that I was challenged by the impetuousness of youth. My brother, on the other hand, was considered disciplined and ready to serve. When my mother died, any chance of getting any of my father's love died with her. He perceived me a little girl with uninspiring aspirations. But, oh no, not Leo! Father bent over backward for him. Leo's dreams are the dreams of the Azdahri race, and, by my father's reasoning, sacred. At the moment, Leo is actually in Aurelia, finishing his last League tour. He'll be returning home sometime in Apus . . ."

"Is that why you left the Xander Youth League?"

"I believed I wasn't needed. I knew I wasn't included in Xander's vision for the Federation. He tolerated me out of respect for my father, but I clearly remembered the day the League performed the 'March of the Azdahri' before Xander. I stood in their ranks, saluting the senator. He approached us individually and shook our hands—nothing less than a divine honor. When it was my turn, his hands hung to his sides while his stare penetrated me. I'll never forget seeing the hate from those dark depths. Later, when I recounted this, my father labeled me 'overly sensitive'. But, Tristan, I know what I felt. That man is . . . vile. Silently, he turned to the next Azdahri. I cried real tears because of that."

"What about your brother? Isn't he half Oxiam, too?"

With just a hint of remorse, she shook her head. "No . . . . He's a bastard, from an affair Father had with an Azdahri aide of his. The woman died giving birth, leaving my father and mother to look after him. My mother is the subservient type. Either take the boy in or be banished from the home herself. Seems my father preferred offspring with appropriate lineage, even if without the legitimacy of marriage. It took years before he showed me any fatherly affection, but he never held back from Leo; my brother has pure Azdahri blood flowing through those veins, his white hair and pale skin a constant reminder."

"I'm sorry, Eliza. That must have been quite painful for your mother."

She nodded wittingly. "In my opinion, that's what shortened her precious life. She treated Leo like her own. She forgave my father, as if she had a choice; but never recovered emotionally. Their relationship only grew worse. Even though my mother seemed happy enough, she really wasn't. Her eyes told it all."

"She would have been proud of you."

He sounded so confident. "You think so?"

"Yeah . . . I think so."

"Thanks, Tristan. That means a lot." She couldn't deny the hopefulness that grew within her.

The door burst open, revealing a highly animated Cole, startling them both. "It's done!" His chest rapidly rose and fell as he met their eyes.

Tristan artfully smiled at Eliza before rising from the couch. "All right. It's about time. We're ready to call Mr. Edde."

Eliza wondered why Tristan's enthusiasm seemed restrained. Maybe he was thinking about *her*? The mission must remain their focus, but just the thought that Tristan might consider her more than a comrade made her feel warm inside.

Cole gave Tristan the thumbs up. "Voleta's on it! Do you know anything about a Serynip chemical bomb—how to detonate it?"

Tristan frowned. "Of course I do. It's actually easier than standard issue explosives."

"Perfect!"

Hardie rushed in, his cropped black hair pushing down on his high cheekbones and thin-lipped smile. "Can't wait to see the looks on those Azdahri bastards once they count up their losses! They'll cry like little girls!"

"Damn right they will!" rejoined Cole as he ran his hand through his medium-length, dark hair.

Hardie stepped back into the hallway. "Lance? How's it going?" he hollered.

"Been ready for an hour!" came a muffled reply.

Hardie smacked his hands together. "I call Azdahri shit on that!"

"Ha! Funny," returned Lance sarcastically, his voice gaining strength.

Cole took charge. "All right, Tristan. Be sure to pack your Droth and anything else you need. We'll brief in ten minutes and take off within an hour."

"Very well," replied Tristan as he closed his book.

"I want to go," said Eliza, afraid of being left behind.

The fish tank's pulsating pump gurgled. The pair of glittering fishes poked their pointed noses at the rising bubbles.

Cole grimaced. "Sorry, sweetheart. You've already done enough. Let the big boys handle it from here."

His attitude disturbed Eliza, reminding her of all-too-frequent past rejections. "I'm not a child. I can handle myself quite well if you please. The Xander Youth League trained me! I'm a marksman with a rifle, probably better than you are."

Cole raised his hand and snickered. "No way. Sorry, but Mr. Edde thinks you're special enough to keep behind. You're our inside man, or woman, or whatever."

"I'm going, and that's that!" She jumped up defiantly. Who did he think he was?

"No, you're not," said Tristan calmly, avoiding her stare.

She turned toward Tristan's reassuring voice, losing some of her animus. Her powder white skin flushed quickly. "You can't tell me what to do." She regretted her words as soon as she had mouthed them. They'd never let her go now.

He ignored her speech. "I know you want to help, but the USC needs you here. Safety isn't our only concern. Don't forget your World Council role. Access to inside Federation information is vital."

Eliza faced Tristan. "I'm not useless. I can do a lot more if you'd let me."

Tristan stared at the tiny bubbles floating on the fish tank's surface, doing his best not to connect with Eliza.

Voleta suddenly entered the room. "I can't link to Mr. Edde!"

"What? Of all the times, dammit! Try again!" ordered Cole.

"I have. His receiver's offline."

"Why in the hell would his receiver be off? That doesn't make any sense, especially if he was expecting our transmission."

"I'll keep trying, but what do we do if we don't hear back?"

"Shit! I don't know! "said Cole.

"We need his confirmation, to take off, don't we?" challenged Hardie.

"I'm in charge. If we can't reach him, we'll proceed as previously directed." Cole cautiously surveyed the group's collective attitude.

"Your call, Cole. You're in charge," said Tristan.

"Maybe there's a storm?" questioned Voleta. "That could cause signal loss. We have no way to know for sure, but we certainly can't sit around and wait. This is the best shot against the Federation we've ever had!"

"You don't have to tell me twice! Let's go! Tristan. Get your flight suits. We need to take the shuttle to the landing pad now! Voleta! Use the portable satellite unit and keep trying Mr. Edde. Try the alternate frequencies." Then to the group, "Let's meet back here in ten. Let's go!" he barked, his confidence regained.

Voleta disappeared in a flash.

"Wait!" Cole handed Eliza a black earpiece, small enough to fit into the palm of her hand. "If you're ever in trouble, you can contact us. By pressing this button, you'll activate this thing and automatically transmit to our station; your signal will appear on the world map monitor. That's how we'll know where you are. Also, Nate has been assigned as your bodyguard. While we're gone, he'll take care of anything you need."

"Thank you." Eliza took the small device, but wanted to smash it against the wall. She nodded and tried to calm her mounting frustration.

Cole motioned to the others, "C'mon!" and took off down the hall.

Eliza, still sensing Tristan's connection, watched him walk out. A whiney song was playing over the sound system, heightening the dread of solitude. "Tristan . . . . Be careful." A piece of her heart walked through that door.

CHAPTER 11

The upcoming mission commanded Tristan's concern more than the routine flight maneuvers en route to the power plant. The thought of a satchel of high explosives on the cockpit floor created a tension he couldn't ignore. He kept wondering how they'd have enough time, after setting the timer, to escape. He had to trust their planning. He reached for the knurled dial behind his right calf and tweaked it gently. The elevator quickly responded to the trim adjustment, immediately releasing forward nose pressure. The gunship leveled perfectly at 3000 feet; the air felt silky smooth. Cole, quiet and pensive, rummaged absent-mindedly through his leather valise. They hadn't made contact with Mr. Edde. Voleta kept trying, but to no avail. The group would have to make important choices without him. Only Cole seemed excited about that.

Lathe's sprawling cityscape slowly crawled beneath the sleek vessel, the tall buildings rising like outstretched fingers. Lance and Hardy were already in motion; proceeding through the underground railway, the same one they had used to reach USC headquarters last week. Once at the zyn facility, control would shift to Lance and, like a skilled surgeon, he would inject the mainframe computer with his coded serum. He'd use a network access port, at the main entrance, to seal all facility doors. There should be no worry about alarms. His virus would render them inoperative. Cole was in charge of the explosives. Tristan eyed the lumpy pack strapped to the cockpit deck. Another nervous bluster rose and fell.

Tristan glanced at the instrument landing system positioning indicator. "We're less than five minutes from the drop zone," he said. "Expect the power plant off the port side at any moment." He scanned the panels again—the stealth indicator, a pulsating blue lamp mounted toward the top right, blinked obediently.

Voleta was strapped into the navigator's seat against the bulkhead behind Tristan. "Still nothing from Mr. Edde," she reported. "There's a weak broadband signal flashing on the frequency monitor, but I'm unable to connect to the carrier. Looks like we're on our own."

"It's all right," replied Cole. "According to Eliza's Intel, security should be minimal, which boggles my mind. At the rate that they're sucking zyn from our planet, you'd expect just the opposite." His bag still rested on his lap, flap open with several papers spilling across his knees.

Apprehension seized Tristan. He felt like a prisoner entangled in the *Marne*'s framework, bound by looming peril. There were only five in their team, a paltry number. Only a flawless plan would succeed. Everything had to go according to plan. "If they spot us, they'll fire up their androids. And I'd also expect more than a few Vutonian guards. I hope this mission won't be as close a call as the last."

Cole nodded. "Lance better disarm security and not screw up again," he said, not kindly. "If he does, I'm firing his ass!"

"If he does, you'll be too dead to fire his ass. He won't make the same mistake twice," said Tristan, concerned that Cole was too tight-assed. The man was under enormous pressure; yet, if his software didn't deliver, the entire mission would fail, to put it mildly.

"Yeah . . . So . . . That Eliza girl. She's cute, huh?" replied Cole.

That's the last thing he wanted to think about. "I didn't notice," quipped Tristan, trying to bat down the unexpected comment.

"For fuck's sake, Tristan. You're young. I can smell the testosterone shoot'n outta your ass! Don't tell me you didn't notice."

"We *really* going to talk about this right now?"

Voleta chuckled. "It's how he eases his nervousness."

"Shut up, Voleta," said Cole. "All I'm saying is . . . ,"

"There it is." Tristan pointed. A montage of tall, gray buildings on the shore of a white-capped ocean unfolded below; high-intensity strobe lights, collision avoidance systems, more affectionately known as "lighthouses", discharged brilliant white flashes from each roof corner. A large cylindrical shaped object rose out of the midst of the tight grouping of structures, its' slanted roof, lined with bright red lamps, angled sharply into the dusky sky.

"Damn. Forgot how big it was." Cole stuffed the scattered papers into his bag.

"Looks like we're not alone. Hope our new transponder code works." He verified the glowing digits, backlit in green, on the transponder's face; if the numbering sequence were off by even one digit, the Vutonian Air Guard would be notified. Several smaller ships circled the field below; one put down atop a runway extending out over the water. Through the darkening sky, several other buildings, their corners and roof edges lined with blue etching, came into view.

Voleta confidently replied. "It will. They'll see our code as a Vutonian civilian vessel; their scans can't detect this as a gunship."

The radio crackled; Voleta tweaked the squelch and listened closely. "We're inside the flight zone," she relayed. "Lance has successfully uploaded the computer code. Right on schedule; he's got total control of the power plant. Bring her down and be quick about it."

"Thanks. I'm taking her in now," advised Tristan. His nervousness somewhat abated as he reduced power and turned the *Marne* sharp to port and into an aggressive descent; another tweak of the knurled knob and the ship hovered over the rooftop landing pad. He glanced through narrow side windows at three smaller ships below. The code had been accepted. "Great work, Voleta."

She nodded and tightened her shoulder restraints.

Tristan further reduced power and nudged the vertical thrusters forward. The craft settled nicely through the moist sea air, thudding to a stop on its extended landing pods.

Hardie's voice crackled again, this time without any distortion, "Once you've disembarked, double-time-it to the door left of the pad. Contrary to expectations, expect high security!" His voice turned raspy. "Take the elevator to *Level Four*! Lance is down there and will assume command."

Cole unstrapped himself. "Good work, boys!" he quipped in a carefree demeanor.

Tristan watched through the forward cockpit windows as two gray-uniformed, Vutonian soldiers warily approached. "You want to handle them or do you want me to?" he asked.

"Don't rob me the honor of taking out these scum bags," said Cole as he hoisted his backpack and hustled aft.

Voleta slapped a full cartridge into her pistol. Its' contact clicked loudly.

The door swung upward, supported on either side by motorized struts. Cole reached the Vutonian soldiers first.

"ID and credentials, please," asked the first soldier.

Cole grinned. "Right here," he smirked and fired. The soldiers crumpled instantly. "Come on!" he shouted. The three sprinted to the reinforced, metal door as instructed. Cole punched in a code; the door opened inward.

A sentry android with twin semi-automatics was waiting on the other side, a head taller than Tristan and outfitted with flashing blue eyes. Its' head tilted slightly as the group approached.

Tristan released a rapid volley, shattering the robot's entire upper body into a smattering of metal and wires.

"Security doesn't seem so tight," declared Cole proudly.

They entered the elevator; Tristan pushed 'UL-4', and the doors slid shut.

A camera, the kind with small lights encircling the lens, protruding from one of the ceiling tiles, whirred, catching Tristan's attention. He worried for a moment, willing his heart to calm while hoping Lance's program did its job.

Voleta must have been thinking the same thing. "Cameras . . . a video loop of a vacant elevator is now cycling. They won't have a clue."

A low volume chime sounded as the elevator settled gently, the doors hissing while they opened. Lance and Hardie grinned at each other as the new arrivals exited the elevator—the laboratory setting was completely sterile—white walls, flooring and ceiling.

"I don't remember an entry as smooth as this one," said Hardie, catching Tristan's eye. "And, we only had to off two guards in the train tunnels." referring to their less impressive arrival.

Lance nodded quietly and continued typing into his tablet. "Maybe they cut back to make it look like a power plant and not a repository?"

"Don't count on it," replied Cole. "There's probably some rocket-shooting robot lurking around a corner. Remember what happened last time?"

Hardie nervously cleared his throat. "Let's stay positive, shall we?"

"This way," said Lance, his ginger hair hung high over a furrowed forehead; his cheerful, gray eyes sparkled like a child's. He cradled the tablet in one arm and hurried across the lobby to a distant elevator.

Tristan took up just behind Lance, still squinting from the brightness of the artificial lighting. "Definitely a repository. This elevator looks eerily familiar, much like the one in the embassy we just blew up."

Carefully balancing his tablet, Lance punched in the access code. The doors slid shut and the elevator hummed during the 15-floor descent. "The Federation won't know what to do once we blow this operation." His eyes sparkled again.

"Damn right! Too bad we can't blow the entire place to hell," said Hardie excitedly. "Imagine the fireworks! The blast radius would be enormous."

"Too many civilians at risk. Remember. We want them on our side," cautioned Cole.

"I know, I know! I was just thinking out loud," replied Hardie sheepishly.

Tristan listened, curious about what Voleta might be thinking. She seemed oddly quiet. Everything appeared to be per plan; maybe too much so. He was used to more activity, especially at a mission's onset. The room lurched when the brakes grabbed. That was the roughest elevator ride he'd been on in quite a while. It prompted memories of summer flights through rising heat waves. His stomach fought to return to normal.

The doors hissed and opened. With Droth raised, Tristan stepped out. He shuffled across the grated, metal ramp. His mind wasn't at ease. His senses were keyed, but nothing caught his eye. He tried to focus his attention; the area smelled more like an office building than a zyn factory. In fact, he couldn't smell *any* zyn, a strong and powerfully familiar chemical odor he had learned to recognize as a child. "I don't smell anything, nor do I see anything that resembles zyn storage or processing."

Cole, Hardie and Lance held back while Tristan and Voleta proceeded.

"Perhaps it's further on, through there?" Voleta pointed to set of heavy glass doors.

The room beyond was nearly obscured by a green tint.

At her prompting, Hardie glanced ahead. "Something seems out of place."

Lance tilted his tablet and concentrated on the display.

Tristan watched as the screen flashed once and then blanked. He quickly scanned his wrist communicator; black too.

"Dammit," whispered Lance. "Signal interference!" He slapped the side of the device. "Something's wrong!" he said edgily.

Cole whispered. "Get a hold of yourself. It's a computer with a mind of its own. Give it a few seconds. It'll be fine."

Lance shook the small, black unit. "No! Of all times . . . Don't do this to me now!"

"Quiet, dammit! You'll bring the entire repository down on us!" hissed Tristan. His tight, black shirt clung tighter. They needed the computer. Could Lance get it working again?

"Is anyone even here?" challenged Hardie.

"Voleta? Is your device working?" asked Cole, eyeing her uneasily.

She flipped the cover and hastily scanned. "Our signal's jammed. My monitor's dead too."

"Is this a trap?" demanded Hardie. "Did Eliza set us up?"

"No way! Don't even think like that," retorted Tristan.

"Come on, man! Something's wrong, and you know it! Where're the fucking guards? Androids? This is supposed to be one of Vuton's largest repositories!" exclaimed Hardie.

Cole challenged again. "Hardie, stop. You're acting like Lance now."

"What's that s'posed to mean?" demanded Lance.

"We hardly know her. And she's the general's daughter! Anyone ever think of that? I seem to remember that even Mr. Edde didn't have much to say." Hardie flushed. His breathing quickened.

Cole jumped in again. "The general wouldn't chance delivering his daughter into enemy hands! Come on now. You sound like a woman! Uh, no offense, Voleta."

She motioned at the glass doors again. "Enough! Eliza didn't betray us. Let's continue with the mission and get it over with so we can go home."

That satisfied Tristan. He wanted to keep moving.

Cole grinned and affectionately caressed his pistol. "Now that's my Voleta. Always straight to the point. Too bad you weren't a man—I'd have you lead me! You heard the lady. Tristan! Take point." He stroked the weapon once more and slung it over his shoulder.

Tristan walked to the sealed doors and pressed a white pressure plate. A moment later, one panel slid open; he gave a swift sideways glance and stepped through. He glanced across the long stretch of grating and identified a cavernous opening filled with an enormous pile of twisted metal and flickering fluorescent lighting, but didn't see any storage vats or zyn transport tubes. "No zyn!" he reported.

Cole raged. "What? No fucking way! It has to be somewhere!"

Tristan glanced down the ramp toward a dimly lit overhang. Several steps led up to a rail in the computer area with various vertical bays of spinning tape drives and flashing indicator lights. On the far wall, he saw two doors. "Let's go up there and have a look around. Maybe we'll find . . ." His speech was cut short by his own intuition; their party wasn't complete; Voleta had disappeared. She hadn't crossed the rubber threshold with them. Turning, he eyed her hand, now resting on the control pad. A second later, the door hissed shut.

"Voleta!" shouted Cole. "What are you doing?" He ran over and pried at the dense plates. They wouldn't budge. He slammed his fist on the shatterproof glass and shouted. "*Voleta!*"

Hardie spun around. "What's going on?"

Tristan's mind whirled. "Voleta? No zyn . . . ?"

Her muffled voice was barely audible. "I'm sorry. I had no choice. You wouldn't understand." She turned away, muttering unintelligibly.

Cole pounded again. "What are ya saying? Voleta! Don't tell me . . . *you screwed us!*"

Tristan waited for her response.

"I'm sorry, Cole," she said, standing further back from the glass.

"Nooooo! Voleta! Damn you! Damn you, you backstabbing bitch!" Cole pried again, glaring.

Tristan scanned the computer area, expecting intruders at any moment. No one had entered through the two distant doors, but he was sure it would not be long before that changed. They'd been set up.

Cole slowly sunk to his knees, dragging his closed fists against the glass. "Voleta . . ." He sounded as if he had lost his greatest love; his voice trailed off in misery.

Voleta formed a subtle frown, "I'm sorry. Your death will be quick."

Tristan knew better though. The woman gave them up, for what?

"Wait! Voleta!" screamed Cole as he rose to his feet.

She turned and stared.

He transformed from a seemingly withered man into one filled with rage. "Tell me one fucking thing." He seethed through gritted teeth. "If I'm gonna die, tell me to my face you're working for the Federation!"

"It doesn't matter who I work for. You're dead."

". . . Dammit, tell me!"

Voleta screamed. "The *Enlightened One*! There! You happy?"

Her voice drifted like a floating whisper. Tristan's heart sank. No one he knew could identify *The Enlightened One*. And now she dropped his name? "Eliza! What about Eliza?" demanded Tristan as he moved closer to the sealed mullion.

She tilted her head and stared. "That stupid bitch did exactly what we expected." She turned again and hastened to the elevator.

Hardie went into full panic. "What do we do? Cole! What do we do?"

Cole squeezed his pistol, knuckles white. "I don't know what you're gonna do, but I'm gonna whoop some ass. I ain't going down like a sacrificial lamb. That's too girly."

"I'd rather surrender!" cried Lance.

"If you do, I'll shoot you myself!" shouted Cole.

Tristan was furious. Voleta had sabotaged their mission so skillfully that no one had had a clue. He watched Lance crumble. Hardie seemed close behind. There was no way that he was going to die here, now. It wasn't his time, but what could he do? He was at a loss for calculating the odds. "Enough! We need to call Eliza! She could be in trouble!" What if the USC location was compromised?

"You heard her! She did what this *Enlightened One* wanted! She's working with Voleta!" said Cole spitefully.

Tristan shook his head. "Bullshit! She fell for this just like we did. They led us here. It's not her fault . . . She was careless . . . Damn it, Lance! Try to reach her!" Tristan believed she was innocent. He believed her stories about her father, being a half-breed, and the outlandish risks she was taking.

Lance lifted the black device to his ear. "It's dead . . . Either she deactivated it, or Voleta blocked the signal. It's totally dead."

Tristan's heart pounded as he considered whether Eliza was compromised. Without a working communicator, protecting her was out of the question. A muted pneumatic hiss and the distinctive sound of weighted footsteps caused him to redirect his attention.

12

CRESCENT 19, 1870 O.C.
CITY: LATHE, USC HQ

Eliza was bored; tired of staring at Mr. Edde's sprawling book collection lining the office walls; filled with the most ancient books she'd ever laid eyes on; and bored of the two fish in the wall tank —a blue one and a lacy-tailed orange one, both with glittering gold—swimming directionless. Passing time like this wasn't at the top of her to-do list. A fitful night's rest only added to the monotony. The office dripped of intelligence and intimidation, strange bedfellows. Perhaps Mr. Edde was one of those precocious exclusives with an unbelievably high IQ? She worried that he couldn't be reached by the highly touted Skyband communications system. His inaccessibility could easily spell disaster. She yearned for Tristan. Maybe he would call? She squirmed on the same couch they had shared just hours earlier, running her hand across the smooth leather, hoping to feel his residual warmth. It gave her a chill.

She wanted her father to be proud; if she failed, it would only drive them further apart. That could never happen to her *brother*. Her thoughts continued to tumble. Tristan had saved her. He had to be concerned about her. She struggled to maintain his fading image. Was his valor simply male bravado? She wished she was ten years older; perhaps it was his dashing good looks. He was hot.

The opening office door made her turn to face a bald man—Nate— her personal bodyguard she had only just come to know. His presence tendered a slight margin of safety, but she wanted more. His pistol bolstered her confidence—barely.

"Hey, Eliza. Just checking in. Everything all right?" asked Nate with a chipper voice.

He had a nice smile; the tension in her neck and across her shoulders slowly loosened its' grasp. "Yes, Nate. Thank you. I've been terribly edgy. Maybe hearing something about the mission would help? Do you think they're okay?"

"Yes. I'm sure they are." His grin widened. "Don't worry. Cole has never compromised a mission. He's a good man with a strong Amstynian army background. Must have taught him some useful practices. I think that's why he's so resourceful."

His fatherly manner continued to knead at her. "A military background surprises me," replied Eliza. "I couldn't tell by looking at him. He does seem to be very knowledgeable about that stuff, and also chemistry. I watched him work on the bombs. His hands didn't shake at all. As for me, the zyn neutralization process was simply too much," she said, stressing. She wondered if that made her sound too elite, as if she was trying to impress him.

They both chuckled.

Nate sat down across from her. His formidable build made the seat cushion wheeze on either side. "His favorite, though, is demolition. He loves explosions. His record with those materials is without equal."

Wasn't he needed in his own country's military? If explosives were his forte, why was he working for the USC? "Why did he leave the Amstynian army?"

"Cole was never one for politics. He hates the system. Couldn't get along with the boss—General Gregson. I heard he had some personal issues. Amstye severed military funding, a move Cole loathed. While the Federation continued to strengthen its military, his country did not. Amstye focused its' resources on culture and economy. Why? They believed that they would never get stuck in a Federation waged war. Foolish bastards."

"I know. It makes no sense. For Xander, Amstye and Reyna are nations of inbred weaklings. He said they were the ones who would eventually throw the world into decline. Wouldn't such profound hate just spawn more enemies?"

"I don't doubt Xander's ultimate quest is a religious war," suggested Nate.

"Religious? Ha! Xander hates religion." She had a tough time relating to Cole's position, but felt more than confident in her assessment of Xander. Most were aware of his disdain.

Nate gently raised his hands. "Don't get carried away. You'll only see that hate manifest when religion and his objectives collide. He's actually a very religious man."

She nearly choked, swallowing hard. "I beg your pardon? I've known him from childhood, and he's always been hell-bent on spreading genetic progression theories."

"Of course he has. But, politically, he wants nothing more than to corrupt other nations' religions. He's eager to turn them against each other. But his misguided ideologies are driven by a distant aspiration— to unify full blooded Azdahris into a common destiny . . ."

"What destiny?" interrupted Eliza.

"That the Azdahri would know themselves as the children of the fallen."

"Nonsense!" She was dumbfounded. "I've never heard anything like that. How could you possibly know this?" Children of the fallen? What was he talking about?

"Because my brother was a surrogate for the Ferian ambassadors," retorted Nate, "He penetrated their inner circles in order to extract information on the senator— if he were to become the next Azdahri sovereign—information helping predict Xander's subsequent moves."

She had to know more. "And what conspiracy did Feria uncover?" She watched the man ponder for a moment, pleasantly surprised by his political awareness. She hadn't expected a conversation of this depth and found herself enjoying it immensely.

"Total war, of course," replied Nate, his body keyed by a series of dull thuds reverberating through the floor. They sounded muffled, like glass being smashed in a thick, cloth bag. "Isn't that the reason we've been battling the Federation to this day?"

Eliza's edginess was fueled by another chain of powerful thumps that shook the couch and caused the fish tank oxygen supply hose to break free and hiss loudly, sending water spraying onto Mr. Edde's desk. She could hear screaming and men shouting. The ruckus was loud enough to force them onto the floor. "What was that?" Eliza's gaze raced around the room. If they were in danger, where could they hide?

"Stay down!" Nate whispered hoarsely, gripping his pistol. He poked his head above the couch, facing the doorway. Several hushed explosions resounded, along with rapid-fire automatic rifle bursts.

Her heart jumped onto the carpet. Suddenly dizzy, she closed her eyes in an effort to steady herself.

Nate snapped. "Damn it!"

"What's happening?" asked Eliza, swallowing hard in an attempt to arrest her pounding chest.

"No time! Push the couch—now!" demanded Nate.

They both pushed. Eliza's periphery caught a corner of upturned carpet.

Nate reached under and yanked, exposing a trap door handle. "When I open this, get in!" he instructed. "Drop down the ladder; it leads to the sewers! Follow the path until you reach an exit! Further down the tunnel, a motion sensor will activate recessed floor lighting; don't worry, you can't miss the hatch with a wheel latch. Be careful!" He lifted the latch. His drawn face glistened.

"No! You're coming with me!" demanded Eliza.

"I have to put this furniture back! If I don't, they'll find you! Trust me! Go!"

The stark reality of isolation in a dark tunnel instantly nauseated her, causing her skin to turn clammy. Nate was her only connection with the familiar. "Nate!" She wanted to scream, to convince him, but it was no use.

He grabbed her shoulders firmly. "Dammit, Eliza! You must survive! Consider this our thanks for your help!" He guided her, making sure she didn't slip on the first few rungs.

Above her head, the door clicked, the carpet slid, and the couch scraped. Muffled rifle blasts infiltrated the obscurity; fear struck her, nearly sending her reeling. Her breathing quickened; she squinted. Faint light eked through a narrow crack; Nate's hulking image was so close. She might never see him again.

Smoke, ceiling light glass shards, and wall fragments blew past. Several men in black shifted through the shredded wall. Nate fired and dropped the nearest one. Another pointed quickly and fired. Nate's body slammed backward; his head bounced off the floor. His pistol flew from his hand and clattered to his side. She gasped. The arches of her feet burned against the narrow rungs. She had to keep watching. Gather information; others would depend on it. Two more black-unformed assailants raced through the opening, followed by a blond-haired man dressed in a flowing dark trench coat. Nate writhed in pain.

"This must be the 'mastermind's' office. Perfect. Who are you, the 'mastermind'?" sneered the man in the trench coat, with a smile on his face.

Nate wheezed.

"Speak up!" He shouted and aimed his weapon.

His weapon was identical to Tristan's. She struggled to see the others, but could only discern thick white letters—VI—embroidered onto their upper coat sleeves. Were they Institute VI men, Tristan's people? How does that make sense? Did Tristan betray the USC? No!

Nate whispered, his breath no longer even. "I'm nobody."

"That's really good, asshole. Bring in the bitches!" ordered the shrouded man.

Eliza could see no more. It was too much to take in, and she would be spotted soon enough if she stayed. She hesitated, considering the darkness below her. "If I can see them, they'll be blowing holes in the floor when they spot me."

Several more black uniforms streamed in, dragging three sobbing women. One of them was a cafeteria worker in charge of the baked bread display. All three women's hands were bound behind them.

The man in white glared down on Nate. "Now .....! I don't have time to kill for this shit. Do you understand me? OK then. We're going to play a game, so pay attention. How many bitches can I kill before you talk?" His words cackled. "The rules are simple. You tell me what I want to know; I'll allow the women to live. If you don't, well … they die for the, oh, what was it I hear all the time …. *righteous cause?*"

"Who the hell are you?" Nate squirmed to reposition himself, groaning when he raised his head.

"Newly appointed, Lt. Erik Gabrio of Institute VI, left arm of the Federation, at your service. That's who the hell I am. Now that we're exchanging pleasantries, who the hell are you?"

Nate pursed his lips and spat.

Erik raised his Droth, chuckling, aimed it and fired. The middle woman's forehead shattered; blood and brains painted the wall.

"You bastard!" wheezed Nate.

The wooden planks under the women carried their screams. They struggled, now pinned by the soldiers against the blood-stained wall.

Eliza peered into the darkness; her hands ached. She had to get ahold of herself. Now was not the time to fall apart. She was better than that. Her muscles spasmed; her arms ached from the constant tension. Hair fell into her eyes, but she dared not release her grip. Institute VI and the Federation in league together? If Institute VI was now with the Federation, where did that put Tristan?

Erik's voice sharpened, "I told you . . . , play nice and they live. Listen! I'll ask again. What is your name?"

"Nate! I'm Nate Haskins!"

"There. That's better now, isn't it, boys?" Erik's thick, black brows were set under a menacing scowl.

They laughed, still holding the hostages against the wall.

"Now for my next question. Where's the half-breed, the general's bitch? We know she was with you."

"I have no idea . . . ," pleaded Nate.

Erik's gun flashed; a second woman dropped. "You piece of shit! I don't have time for this! Tell me where she is!"

The last hostage, alone and dripping in blood, wept with dry heaves. She shook uncontrollably and fell to her knees. She crumpled forward; it shaking with each tearless gasp.

"She left! I swear! She left this morning! She said she was going back to her father! That's all I know! I swear on my life!"

"Liar!" Erik shoved the Droth's cold, black barrel under Nate's chin. "I hate liars. Tell me where she is, or I swear by whatever god you believe in, I'll blow a round through your neck, and I'll take out that woman on her knees too. Do we understand each other?"

Nate's voice gained strength. "She's gone! She left! That's all I know! I swear on my life!" His glassed-over gaze fell to the floor.

Eliza's throat tightened. The gunshots had been muted, but not unheard. Her only option was to descend. She'd be the only surviving eyewitness. That kept her quivering hands and feet attached to the rungs. What would Tristan tell her to do? Wait. Did he, like Erik, suppress a veiled evil streak? Were they all so stoic, unemotional? How could he kill without mercy?

She saw Nate's still body.

Erik grabbed a handful of the prostrate woman's blood-soaked hair and yanked her from the floor, pressing the Droth against her head. "Don't tempt me, asshole. I'll blow her brains all over this room if you don't tell me where Eliza Nyvala is!" Erik rushed over, and jammed the Droth's nozzle against Nate's neck. "Where is she?"

As if giving a final farewell, Nate's passionless gaze shifted toward the ruffled carpet. His eyes shifted back. "I don't know anything . . ."

Erik's bladed gun exploded, blowing the third woman against the wall. "I hate you. I fucking hate you! You had to be a tough guy, didn't you?" He slowly brought the Droth to bear against Nate's temple. "Don't make me waste my ammo! Last chance!"

"Shoot yourself, you son of a bitch!" shouted Nate in a burst of courage.

Erik fired. Eliza's stomach tightened. Nate was dead, and she practically fell down the rungs. She couldn't move; her legs shook—it was so cold. She felt utterly helpless, quivering. This was the worst day of her life.

Erik spoke, "Guess the bastard was telling the truth. Maybe she *did* leave this morning. Shit. Mawson ain't going to be happy about this."

One soldier quipped. "You think Voleta took her to the power plant?"

"No. Doubt it. That slut wouldn't screw up like that. Anyway, Tristan wouldn't put her in any danger. He had orders from the Headmaster himself to keep her safe."

"At least one of our guys is with the group," added the soldier.

"Ha! Tristan doesn't even know he's in this grand scheme. But he will soon, and he'll probably get a big, fat, shiny medal for it, too, after

Zeddicus tells him he was USC bait. Bastard. Wish I could see the look on his face when he realizes that he was nothing more than a worm on a hook. I'm sure he'll come home bragging about how he was wise to it the entire time."

"You don't like Hart, do you?"

"No. In fact, part of me hopes that those idiots persuaded him to see their perspective. Then he can die for the . . ." Erik finger-quoted his next words, "'*righteous cause*' and get the hell out of my way. But, it's just a dream." He broke out in laughter. "Let's get out of here. Burn the building. Enjoy yourselves, boys. You're now Federation heroes! The USC is no more!"

The men launched closed fists upward and cheered.

Eliza rubbed the back of her wrist against tear-soaked eyes. The darkness caused her to fumble against the cold metal rungs. She had to warn the others. She struggled along the uneven stone floor and remembered the communicator. She pressed it twice. Nothing. She doubled over and spilled her guts. They were nearly dry; she hadn't eaten anything since the night before. The pain was too much to bear; her heart sunk to the stone floor. Tristan .... Was he another Erik? Would he kill Cole and the others? And her father? He *must* know about this. If she was caught, would he execute her himself? All seemed lost as she groped ahead, hoping to find that hatch.

CRESCENT 19, 1870 O.C.
CITY: LATHE, POWER PLANT

Voleta—a traitor—gone, but not forgotten. The cramped office space was like being forced out into the open. Desks lined the walls, a few chairs, a row of switches on an adjoining wall—nothing useful. Footsteps, the penetrating kind that heel taps made, closed in on them. Tristan, crouching, took another careful look. Whoever was on the other side of that glass wall definitely had the upper hand. Computer equipment blocked his view, but theirs too. He eyed Cole, Lance and Hardie, worried for their safety. They crouched adjacent the desks, their gazes fraught with dread. Lance was a bundle of nerves; his tan shirt was stained with worry and clung to his shaking body. A shadowy image formed in Tristan's periphery. He immediately recognized the black mask—Zeddicus Sangray. Red lights flashed along his shoulders and down his legs. Bewildered, Tristan stared restlessly; his blood pulsed feverishly and flooded his thoughts. More footsteps produced a covey of Institute VI men. First Voleta, and now this. He thought back to the conference room when Sangray had received an assignment. His emotions shifted between anger and shame. 'Damn,' he thought. 'This jokes on me.' He gripped his Droth—at least he still had that. His fingers tingled.

"Game's over, USC scum."

It took a second to recognize the voice—Lord Commander Seryth, the white-haired politico from the Ball. His mind reeled as he analyzed the game; he felt like a pawn; Sangray, Seryth, Institute VI. Too enraged to die, he could only wait. If he opened fire—they'd be expecting that—escape would be impossible, especially with Zeddicus there. Tristan threw up his hands; his Droth dropped to his side.

"There are a couple dozen of them!" shouted Cole. "What's wrong with you? We can take 'em! Oh, I get it. You and Voleta did this together. Huh, you bastard?" He turned his pistol on Tristan. "I'll make sure that you're the first to die!"

Held between deadly rage and the unknown, Tristan could only hope that Cole would come to his senses. "Dammit, Cole!" hissed Tristan, scowling. "Put it down! I did no such thing!"

"Like hell you didn't . . . !" snapped Cole.

The glass partition parted—a shrill of air—and forced Tristan to turn.

"He speaks the truth, Corporal Ashbury, or shall I say ex-Corporal?" said Seryth, dropping his hand from the door entry pad. "Oh yes, I've reviewed the facts; you should have stayed in Amstye!"

Cole sounded powerful but looked so helpless rising from a crouch. "Shut up or I'll finish your pathetic excuse for life right here, right now!"

Tristan had no idea what to expect from Seryth, and the Institute VI men, especially Sangray, couldn't be trusted. Cole needed to chill out or they'd all be shredded meat.

"Cole!" shouted Lance. "Are you blind? We're outnumbered! Don't be stupid; surrender or they'll kill us!"

"I'd rather die than serve the cursed Federation!" Cole held his aim.

"Cursed? Tsk tsk," chuckled Seryth. "I'm afraid you heard wrong, Ashbury. No, I believe you're the cursed one. Now, we can discuss your predicament if you like, if you lower your weapon. If you don't, I'll shoot you myself. What's it going to be?"

Lance dropped his, its clatter a warning shot.

"Pansy!" hissed Cole.

"Cole! Please!" pleaded Lance. "Put down your pistol!"

"Over my dead body!"

Cole's craze meant sure death. "Cole!" demanded Tristan. "Listen to him! We can live to fight another day!"

"Yeah—you would say that, wouldn't you, traitor." Cole exploded.

"Tristan? What's going on?" demanded Hardie.

"I don't know . . . ," said Tristan, eyeing Seryth.

"Cole. It's over." Hardie lowered his pistol, nervously eyeing Sangray.

Cole's eyes watered. "It ain't over till we take our last breath! We're freedom fighters and we're supposed to be fighting Federation tyranny." He leveled his glare at Seryth. "Him! Or maybe you've forgotten?"

"Cole . . . ," said Hardie.

Cole flung his weapon. Against the wall, the handle splintered and tumbled to the floor. He wistfully eyed the useless pile of debris.

"Tristan . . . . Collect their weapons." Zeddicus's monotone resonated from his face grill.

Tristan cringed when Cole started up again.

"Damn you, Tristan. Damn you," spit Cole.

"I don't understand," said Tristan, his eyes meeting Zeddicus's dark probes.

"Forgive me, Tristan." Seryth stepped in front of Zeddicus. "I kept you in the dark on purpose. If you had known, well, we wouldn't be here today. It was best to keep you in the dark. You're fortunate that Mawson agreed to spare your life. He considers you the most accomplished pilot he's ever known."

"But why this?" Tristan asked. Both sides were leveraging him. And if Mawson was in on it, where did that put Mr. Edde? That's probably why they didn't raise him on the Skyband.

Seryth's pale face nodded toward the downed pistols. "Weapons, Tristan."

Tristan snatched up two fallen pistols and shuffled over to Cole's.

Cole cleared his throat and spit at Tristan.

Skirting him, Tristan began to fear for the others. Zeddicus grabbed the weapons from Tristan and shoved him down the ramp.

Perched above, Seryth laughed again. "Mr. Ashbury, I want to thank you for your contributions to the Federation's cause. I truly owe you more than, well, I'd care to give you."

"What the hell are you talking about?" fired Cole.

Seryth walked up to the rail and looked down on the men.

Zeddicus ordered the soldiers to bind everyone but Tristan. Only Cole resisted.

"Isn't it obvious?" started Seryth angrily. "Oh, I forgot. You're from Amstye and are too stupid to understand. Let me explain. Mawson used the USC to unite the Azdahri. You were the terrorist that we needed in order to strike fear in their hearts."

"We fought *for* the people!" exclaimed Cole.

"Unfortunately, they won't see it that way. No. Instead, they view you as monsters!"

"What?" yelled Cole.

One of the soldiers wrenched off Cole's backpack and dug out the bomb. "It's a chemical bomb, sir. No explosives."

Cole stumbled, nearly falling to the floor.

Seryth frowned. "Child's play. Glad we brought our own."

"What are you talking about?" asked Cole.

"Destroying the repository and power plant, of course."

"You're mad!" exclaimed Cole.

"On the contrary. Half of Lathe will be without power, hundreds of thousands, even more, will die—suffer from extreme cold, blah, blah, blah. With the USC taking the fall. And the Federation—saviors, of course—will exterminate them all. By now, I'm sure Institute VI has already destroyed your little USC Headquarters."

"What!" exclaimed Tristan. What of Eliza? They'd be after her too! Or had he been deceived?

"Is there a problem?" asked Seryth, sounding strangely empathetic.

Cole shouted. "You're a sick, demented lunatic!"

"Yes, yes, but the people will rejoice! The Federation will be Vuton's savior, and together, they'll welcome Xander. We'll come in, restore Lathe's power, and then they'll owe *us*! They'll unite with Atomia, and all of your efforts to squash our plans will have been destroyed! It was in vain, Ashbury! Everything you've been fighting for has amounted to nothing! Think of it. A united front comprised of the world's two most powerful nations!"

Cole stared blankly, sweat dripping from his forehead.

"But, I can be merciful. You wished to destroy this repository, and so you will. I'll bind our weapon onto you; your greatest act will take you out in a blaze of glory, you stupid, Cintarian trash! And you thought you could thwart the Azdahri race? No, today you die!" Seryth paused, seething. "Tristan?" He turned and faced him.

Tristan bristled. He should have seen it coming through Seryth's veiled politeness at the Ball. Anyone acting so pleasant hid ulterior motives—Tristan had been too distracted to heed his own advice.

"These fine soldiers will strap the bomb to Ashbury. As for the other two, taking prisoners is against our code. Kill them." ordered Seryth.

"No! We surrender! Please!" cried Lance.

Tristan couldn't bring himself to look at Lance.

"Go on, Hart. The Federation now owns Institute VI; consider it Xander's left hand. I'm here to determine who's worthy and who's not. Prove yourself to me, the Federation, and the Azdahri . . . ." Seryth motioned toward Lance and Hardie. A deadly hush gushed from his hand. "Make sure it's slow, Tristan. They're traitors to all Azdahris and deserve to suffer. Open them up with your blade? That would be fitting! Go on, cut that one's neck; let him bleed out. I want it painfully slow."

Tristan couldn't move. He seethed—a volcano about to explode. The pressure was too great. He lifted his head and faced the gut-wrenching sorrow on Lance's face. He'd never forget that look.

Lance wavered, ghostly pale, the front of his trousers soaked.

Tristan glanced at his hands, unable to picture them as weapons. He couldn't murder his friend.

"*Now!*" screamed Seryth.

Tristan twitched. "I can't." His words tumbled through to the floor.

Seryth glared. "Well, now! That was disappointing. Zeddicus! Please show our dear friend how to follow orders."

Zeddicus stepped forward, joints whirring.

Lance began to mouth silent pleads; Hardie's gaze was frozen to his feet; Cole stared at Tristan.

"I'm afraid we don't tolerate cowards, Tristan," chided Seryth, glancing over at his soldiers. "Let's ignore my deal with Mawson. Strap Hart to Ashbury since that's where his loyalties lie. How fitting!"

A soldier grabbed Tristan's Droth and flung it away. It clattered loudly and slid under a desk. Two men yanked him around and cinched a rope around his wrists.

Zeddicus faced Seryth.

The Lord Commander nodded. The soldiers stepped back and Zeddicus pressed the nozzle against Hardie's temple and pulled the trigger. The explosion was ear-shattering. Blood drenched Cole and splattered on the soldiers. Lance gasped, gagging. He shrunk to his knees as Zeddicus released his blade and severed Lance's neck.

Agony overtook Tristan. He couldn't believe what he had just witnessed. Helplessness swept over him, like when his friends and family were murdered. His ears rang, at first a dull throb. His muscles shook uncontrollably.

Sobbing like a baby, Cole fell to his knees.

"Now, that's how it's done. And we shall treat all Federation traitors this way. Oh, Ashbury. We have a special plan for your precious Amstye. Too bad you won't live to see it. Thank you again for your commitment to the Federation. You have our gratitude. I trust that the fireworks display will provide a fitting finale." A sly grin stretched across Seryth's darkened face as he turned toward the door. "Enjoy!"

"Strap them to the computer railing," ordered Zeddicus, his metallic voice loud and grating. "Set the timer for thirty minutes . That's enough time for us to escape the blast zone. Evacuate the building!" He bolted past Tristan, a rush of motors and flashing lights.

Tristan watched a soldier drag Cole across the floor and slam his rifle butt into the back of his head.

"He's coming! Run! Save yourself! He can't be stopped!" Tristan twitched. Gray fog surrounded him. He tried to swish it away, but it merely swirled around his hands. A moment of clarity quickly blurred. He was aware enough to realize the haunting dream, but couldn't escape it. A blur of alien idols gaped wantonly as if he were their next sacrifice. He shuddered and groped through the gloom.

"He's coming! Run! Save yourself! He can't be stopped!" The words repeated, as faint as his eyesight was dim. Frigid fingers gripped him; his head ached against a cold surface. He struggled in the dark eddy. His tongue cleaved to the roof of his mouth. He cried out. "What? No. I won't leave you!" Yet, his throat was still.

"You must! He'll kill us both!"

Tristan eked out a reply. "I won't!"

"Tristan. He's here! He's here! Run! Now!"

The insistent commands vanished, his attention shifting to throbbing muscles. His knees ached, raw and bruised against the hard floor. "No!" he shouted. He came to, sure that he had been screaming, only to realize his throat burned with dryness.

"Wake up, dumb ass!"

"What?" he mumbled.

"Wake up!"

"Huh . . . ?"

Cole appeared through his squint, but the dizziness was too great. He closed them again. The floor vibrated. It wasn't stone, rather raised computer flooring. He glanced around. Were they still alive? He struggled to raise his head. His arms were cuffed to railing surrounding the computer walkway. His wrists burned. Cole dangled adjacent to him.

"Wake up! Wake up, you . . ."

"I'm awake! Stop yelling at me." His head dropped, lazily, lifeless. The agony grew worse.

"Damn it! Twenty minutes and counting. Do you know what that means?"

"Stop talking! I can't think straight!" Tristan willed the pain to stop; he felt sick when it didn't. The bomb had been set for 30 minutes. Lance and Hardie were dead. Their bodies lie in the adjacent room. He felt like he would puke.

"If we don't free ourselves, we'll be just like them!" shouted Cole. He lowered his indolent gaze.

Gripped by wasted time, Tristan recoiled. "You think I don't know that?" He yanked again; a searing pain shot through his skull.

"What the hell went wrong?" demanded Cole. "Your own I6 betrayed us! What deceit did you actually devise?"

"How should I know? If you haven't noticed yet, I'm tied up just like you."

"I don't trust ya! Voleta, Eliza. Damn every one of you backstabbing freaks!"

Cole was an idiot. There *had* been more than enough proof that Tristan hadn't brought this on them. Time continued to waste away. "That's insane! Eliza didn't backstab anyone, and neither did I."

"She told us about this blasted location in the first place!" exclaimed Cole. His daze darted frantically.

"She couldn't have known. Someone else has been tracking her movements." Tristan thought back to Mohawk and his would be assailants.

"I don't care! If I get out of here, not even the Deity will be able to save her!"

"You won't lay a hand on her!" Tristan's anger swelled. Escaping was the priority and time was slipping away. He yanked the railing again; it shifted.

"Ha! I knew pissing your wimpy ass off was a good thing. Keep doing that! We might get out of here yet!"

Tristan tugged again. The rail flexed after a few more heaves. It snapped loudly and popped out of the fitting. He looped around the pole and was free of it, but his hands were still bound. "Now what?"

"In my boot, there's a lock pick! Can you reach it?" Cole, caught against the railing, shoved out his left leg. "It's hidden, half way down. Just feel for it."

Tristan grabbed Cole's pant leg. He found the tool and fumbled with the blade and lock.

"Hurry up! Seventeen minutes!" pleaded Cole.

The tumblers shifted; *click!* The lock sprang open; Tristan was free. He shook off the restraints and reached for Cole.

"Those monsters," seethed Cole. "They killed Hardie and Lance. Dammit. I shouldn't have been so careless. Why didn't I suspect Voleta? Why?"

"Wait till we're out of here," said Tristan. "C'mon!"

"Hold it! They've locked everything down. We need to retrace our steps. I'll try the computer—activate the controls that Voleta killed."

Tristan nodded. It might work.

Cole reached for a key board and pounded out a few swift strokes.

Tristan wanted his Droth. Maybe it was still where he'd dropped it? A quick glance—it was. Elated, he jumped over the railing and retrieved his weapon. Feeling the cold steel in his hand gave him a surge of confidence. No one could stop him now.

"I did it! I'm a damn genius," said Cole. "System's unlocked, and with fifteen minutes to spare! Damn it. My weapon's shattered—idiot!"

Tristan eyed his friends' lifeless bodies. "Let's check Hardie and Lance." Tristan fought to bring himself close. Sadness froze him in his tracks.

Cole slid past, and dug into Hardy's boot. He came out with a small hand gun. "So sorry, old friend," he said.

Tristan's throat tightened at that fledgling eulogy; they ran to the elevator and Tristan hit the up arrow. Nothing happened.

"Shit on me," mumbled Cole. Now what's the matter?" He pried at the control plate; it bent back, exposing a bundle of colored wires.

"Ten minutes," said Tristan, gazing back at the main computer. They were cutting it close. They needed 30 minutes to clear the blast zone.

Cole yanked out two wires, yellow and green, and twisted them together. "You think I don't know that? Oww!" he shouted when sparks flew. "That should do it." The elevator opened, spilling green lighting at their feet.

"Didn't know you had it in you," exclaimed Tristan.

"I'm a jack of all trades. Ya have to be if you wanna be a leader."

The elevator crawled its way back up, shuddering to a stop at the rooftop. The doors hissed, exposing the Marne, a truly welcomed sight. It sat, armed and waiting. Hopefully, Seryth hadn't sabotaged it.

Four canine-droids, quadrupeds that looked like dogs, paced just past the gunship. 10mm, neck-mounted turrets, jutted out from beneath oblong heads, completely unnerving him. The shortened barrels were twice the size of Tristan's Droth.

"Looks like they expected company."

"Get their attention," said Tristan.

Cole cocked his pistol. The sliding mechanism clicked loudly. The hounds pivoted and aimed their sensors directly at him. "Whad'ya say?"

"I said, get their attention. Get them to fire at you. I'll run to the ship, get the guns online and blast them to bits," said Tristan, ready to run.

Cole looked at Tristan like he was crazy. "Oh, no. I don't trust ya. What's stopping you from deserting me when you climb aboard our only way outta here?"

"Cole! Really! We don't have time for this! If I wanted to betray you, I would have killed Lance and Hardie, and then you! Now, get over your arrogant self and work with me! We have less than five minutes!"

"If you leave me to die, I promise I'll find you and kill you."

"Fair enough," replied Tristan smugly, annoyed with the dawdling.

Cole bolted across a walkway, screaming and waving his arms. "Over here, you shit eaters!" He fired into the bunch of canines; his bullets glanced off a polished, angled back. All four canine heads swiveled in unison and released triple volleys. Cole threw down behind metal crates, just out of reach of the exploding shells.

Tristan sprinted and activated the Marne's ramp. A thumb print later, ramp motors whined, lowering the shiny metallic surface. He slipped through the opening and made for the cockpit, hastily settling into the captain's chair. His chest heaved and his palms were sweaty, but not enough to deter him. The faint, familiar sounds of the craft were comforting—cooling fans whirling overhead, the steady drone of the AI taking control, and muted beeps of the instrument panels. After punching in an armament sequence, a high-pitched trill warbled while the front-mounted guns thrummed to full power. He eyed the crates Cole was hiding behind. If he took out one of the canines, Cole could dash to the ship. He grabbed twin joy sticks, aimed and fired. All four robots shattered into a dizzying array of red fluid and metallic shards. Unspent bullets exploded, blowing a ragged hole in an adjacent wall. That was better than Tristan had expected.

Cole shot across the graveled surface and leaped onto the ramp.

Tristan ignited the thrusters, hovering the craft above the deck just long enough to reach full power. Both men were slammed into their seats when the Marne shot over the roof's edge.

"I hope you know what you're doing," yelled Cole.

Tristan reached for the communications dials on the overhead panel. Green indicator lights flashed as he changed the frequency.

"What the hell are you doing?" demanded Cole.

"Contacting Eliza!" answered Tristan.

Cole yanked Tristan's arm down. "No! We contact no one! We can't trust a single soul! We're dead as far as anyone is concerned. Don't ya see? There's only one man we can trust—Mr. Edde."

"He could be a traitor too! He and Mawson could have masterminded this entire debacle!" retorted Tristan angrily.

"No! Not Mr. Edde! I trusted you and now you trust me! He's one of us! I promise! I know him personally and he hates the Federation more than anyone I know!"

He couldn't deny that. Eliza could wait, but not for long. "Let's return to Headquarters. Seryth mentioned they had sent men there."

"Glad we agree on something," said Cole.

A shattering detonation rocked the ship's stern, sending muffled shock waves forward. Tristan grabbed for his armrests, eyeing the aft monitor. The power plant roof had transformed into an inferno; flames clawed relentlessly skyward. A yellowed, orange reflection mirrored into the cockpit. The building swayed, and began crumbling in on itself. Tongues of fire and black smoke filled the sky. In an instant, except for the raging torch-like effect of the fiery eruption, the cityscape disappeared. The sprawling city of Lathe was blanketed in black.

CHAPTER

15

At 30,000 feet, the sleek craft slid effortlessly through driving rain. Trailing aft, its opaque vapor trail collapsed at a dizzying speed. Cloud bursts tore arduously at the vessel, in no wise impeding it as it hurtled toward Lathe. Tristan eyed the instrument panel, satisfied and unusually tranquil. Mr. Edde's disappearance worried him. The breakdown could have been caused by many things—weather, more pressing issues, even sickness. Tristan was more concerned about the USC Headquarters, Eliza's safety, and the possibility of hostile forces when they landed.

What if the USC no longer existed? If Mr. Edde had turned traitor, the situation would quickly advance from bad to worse. A trip to Aurelia did raise questions. He didn't trust him; not now, and he wasn't sure if he could trust Eliza or anyone else. By all rights, with the world powers assembling, a real threat to lasting peace seemed imminent. Xander's new world order fantasy bothered Tristan to no end.

Where could they turn for help? Vuton had probably already labeled the USC a terrorist organization. With open arms, the Federation would be welcomed as elite demigods. That's what Eliza had been saying all along. Maybe she was right? He hadn't credited her and probably should have. His allegiances became more and more blurred.

Lathe's Outer Marker signaled the beginning of final approach and he began the descent toward a brightly lit runway.

Cole suddenly shouted. "There!" He pointed out the port side window to their distant objective.

Smoke ballooned skyward, billowing and wavering like heat undulations above desert sand just minutes from touchdown.

"No!" Cole's fist smashed into the seatback in front of him, leaving knuckled impressions. "No! Land the Marne now!" he shouted, frantically pointing toward the smoke.

"We don't know if Federation troops are there!" retorted Tristan. "It could be a trap."

"I don't care! Do it, Tristan! Take this hunk of metal over there and put it down!" returned Cole with desperation.

Tristan's gaze darted between radar and window. Nighttime and the upper level's shadow lowered visibility to less than 2000 feet; the ship shuddered as Tristan forced a turn and kept the ship airborne. Darkened streets, lifeless and empty, offered few traces to recent activities. By the time he brought the vessel about, any semblance of tranquility had eluded him. The USC headquarters was an enormous mound of smoldering rubble. He could feel the wet of his palms as he edged the nose forward. Bodies of USC soldiers scattered throughout appeared in the obscurity. The torrid sight numbed him beyond words.

"The Federation, the despicable Federation! Nothing but executioners!" Cole's reaction was filled with venom.

Tristan altered the wing configuration and hovered the screaming cruiser. A great wall of water sprayed in all directions. The ship floated as if hung by invisible wires while it transferred its weight, and then settled onto the street gracefully like a swan.

Cole didn't wait for the engines to spin down; he jumped up and bolted to the rear.

A scream of power ravaged the cabin through the raised aft door. Tristan jolted, hastily glancing over his shoulder. Unnerved, he caught a glimpse of the disaster through rising steam and sheeting rain. Cole jumped onto the swampy street and raced to the nearest corpse. Tristan joined him and peered over his shoulder. The victim's jacket was shredded from multiple lacerations. Whoever caused this problem wasn't taking any prisoners. Cole fell to one knee, turning his face skyward. Rain veiled his anguish, but not his heartfelt cries.

A shrill chirping from inside the ship drew Tristan back to the cockpit. Dripping wet, he crouched beneath the overhead console, studying the flashing lights sequence. Satellite five—Mr. Edde's satellite. He shouted for Cole and plugged in his headset. The monitor sprang to life. He wiped the rain from his eyes and squinted at a grainy image of Mr. Edde dressed in a dark gray suit, white shirt and black tie.

"Mr. Hart! You're alive!"

Cole burst into the cockpit. "Mr. Edde!"

"Mr. Ashbury! I can't believe it! I heard a most atrocious account. The USC Headquarters was attacked by Institute VI and Federation troops?"

"Yes, sir! We arrived on location barely five minutes ago," replied Cole with heavy breath. "As far as we can tell, they took no prisoners! It was a set up! That Nyvala girl gave us false information!"

"We don't know that yet!" exclaimed Tristan. "She might not have known!"

"She had to have known! And that's not all! Voleta—Voleta turned on us! Said she was working for the Enlightened One! The Federation used us to fool the populace! They destroyed Lathe's main power plant, robbing half the city of power, and they're blaming it on us! Everyone else is dead! Hardie, Lance." His voice trailed off. "The USC no longer exists!"

"Some did survive the attack, Mr. Ashbury. That's been confirmed, so all is not lost. In this time of crisis, we must stand together." The audio crackled, distorting the transmission. Tristan tweaked the dials. "We've gained an even greater understanding of our enemy. I've been in contact with various Federation sources; their objectives are now clearer than ever. My previous assumptions have been validated by their barbaric actions against our people. Xander intends to build the Federation into what he deems its destiny—an iron-fisted Empire bent on world domination. He's plotting ways to expand its borders to the world's far reaches and to wage war against all Cintarians including their home nation of Reyna. He's destroying everyone in his path."

"Cintarians? Is this a holy war?" said Cole, sitting on the edge of his seat.

"That's irrelevant. They'll wage war against any opposition. And now, they have the power to do so. Ultimately, Xander will be elected sovereign, able then to realize his insane ambitions."

"What do we do? When will you return? We need you," pleaded Cole.

Mr. Edde paused. "—I'm afraid I won't be returning—at least, not right away. I'm now on Institute VI's most wanted list thanks to Mawson. A wrong move could prove fatal. They can find me as soon as I set foot on Eshen soil. I have no choice but to remain in Aurelia. Hopefully, our communications breakdown was only a fluke."

Tristan remained skeptical. "How convenient. We really could have used your expertise *before* we started this mission." He was well aware of satellite reliability.

"Tristan!" Cole scowled.

"It's fine, Mr. Ashbury. He has every right to be suspicious. I'm sure that you would agree how difficult it is to trust anyone these days. It's onerous to trust even yourself."

"What's that supposed to mean?" Tristan was ready for a fight. The loss of the USC HQ building was only the beginning. Now, without leadership, what would prevent something worse?

"I also have to trust that *you* aren't working for our enemy. What side are you on, Mr. Hart?"

"After risking my life to save Cole, my intentions should be obvious," replied Tristan.

"But for how long? You're a mercenary for hire, one who bows to the highest bidder? That's what you told me, is it not? My pockets are full, but the supply is not endless. I'm not able to match a hefty Federation offer. How long do you plan to stay with us, sir?"

Cole's disdain burned into the side of Tristan's face like a branding iron. "It's not about the credits." Why did he think it was? Tristan considered himself more loyal than most.

"Your sudden change of heart has inflamed my curiosity. What could have sparked such a change? Was it the deaths that you recently witnessed? Was it the Federation and their undying commitment to terror and fear? Or was it," his voice lowered tauntingly, "—our little informant? She's inspiring, isn't she?"

"Eliza?" Absurd. He was drawing for straws.

"She's a natural speaker capable of moving a man's soul. Her beliefs and convictions have . . . even encouraged my own faith."

"Do you know where she is? You do, don't you?" Maybe Mr. Edde's perceptions were correct. He had no idea the teenager had impressed him so much. Tristan was concerned for her safety, but was unable to protect her. She could be anywhere, lost, alone, desperate. She might even be dead.

"I don't know, but I need you to find out. She contacted me shortly after the attack."

Mr. Edde's response drove through Tristan like an auger. "What! And you didn't tell us?"

"Your emotions betray you, Tristan. You seem to care for this girl too much. I'll be honest with you. I can easily use this to my advantage."

Advantage. They were on the same team. This was a side of Mr. Edde he hadn't seen coming. "Are you serious?"

"Very much so. You're a mercenary for hire, but your heart blinds you. That's good for the USC; you won't betray us, because if you do, you'll betray her."

Tristan couldn't extinguish the flames igniting his thoughts.

Mr. Edde lifted a shoulder. "I lost contact. She escaped headquarters and informed me of the tragedy. Apparently, Mr. Gabrio led the attack."

"Erik?" That made sense. Erik had sold out completely. Had he no soul? All of those deaths? Their blood was upon him.

"He was merciless. He's searching for her, Tristan. You must find her first!"

Tristan's stomach knotted. Erik was never a leader. Yet, those deaths were on him.

"I can tell you her last location. She's in grave danger, Tristan. If we're not quick, the Federation will find her."

"And what of the Enlightened One? He sent men after her as well. That was who Voleta was working for, right?"

The camera followed Mr. Edde as he pushed back in his padded chair and rested his chin on his hand. "Yes. Eliza mentioned that too. The Enlightened One is a criminal master mind. He's globally recognized as the epitome of knowledge and foresight. Supposedly, he's involved in criminal transactions with nearly every nation. There's rumor that he even has dealings in Aurelia. I have proof that he's well connected to the Federation."

Cole calmed. "Must be, especially if Voleta was involved."

"Don't trust anyone, men. Find Ms. Nyvala. She's the key to unraveling this mess and must be safeguarded at all costs. Don't contact me; I'll contact you—plan on providing frequent updates. Any questions?"

"Do you trust her?" asked Cole.

Tristan wondered the same thing.

The rain continued to run down the Marne's windows.

Mr. Edde nodded. "I do. The general's daughter can be a great weapon against the Federation. With the information she has gathered, she has the ability to expose them—all of them."

"I understand. What's the situation in Aurelia?" Cole nodded.

Mr. Edde sighed. "It's been difficult. The country's facing Thracian hostilities and is on a heightened state of alert. Troops have been ordered to Tarrant. Rebels have mounted surprise attacks against Imperial encampments. Crime and sex trades are at an all-time high. I don't want to get into it, but it's a lawlessness country, to say the least. My southern propaganda efforts have fallen grossly short mainly due to some mad man burning people throughout that region. They call him the Man Burner, a monster from the underworld. They are original, are they not?" Mr. Edde chuckled quietly. "What a superstitious people!"

"Sounds like a waste. What do you hope to accomplish?" asked Cole.

Tristan feigned ignorance, angry that they were wasting precious time. He didn't care about Aurelia; Eliza's life was at stake.

"The soon to be Sovereign Xander has a proven fascination with Aurelia's Emperor. Emperor Nebekon is a demagogue, populist, and dictator all rolled into one. Similar qualities are shared by the senator himself. Let's hope that we can dissuade the emperor from plunging his country's freedoms into Federation enslavement."

Cole scoffed and squirmed against the firm padding.

"What do we do when we find Eliza?" asked Tristan.

"Keep her safe. Keep her hidden. She's our last hope for availing Eshen. We must bring her before the Reynan World Council. Give me some time and I'll provide you with a workable strategy. She's top priority. And if your feelings change about credits, I'll pay you double what anyone else would, Mr. Hart. Whatever you do, bring her to me."

CHAPTER

16

Senator Xander's portrait hung on the far wall, his flowing white hair awash in red and black from a backdrop of Atomian flags—black discs set atop flaming red. The flags were draped around the conference room and boldly represented Federation power. Salvador Dukes Seryth, Valkyrie Lord Commander, stood before six national-planning session members, his back to the painting and his stare spotted with trepidation. He hid it well before the emblematic symbols. Assigned to implement Xander's plan, he was intent on a stark representation of Atomian power. He gloated about the Vutonian power plant's destruction—his latest triumph—nothing short of magnificent. Daily reports confirmed that many Atomian and Vutonian Azdahri were proclaiming Federation allegiance. Senator Xander's election was eminent and would undo centuries of Vutonian separation by aligning them with Atomia. By this, Atomia would become the world's most powerful nation.

What better place for their top leadership to convene than under these daunting banners. The harvest was ripe, and the attendees were eager to offer fealty to Xander. Even more thrilling was that he had been chosen to deliver the confidential discourse to these hand-selected men. Never in Atomian history had so much power been assembled for such a renowned cause. He was honored beyond words, his mind euphoric as he studied each distinguished principal seated around the polished-wood conference table. Thin lipped and smug, he stroked his white hair and reveled in his non-conformity.

Headmaster Mawson, newly recognized as Xander's left hand, hailed from Institute VI. Salvador knew, all too well, that money could easily shift a man's morals and ethics. Mawson was no stranger to such leverage. For this new position, his compensation had tripled. His gray hair, wavy and thick, was combed back, exposing a scar running diagonally from his left eye toward his right forehead. His cheeks drooped, framing a downturned smile. He tapped the table nervously, seeming eager for the meeting to begin.

Next to him sat the white haired Prime Patriarch Ransom Penney. He appeared quite stern; wrinkled forehead, white eyebrows and unyielding eyes. Impatience exuded. His input, though, was generally rehearsed and welcomed.

Admiral Preston Thorne, a fairly pleasant military mogul, was superbly capable of running the country's naval resources. Kind smile and pleasant eyes had won over many an unsuspecting rival. Early on, Salvador had learned never to underestimate the admiral's negotiating skills.

He had reservations about Homeland Security Advisor, Dobbs Appleton. He planned to keep his eye on the surprisingly inventive man. He didn't appear well-suited to such assemblies, what with unkempt, graying hair, and white, bearded stubble. The man's raised caterpillar eyebrow gave Salvador pause; he appeared doubtful, albeit inquisitive.

The only invited senator, Jonas Bristol, bespoke aged wisdom, and was entrenched in government circles deeply enough to profit Seryth. His entry into governmental confidences remained elusive to others. Although still distinguished with thinning, white hair shaped over the ears, his countenance had seen better days. Several large, fleshly moles dotted his face and neck.

He studied the last astute figure, Head of Science, Professor Oswald Godwin. They thought alike. He celebrated a depth of scientific knowledge that even the most notable religious leaders shunned. His demeanor bespoke tranquility—white hair, short and brushed back over a high forehead. Sleep had forsaken him years past; drooping bags attested. Yet, his dark eyes could penetrate his subjects and reign down a torrent of intimidation.

The retinue shared one distinctive trait—pride! Salvador expected as much. Coupled with unwaning passion for success, they were courageous and intelligent men with the necessary will to forge the Federation into an indisputably supreme global force.

Salvador took his seat centered before a gaping Atomian flag. "Good evening and congratulations, gentleman. Our efforts have proven prolific. The USC has been destroyed; its remnants are now a fertile conveyance for Vuton's imminent transplantation into the Federation. Vuton's Sovereign Drakkar informed Senator Xander that, once elected, his first order of business would be to reunite our two countries— Atomia and Vuton will become one!" The men stirred, each nodding their approvals. "This grand achievement, the fruit of your labors, with no small credit to our founding forefathers for sowing these seeds, is soon to be harvested. We must not delay the inevitable aggregation of our succulent harvest."

Salvador pressed a button on his console; motors hummed; six tabletop doors slid open. In unison, personal monitors flickered to life. "If you'll focus your attention on the displays, I'll begin with Senator Xander's itinerary starting Apus 10th, barely two months from now. The senator is a man of action. Two years will be upon us before we know it, during which we intend to wage war on Reyna. Expect to be busier than you've ever been, gentlemen." His admonition encouraged a light chorus of murmuring. "Much is riding on our collective preparedness."

A thin, boyish-looking steward entered to deliver a folded note to the admiral, the draft fluttering several flags.

Salvador eyed the disruption warily and continued once it was past. "Xander's war plans include striking Amstye and taking her to her knees. Infiltration into their government and military has already commenced. Additionally, in order to promote a noninterventionist perception, we are working directly with the Amstynians. Clexor, their president, must remain in power to have time to dismantle their military. The Amstynian president will be tasked with eradicating Amstynian culture and philosophy from the very fabric of their society. Without Amstye as their ally, Reyna will crumble. This alliance will be destroyed: Amstye will either destroy itself from within, or *we* will destroy Amstye, but they will no longer support Reyna."

Patriarch Penney's forehead deeply creased. "I still disagree with this," he said, locking stares with Salvador. "If we allow their current leader more time, certainly he'll be better positioned to meet our demands and avoid the possibility of exposing our prejudices."

Salvador swallowed hard to appease his knotted stomach. War was the only answer; diplomacy was for the weak and would be a complete waste of time. These times demanded iron-fisted rule. "Necessity dictates a staunch, offensive posture," continued Seryth. "Xander has mastered the ability to leverage fear. He's taught us, that when fear reigns, nations quake and eventually collapse. Diplomacy is a mortal enemy. May I provide an undeniable example? Reyna, the recognized World Council, is our sworn adversary. No amount of talking has produced any degree of unification; diplomacy produces failure. Our New World Order initiative will ultimately dissolve under democratic ambitions!"

Admiral Thorne sat searching for a comfortable position. "You speak of war. With Vuton as our ally, Amstye does not stand a chance. But what of the rest of Eshen? Feria will surely come to Amstye's aid. Even the fanatical Oxium will join them if they perceive a threat to their well-being."

"Oh, yes. Lest we forget—Feria and Oxium—two countries occluded by religion. Subservience to any religion can be manipulated if the price is right. Xander has unlimited funds at his disposal and is prepared to fully employ this advantage. Feria is weak, and compared to the rest of Eshen, is a technology bottom feeder. When Xander offers them protection against our iron fist, they'll have no choice but to lay down their arms. Amstye will no longer be their great protector."

"And how will we handle Oxium from the West?" Senator Bristol's voice resonated with foresight.

"For quite some time, Xander has maintained a strong relationship with Oxium. This relationship is rife with contempt, propaganda, and stealthy collaboration. Certainly no secret, cooperative relationships are usually founded on shared hostilities. We share a common enemy— Amstye. He took a few moments to allow his words to resonate, surveying their faces for hints of rejection. There didn't seem to be any. "Oxium will be without resources. They are stupid and will fall to their own devices. No one will be able to match our superiority." He smiled at the admiral. "We must feed their war hungry bellies, and then slit them wide open. They'll have no choice but to capitulate to our demands."

"And what of Senator Galik? He continues to be a thorn in our side. He wants to sway the populace and ruin Xander's chance of becoming sovereign. Our fear is that he could end our vision with one well-orchestrated ploy." Bristol maintained a hardened stare.

Salvador scoffed. "He can't stop us. Soon, he'll be seen as a traitor; when the time is right, we'll punish him as such. Let him stir the pot a bit longer. Don't worry; we monitor his every move." He was disturbed that the consensus respected a weak senator and made a mental note to privately discuss this with Bristol.

Mawson stirred. "And what of the general's daughter, Eliza? She poses a threat perhaps greater than Galik. She stole top secret Federation military documents. What else did she have access to?"

He was irritated that Eliza had been brought into the discussion. They didn't need to be concerned with such minutiae. "Don't be foolish. Our eyes and ears are everywhere, Mawson. Soon, you'll understand that. I know she hates the Federation. However, she's young and the general's daughter. I charge you that no harm befalls her. Find her and bring her to me."

Mawson issued a challenge. "Alive? How do you know that those are the only documents she's viewed? She's a traitor to the Federation and must be dealt with accordingly, even if she's the general's daughter. Surely, he would understand."

"He would," replied Salvador. "General Nyvala is a patriot to the highest degree. But I want her alive." Salvador tried to mask his irritation.

"If so, then why do you want her alive?"

Salvador hadn't certified Mawson's full confidence, and this was more disturbing than he had anticipated. "My reasons are far more substantive than your objections. Remember. You were placed in your position only recently, and you can be removed just as quickly."

Mawson's eyes bore into the table.

"Next on the list. When Amstye is destroyed, the war with Thracia and Aurelia will begin. We'll forge into Aurelia as knights in shining armor, saving them from Thracia's grasp. Then, we'll have gained access to their land to establish advanced military bases and begin preparation for the Reynan invasion. In the mean time, Professor Godwin, are we ready to test the Supernova and Iomega?"

"Yes, of course, Lord Commander. I've prepared a detailed briefing."

Salvador punched a button on the console, distributing electronic images of an enormous Iomega android. "Please. We don't need to be bored with too many details. A synopsis will be sufficient."

"Politics are for the moment, Lord Commander; science is for eternity. The Supernova is a solar-powered, explosive device, fusing together a mass of highly-focused destructive power. Once formed, the discharges are capable of releasing vast quantities of ..."

"Professor!"

"Of course. In four months, the Supernova will be ready for testing; the date has been set. After successful testing, we plan next generation deployment—the Eternity. Iomega testing will last just over one month, after the elections of course. Xander wanted to personally witness the robotic monstrosity. Battle-readiness will be sanctioned several weeks before the initial Reynan attack."

"And there you have it, men." He rearranged a stack of papers and casually met the Professor's gaze. "Since we're on the topic, what of the human weapons, Subjects Six and Thirteen?" Smugly satisfied that he was in control; he had just navigated the most difficult portion of the conference.

The professor hesitated. "I would rather discuss that in private, Lord Commander."

"Nonsense. We're all on the same side. Please, continue."

"Of course. As of yet, Subject Six's location has not been discovered."

"After five years? Professor, professor, professor. Tsk, tsk. I'm not impressed." He relished challenging the man. Even though an intellect, Salvador enjoyed intimidating him. Intelligence wasn't everything. "And of Subject Thirteen?"

"A true success. We unleashed her south of Jador."

"Good. And ..."

"She went missing." Silence blanketed the room.

"Of course she did."

"However, we've dispatched our best operatives to locate her. But, the project was a success, Lord Commander. We just …"

"I know. You lost her. You told us."

The admiral's casual smile faded. "Human weapons—is that necessary? If others were to hear of this …?" questioned the admiral.

"What would they do, Admiral? Would they attack the Federation? I think not. Believe in our system and you'll become better for it. Well, gentleman. That's all. I prefer succinct meetings. Senator Xander extends his regards and believes in each and every one of you. He harbors no doubt that you will soon unleash your full leadership potential." He rose from his chair, lifting his arm, palm up. "We salute Xander!" Behind him, the Atomian flag glared knowingly.

The men hastily followed suit, chiming in as their palms rose in unison.

Thoroughly satisfied, Salvador's anticipation for his next meeting with Xander began to take flight. Their plans were in motion. Any hindrance would be met with absolute force.

URSA 16, 1870 O.C.
COUNTRY: AMSTYE
CITY: TIBUR, BORDER CITY

Tristan pictured the Embassy bombing from nearly a month ago; he'd been searching for Eliza that entire time. He remembered Lance and Hardie and felt sad until he remembered Voleta running away. He was pissed; she caused their deaths. On every call, Mr. Edde repeated his impossible demand to protect Eliza. Tristan finally stopped arguing with him. Her disappearance might be linked to the upcoming Federation elections which troubled him all the more. The world's fate rode on the election outcomes. Border skirmishes between Oxium and Amstye were on the rise; talk of war at dinner tables across Eshen was rumored to be commonplace. The Amstynian president, Acsel Clexor, had repeatedly appeared on public broadcasts assuring stability. Tristan didn't believe a word of it.

On last night's call, Mr. Edde had been livid over not being able to find Eliza. High-profile people didn't just vanish like that; a ransom was usually involved. Even so, Cole had been credited with a long-awaited breakthrough, yet Mr. Edde turned the assignment over to Tristan. A well-known journalist, Bailey Scovlin, had uncovered secreted meetings between Eliza and Amstynian officers. After publishing incriminating evidence on Federation involvement in Amstye, her readers demanded more. Some considered the works a conspiracy, but Tristan knew otherwise. Cole was convinced that Bailey knew where Eliza was; she had agreed to meet.

Tristan had spent two miserable weeks searching for leads around the USC Headquarters' neighborhood. Most buildings were vacant and the people he had talked to feared for their lives and refused to talk. He was anxious to find Eliza, the gleaming prize at the end of a dreary road. According to Cole, Eliza had been sighted in Amstye. Bailey had also disclosed that President Clexor was suspected to have Federation ties.

Tristan and Cole boarded the Marne for Tibur, a bustling, albeit no-name town on the Amstynian/Atomian border. Feria and Amstye boasted astoundingly beautiful scenery, something that Tristan greatly enjoyed. Two hours into the four hour flight, the landscape began triggering childhood memories—playing in open fields and swimming in crystal clear streams on robust summer days. Tristan transferred controls to a droid, a wiry robot with four arms, and claimed the navigator's chair, a seat with the best portside view. Unending grain fields unfurled beneath him as far as the eye could see. They were golden and wavering, yet foreboding under a formidable ridge of lingering storm clouds. Rain was coming. He mused, enjoying the engines' hum and feeling the ship's power. Excitement swelled within—lush green peaks, toppling waterfalls, and winding blue rivers had sprung into view. Feria was truly beautiful, second only to Reyna.

Tristan reassumed control and flew the last hour into Amstye along the Hernas River, substantially wide, twisting and turning through green valleys sprinkled with orange trees. The late-afternoon sun shed rich purples mixed with white and gray swirls. He didn't relish a nighttime landing, but it was unavoidable. Tibur's lights glittered in the dusk across the bordering hills.

Tristan guided the powerful gunship toward the eastern docking station, just a stone's throw from the entertainment sector. They cleared customs with ease and made their way toward the city lights and evening bustle. Bailey had provided directions to a local tavern. Tristan wasn't excited to take a jaunt through the dimly lit streets, but as they made their way, he soon lost his apprehension. Very few people were out, and a cozy tavern sounded inviting. A street shuttle pulled by underground cables glided by, as did motorized vehicles sloshing through wet streets. There was a quietly busy, yet quaint sense to the surroundings. Power lines draped across the wide thoroughfare, and gas lamps burned bleakly under pregnant clouds.

Cole outpaced him, reaching the tavern a few steps ahead. The room was bathed in subdued lighting generous enough to identify a woman's silhouette alongside a heavy-headed creature. An Acrolyte—in Eshen—Tristan was stunned. Lion-men were generally found in the opposite hemisphere, mainly in Kania and Antegon. The blonde woman captured his imagination; her penetrating gaze gave some reprieve from a glaring lion face. Tristan took in the journalist, lingering on her breasts bursting through a snug white blouse. That's not what journalists wore. Journalists were prying and inflexible. Far too much woman had been packed into that revealing outfit. He studied the beast, eyeing its braided mane—a first for Tristan. Its jaw, lined with jagged teeth, appeared deadly. The Acrolyte had woven several brass rings into his thick, brown hair—a curved fang was suspended from each.

"Ms. Scovlin. I'm Cole Ashbury—thanks for meeting with us. This is Tristan Hart."

The Acrolyte growled.

She embraced Cole's hand. "Please call me Bailey. I have a feeling we'll be getting to know each other very well."

"Okay," replied Cole.

"Nice to meet you." Tristan smiled and warily eyed the beast that stood a full head taller than himself.

"Please, Tristan. The pleasure's all mine. Oh, this is Atlas, my bodyguard."

Should Tristan shake his hand? He didn't know Acrolyte protocol and he didn't want to piss him off; he just nodded.

The creature shuffled clodded feet and snorted.

"You must put your butt on the line a lot to have an Acrolyte bodyguard?" queried Cole.

"My type of journalist is always in danger. The amount of hate mail I receive every day would surprise you. My publications are not appreciated by everyone. I'm fortunate to be able to afford Atlas. Would you believe that no one dares trouble me anymore?"

"I see," said Cole. "What about our arrangement? We're worried that Eliza might already be dead. If not, close to it."

"Ah, yes. Sweet, little Eliza. She's a handful, you know, stubborn and arrogant." Bailey chuckled. "I suppose it's her shared blood. Azdahri arrogance—Oxiite stubbornness."

That caught Tristan's attention. "Is she all right?" Bailey tone was casual, yet Eliza's peril demanded otherwise.

"She was, last I heard. But she's wandered off again, trying to fix the world's problems all by herself. She doesn't listen to anyone. I don't think she understands how important she really is."

"Where is she, Tibur?" asked Tristan abruptly. Bailey's disregard seemed incautious, and he didn't like how things were shaping up.

"No, no, no, Tristan. First things first. I need something from you," replied Bailey.

Atlas rumbled.

"What?" said Tristan. "Eliza's in danger if you didn't catch that!" Tristan wanted to explode.

Atlas's roared.

The group jerked in alarm.

"Don't do that again, please," asked Bailey, eyeing Atlas nervously. "As you can see, he's very sensitive. Now, where was I? Oh yes, of course. Before we move any further, I need some answers." She pushed her glasses against the bridge of her nose and tapped her pen against her cheek.

Who was this woman? wondered Tristan. "This could take all night," he said. "And we don't have …"

"I only have a few," she said. "You don't come off as very perceptive, so it shouldn't take long."

Tristan fumed.

"Good. Now that we're on the same page, prove to me that Institute VI hired you." She stared at Tristan blankly.

"I carry a bladed Droth; a weapon only issued to select I6 mercenaries. I'm captain of a gunship registered under …"

"Please, Tristan. You could have stolen them. How about something more substantial? I know. What's the I6 chain of command?"

He glanced at Cole. Was she a school teacher and he a child sent to the corner? He didn't want to divulge anything. "Headmaster Mawson is the head of the organization and Loci Talbot's his second. She's as dangerous as she is intelligent. There were fifteen thousand members last I heard. That number's probably doubled to keep up with the Valkyrie. The Institute was founded in 1787 as a militia group. Around 1815, its charter was changed to a mercenary focus. There have been six Headmasters since then. Each ..."

She raised her hand. "Okay, I'm convinced. That's good news. Next question." She set a small recorder on the table. "Mawson. Surely you knew that he was going to off-load the Institute to the Federation? Why didn't you leave when you found out?"

"I knew. He had mentioned it, but honestly, the possibility seemed remote. He told me that his men's best interest was his greatest concern. He hated the thought of becoming a Federation lap dog. That's what drove him to continue as a mercenary. However, I often believed that he was feeding the Federation my reports. In the end, I was caught off guard and didn't want to accept the truth. After he sold the institute, the gavel came down on us with astonishing brutality. I've killed before, but never innocent people. There was no judge; there was no jury, there wasn't even judgment—the only 'due process' we received was condemnation. The Valkyrie Lord Commander carried out the USC HQ destruction showing absolutely no mercy. No one made it out alive—except Eliza. If I *had* anticipated such cruelty, we wouldn't be talking here tonight."

"Feed my curiosity. What made you join Institute VI?"

Tristan bit his tongue. He hated his past haunts. "What does that have to do with anything?"

"It could have everything to do with our arrangement. From what I understand, Mawson is known for his recruiting selectiveness. That makes you quite special."

She really knew how to dig. "I pilot aircraft better than most. As a teenager, I used to fly experimental aircraft made by an old neighborhood codger. That's how I logged my hours and practiced maneuvering skills." Maybe giving her something general would settle her down?

"I'm not buying it. Look, we can continue like this all night. But I promise you, if I don't get what I want, you can kiss your chances of finding Eliza goodbye."

"Get off your pedestal, Tristan!" Cole said.

The ensuing silence fit like a muzzle. His old memories were painful. "My hometown was destroyed," began Tristan reluctantly.

"Destroyed? What do you mean?" asked Bailey.

"By a man, someone or something, I'm not sure."

"Where was your hometown?"

"Southaven, Feria."

Bailey gasped. "You—you survived? That's impossible! No one lived through that incident—I read the original reports. The Federation blamed the destruction on zyn repository explosions! Is that true?"

"Far from it." He didn't like talking about the most traumatic event of his life.

"So, it *was* a cover-up. What really happened?"

"What's the point in hearing about my childhood? This isn't fair. You wanted information on I6, not me."

"But there had to be something?"

"I wanted revenge," blurted Tristan. "I wanted to search for whoever it was that destroyed everything important to me. I swore that I'd have it. Mawson just happened to provide me with a golden opportunity. I was a perfect I6 candidate, young and full of hatred. Now, if you don't mind, I'd prefer you change the focus to our original purpose for coming here."

The main entrance burst open, and a group of girls with purple-red hair cut short and spiked barged in. Their routy singing captured the tavern's attention; they sounded drunk, were off key, and seemed oblivious to anyone but themselves. The first one stopped short; gasped, and stared at Atlas through bulging eyes lined with black makeup. She thrust her arms out to her sides, stopping the group's advance, and began pushing them backward. They ran back out the door, several screaming.

Bailey scowled and continued. "Of course. That's only fair. My next question relates to Mr. Edde. I'll talk to him soon enough, but I'd appreciate your perspective. Were he and Mawson acquainted?"

"Yeah, they were. He told me they used to be friends."

"Is that all?"

"Pretty much. Nothing else stood out. Said they went way back. Mr. Edde prefers to associate with powerful people."

"If this is true, then perhaps Mr. Edde knows?"

"What are you getting at?" asked Tristan.

"What every career-oriented woman wants—recognition. In my line of work, I have many adversaries, and it seems they're always one step ahead. However, I believe there are two crucial ingredients that could significantly level the playing field. One: uncover the truth about the Federation. I run with a select group of journalists that believe a few powerful men control our world, ones who determine wars, politics, weather, famine; you name it. I believe that the Federation is the breeding ground for these elusive parasites and their covert activities. The Federation wants to become the world's police and no one will be able to derail their ultimate plan, whatever that is. The reason for my questions is simple—I believe that your Headmaster is the Enlightened One and that he's been in league with the Federation all along."

"The Enlightened One, the one after Eliza?" exclaimed Tristan, unable to contain his surprise. She knew of him?

"They're all after her, Tristan," said Bailey. "You don't really appreciate her true importance. She's the only one who's dug up enough evidence to convict them. If the daughter of the great General Nyvala were to address the Reynan World Council, she could obtain much-needed support, and prevent the Federation from gaining a foothold."

That made perfect sense. "Then why isn't she already in Reyna?"

"It's not that simple. The Federation's military has almost complete control of the seas. Amstye's president has no backbone and won't make a case against the Federation while they're in Amstynian waters! Perhaps now, you can see why Eliza can't trust anybody. Political corruption is choking our country. Only a fraction of us notice these warning signs. I've spoken with Eliza, but she doesn't trust me. Bad for me, but it's good that she's not very trusting. Apparently, what she experienced at the USC's Headquarters traumatized her. She kept referring to 'Erik Gabrio.' Said he haunts her dreams."

Tristan shook his head. Poor Eliza. He had no idea how Erik could have corrupted so quickly. Was this his destiny too?

"And that's that. I believe there are more enemies surfeiting freedom's plight than we're aware of. I plan to find every last one of them. That's my unshakeable conviction."

Fair enough. She talked a good talk even for a journalist. He'd have to trust that she had the essential connections necessary to fulfill her dreams. "What's your second crucial ingredient?"

"Oh, yes. Number two is to publish the greatest story ever told. Of course, to do that my main character would need to have moved the world. I'm quite familiar with Eshen and have some noteworthy possibilities, but nothing that really pops! Hey, I have an idea. Maybe I could shadow you? I need a unique story, and you're in the middle of the action. I mean, you're still working for the USC and you want to save Eliza, the key to the Federation's demise. The Federation sees you as a traitor—that carries a death penalty. If I stay with you, I could find more dirt than I could by squandering my energies in Amstye. Plus, when you're caught, I'd see your reaction from a front row seat. Will you concede to the Federation or will you die a martyr? Will you succeed or will you fail? I can't believe it myself, but in the short time I've been with you, you've become very interesting."

When he was caught? What did she mean by that? "No thanks."

"You don't have a choice. I know where Eliza is, and as a journalist, I have no problem attaching myself to very sticky situations. I have access to almost everything you'll need, promoting me into a valuable position. Plus, you'd gain Atlas."

Tristan felt the table vibrate from the animal's rumble. He had already grown tired of that annoying sound. He had to stay level-headed on this one. No emotions. It seemed like a fair trade even with Atlas hanging around.

Cole had been listening intently to the entire conversation. "As a journalist, you're able to push through closed doors. It sounds like a good idea except for the part about Tristan being interesting."

"He certainly is, especially being a Southaven survivor. I can't wait to publish that story. By the way, I intend to pick your brain." Bailey's eyes sparkled in the tavern's dim lighting.

"You won't get anywhere." Tristan had no intentions of disclosing more of his personal life, at least, not without a compelling reason.

"I can read people like a book."

"What page is Eliza on?" asked Tristan, smirking.

"I left her with a friend named Jo, but I call him Baby Jo."

"Baby Jo?" That sounded nonsensical. No one he knew had a name like that.

"You'll understand when you meet him. Shall we be on our way?"

Tristan nodded. Finally, after four weeks of searching, he'd find Eliza. He was sure that she was scared to death. His 'victory' partner was turning out to be far more important than he'd ever imagined.

Provoked by Bailey's questions, Tristan was at a loss. She knew what she wanted, but her method was aggravating. They chose to walk back to her place even though a light drizzle was in the air. That could have made her strangely reticent. Tristan expected more of getting put on the spot, but she barely said a word. Atlas stayed close, never more than an arm's length away. Some of Tibur's night folk stared; others crossed the street. Outside a cigar shop, they happened upon two Amstynian soldiers huddling under its portico. They were dressed in dark green woolen uniforms with no significant markings. Tristan hung back while Bailey quizzed them quietly. She reported back that Enlightened One bandits had been engaging against the military. Oxium was amassing troops to the west while the Federation continued building its forces to the south. Tibur had been a haven. No longer.

They turned down an alley, and then onto a narrow side street lined with neat, two-story row houses. Bailey climbed the steps and punched in a code. The door swung open, offering an inviting setting, warm and dry. The apartment was quaint, cozy, and definitely lived in, but no sign of Eliza. A stack of newspapers teetered in the middle of the living room atop a worn ottoman. Two floor lamps shed a warm glow throughout. The couch, somewhat dated with muted beiges and greens, had a wide, arched back complete with several throws. Tristan breathed deeply, enjoying the smell of freshly baked bread. He stopped at a small picture and was instantly captivated.

"Baby Jo!" shouted Bailey as if she hadn't seen him in years. She tossed her jacket onto a wall hook—it caught—and turned back to him.

"I told you a thousand times not to refer to me like that!" came a high-pitched reply.

Tristan turned toward the voice, surprised not to see anyone. He glanced down and promptly stepped back, trying to hold back his astonishment. He towered over Baby Jo, a tiny creature reminding him of a monkey, but not exactly. Maybe more a gopher-like the ones in the desert around Institute VI. Then again, not really either. Delicate round ears poked out the side of a soft, rounded head. He didn't have a nose and his eyes, under cover of a slightly protruding forehead, were set far apart. His rough fur appeared sparse and somewhat prickly as he stood just below Tristan's knees. He moved his long, skinny arms when he shuffled, barely able to keep his tiny hands from dragging. His protruding belly under a bright red robe overshadowed his three-toed feet. What stood before Tristan was unlike any creature he'd never seen.

"I see you brought company! I would have appreciated being informed. I could have prepared something special for dinner." Jo wasn't the least bit bashful as he craned his neck to size up Tristan.

Tristan, self-conscious that he giggled when Jo talked, was pleasantly amused at the small and unexpected sight. He glanced at Bailey. "How do you find these creatures? First, an Acrolyte, and now this."

"Excuse me, sir." Baby Jo tapped Tristan's knee. "Please do not speak of me as if I am not present. It is exceptionally discourteous."

"Sorry . . . I . . ." stammered Tristan, caught completely off guard. He didn't try to suppress a chuckle.

"And I'm not a creature; I'm a being very much like you. You, sir, are a human; I'm a Paputa Nagori."

Cole snickered. "A paputooo what?"

"Paputa Nagori."

Bailey leaned and dotingly patted his head. "He's an artist, but no ordinary artist. He produces extravagant paintings." Her eyes gleamed. "They're . . . beyond reproach, alive." She eyed him tenderly.

"Alive?" returned Tristan, reflecting on the lone picture he had passed.

"That's what I said, isn't it?" replied Bailey.

"So, Baby Jo . . ." Ignoring Bailey's sharpness, although smarting, Tristan decidedly enjoyed the miniature being.

"My name is not Baby Jo! That's a title Ms. Scovlin afforded me for reasons unknown!"

Another chuckle.

"There are many reasons! For starters, you look like a cute baby!" She gently stroked his head.

"My name is Thuloritoid Kunzspinel, but I allow my acquaintances to address me as Jo."

"I'm Tristan Hart, and this is Cole Ashbury. It's a pleasure to meet you, Jo." The little creature was quite approachable, although extremely forward; Tristan liked him from the start.

"The pleasure's mine." Jo managed a slight bow, dipping well below Tristan's knees.

"All right. Now that we're past the introductions with the puti . . ." said Cole impatiently.

"Paputa!" Jo sneered through tiny, clenched teeth.

"Whatever. Where's Eliza?" demanded Cole. "She's coming with us."

"Jo? Where is she?" asked Bailey.

Jo pressed a hooked finger against his lip. "Umm . . . oh, dear . . . ."

That's not what Tristan wanted to hear. "What happened?" he asked.

"She seems to have misplaced herself," said Jo cautiously.

"Dammit! What the hell does that mean?" demanded Cole.

Jo's pitch crescendoed. "It's my fault! I told her not to leave, but she wouldn't listen! I tried to stop her! I used common sense, logic, and a good bit of charisma! But nothing worked!" Jo fought to catch his breath. "It was as if she didn't take me seriously, or worse! It was like I wasn't even there!"

Tristan saw why Bailey named him Baby Jo. He felt sorry for him standing there ready to burst into tears.

"Jo!" exclaimed Bailey. "That's quite sufficient. Where did she go?"

Jo began patting his plump cheeks. "To the pits of the underworld. To her death, or worse! She's thrown herself into the serpent's den! It's likely we never see her again."

"What do you mean?" asked Tristan, panicking. "Where is she? Tell me now!"

Bailey turned to him. "Tristan! He . . ."

"No! We need to . . . !" continued Tristan, his tone sharpening. Atlas bellowed.

Tristan stumbled backward. "Dammit. Can you please ask him to stop doing that!"

"He's on my payroll, and I think he needs to keep order. Listen. Jo can become extremely pessimistic. It's in his DNA. He'll be fine if you're patient with him. Now, Jo. Please tell us Eliza whereabouts," coaxed Bailey.

Still patting his face, Jo glanced up. "She went to Choppa's bar." His ears twitched nervously.

"That impatient child! Why couldn't she wait for us?" Bailey sighed.

"Why did she go to Choppa's bar?" queried Tristan. "And why would she go there alone?"

"Choppa's bar is owned by Sullivan Byrd, a complete pervert." Bailey scowled as she explained. "Every weekend, he enlists five girls to fuel his perversions on stage. The one who succeeds in capturing his attention receives a ton of credits and one night with the Byrd. If he really likes the winner, she's awarded an entire weekend."

"What was she thinking?" asked Tristan. "Why would she do that?"

"Because of his connections to the Enlightened One, who, I might add, has discovered that she's hiding in Tibur," said Bailey, glancing back down at Jo. "What else are you keeping from us?"

Jo dropped his hands; his ears twitched freely. "She might have mentioned that she was going to get close to Byrd and interrogate him. She's entering the show! You should know that she's confiscated a stunner, a small weapon used to shock someone. It fits in her boot, but it's not powerful enough to waylay Byrd, especially if he has back-up. She could be in serious trouble."

"She went alone?" Tristan was livid, knowing that those men could easily overpower her.

"No, of course not! Jase accompanied her. He persuaded her that she'd have a better chance, with him as an accomplice, infiltrating Byrd's organization." Jo's hands went back to his face.

"Jase? Of course, he would!" said Bailey angrily. "That daredevil! He'd put anyone in danger without considering a single consequence."

"Who's Jase?" asked Tristan, not sure if he'd like the answer.

"Jase Foard, an Amstynian ex-Army pilot. He's as cocky as they come. I asked him to protect her and specifically avoid any altercations with the Enlightened One's men."

"Are you sure he's on our side?" asked Tristan, thinking that Jase must be daft.

"Yes, I am. Don't worry," said Bailey. "He's just young and dumb."

"And he's putting Eliza's life in danger! We have to do something!" demanded Tristan.

"There's no time to waste!" said Cole. "Where's this Chopper's bar?"

"It's Choppa's! Do you have a problem with your short-term memory?" asked Jo, expressionless.

"I have a problem with you," fired Cole.

Jo covered his ears and hid behind Tristan's legs.

"Enough!" Bailey threw up her hands. "Atlas and I will accompany you. Eliza's important to every one of us. We must rescue her and then rendezvous with General Braxton. He'll evacuate her to Reyna. But, before we go back out into that rain, I need to change into something more suitable! Don't worry. I'm a quick change artist!"

"We need to get a head start!" said Tristan nervously, moving toward the door.

"You won't be able to get in without me!" said Bailey. "I'm a journalist, remember? I can get in anywhere." She turned and ran up the stairs.

Tristan grabbed at his hair. Jase sounded like a total idiot; Eliza's life was in danger—because of him.

"We'll get her back," said Cole confidently. "Plus, this could be our chance to do some damage to the Enlightened One. We'll make sure he gets what's coming!"

"She doesn't think," exclaimed Tristan, perplexed why Eliza would've compromised not only herself but the rest of them.

"You can't blame her," said Cole. "She probably thinks she's all alone, maybe feels like she has no one to turn to. Same position we're in."

Tristan nodded and walked into the next room. He wanted some peace. His head felt like exploding. Had he made the right choice by leaving 16? It was too late to back out; he was now forced to live with his decision. Why did he choose sides? Mercenaries didn't do that. Extracting Eliza seemed more doubtful with each new twist.

Sensing an unexpected calm and instantly transfixed, a second painting drew him into the next room. He craved peace and quiet—no questions, no answers, just solitude. He studied the luring image; it was as if he was looking through a window frame, yet standing past it at the same time. He wanted to touch the canvas, but he knew better. Mesmerized, nothing seemed real, not even the room around him. It truly seemed that he was part of the picture. The clarity made him not want the moment to end. A castle was nestled into a hillside on his right, and straight ahead, three magnificent rock arches loomed, one beyond the next, vaulting a verdant vale. He walked forward and felt himself flush while he wrestled with his perceptions. It was impossible, but as surely as he was breathing, he was standing in lush, green grass in a valley. Water splashed against river's edge; *it couldn't be,* he thought. He glanced behind; only a river running through a valley appeared. He was dwarfed by spanning arches crossing high above. Their surfaces were sculpted as if by a baker's knife, smooth, long, interwoven streaks of molded rock. On the far hill, at the base of the nearest arch, lies another castle. With teeming towers—banners flying—thick stone walls, and jutting turrets, both castles appeared majestic. Silky, jaded shades of luscious grassy meadows nestled serenely alongside each. He peered into the distance at a spectacular repeat of castle and arch, over and over as far as he could see. He glanced over his shoulder, sure that the serenity he so longed for, that now was upon him, would be shattered by Cole, Bailey, or worse yet, Atlas. "Cole! Jo!" he yelled. Silence was the sole reply; he was alone in a strange, new world. His voice echoed off jutting rock formations and inviting green radiance. Should he step further in? Should he reach out and touch the arch's mighty base? He took several steps and reached his inquisitive fingers forward . . .

"Don't touch it!"

Tristan jerked. "What?" he asked, startled. The transition brought a fleeting wave of dizziness. That high pitched voice seemed only to shatter his tranquility. And it did. His eyes focused on the wall painting. He was back in the room, but he wanted to return—to the valley, the castles, the river, and the magnificent arches. What had just happened?

"What are you doing? You're ruining my beautiful masterpiece! You devil!" Baby Jo pounded his closed fists against his head and ran in circles around Tristan's legs.

"No . . . . I mean . . . , I'm sorry. What happened?"

"You were in my painting, of course. But if you touch anything, it will leave a mark!"

"That was incredible! How does it work? How did you produce it?"

"I'm a Paputa. It's magic."

"Magic?"

"Oh, that's right. People from Eshen don't believe in magic. They're all about technology. But can technology do this, my friend? I think not!"

"Where are those castles, those arches?" Magic or not, the painting now lived inside Tristan.

"I painted that in Tholiad, a rather interesting place—the only country I know ruled by women. That was the town of . . . , oh hang it all. I forgot." He stopped circling and began tapping his foot. "Magerock! That's it! They say a great wizard created those arched formations long ago in order to defend against some mystical creature."

Now it sounded outlandish. "Funny. Keep your myths to yourself," chided Tristan. He'd been warned against magic since a child.

"It's no myth. It's true!" He thumped his foot harder, shaking a crystal decanter on the end table.

"Can you perform that with people?" That would be fantastic? Jo was one of the most intriguing beings he'd ever met.

"Why, yes! That's where I made my fortune! I'd paint a portrait of someone, but it usually only became beneficial after the person had died. I know. Pretty morbid, but let me explain. When one can't experience a loved one for any reason, death included, he can enter that special world and experience him or her again! The painting reacts with him, well, most of the time. But the person can see his loved one in the flesh. Of course, touching isn't allowed, or the painting will be ruined! But, yes, it's extraordinary. Because of my works, people have released floods of joyful tears."

"Incredible." Tristan was stunned. "Once in the paintings, can they talk?" If Jo could do that . . . , the possibilities were endless.

"No! That's ridiculous!" Jo waved a tiny, sharp finger.

"Shall we?" asked Bailey in a full length, royal blue evening gown, standing at the room's entrance. The dress delicately clung to her shapely form. A long stem, yellow rose in her hand did nothing but enhance her trim figure.

Tristan glanced at the picture once more, unable to quell his curiosity. He had to visit it again. What kind of people lived in those castles and what were they protecting? "I hope you're ready to go undercover," asked Tristan.

"I am," replied Bailey. "It's one of my exceptional talents." She grinned.

She was definitely a quick change artist. The evening was turning more promising—a beautiful woman with lovely blonde hair dusting her shoulders. For a moment, Tristan forgot the picture.

"Let's go crash a party," said Bailey as she headed for the door.

19

Baby Jo's little round face scrunched like a dried prune when Bailey told him he had to stay home. A bar was no place for a Paputa. In a sulking burst of emotion, he climbed onto the back of the divan under the painting Tristan had just experienced and huffed. He slowly turned, wiping a tear from an eye and gazed into the painting. Tristan caught a glimpse of him before heading out the door, relishing the extraordinary union.

Pulling up his hood, he joined Bailey, Cole and Atlas on their way to the neighborhood transfer station. The brightly lit facility, a large, flat-roofed, four-story building lined with slowly pulsating, green and blue strobes, loomed two long blocks away. A shuttle had just landed, it's engine a hushed but powerful thrumming. Bailey explained shuttle operations, informing them that the next flight was non-stop and would deposit them within walking distance to Choppas. The one-way discussion faded in and out; Tristan was hoping against hope that he could stop her before she found herself in too much trouble. Inside, dull green shuttle walls and glaring white tube lights proved annoying. He wanted to check out the town below, but the glare on the windows from the lights made that nearly impossible. Bailey rambled on, reviewing their options and increasing Tristan's tension; he wondered if Eliza might elude them again. Maybe she wasn't even there? Jase shouldn't have pressed Eliza like he did; Tristan could only imagine what she must be going through as the shuttle sped above Tibur's southernmost neighborhoods.

He squinted at flashing red, green and blue neon lighting on Choppa's signage. It was the largest building in the vicinity. A string of shuttles queued for entry into the shuttle port; a small mob milled about at street level, making their way to and from the entertainment district's clubs. Once docked, they disembarked and took two escalators to street level. The overall tone was excitement—lots of people, colored lights, and a steady drum of hovering shuttles, but Tristan wasn't ready for the hubbub. He wished for more reserved surroundings.

The Choppa had been designed with an open architecture, arched façade, and dazzling, clear lights on all exterior lines. As they approached, a smartly dressed doorman tipped a black top hat, bowed slightly and motioned them closer. His red jacket, lined with gold, double-breasted pleating, was loosely draped around a portly frame. "Are you on the list?" he recited as stoically as a mechanics droid and raised an electronic tablet over a distended belly.

"No, we're not," answered Bailey, switching to a coy smile.

"Then you shall not enter. Only members on this list may enter." He rapped a chubby forefinger against the screen. "This is Mr. Byrd's private bar, you see."

"We understand," replied Bailey. "However, I'd like to suggest a joint proposition that could redefine your rules. I'm Bailey Scovlin—journalist." She pulled a reporter's card out from a small handbag and displayed it prominently. "This elite club, renowned the country over, deserves notoriety I could easily provide from a private interview featuring Mr. Byrd. I'd like to do a piece on the special live auditions currently being conducted; my editor in chief insisted I deliver an article for next week's publication."

He eyed Bailey warily. "I suppose I could ask him. But what's your real purpose? Mr. Byrd has many enemies, and I'm concerned that you might be among them. We can't extend trust to just anyone, journalists included."

"Fair enough. I'm seeking to better understand Mr. Byrd's position on legalized prostitution. Rumor has it that such services are abundantly available on these premises and with President Clexor so keen on best business practices, word on the street is that prostitution could be legalized before next season's elections. There's nothing wrong with such wonderful services as long as adults are consenting and no one gets hurt, right? Plus, think of the economic benefits. But I'm such a small voice. With Mr. Byrd's backing, we'd be able to influence key lawmakers and perhaps bring about much-needed change. Do you understand my real purpose now?"

Tristan found himself pondering the benefits of legalized prostitution, unexpectedly lured into her ruse. He gave himself a quick flinch to shake off the unwelcomed train of thoughts.

The man nodded. "You've made it sound like a great opportunity, and I know that Mr. Byrd is in favor of free advertising. I'll do you a favor this time and discuss with him your proposal. Who are these other individuals?"

"The Acrolyte is my bodyguard and the rest comprise my technical crew. A girl can't be too careful nowadays."

"Most definitely, but the beast won't be allowed in. They can't be trusted."

Atlas snarled.

"So be it. He'll wait outside," returned Bailey.

Atlas whined quietly and stared down at the doorman.

"Remain here. I shall return momentarily." The porter disappeared through swinging door.

"Do you really think your plan will work?" asked Tristan while the messenger disappeared into the club. He had his doubts, but, he had to admit that the effort seemed plausible.

Bailey lifted a shoulder. "It has to. Why wouldn't it? It's all about publicity for these scumbags. They love opportunities to promote their scandalous activities, especially if legalization is a possibility."

"What if they don't let us in?" asked Cole.

"Then I'll go by myself. I'm a lady, and they see me as a piece of ass. I'm sure that I'll be able to find Eliza on my own."

"I don't think so," scoffed Tristan. "I'm not going to let you do that. We'd have to find another way."

"Thanks for the fatherly disposition, Tristan. But honestly, I've been in stickier situations and survived."

"This is no random band of mobsters," exclaimed Tristan. "They work for the Enlightened One! They have no regard for human life, especially those they deem threatening."

The double doors flew open, depositing the doorman back onto the red carpet. "I spoke with Mr. Byrd. Miss Scovlin and only one member are allowed entry. No more."

Another red-jacketed porter stepped onto the carpet, this one more corpulent than the first.

"I'll attend her," said Tristan, eyeing the newly arrived attendant. He sensed Cole's displeasure immediately.

"Damn, man. Leaving me with the vicious-ass kitty cat?" asked Cole. "That ain't right."

"He doesn't bite . . . most of the time," giggled Bailey, turning to leave.

Cole eyed the man-beast warily, frowning when Tristan grinned.

The doorman turned to the new porter, motioning discretely for him to adjust his puffy, red tie. "Mr. Bosno will escort you to Mr. Byrd's private salon. Leave your weapons outside."

Mr. Bosno held the door and motioned ceremoniously. Cole slipped a hand behind Tristan's back and grabbed the bladed Droth. I6 weaponry would be a dead giveaway.

"Thank you." Bailey dropped her name card back into her bag, rearranged the front of her low cut dress. She handed her coat to Atlas and followed the red-jacketed man.

The vestibule opened into a spacious, circular hall. A round bar took up the entire central area; three bartenders busily loaded serving trays with mixed drinks. The bar was only partially occupied but wasn't the main event. That was upstairs where music blasted. A circular staircase clung to the curved wall, opening the way to a dance floor occupied by a small troop of scantily clad dancers. Tristan studied each woman, hoping for Eliza, but she wasn't there. The music was grating—powerful beats accompanied by raspy voices, mismatched and out of tune. Couples clung to each other; some swaying more than dancing. He wanted on that floor for two reasons; that's where Byrd's weekend show would take place, and that's where he would find Eliza.

The porter led them away from the staircase, across the room and down a narrow hall. Tristan's senses were immediately keyed; three men huddling against a wall looked just like the three who attacked them at the ball. They were dressed the same—thick leather gauntlets, wide shoulder and form-fitting torso armor. He didn't want to gawk but needed to ensure they indeed were the same. He concluded that they worked for the Enlightened One; Eliza was in grave danger. He pulled his cap bill low.

"Second room on the left," said Mr. Bosno, pointing.

Bailey nodded.

The man gaped at Bailey, pausing at her breasts, riling Tristan, and then walked back down the hall without saying another word.

"Go find Eliza," ordered Bailey. "I'll distract Byrd until the show. Hurry! I can't divert him forever."

Tristan appreciated her focus. The setting reeked of booze, cigarette smoke and danger, especially next to those goons. "Will you be all right?" he asked nervously.

"Tristan! For the last time, I'm quite capable. You don't need to keep checking on me. Go find Eliza! There's more security than I expected, so we need to hurry." She pushed open the door and walked in. "Hello, Mr. Byrd!"

Tristan caught a glimpse of Byrd's backside, but the opening was too narrow, and the door closed too quickly to see any more. Where would Eliza be in these dodgy surroundings? He walked down the hallway, halting uncomfortably at each door. He could already tell it was going to take longer than he wanted. He struggled to uncover any clues, but the booming music was too loud. Behind one door, a woman groaned; he quickly moved on. Behind another, two men were arguing about losing bets at dog races. Behind the next two, silence. The door at the end was cracked open enough to expose a steep stairwell. Out of options, he cautiously nudged it and listened to an indiscernible conversation. They spoke again, louder. His heart quickened; the woman's voice was Eliza's. He couldn't believe his good fortune. Not enough time to tell Bailey.

He stepped as lightly as he could. The air was dank from years of cigar smoke. The man she was talking to had his back to the stairs; he could only hear Eliza's voice. He eyed the man—blond spiked hair, skin tight on the sides, then recognized his outfit of thick gauntlets, shoulder pads and torso gear that the three thugs wore. Those clothes must be standard issue for the Enlightened One's hooligans. Eliza was in immediate danger, and she didn't know it. But the man sounded too casual, too friendly to be troublesome, an unexpected development.

Without warning, Eliza stepped around the corner, appearing more radiant than he could have possibly imagined. Her hair graced her shoulders, full, teased, with a nice sheen caused by warm lighting. Her beauty stunned him, eyes dressed with muted hues, eyelashes longer than he'd remembered, rouge softly embellishing her cheeks, and a light pink shade covering full lips. His heart pounded. He held his breath, taking in her mystique—a handful of thin straps connecting black vinyl panels—concealing her body from her breasts to the top of her thighs. Her back was completely exposed except for the straps. She was dressed too racy, too provocatively, and too sensuously; she was not going on that dance floor. Dazed by this turn of events, he was forced to approach.

"Tristan! Is that you?" Eliza exclaimed, instantly blowing his cover.

The man spun around. "Who is *he?*"

In celebration, Eliza's embrace knocked him backward, causing him to relinquish his scowl.

"I'm so glad you're alive," Eliza exclaimed. "I feared the worst! What are you doing here?"

Tristan eyed her suspiciously, enjoying the sound of her voice, elated that she didn't seem to be upset. "I could say the same thing about you. What are you doing here?" He lowered his voice to barely a whisper. "It's dangerous, Eliza," hoping for a sane response.

"I had no choice. This is the closest I could get to the Enlightened One. Sullivan Byrd is actually one of the few people who has personally encountered that chimerical individual! I'm so close. If I could identify him, I might be able to secure assistance from the USC, its allies, and even Mr. Edde and General Braxton!" She rushed excitedly.

She spoke from the mental playground of a misguided teenager. Extracting her from Choppa's wasn't going to be easy. "Eliza." He glared at the man. "Mr. Edde's been attempting to contact you. For your own safety, he's ordered me to extract you to safety. You're far more important than you realize and can't continue with such risks."

"I'll prove myself this time. You'll see. Others will believe in me!"

Her body language, stiff from anger, took the wind out of his sails. "This isn't the way, Eliza! Haven't you noticed the security? There's no way you could escape on your own!" *Was she even listening?* He questioned, trying not to bow to a rising tide of exasperation.

The man stepped forward, pressing his hand to Eliza's shoulder and nudging her to the side. "Hey, don't scare the woman. Everything's under control."

It finally clicked. He was the man Bailey had mentioned. "You must be Jase," queried Tristan, not kindly.

"Yeah, that's right. And you must be . . . Oh, what was it . . . , Stacey?"

Stacey? First impressions were ruined; Tristan didn't like him. He turned to Eliza and continued, ignoring Jase. "Eliza, your safety is imperative, and it's time to leave."

"I have back up, Tristan, and like he said," pointing to Jase, "everything's under control. Jase is one of the best pilots in the Amstynian military. He's undercover so give him a break. I couldn't have acquired a better agent!"

"Eliza. We'll find another way," exclaimed Tristan. "I didn't travel all this distance under Mr. Edde's directives to leave your life to chance."

"Give it a rest, will ya?" Jase reached over and pushed against Tristan's arm. "I heard about you. 16, right? I'm not impressed. I've had my run-ins with your kind. You think you're tough, but when you're caught, without weapons or back up, you squeal like pigs. You can relieve yourself in the ladies room down the hall."

Tristan smacked Jase's hand. "If you're Amstynian military, you're already aware that General Braxton is expecting Eliza."

"I'm Air Fleet; he's Army. Our paths don't cross. If we have to take Eliza to him, why not go with as much Intelligence as possible? We can use this to our advantage. I'm surprised that you didn't come up with the idea first!"

"Is every soldier from Amstye such an ass?" demanded Tristan.

"What? Say that to my face!"

"I thought I just did!"

"Enough, you two! I'm doing this no matter what you say, Tristan. You can help me if you want, but if not, please don't stand in my way. I have to do this."

Both men paused, creating an awkward silence.

"What would you have me do?" asked Tristan.

"How did you get in?" Eliza calmed slightly and turned curious.

Tristan pointed upstairs. "Bailey. She's interviewing Sullivan now."

"I didn't want anyone else involved," said Eliza.

"Too late. We already are. Eliza! You're far too important," pleaded Tristan. "Please try to understand. You're being chased by more people than you realize; you'll be safer with us than alone with Jase."

"Go with Bailey. She needs you more. Besides, Jase has a pass to be my personal escort, something that you don't have. When I'm chosen, he'll be there every step of the way."

He couldn't believe it. "How do you know you'll be chosen?" demanded Tristan.

"Are you blind?" snapped Jase. "Check her out! Plus, she has youth on her side; Byrd always goes for the young ones."

"You would know that, wouldn't you?" chided Tristan, challenged to maintain his composure.

"Is anyone else with you?" asked Eliza.

"Cole and Atlas."

"Well, that's substantial," said Eliza, smiling.

"It's time, Monique!" came a voice from the top of the stairs.

"Monique?" said Tristan, eyeing Eliza suspiciously.

"It's my stage name for obvious reasons," replied Eliza.

Jase stepped around Tristan and started up the steps. "Showtime! Come on, Monique. I guess we'll see you outside, Stacey."

Tristan clenched his jaws as Eliza and Jase answered the call. Had Bailey finished with Byrd? He wanted to hurry, but paced himself, allowing the two to reach the top before he followed. As soon as they were through the door, he bound up, stopping abruptly before entering the hallway.

"Aw! Come on, honey. Show us one of them! Just one! We can always imagine the other!" sneered an aggressive male voice. "Come on! One date?"

Through the fragile opening, Tristan observed a goon accosting Bailey.

"Dream on!" exclaimed Bailey.

"I don't believe that? You can't resist a real man, can you?"

"You're hardly a man. And how can you consider yourself a man when your friend here wears pigtails?"

Tristan waited nervously, hidden and listening to Bailey 'hold her own'.

"It's a new style! But enough of that. Why don't you go on stage and take off those clothes? We'll be right there cheering you on!"

"Urgh! You're disgusting!" said Bailey.

Three men surrounded her, the same three from the ball, a mohawk—Tye; one bald and masked—Wally; and one with two ponytails sprouting from a shaved head. Tristan wished he had some of Eliza's repellant, even more, his Droth.

"See you around, sweetheart, sooner than you think!" said Tye, turning to leave with the other two following.

Bailey waited briefly and then continued on her way.

Tristan pushed open the door, fuming from the encounter.

"Tristan! Don't do that! You scared me half to death!" whispered Bailey hoarsely.

"Sorry. We're in trouble." He glanced nervously past Bailey's shoulder.

"What do you mean? Did you find Eliza?" asked Bailey under an entrenched brow.

"Yeah. She's going through with it. I couldn't stop either of them." He removed his cap, shoved it in a back pocket and mussed up his hair.

"Damn teenager!"

"Your Jase convinced her that it was okay."

"That little . . ."

"That's not all. It gets worse."

"How much worse?" Tristan didn't want to tell her.

"Much worse. The three goons you just spoke with can identify Eliza; those creeps attacked us at the ball. They'll recognize her as soon as she steps one foot onto that dance floor. It'll be game over the moment they sound the alarm!"

With arms crossed and long-billed hats pulled low, two men lurked in the hallway, sizing up Tristan and Bailey behind Eliza. Tristan slowed his gait and focused past them, making sure to avoid eye contact. He wanted to reach Eliza before she was completely out of reach, but couldn't without raising too much suspicion. He was surprised that she discounted jeopardy; sanity demanded acceptance, but she kept tying his hands. Eliza was his responsibility. He couldn't merely waltz onto the dance floor, scold her, and whisk her away. Once past the men, he reached for Bailey's hand, and together, they ran to catch up. An oppressive blending of notes and harsh vocals, echoes of discombobulated styles, created a surreal outlook and built a profound sense of unruliness. Tristan was a music lover, but he preferred older genres to modern. Taste of Everything from Feria was his favorite group.

"What do we do?" asked Bailey as she stumbled along behind, unable to match his stride.

"I don't know," replied Tristan. "I knew this would happen. She doesn't think!"

"At least Jase is with her."

He felt absolutely no consolation, still fuming at how precarious the situation had become. "My first impression of him was awful," retorted Tristan angrily. "He only makes matters worse. He's way too brassy and short-sighted." He stopped before a pair of closed doors smudged from grimy handprints, carefully pulling on the door. Once his eyes adjusted to the dimness, he found himself facing a wall decorated with stage ropes hanging from trusses. On the far side, patrons mingled at the edge of the dance floor and in front of the bar. Further left, a ragtag band beat out a hardened melody, hardly the size he had been expecting; such a small band for so much racket. Three members were covered with tattoos and decked with long, stringy hair. That no one was dancing didn't come as a surprise; the music was as offbeat as it ever could have been. Tristan glanced at Bailey, hoping that she wouldn't interfere. "How'd it go with Byrd?" he asked.

"Byrd's nothing but an arrogant ass, dangerously baneful. His office was filled with all kinds of adult novelty products. If that's any indication of perverted mentality, we can't afford to allow Eliza out of our sights. Tristan, I have to agree with you. Eliza is in way over her head. We might not make it out of here alive."

That was the first time he'd noticed her guard dropping, subtle but definite. "We'll figure it out. I don't plan to die at the hands of these scumbags." He studied the bar area again, this time shielding his eyes from the newly lit spotlights panning a dusty dance floor. The three adversaries from the ball were throwing back drinks, slapping each other and hooting loudly. Their voices carried across the floor.

Bailey noticed them as well. "It's scary to think that the losing contestants are thrown to those monsters; they're gang-raped with no one to protect them. What is Amstye coming to?"

Tristan hoped he'd have the chance to silence them for good. If it came to that, he'd be overjoyed, but his priority was Eliza's extraction. "Did you get anything on Byrd?" he asked.

"No. He had no patience for my questions and eventually turned hostile. He was way too irritated to continue a comprehensive interview; he's hyper-focused on the show. Speaking of the Dark Lord . . . ." She nodded toward the far wall.

Cheering made it too difficult to continue their conversation. A sunglassed character moved toward center stage. The brightest of three spots glared against his black hat, ominously darkening his face. Tristan quickly pulled Bailey behind a rack of colorful costumes. The man twisted at a black mustache, and then straightened a loosely fitting beige suit under a white fur coat.

"Feast your eyes on Mr. Sullivan Byrd," said Bailey as she peeked between hangers.

Byrd's glittering fingernails flashed—long, silver, curved extensions. His hands wrapped around silver atop a black cane. The thought of that man touching Eliza turned Tristan's stomach. He had to stop him, but Byrd wasn't Tristan's only trouble. He glanced at Tye just wiping a sleeve across his chin. That was good; the drunker he was, the easier he would be to eliminate.

Sullivan aimed for a high back chair set on the stage's periphery. No sooner than he sat down did five women, practically nude, promenade toward center stage. Each wore a brightly painted mask. Camouflaged. More good news because Tye or his buddies wouldn't be able to recognize her. Combined, she wore more clothes than the rest and looked better by a long shot; Byrd was sure to choose her. He watched her, stiff and icy, struggling with offbeat strains. That might work to their advantage. Tristan was torn. He'd want a friend to win, but never a competition like this. They sashayed through a temple of unbridled lust, about an altar of desire, pulling frilly neck wraps and allure across wanton's vicar. Byrd sat, legs outstretched, his grin growing with each passing tempt. This was his world, and he was submerged; under a steady thrum of drums or audience din, nothing distracted him. Like sacrificial lambs, they passed twice more, until a flick of the wrist. Eliza glanced about, unsure, quickly falling in line behind the four and a score of libidinous eyes.

"My, my, boys! We have some nice pickings today! Look at dem hips, dem legs, dem jugs! It's going to be one hell of a night!" He grinned at a bodyguard, an enormous man, bearded and shaggy, in a quest for approval.

Tristan glanced at still crouching Bailey. "Get Cole and Atlas in here," he whispered. "We're going to need them." Along the side wall, he picked out Jase behind a column of tightly pleated curtains. A rack of bulging ropes tied off on large wooden pegs hung just over his head. Tye's gape was fixed on him. Tristan's anger flushed. "You need to leave. It's not safe." Tye and the others toned down their revelry and studied shadow's dark reaches.

"If Eliza can stick it out, so can I," returned Bailey candidly.

"Go get my Droth. If you do nothing else, do that!" Piercing stares stung like pinpricks; they were too exposed in this position.

Bailey threw up one last wall of defiance, forcing Tristan to plead. "Please! Go!"

She took one last look at Eliza and then slipped through the doorway.

The contestants began solo performances, attempting to exploit Sullivan's insatiable perversions. The first woman spun tauntingly; the music gyrated. She dangled her wrap, allowing it to linger as she drew it past closed eyes, cunningly wheeling her hips. Tristan fumed at images of Eliza doing the same. He had worked his way through broken cover, nearing the bar area, and stopped behind an oblivious couple. Tye's group hadn't detected him yet.

Like a human elixir, the woman continued, sliding gracefully from side to side. It reminded him of a vintage Oxium dance. She pirouetted several times and rested on the flats of thinly-soled slippers.

The men, Tye's voice rising above the rest, shook their fists and bleated. "Give the man some rubbing! What are you waiting for?"

It was Eliza's turn; Tristan prickled when she swooned and dropped into the splits. Tristan's shock turned to embarrassment. He followed her moves, wishing he could will her invisible. Boos abruptly stopped, transforming into ecstatic cheers. Eliza wasn't helping the situation at all. She pushed off the floor and spun to either side. Men cackled in rutty groans, blind enough for Tristan to edge closer to Jase. Sweat poured down his back; it chilled him as he pressed against a wall, practically hovering over an enormous belly of a man swigging from an oversized mug. Jase caught Tristan's eyes and nodded, but Tristan ignored him; his attention was on Eliza. Byrd could practically breathe on her. She finished with a bow and fell back in place. Three more dances were excruciating. Finally, the last dancer sauntered away; Byrd tapped his fingers and began stroking his face.

Tristan needed a weapon; Bailey hadn't returned, and he was growing desperate. Jase had two pistols, but he was still through a crowd of clamoring drunks.

"All right, All right! Order!" All eyes turned to Sullivan.

Tristan was stricken with anxiety. If Eliza was chosen, what would he do?

"I've been rewarded! Oh, how I'm tempted to choose all five! We'd have a spectacular affair!" An angry rumble rose. "I know, I know. That wouldn't be fair. It should please you that I've made my decision. Tonight, I select the only one playing hard to get. I think it's time to anoint her into true womanhood!" He motioned toward Eliza. "You're just too bashful, sweetheart! It's time to break you in!"

Tristan hated Byrd for that, his mind helplessly reeling.

"But, before I pass these beautiful women to you hard-working sons-of-bitches, I want this lovely young beauty to tell us her name."

She edged forward, slowly, somewhat coy with hands loosely planted on thighs. "Monique . . . ," she whispered.

"Ah, yes!" He swiveled to face the bar. "As compensation for the many benefits I provide, and on your behalf, Monique will demonstrate appreciation! Ha. Interesting. She'll become, well, a little responsible . . . ," he chuckled again, ". . . for installing us as this damned country's true politicians! Now, sweetheart. I want you to remove that mask, drop down to your knees and wet these boys' appetites real nice!" Sullivan threw back his head in laughter and reached for his belt buckle.

Tristan wanted to kill him. He looked at Jase; both men scowling. Eliza hesitated.

"Go on, beauty! Down on your knees! Don't disappoint my men!"

Tristan had to intervene. A wrong move could ruin the mission, but it no longer mattered. Eliza's safety was the top priority. He had no choice. He pushed through the throng; several drunks shoved back in return.

Sullivan rose from his chair, turning his backside to the bar. "Here. Let me help you." He dropped his pants, exposing baggy, red and white dotted underwear. "I'm ready!"

The crowd went wild, filling the haze with a flood of obscenities!

Tristan stepped into the misty beam; all eyes were on Eliza.

Sullivan slapped her; the mask skidded across the floor. "I said, get on your knees, bitch!"

Tristan cringed, a second away from Byrd's throat. He glared at Tye.

A mug dropped, shattering. Tristan's time was up; Tye had recognized him. He grabbed a rum bottle and lunged. The hush was stifling. Eliza glanced up; Tristan smashed the glass on Sullivan's head, collapsing him in a heap.

"Tristan!" shouted Eliza.

"Run!" He scooped her up and twisted her around, practically carrying her in a run for the double doors. Jase bolted behind.

On his knees, Sullivan rubbed his head and pounded the air. "Get him! Bring me that twit! I want him alive!" He slumped back.

They bound through the doors and down a narrow stairwell. Tristan was glad he knew what to expect. Sensing only the slightest relief, they raced hard and reached the landing where he had first discovered Eliza and Jase. He scanned frantically for an exit. Footsteps echoed.

Eliza shook her hand loose and shouted. "This way!"

Jase sprang from behind. "What the hell were you thinking? I had everything under control!"

"Not from where I stood!" Tristan eyed a door further down the hall lit by a single hanging bulb. Without warning, it blew open, flooding near obscurity with a greenish tint and releasing a slew of blazing guns. Tristan shoved Eliza behind some crates; Jase followed.

"Great! Now what? Did you think this through, mercenary?" said Jase with an undeniable tone of spite.

"Give me one of your pistols!" demanded Tristan.

"You sure you know how to use it?" Jase slapped the weapon into Tristan's hand. "We're surrounded, you know."

"Then quit talking and use it!" Tristan peered over the crates and opened fire. The thugs retreated into the green, relentlessly firing. Shredded ceiling tiles, plaster and wood showered down. Tristan managed two triple bursts.

"Stop wasting your bullets! We're almost out!" hissed Jase.

Tristan wanted his I6 Droth. When it seemed like things couldn't get any worse, Tye and several more men advanced, blasting away. Tristan shoved Eliza into a shallow alcove, shielding her as best he could. Jase aimed at the approaching men.

Tye's laughter echoed. "I know it's you, Nyvala! You're pretty stupid to come here! There's no escape! Mr. Byrd and his boys are planning to have fun with you before we deliver you to the Enlightened One!"

"What does he want from me?" said Eliza. Her voice quivered.

Tristan flared. "Don't bother. You won't like what you hear."

The laughter continued. "You make dicey choices, Eliza! Can't have you freelancing, working-over Federation's enemies this way! We'll get you a real job, like standing on street corners! Everyone loves a half-breed!"

Jase fired a triple volley.

"Is there a problem? Ha! Don't be a hero! We'll hang you upside down above our bar and slit you so your guts dangle across your face!" mocked Tye.

"Tristan . . ." Eliza's voice weakened.

He gazed into frightful eyes. "They won't lay a hand on you. I promise." He could sense her heart pounding furiously.

"Dammit. If only you would have waited! Now, there's no way out!" said Jase frantically.

"Wait for what?" asked Tristan. "You know what Byrd wanted! Don't be an idiot!" Tristan was right. Jase had no awareness of the dilemma he had created.

Sounding like angry bees, explosive bursts zinged by; plaster shattered. From down the hall, more screams and another body thudded to the floor.

Tristan's grin spread at the sound of a deep, guttural roar—Atlas!

"What the hell is that?" shouted Jase.

"Backup," replied Tristan eagerly. Dropping to one knee, he stole a glance. Cole unleashed his fury. Tye and his men disappeared down a side hall.

Cole waved. "Come on! I'll cover ya!"

Tristan opened fire, sprinting with Eliza close behind. Clear. They bolted through the exit, thrilled to see Atlas towering over three blood-drenched men. That was Tristan's idea of a bodyguard.

"Eliza! You're alive!" Bailey ran over from behind a dumpster. "Here!" She handed Tristan his weapon.

Better late than never. He snatched it and turned, locking onto two confused faces, and fired.

Cole rolled a dumpster against the door. "We need to leave!" he shouted.

The five dashed to the shuttle port and up the escalators. They broke through the crowd, lunging into the awaiting craft. Tristan's heart raced, pounding like storm surf beating against a rocky shoal as he stared through closing doors. The shuttle broke free, hovering momentarily while a brief safety announcement played. The engines roared, shaking the vessel as it shrank into darkness. Eliza clung to Tristan, her heartbeat matching his, a blank stare bespeaking her fear. Tristan studied their reflections, pondering over unscathed fortune. He ran his hand through his hair, prompting Eliza to mimic. They looked deeply into each other's eyes, accepting that this was the beginning of a very long journey.

CHAPTER
20

It was time to leave Tibur behind. Tristan studied his newly formed, seven-member team as they boarded the gunship through the aft door. Cole and Eliza each held their own unique quirks—nothing Tristan couldn't manage. Bailey was full of surprises; she had impressed him at Choppas. He was more concerned about Jo than the others and decided to watch over him to make sure he remained unharmed. Jo worried that the Enlightened One would find Eliza; he donated a few pieces of his artwork to decorate the Marne's conference room. Tristan caught himself pondering magic pictures throughout the day, pleased by their stress-relieving attributes. Atlas and Jase troubled him, the former for obvious reasons. The Acrolyte carried a marked degree of anguish, but he was an Acrolyte—unfamiliar territory; the creature was calm enough when with Bailey. But Jase was the wild card, challenging his every plan.

Tristan showed them where to stow what little belongings they brought onboard. Jo's were the most cumbersome; Jase and Atlas carried two of his pictures and deposited them in the conference room. Jo quibbled, talking about how fragile the art was, and wouldn't stop harping about it. He acted like he enjoyed barking orders, but no one seemed to mind.

They had only a couple more minutes until Mr. Edde's call. The conference room, a fairly compact room, sat directly behind the bridge. Tristan adjusted the lighting, pleased with the subtle blue hues. A narrow, metal table took up most of the space, dim streams of warm light bathing each position. The team entered, chattering amongst themselves and found their seats. Bailey set her electronic notepad down and helped Jo climb into a chair. Tristan was usually eager to talk with Mr. Edde, hoping for his direction; he hoped that they wouldn't be disappointed and pressed a flashing green button. A hologram bust of Mr. Edde materialized, wavering slightly, then stabilizing.

"Good evening, everyone. Some of you know me personally. But first things first, I'd like to personally thank you for ensuring Ms. Nyvala's safety. When the USC headquarters fell, I feared the worst. The likelihood that we wouldn't have the much-needed pool of resources to draw from became painfully obvious. But now, due to your valiant efforts, I have full confidence that our reserves are largely intact. Mr. Ashbury forwarded me your credentials, and I'm pleased with what I've seen. I anticipate a solid team and, with united efforts, a boon to our cause."

"Wait a minute," exclaimed Jase, his tongue sharpened. "Who said anything about a team? No offense, Mr. Edde, but I'm not here to be anyone's lap dog. My sole intent is Eliza's safety."

"Mr. Foard, your piloting credentials are outstanding, however . . . ," A calculated pause hung in the air. "Don't forget. Your reckless flying habits had you disbarred from the Amstynian Air Force. Pity."

"Don't act like you know me."

"Oh, but I do. Born 1848, you grew up in Framus, Amstye—a city boy who ran with the wrong crowd--a gang if memory serves me correctly. Weren't you apprehended for illegal oje grain trading and sentenced to six years in prison? Isn't that why you chose military life? After completing nearly four years of service, your reckless behavior overcame you. You were discharged, only to become a paltry bounty hunter. How'd that work out for you?"

"I don't appreciate your exposition, or your tone."

"Forgive me, Mr. Foard. I had to correct you. I do know you, very well."

"Well, now that we're past the pleasantries, what's our next move?" asked Cole.

Mr. Edde nodded. "Ms. Nyvala's special undertakings determine that. Would you please provide the team with an update, or should we expect a continuation of your recent ventures?"

"I'm finished, and I apologize," said Eliza sheepishly. "I had to track down my only Enlightened One lead; he was far more influential than I had supposed."

"Don't fret. Your frustration is warranted. I've been busy gathering leads on him as well. You're probably aware that he's extremely difficult to track. Don't panic, though. It'll only be a matter of time before something more promising is uncovered."

"Thank you." She glanced through the rotating hologram at Tristan.

"Eliza. You're the key to our success. You need to trust this team and me, and then divulge what covert knowledge you've acquired. I'm well aware that you've accessed proprietary data capable of rendering the Federation's advantages useless. I understand there's secrecy involved. That's why you must present this information to the Reynan World Council. As such, you're quite possibly our last hope to solicit their involvement. Without it, the Federation will soon become too powerful to control. Their elections are nearly upon us; those results will likely initiate an unstoppable chain of chaos."

Bailey slid another book under Jo, raising him high enough to view the hologram. "It seems hopeless," she claimed. "The Federation is deeply connected throughout Eshen. They're now able to reach countless scumbags, people so ruthless and committed to the Enlightened One that our enemies list has become recalcitrant. We can't trust anyone."

"I understand how you feel, Ms. Scovlin, but let's not throw away our hope. With the information Ms. Nyvala holds, we can stop the Federation dead in their tracks. Look around; there sits nearly unlimited potential. Align your abilities and garner the opportunity to accomplish the grandest of endeavors. If you set your mind to succeed, failure will not be an option. The decisions you make today will directly affect tomorrow; make the right ones! To the Federation, acts of war are nothing but a game. Today, they have military superiority which means one thing—that we're going to have to become better at everything we do. In your presence sits an ex-Amstynian pilot, an ex-Institute VI mercenary, an ex-corporal, a renowned Journalist and her unquestionably fierce bodyguard, and a woman of Azdahri nobility, well-versed in her country's politics and ready to fight for freedom. And of course, let's not forget," Mr. Edde looked down toward the Paputa. "Mr. . . ."

"You can just call me Jo. It would be easier." He cocked his small, round head toward the hologram.

"I would hate to break my rhythm." Mr. Edde quietly chuckled.

"He's the most extraordinary of us all. He can paint!" said Cole stoically.

"Do not belittle my expertise! I'll have you know that . . ."

"No need. I understand your importance," quipped Mr. Edde confidently. "We'll find a use for everyone's unique abilities. Rest assured, everyone will be called upon before we're finished. Please take some time to consider our plight; this team's formation could mark the genesis of a new USC.

We could build on this moment and move forward, unified in purpose. Are you committed to this—our cause? I ask everyone to decide and to submit your answers by morning. If you've already decided, please remain after I finish. I'll provide further direction at that time."

Tristan studied the faces around the table, noticing that each person was doing the same, especially Eliza. She sat fidgeting with a small paper clip as she glanced around.

Cole pushed back. "I'm in, dammit. Have been from the start."

Atlas growled when Bailey answered. "Count Atlas and me in. We have to see where this story will end."

Baby Jo stood up on the stack of books. "I believe in Eliza's purpose. I want to see her safely to Reyna. If the Federation is in control, then all the different peoples of the planet will suffer. It's nothing short of a privilege to be part of this august assemblage."

All eyes were on Jase. "Ah, I got nothin' better to do. I'm in."

Tristan peered through the hologram and met Eliza's gaze. "I'm in."

Mr. Edde sat back, content and smiling. "Then let's get started, shall we? Your first stop will be Amstye's westernmost city of Ncopolis, a border town between Amstye and Oxium. General Braxton is already posted there and is expecting you. I've provided him with your arrival details; everything that you'll need has already been shipped. Take Ms. Nyvala directly to Braxton. As one of the few trustworthy Amstynian officials, he's promised safe passage and has assured her safety. I am en-route from Aurelia to Neopolis as we speak, but you'll arrive before I do. Until then, her safety is your top priority. Be aware that you're entering very dangerous territory. Oxium is on the offensive and has deployed troops along the border against Amstye. Ongoing negotiations have failed; they refuse to withdraw. They claim that Amstynian forces are actively infiltrating their borders. We're convinced that the Federation is behind these lies, instigating the conflict with relentless cunning. Our Intel tells us that the Federation has been smuggling Amstynian-produced arms into Oxium with the consent of President Clexor. If war breaks out, Amstye will be attacked by their own weapons. In the midst of this uncertainty, General Braxton has intensified his efforts to provide border security."

"We'll do whatever we have to!" interjected Cole.

"An interesting note—Senator Galik plans to make an appearance. Because of his peace efforts, we've deemed his motives genuine, but with a certain risk. I warn you—expect extreme resistance! Oxium and Federation troops are reported to have arrayed themselves in Scoria across the river from Neopolis. We've been informed by highly reliable sources that they are fortifying their position. The Federation has deceived the public by declaring that this military effort is not an act of war; rather, they are searching for a dangerous experimental subject who escaped their testing facilities some years ago. Supposedly, this individual was capable of massively powerful attacks, even to the point of destroying entire settlements. Personally, I think that this is a ruse and refuse to buy into it."

Tristan let Mr. Edde's words sink in, adjusting to the new developments as they related to his past. After all he had heard, the war the free world most dreaded was upon them. He wondered what Bailey thought; was she worried, hopeless, or somewhere in between? Curiosity struck with the phrase, *a dangerous experimental subject.* He had to ask, "Could this person be the one reported years ago in Southaven?"

"I recall something of the sort," said Mr. Edde. "Of course, the Federation deemed it an accident. Ah . . . , now I remember. Mawson had informed me that you were the only survivor of that tragedy. This could be something of great interest to you, Mr. Hart."

"Very much so," said Tristan, trying to suppress surprise. He felt instantly overwhelmed with thoughts of encountering Viktor again. His past stood before him like an incoming tidal wave.

"I hope that your curiosity won't jeopardize our mission?" said Mr. Edde candidly.

"No, sir. Not at all." Mr. Edde had no clue of what he had just triggered. Shadows leapt across the arena of Tristan's mind: unstoppable, painful memories. For years, through so many missions and with so many companions, he had successfully avoided the subject, but now, his past was circling back, like a sleek fighting vessel, banking hard to port and lining up again for the kill. Was he ready to face it, to bring closure to his agony?

CHAPTER
21

Tristan snickered to himself when he remembered a redeye, ultra economical flights that used to crisscross the continent during early morning hours. He used those years before to go travel on leave from Institute VI. Cost savings and deserted cabins were the perfect way to commute. The Marne's atmosphere echoed the same solitude. The trip to Neopolis was a long one. They would fly through the night and land late morning. Someone entered the cockpit; it was Jase to relieve him. Good enough. The strain of piloting, tired eyes, hunger pains, and slower reactions to occasional traffic were getting the best of him. Jase slid into the co-pilot seat and nodded. The ship was on autopilot and he'd be back in six hours to do it all over again. He watched Jase run down the checklist, flipping switches and turning dials. True to his reputation, he was an experienced pilot.

Tristan vacated the cockpit and walked toward the conference room. Eliza was inside, gazing at one of Jo's paintings. He immediately wanted to join her.

Startled, her expressive brown eyes caught the intruder. "Tristan?"

"Shouldn't you be asleep?" he asked. It was the middle of the night and she was probably exhausted.

"How can I sleep after everything that happened tonight? I really thought that I had experienced a lifetime of evil, but I was completely misled. I'm so naïve. How do people become so corrupt?" Her finger traced the frame's embossed edge.

He wanted to help, but was drawing a blank. "I don't know." Feeling awkward for not providing a better response, he tried again. "I suppose that there are many theories, but I like 16's take on it—all men are capable of killing; war is the result of collective ills. Governments and civil societies should guard against such brutishness. Sadly, they're corrupt too."

"Well, I don't see it like that." She leaned closer to a collection of vibrant mountains. "Even if my life depended on it, I don't think I could kill someone. The thought of doing that turns my stomach. What about you?"

"Most people don't have it in them to kill," he replied, not anxious to upset her.

"When driven by desperation, people allow themselves to become that way. They lose any semblance of morality and don't care what it takes to get what they want."

He liked being with her, hearing her talk, learning her interests. He also liked Jo's painting and wondered what it would be like to stand in the grass on that mountaintop. Eliza was definitely more complex than she had initially seemed. He was tired and didn't want to dive into a deep conversation, but he didn't want to leave either.

"Have you tried any of Jo's paintings?" she asked.

"Tried? Actually, one," he replied. Did Jo tell her?

Her eyes sparkled. "Aren't they grand? You can experience a brand-new world; it's like a dream coming to life! That tiny creature captivated me the first day I met him; he has hundreds of magical stories."

"Illusion, Eliza. That's what magic is." His tone was level.

"Nonsense! Magic is real, but you have to believe! Countless fables *have* come to life—every culture in the world will tell you that. You're Ferian, that's your problem—too much science. It keeps you from believing. Too much technology will do that to anyone. I want to live in a place without technology."

Science was important and he wasn't prepared to change his beliefs, but he couldn't deny those castles and enormous arches. "Maybe you can? Thracia, Antegon, and Kania are only a short trip from Reyna. Aurelia isn't very advanced either."

"I suppose you're right," she said softly. Suddenly, her eyes lit up. "Would you go with me?"

"What? Where?"

"Would you go with me?"

She was a typical teenager and was doing that to him again. "It's … if Mr. Edde ordered me to, I would," he replied, feeling like he was stumbling down the painted mountainside.

Eliza stomped her foot. "Urgh! Can't you make your own decisions? What's wrong with you? It's not manly!"

Manly? Of course, he could decide for himself. He could decide anything. "Whoa, there. My job is to escort you to Reyna!"

"You were an I6 mercenary and look what that's done for you."

"Hey, careful! What're you saying?"

"Nothing. Sorry. I shouldn't have said that. My lack of patience sometimes gets the best of me. Okay, I have another idea. I don't want to travel to Reyna alone, but if you joined me there, that'd make up for it."

"Look."

"Don't try to talk me out of it. Even though it was nearly impossible, you rescued me from Sullivan Byrd! You were outnumbered a thousand to one, yet you risked your life! Deny your feelings, but I can see right through them!" She winked. "You have to stop being so serious; let's try out a painting, shall we? Pick one that will help you remember me."

"What's up with you and remembering? You said that when we first met."

"Oh, Tristan. I'll explain later, but, first things first." She pointed at the picture with sprawling mountains, the same one he'd been eyeing. "Let's experience Reyna." Her voice sounded like it was floating on clouds.

"Eliza!"

"Not the real Reyna; Jo's Reyna. That's a Reynan sunrise, so beautiful. We can enjoy being together in another land! Trust me. You won't regret it."

Why was she pressuring him so? "Haven't you already done this one?"

"Well, only five or six times," she said coyly. "Come on—take my hand." She reached out. "Don't worry. There's nothing to fear." She touched him. "Hurry up! By the time you decide, it'll be too late!"

Their eyes locked. A vacuum droid whirred down the corridor, not enough distraction to keep her from noticing Tristan's sweaty palms.

Why did she affect him like that? He yielded and realized her's were also damp.

"Okay, good," she said excitedly. "Step one complete! Now, eyes on the picture. Absorb every detail and you'll be on the other side before you know it!"

The engines' steady hum helped settle his nerves. He had nothing to fear. He started thinking about the colors, how sweeping the terrain was. Deep in his chest, he sensed a flutter. The next instant, his heart pounded like he'd dropped into frigid water; he was engulfed by those same colorful swirls draped across flowing peaks and valleys. He became lost in a brilliant blue river that curved around fingers of land, playfully toying with everything it touched.

Early morning shadows struggled to conceal the unfolding spectacle and created suspense too intense to comprehend. The changes made him gasp. The sun crawled toward the horizon. Billowing tufts of clouds, dark blue hues not quite ready to be revealed, wrapped the emerging, yellow ball. How did Jo create this? A single golden ray settled on the furthest ridge. He strained, allowing the mural to expand. It was then that the magic claimed him. He breathed quietly, timidly, shut his eyes and entered timelessness. A moment later, it could have been eternity, he open them. Incredible. He made it. But where was Eliza?

Her voice had lost its tension. "You took long enough."

How surreal. He felt like a time traveler if ever there was such a thing. He could hear her, but no other sounds. Trees swayed in silent wind, clouds floated and rivers flowed—all mute, just like the first time.

"You know, I was talking to Jo. He told me about a Grand Master Paputa who has lived for thousands of years. He has experienced countless wars and even the golden age of peace. He has outlived the rise and fall of great nations, and seen cultures blossom and wilt away. But his paintings are more than that; they are portals."

"Eliza!" He didn't want to spoil her experience, but portals didn't exist. She had to be referring to time travel.

"Don't do it, Tristan!" She fixed her gaze on the golden rays. "I think it's true. I mean, at first, I didn't believe this either. Look where that got me? Maybe one day, when our fight against the Federation has ended, I could live in a painting, maybe disappear into history? Jo told me that a civilization once lived in the clouds. Perhaps I could too?"

He imagined a city in the clouds and tried to dismiss it as the sun continued its sluggish ascent. The land exploded with brilliant hues, most too radiant to describe, shades he never knew existed. From river valleys to mountain peaks, morning dew sparkled. The sparkles pulsated, sweeping to and fro. Eliza's dream melted into his thoughts.

"Thanks for coming with me. It means a lot. Everyone is always so serious. I understand that our situation is dire, but grave mindsets will blind us; we won't be able to enjoy life's beauty."

"No problem." He didn't consider himself a serious person. He did dance with her.

"My mother taught me to remember people and events that were important to me. And you know what? I've never forgotten one. Before she died, she asked me to remember her. And I do, every day. I remember those moments like they happened yesterday. It's so special."

She was so innocent. He hoped she'd never lose that quality. Perhaps he would have been like her if his life had been different?

"So, anyway, remember this moment."

Her smile warmed him and her hands too. He wanted to pull her close.

Tristan was mesmerized. Water shimmied under the sun's fiery glow; flocks of birds, as if by design, danced in harmony before them. He spotted wild horses galloping across a meadow. He glanced at Eliza, her skin glistening, smiling as if this was her first time.

"Well?" She smiled again.

"It's …"

"Amazing? Marvelous? Shocking?"

Tristan had to chuckle. "Yes." Not just because she was right, but because she sounded so much like a little girl lost in childhood.

"I'm so glad you like it!" She rested her head on his arm. "Whenever you have Eliza withdrawals, just remember this, okay?"

He smiled within.

A loud "humph!" startled them and dropped them back into reality.

Tristan blinked and realized what had happened.

A demanding voice. "Eliza. You're still here?"

"Yes. Sorry. I couldn't get enough of these works of art. I had to share them with someone." She dropped Tristan's hand.

"I see. Did you touch anything?"

"No! I promise! Not after the first two times."

The little voice stammered. "Two times!"

"Oops! Sorry, Jo. I just get carried away. They're so real."

"I know! That's the point! Do you know how long it takes to paint them; what trouble I endure to create those experiences? Oh, the patience you strain out of my tiny self. Have you considered the finances involved? It does cost to produce them!"

"You're right. I'm sorry."

Jo flicked his tiny wrist. "Please. Off you go!"

Eliza bowed in submission. "Yes, Jo."

Still flicking his wrist. "Thank you!"

Tristan and Eliza scooted past Jo and into the passageway.

Eliza kicked at the gunmetal-gray floor. "That was a total bummer. It ruined our moment."

"We need some shut eye anyway." Tristan shrugged, wondering if he could sleep after that.

"I guess you're right. Thanks again." She lifted her arms for a hug.

Tristan froze. They were getting too close. He stepped back and awkwardly glanced away.

"Come on! You can do it!" coaxed Eliza.

"I don't think," stammered Tristan.

"You marked my Jadorian painting!" shouted Jo, a sharpened voice piercing the bulkhead.

"Uh, oh." Eliza grinned.

"I'll take care of it." Tristan quickly took his leave and walked away.

22

Tristan only managed to catch a couple hours of sleep, accomplishing nothing more than waking up groggy. Tossing and turning, anxious to shut down, the fitful sleep afforded no rest. He climbed off his bunk and immediately thought of Jo's painting. It was the most astounding sunrise he'd ever seen. He not only saw the golden rays, but he felt them as well—that was the most pleasurable part of the experience. He wanted to encounter it again with Eliza.

He needed to clean up and relieve Jase at the helm. Cole poked his head in, a big man with a sleepy smile. A second berth in Tristan's quarters wasn't being used. Its curtains were drawn. Two personal lockers were fitted along the adjacent wall. Tristan snatched his toothbrush and headed to the head down the hall. Cole mumbled something; probably "good morning." Tristan was *not* a morning person, a condition now compounded by a lack of restful sleep. He grunted and splashed water on his face. As his mind came out of the grog, he heard snoring through the wall. It was Atlas. Someone knocked on the doorframe and Tristan glanced over; Bailey stood nursing a mug of coffee.

"Good morning. Rough night?" asked Bailey, not seeming to be bothered by his dour expression.

Tristan eyed her recorder. "You could say that."

"The snoring kept you up too? I thought the ship was falling apart. Wasn't sure if it was that or Atlas."

Tristan grinned as he dried his face. "I would have told you to go in there and plug his nose or something, but then we'd be cleaning parts of you off the wall.

"You're a riot," meaning he wasn't. "Since we'll be arriving later this morning, I was wondering if I could ask you a few questions."

"Do we have to do this now?" asked Tristan, checking the time on his personal communicator and thinking about Jase. He hung the towel next to the sink. "OK. The answers are 'no, no, yes, no,' and 'none of your business.' How's that?"

"You're a real comedian. C'mon, you agreed to allow me to follow your story. My audience will expect to know what made you into the man you are today. What happened in Southaven will go a long way toward that. You might not know this, but the truth about Southaven has never been uncovered."

He took a few seconds to find his thoughts. "I'm struggling with your not-so-subtle technique, and right now, I need to relieve Jase."

"I understand, but if the truth is to be made public, we need to talk. Perhaps it will bring you needed closure, eh?"

What was she, some kind of psychiatrist? "Closure? There's no *closure* until the score between me and Viktor is settled. You can record *that*!"

"OK. Let's start from the beginning, shall we? Before the, er, ... event, did anything happen out of the ordinary?"

He grunted again, crossed his arms and leaned against the sink. He had to go through this again? He rubbed his eyes, hoping he'd have time for breakfast. His mind kicked slowly into gear.

"Six years ago, Southaven was a busy mountain valley town, mainly home to a lot of farmers. Its homes maintained really unique appearances, maple-planked rooftops and split elm walls. Lots of good, rich, fertile farmland covered the valley floor. The place was beautiful. The main attraction, though, was Viktor's Peak, a mountain with foothills reaching the city limits. Tunnels had been bored through it, but a lot of residents kept their distance, from some kind of fear, or whatever. I hated what zyn production represented. My dad told me it would destroy our town. I discovered just how dangerously profitable zyn sales to both the Federation and Amstye really was. After my father passed, I was their last qualified pilot. I maintained my skills by crop-dusting fertilizer and pesticides from a specially rigged airship. I'd spend the entire day in that thing and loved every minute; my work was critical to Southaven's farming economy." Thoughts of his mother made his throat tighten. "After my father died, my mother suffered more than I did." Sighing, he glancing away, pained from the remembrance.

"One day I'll never forget. I was flying as usual, but that day felt weird from the moment my feet hit the floor. My friend, Ganer Weatherly, was with me. He'd begged me to teach him how to fly the G-43—my airship. It was a sorry-ass heap and I didn't want him in it; too dangerous, but I finally gave in. Here's how old it was - my father flew it when he was in the Amstynian Air Force over twenty years earlier. It went obsolete, so he bought it off the government when he retired from there. Some days, I was surprised it would even crank over. Fertilizer or pesticide, definitely poison, whatever, was stored underneath in four long cylinders with release valves. It had two engines—one fore, one aft—a push-pull design that made it look like a pregnant pigeon. The first time I saw it, I didn't believe it could fly." Tristan mused quietly before continuing. "I guess it took an engineering marvel to handle such a huge payload, even if it was butt-ugly.

"Ganer and I shared birthdays and had both recently turned 17; the girls loved his blonde hair and cheesy smile." He chuckled again. "He was a cheerful guy and quite pleasant—great friend. We took off, steering clear of the village, and began dropping our payload as soon as we reached the designated acreage. From where we were, Viktor's peak was an impressively rugged sight—five jagged crowns up in the clouds—all framed by a sun rising behind; a long shadow had formed on the near-side. Ganer was really stoked. He held onto his glasses and kept looking down."

✕✕✕✕✕✕✕

"Not bad!" he kept repeating. "I can't believe I was scared about stealing a ride in this bird! It's *made* to fly! I wish Feria wasn't so damn religious about this stuff. We should have done this a long time ago!"

Tristan grinned from ear to ear. "This was one place where I never worried. When my dad taught me how to fly, he gave me the greatest gift ever."

"You're the stud in this sky! I'm blown away."

"Lots of practice," said Tristan, feigning modesty. It felt good to be noticed by his friend.

"What do you plan to do with these skills?" yelled Ganer over the exhaust manifold's clacking.

Tristan shoved in the throttle and banked hard left; the G-43 moaned in complaint. Ganer's voice vanished.

"If I can talk my mom into it, I'm gonna join the Amstynian Air Force! Way more opportunities there than here."

Ganer's eyebrows touched the top rim of his glasses. "What? You'll be looked down on for sure! They hate adrenaline junkies!"

Tristan remembered scanning the horizon. "Ah, only if they don't need 'em. You'd be surprised how many men our age have gone to Amstye. They all come back with excellent training and are able to use those skills like my dad did, but they've come and gone. It's just me now, but it's something I still have to do. Four years isn't a long time; I'd earn all my ratings for free. That's something I can't do here! Maybe I'll make a difference in this deity-forsaken place!" He glanced back at the trail of white chemicals.

"I believe you will, Tristan. I believe you will. You'll blow the socks off every other recruit!" admired Ganer.

Tristan smiled. The craft lurched; his butt grabbed some air.

The boys looked over at Viktor's Peak. An enormous column of gray smoke raced skyward. Tristan grabbed the yoke and shoved it forward, sending the G-43 into a whistling dive. A ring of flames shot out from the column of smoke.

"What is that?" asked Ganer, his glasses sliding down his nose.

"I don't know. Maybe an accident? Let's check it out!"

"What? No way!"

"But, they might need us!"

"Shit, I was afraid you were gonna say that."

Tristan pulled back on the throttle and slowed the descent, excited to close in on his destination so quickly. He felt free. The peaks rose like giant sentries; the mine's dirt strip flattened before them. He was too high and did a go-round, finally gently settling her. He taxied, spraying dirt everywhere as they approached a small crowd. The engine never sounded so loud. A body was on the ground. Miners wearing yellow hard hats and grimy coveralls surrounded it. They didn't seem to notice the G-43 until someone broke from the crowd and ran toward them, waving. It was the Nigel Tomlin, an old family friend—the mayor.

A tuft of wavy, brown hair fell into his eyes. "Tristan! Praise the Deity!" exclaimed Nigel. "You have to get this contraption right back into the air. This man needs a doctor, now!!

Tristan was caught up in the moment, straining to get a better look. Southaven was never this lively.

"I don't know what happened. He just …" Nigel voice trailed off.

Another man approached. "… Came out of nowhere, just dropped out of the sky! I saw it with my own eyes, I did!"

The man was lying on his back and hadn't moved.

"He's not dead?"

"No! Tristan! Help me load him in the cargo hold!" barked Nigel.

"Offload those bags covered in white power," said Tristan.

They picked him up; he moaned and mumbled all the way. They threw a jacket over him and strapped him down. His chest was skin-bare and bulging in a tight blue outfit; a cape was belted at his waist. He was strikingly handsome, angled brow, clear skin and tied-back indigo hair. Tristan had never seen a man so fit or blue hair like that. His features were pretty like a woman. A sword was attached to his belt along with an enormous silver belt buckle. A sword? No one carried swords anymore. Even buckled down, he was an intimidating sight. Tristan jumped into the pilot's seat and headed back to Southaven, half-wondering if he was flying into some kind of trouble.

"This is bad! What kind of man is he?" asked Ganer, sounding confused.

"I don't know," replied Tristan. "What did that miner mean, 'Out of nowhere'?"

"You heard that, too? He fell out of the sky, out of nowhere!" said Ganer as he glanced over his shoulder.

"We'll find a logical explanation," said Tristan, assuming the man wouldn't die.

The man murmured. "Annihilation … mission … I am …… Subject Six ………"

Ganer turned and stared. "He looks bad, Tristan! Can't this thing fly any faster?"

"Sure, Ganer, I'm at half-throttle, dummy," dripping with sarcasm. "I'm pushing this piece of junk as fast as it can go!"

✕✕✕✕✕✕

Bailey tapped her recorder, seeming satisfied. "Subject Six. He's the one! Mr. Edde talked about him in his last report," she exclaimed.

"I was completely intrigued by everything about him—his clothing, his hair, his powerful frame. I've never seen a man like him. Where did he come from? What did he mean, 'Annihilation, mission, Subject Six?' I wanted to talk to him, but he wasn't coherent. We landed in a field opposite the infirmary. They whisked him into the building and that's the last I saw of him that day. I stopped by several times, but they said he had a bad case of amnesia."

"How convenient! I don't believe it," blurted Cole.

Bailey looked up at him. "Does anyone care what you believe? Butt out! I'm right in the middle of this," said Bailey curtly. "Let's move to the conference room; it's more private."

That didn't deter Cole. "Yeah, in the middle of talking. Good thing for me, I can talk, too. I couldn't help but overhear your story."

"You were eavesdropping?" demanded Tristan.

"Nah, but what I heard got my attention. Bizarre! Last time I heard about anyone falling from the sky, he landed head first up to his waist; dirt dart!"

"Shut up. You're interrupting," chided Bailey as she sat down.

"Okay. Geez, sorry!" said Cole, finding a chair for himself, ignoring the word "private."

"Should he stick around?" asked Bailey.

Tristan wondered about Jase; it probably didn't matter. "It's fine. Cole, could you let Jase know that I'll be late?"

"Oh, OK. No problem," said Cole.

Bailey clicked the recorder. "Pick up where you left off."

"Yeah, even though my mother told me to stay away, I went by every day to see him. The hospital staff started calling me his shadow, and him Viktor, after the peak where I picked him up. I don't think he ever told anyone his real name. I spent as much time with him as I could and learned a lot. He could do extraordinary things, impossible things no one knew about. I guess that's how he became Southaven's 'big hero'." Tristan's eyes fell and he realized he was wringing his hands. "In retrospect, saving him from that mountain turned out to be the greatest mistake of my life."

23

"Tristan Aaron Hart, I said 'no'!" announced his mother, loudly, sending their large cat scurrying. "There's no good reason for you to visit that man Viktor! Every day's the same thing! We barely know anything about him! He doesn't even have a real name. Has he ever bothered to tell you what it is? Listen to me!" Her ginger hair, neatly coiffured and beginning to ruffle, revealed a serious face. Full amber eyes set low within their sockets, settled somberly upon her only son. Soft skin gracefully complimented high cheekbones, creating a pleasurable impression. There was something charming about her, thought Tristan. Perhaps it was her nurturing personality, or perhaps her wit.

"Mother! I'm an adult! I'm seventeen!" shouted Tristan. "Why can't I lead my own life? I hold down one of the most important jobs in all of Southaven! Our friends and neighbors respect me. Why don't you? Viktor isn't bad. You're the only one that thinks so, and for no good reason. It's been a month since we rescued him and he's been nothing but a model new citizen since!"

Her lips firmed; her eyes flamed. "Tristan, you have to trust me. Your father would have agreed with me. Every person has two sides, like a coin. Just because no one has seen it so far, doesn't mean it isn't there. By the time anyone finds out, it's too late."

"Father isn't here anymore, is he? Stop using his memory to judge me." Tristan's voice broke ever so slightly as he eyed the front door. "He was a courageous man, took risks and had an open mind. His memory inspires me, especially when I'm uncertain about something. But you make him out to be some kind of frail shadow-boxer. I'm going to follow in his footsteps and join the Amstynian Royal Air Force. That's my ticket out of Southaven!" Tristan bolted for the front door, his dark hair flying. The door slammed behind him and his heart swelled felt like it would explode. Viktor was a good person. He quieted Tristan's inner pains. He was someone to admire and respect—he was going to visit him no matter what. This time, his mother just didn't understand.

Sweat burned his eyes as he ran down his street, winding through the neighborhood. The inn where Viktor had been provided a gratis room was on this side of town. Tristan hated fighting with his mother, but he needed his space. It seemed that everyone in town liked Viktor but her. She never told him why she didn't approve of him. The inn was just ahead; Tristan worked his way through a gathering crowd, his ears ringing from the run; so loudly he didn't hear Viktor talking right beside him.

"Now, look closely ..." Viktor clung to a small cup, pouring water over his fingers. He swept his hand and a glowing, vibrant rainbow settled on his hand.

The crowd gasped, and then cheered this marvelous wonder. "Bravo! Excellent!"

"That's all for today. Thank you," said Viktor, bowing gracefully and grinning from ear to ear.

The colorful vision made Tristan even more anxious to reconnect with his friend. He wanted to tell him how upset his mother had made him. Viktor certainly could help him sort out his emotional pain.

"Hello, Tristan. It's good to see you."

"It's good to see you, too. You've become quite the celebrity. You're the only one people talk about now; they love seeing you do these thrilling illusions."

"Well, they're a thrilling lot so it's the least I can do," replied Viktor, pulling his neck wrap tight. "While I convalesced, their nurturing kindness has been far more than I ever deserved. I pray the knowledge I share will repay them in some small measure."

"I'm sure it will. It already has; I just wish my mother thought so." A troubling memory of his mother's last words flashed, making him feel guilty for even talking to Viktor.

"Give her more time. A mother's love should not be taken for granted."

"You're right. I need to calm down. Sorry."

"There's nothing to be riled over. We have to be forward-minded. Anything less would cause us to forfeit the tranquility to come from what we've started. We need to better ourselves. Time is fleeting; becoming shorter and shorter with advancing years. You'll find proper motivation when you grasp the bigger picture and see your own looming mortality, as the timepiece that is your life winds down. Time is your friend, and wants to mentor you. With enough of it, you can accomplish the impossible."

"I wish you could remember your past. You seem so learned, more than anyone I've ever known. No one talks like you." He wanted Viktor's insight into everything and felt a little guilty about that. It seemed silly at times.

Viktor smiled, a gust ruffling his blue hair. "Perhaps I'll remember one day. Who knows? Forgive me, Tristan, but I have to go. I was invited to the meet with the Town Council. They want me to help them with future plans for development of this fine city."

"Oh, okay. Don't let me hold you up. Good luck." For a second, Tristan's heart dropped. He still had more he wanted to talk about.

"There's no such thing as luck, my friend; only destiny." He move quickly down the steps and across the street and was greeted by several men standing outside the Town Hall.

Tristan watched his friend become absorbed by everyone around him, wondering what it would be like to be him.

✕✕✕✕✕✕✕✕

"This Viktor guy sounds like a real loon," quipped Cole. "Surprised you saw anything in him. Then again, not so much."

"He seemed like he wanted to help," said Bailey while she typed away on her pad.

"He did help," exclaimed Tristan, abruptly toning down his enthusiasm. Sadness and anger returned every time he reminisced about Viktor. No one really saw him as he did and the conflict left him depressed. "His perceptions were astounding. He perceived reality from impossible perspectives. His ideas for development were so futuristic and "out of the box", they astounded everyone. His knowledge seemed to have no bounds. He taught men how to forge a blade that melted rock and metal like a hot knife through butter. He showed us how to shield ourselves from Federation firepower. He taught metallurgy, how to mine unheard-of minerals, and then how to use them for new applications. He even reengineered the mountain's zyn extraction methods. Production shot from mere hundreds of pounds a day to thousands. He taught technological skills, magic…and the occult." Tristan chuckled quietly and waited for his racing heart to subside.

"His contributions were bizarre, but that's not all."

"He actually taught women how to design exquisite jewelry from precious metals and stones —bracelets, ornaments, rings and necklaces! He taught the ladies how to wear them as well as basic cosmetology, if you can believe that!" He paused again to allow his enthusiasm to wane. "Sadly, those things changed Southaven. Everyone was affected. Our traditions became replaced by Viktor's practices and "wisdom." People abandoned their beliefs. The older folks were harmed far more than the younger ones. Troubles mounted—unplanned pregnancies, rapes, worse. People became greedy; mutual trust disappeared. In retrospect, Southaven was devastated. Within a few months, the majority were turned into fanatical followers of this new "prophet." They made Viktor into a god—well, everyone but my mother, of course."

"What was up with the magic? How did it play out?" asked Cole.

Eliza stuck her head into the room, a towel draped over her shoulder. "I thought you didn't believe in magic?"

Tristan smiled and motioned her in. "It's not that I don't," he explained with newfound confidence. "It's that I don't want to. Magic is nothing to be fooled with and can end up being destructive; I keep my distance."

Eliza shrugged and sat beside Cole. "Not all magic is bad," she said.

"We're straying from the topic at hand," warned Bailey. "Can we refocus, please? It's okay if you stick around, but please, no interruptions. Go on, Tristan."

Tristan nodded. "Viktor never stopped his "lessons." There was something new every day. He taught the art of root cuttings and how to use enchantments. He taught Astrology, knowledge of the constellations, but in a totally unfamiliar way. Our books and schools couldn't reach his level of expertise; it was as if he truly was a fallen star. He foretold of eclipses thousands of years in the future. He cited moon cycles as if they were common knowledge. He even taught how to cure diseases that until then had been impossible to treat and were sometimes deadly. He became famous, not just in our small town, but throughout all of Feria. That's when the Federation got wind of him. Then he changed."

That particular memory jolted Tristan. Until that fateful day .... Viktor had meant the world to him. He now wished the interview would stop. He just wanted to be alone; his mother had been right all along.

XXXXXXX

Just outside his bedroom window, Tristan was shaken out of a sound slumber. People were arguing and shouting, hostility usually nowhere resembling his peaceful neighborhood. He dragged himself from beneath the covers, reluctantly, and peered out the window. He felt his blood immediately freeze; men in black armor—Federation troops— their helmets, gauntlets, and leggings displaying a look of determined malevolence. They were everywhere, walking up to houses, pounding on doors and shouting orders at the occupants. Out on the street, Viktor and the town council members were being detained, or so it seemed, by the intruders. Nigel was shouting and raising his fist at a soldier. The mayor was usually more reserved than that. Tristan threw on some clothes and made his way to the door.

His mother tried to stop him. "Tristan! Stay inside! Don't go out there! Please!"

"Not now, Mom," said Tristan, reaching past her small frame and yanking open the door.

Nigel's manner frightened Tristan. He was in trouble. What was the Federation doing in Southaven, and why so close to his home?

"No!" shouted Nigel. "This is Ferian territory! You have no right to our land, our belongings!" "Viktor is a free man and stays. I don't care what kind of scientist you claim to be, Hemis!"

Tristan studied a bald, portly man, his white mustache and goatee in stark contrast to his brown leather jacket.

Hemis laughed and tossed his white scarf over his shoulder. "But you see. Viktor *belongs* to us! He's a serious threat to every man, woman

193

and child here! You claim that this is your town, your country; but yet, we're the ones who industrialized the mountain's zyn production. But, let's not get ahead of ourselves. He's ours and we want him back. Viktor is not what he appears to be."

Tristan listened, angered that Hemis had taken his mother's side.

Viktor stepped forward. "Don't pretend you know me. Like you, I am free, and I choose to stay in Southaven. My work is not finished," he said, his chest bursting from his blue body-suit. His blue hair blown by the wind.

The crowd had grown.

"What do you mean, your work? Do you actually believe your purpose is to promote some backwater, podunk village? Oh no, my dear specimen, no. Your purpose is far grander than that! How did you come to be so knowledgeable? How do you know things that the human race has yet to conceive?"

"It doesn't matter! I am not who you think I am."

"You can't undo your past; its inseparable; it courses through your veins. You cannot elude your very essence!"

"I am human, nothing more!" Viktor's gaze bore across the distance.

"Do not degrade yourself in my presence! I did not spend two decades developing you to allow you to regress into a common peasant!"

Tristan was sickened. Developed? Peasant? What did that mean? His senses came alive. A familiar ache surfaced, an unquenchable yearning, the same one his mother had attempted to quash when she demanded he disassociate from Viktor. But, was it based on the same reasoning? Of all the possibilities, why the Federation? Was it a ruse? Surely, they wouldn't risk political turmoil.

Nigel continued, unrelentingly. "Leave now or I shall report this scandalous act to the Ferian central government! Amstye and Reyna would be more than happy to intervene and introduce you to a world of trouble!"

"It will not be long before threats like that are completely empty! Fine. We'll leave. But, before I go, here's a little gift," submitted Hemis, turning to an approaching soldier holding a small, draped parcel.

Viktor glared. "I want nothing from you."

"Hear me out and receive this book. Aren't you the least bit curious to discover your past?" Hemis held out a small brown book. "Read this. If you're still not convinced, I shall refrain from bothering you anymore."

Viktor glanced at Tristan, and then the book.

"Don't listen to him, Viktor! It's filled with lies!" Nigel grabbed for the book.

"Ha! You sorry little man. You don't know anything!" Hemis glared at Nigel, then turned to Viktor. "Why do you let them call you by that name; your title is 'Subject Six.' Enjoy those pages!" He spun on his heel and led his men to the adjacent field and an awaiting Federation gunship. The gray, angular craft looked like something out of the future.

The crowd was silent, dazed. Nigel touched Viktor's shoulder.

Tristan approached. "Are you all right?"

"Yes, yes, Tristan," answered Viktor. "Thank you."

"Are you going to read it?" asked Tristan. He glanced at the retreating soldiers, squinting from sunlight gleaming off the ship's metal skin. Hemis and his entourage were already half way across the field when the ship's engines fired up. Tristan's chest rumbled in resonance, even at the considerable distance.

Viktor flipped the book over. "Since the day I was discovered on the mountain, I've questioned my origin. Having no answers has caused me to doubt myself and my purpose. Perhaps …?"

"No," said Tristan. "Don't listen to them! The Federation is evil! Everyone knows that! This book is a lie! You can't trust them."

"It might not answer all my questions, but perhaps some? I have to know. I don't know what this is, but I'm going back to my room to see."

"Viktor." Tristan wanted to plead, but stopped.

Viktor started down the street, and then turned back, smiling. "Thank you for your concern, Tristan. Really. But we both have our destinies. We need to give each other the freedom to explore. Thank you."

The words pierced him like nails in a coffin. His heart gripped him in inescapable despair.

XXXXXXX

"He didn't leave his room for days," said Tristan, sounding melancholy. "No one saw him. We left him alone, hoping against hope that he would not return to his past, whatever that might have been."

"This is a weird story," said Cole absently.

"What was the date?" asked Bailey, still typing feverishly.

"Serpens 24, 1864 O.C."

"The date of the explosion!" Bailey shouted, jumping to her feet, nearly sending her pad flying.

A hush enveloped the room.

In the silence, Tristan realized that Bailey had been right both about the date and his need to get the story off his chest. He did feel relieved, not completely, but six years of pain had begun to diminish. He didn't understand why he yearned so much for Viktor at the time. Was Viktor the father figure he had lost? He didn't know, but he did know that he grew to admire the man's uncanny abilities and knowledge. He had become like family. What would Viktor be like now? Would their paths ever cross again? "No. The day of the attack," Tristan whispered hoarsely, his eyes downcast.

"Typical that the damn Federation was involved! They get their dirty hands on everything they see! I'll wager most global tragedies can be traced to those bastards!" retorted Cole.

"The Federation is involved in many global activities largely viewed as magical or other-worldly, including high level atmospheric travel. I've heard rumors of cloning and mind control experiments, but could never confirm them," replied Eliza.

"Ugh!" said Cole.

"Are you ready to finish your story?" asked Bailey.

Tristan swallowed hard. His past had surfaced once again—the horrors of Southaven, the merciless killing—he wasn't ready, especially for the spectre of emotional pain he had learned to dread. There was no way he could have prepared for this. The click of the recorder's power switch cued him that his fear no longer mattered.

CHAPTER

24

Tristan sighed, marking his first recounting of the Southaven story in years. He wondered what emotional dangers awaited. The time had arrived to expose his bruised and aching heart, but he still hedged; they probably wouldn't believe him, anyway. Cole, Eliza and Bailey waited, pensively, shrouded in the conference room's dim blue lighting. Plainly, his words had wedged an unanticipated degree of reflection in each of their minds. Not with her usual candor, Bailey was the first to move, nodding to Tristan to continue rendering the Southaven episode.

✕✕✕✕✕✕✕

After accepting Viktor's appeal, Tristan grappled with complacency. Compelled to somehow turn the situation around, he tried to let Viktor go, but after nearly a week, worry tinged with sorrow crept into his brain. Vacuity only served up pounding headaches. He wasn't built that way and he wouldn't give in to it. That's when he decided to go to the inn and speak with his mentor. What harm could that do? Surely those solitary days were more than enough time for him to digest that book, whatever it contained.

After leaving his house, he quickly reached the inn, paused and stared at curtained windows high over the street, searching for a sign of life. Painfully slowly, he approached the door, nervous about Gilbert's possible reaction. The innkeeper was generally easy going, but he was known to harbor a stubborn streak. The hinges creaked; he entered a cozy lobby and glanced at the central spiral staircase. If he hustled, he'd be outside Viktor's room in a heartbeat, yet he still didn't feel ready.

Behind the counter, Gilbert, in a dingy, sleeveless shirt, stuck to a portly frame, leaned on elbows and eyed Tristan curiously.

He lost the urge to bolt. "Hello, Gilbert," greeted Tristan warily, but tried to appear as confident as any other 17 year old would. He brushed down his leather vest, and aligned the snaps.

"Why hello, Tristan! How are you today?" asked Gilbert, seeming none the worse for Tristan's presence. "Sharp vest."

"Super, thank you," immediately feeling overdone. "I'm here to see Viktor."

"I'm afraid Sir Viktor has requested privacy. It would be unwise to disturb him," replied Gilbert softly, a gentle grin fading.

"It's been days since he's been out. Is he okay?"

"I can't stop you, but it's your head to lose." Gilbert ran his thumb across his neck and motioned toward the landing near Tristan.

Tristan's eagerness overtook him; he headed up, two-steps-at-a-time. That seemed to go more smoothly than expected, but he wasn't sure what to do next. Because of the notion of relief, he now worried about his expectations. The sight of Viktor's door flooded him with uncertainty. Why did he demand such solitude? Viktor was a good man, despite his mother's incessant harping. Southaven was emerging from abject poverty. People, no longer living under the old religious scrutiny, were now free. Each step toward the door seemed slower than the last. When he finally reached Viktor's door, it seemed an eon had passed. He pressed an ear against ornate designs, more than anything searching for the courage to knock. Viktor commanded respect. Would he be angry? Shuffling, perhaps papers, and incoherent blathering. He knocked. A hush descended. Tristan rapped again. He had every right to visit his friend. If the door was unlocked, he'd open it himself. The handle felt cold, nearly freezing. The door cracked, sending a flood of chilly air into his face.

Viktor sat at the desk, rocking; his hands gripped his hair.

"Viktor?" Tristan wanted to run over, maybe embrace him, but his emotions suddenly felt challenged.

Victor cast a distant stare. His lips quivered, the sounds barely audible.

"Are you all right?" Tristan ignored the first impression and continued to stare, shivering from a strange coldness, but he didn't question or care. He'd waited an entire week; he wouldn't back out now. Besides, Viktor was his friend and he wanted them to need each other.

Viktor closed his fists; his indigo hair wildly protruding. He broke out in laughter—raspy, hollow, crazed. "I'm more than all right. I'm absolutely extraordinary." he announced, gazing from a tilted head.

"Are you sure?" said Tristan, apprehension beginning to grip his consciousness. The man's deportment actually startled him. Nothing seemed as it was a few days past. Viktor was suffering; his emotionless expression and tarnished eyes had aged him a good decade or more.

"And what do you think you know? Certainly nothing about me. You're a child and barely know yourself." chided Viktor, brazenly.

"Viktor," said Tristan, suddenly emotionally bruised and uncertain. "What's happening with you?"

"Knowledge, power, eternal salvation. What's gotten into *you*?" he rebutted, not kindly.

"I don't understand." The tension escalated. This was no longer a friendly conversation. He sensed animosity; previous affinities blurred. The hallway lured him, a less hostile place, but certainly no refuge.

"Of course you don't." Viktor's tone sharpened. "How could your psyche even comprehend the reality I now fully understand? You were formed from clay and I will return you to dust. You're bred to live simple, despondent lives. Insects are more developed than you! Yet, you consider yourselves great intellects. Such a ruse surely ushers in some comfort. But, lacking true direction, fear dictates your every move. Why drive yourselves like this? Why? You believe your opinions matter; each of you demand an audience as if you're divine! How nonsensical. True intelligence resides with those who were here before this world was ever created. Your foolishness and corruption mimic the Federation's."

What? Was he talking about Tristan, or everyone? "That book you read, what did it tell you?" asked Tristan, stumbling. Viktor's words had pierced like a serrated dagger. The indictments were dispiriting, his own strength seemingly pouring from him.

Viktor hurled the book.

Tristan shrunk away, but not quickly enough. He winced at a throbbing arm and dropped to his knees.

Viktor's laughter turned the room frigid, bluish, his breath fogged. "I'm a tool designed by and for the Federation! I'm their servant! But in their haste, they made a glaring oversight .... They underestimated my powers."

"What do you mean, designed?" asked Tristan, squeezing the birth of a bruise. Viktor resembled friend and fiend, rending his ability to think, feel, and even breathe. His rant soured into the peculiar, bizarrely out of touch, otherworldly. Did they reach Gilbert's ears?

"One third human, one third machine, and one third Fallen."

"Fallen? What are you talking about?" He drew himself up, moving along the wall toward the window.

"Don't you see? I'm a perfect specimen. I enjoy a highly-tuned human body, interfaced with a perpetual machine. It's inside me, a design that will endure countless eons! In me, the Fallen ... grants limitless access to knowledge! I am the future! I can manipulate nature! I can destroy or create. I am a god!"

"What happened to you? Stop! You speak nonsense! Do you hear your own words?"

Viktor slid a double-edged, serrated blade from a sheath lying on the desk. "And I'm not the only one!" His piercing glare scanned the room, searching, staring; and ended at the window. "Another specimen survived, one able to diminish or ruin my glory. Subject Thirteen. I'll find her—I'll kill her. After that, I will be the Federation's demise." Viktor erupted in another burst of icy laughter.

"Viktor! Enough!" Tristan's teeth chattered as if he was standing naked in a blizzard. He wanted to leave, but his feet had rooted into the floor.

"Fool."

"Don't do this. Please. Listen to me!" Hopelessness saturated every attempt to convince this now seeming adversary; he glanced at the sword, wondering ... He began to shake.

From across the room, Viktor widened his stance, blade in hand, muscles flexing beneath a tight blue shirt. "You would like me to listen to you, to serve your kind, wouldn't you? I've wasted months making your city prosperous, serving you, in virtual servitude! In truth, you all should have served me! I'm your superior! I'm the foundation of your future, if you even have one! You are mindless beasts, caring only about your selfish lives, ensuring full bellies, not to mention purses! But, not anymore. I decree divine justice on Southaven! You took full advantage of my amnesia and now, I'll take advantage of you—all of you!"

"No! You can't!" Tristan's skin frosted; he had to warn the others. There was no doubt that Viktor had the power to back up his words.

Viktor extended his palm. An invisible force slammed Tristan so hard that it blew him toward the window. Another came and sent him the rest of the way. Glass shards shredded his skin. He tumbled two stories, and thudded onto stone pavement. He lay, on his back, gasping. Darkness soon descended.

XXXXXXX

Tristan came to, still sprawled across the stones. His leg was pinned underneath, without movement; in agonizing pain. Searing heat, ebbing, burning, almost too great to tolerate, scorched him. His back throbbed. He remembered Viktor's palm, a pulse of power …. He shuddered, struggling to straighten the useless limb and rise. Each movement crackled caked blood covering arms and face. He had to move; it seemed impossible. Flames erupted from second floor windows; the stink of char and a blanket of gray haze disoriented him. Still dulled, muffled screams and shouts fed his passion. Wincing, he lifted his arms; they obeyed. Others needed his help. He pushed off, wanting to scream, and stumbled ahead, a shattered fountain on his right. His senses were awry; dizziness swooped like some strange carnival ride. The ground buckled. The entire settlement was aflame under smoky, orange and yellow fury. Fire burst from a hundred windows. Tristan grimaced from the deafening roar, in absolute horror. How did Viktor do this? Death was everywhere. Life, in which he had grown so comfortable, would never be the same.

He hobbled through the ruin, stopping in disbelief before the bank. Ganer, his friend since childhood, was impaled on a wooden pike. "Ganer!" shouted a stricken Tristan.

Ganer's voice gurgled; red life flowing out of his mouth. His glasses lay shattered below. "Help us. He's killing everyone …"

Tristan would never forget that plea—a lifetime buddy, his closest friend. "Save your strength!" he called back, both frightened and sickened by the incomprehensible sight.

"Your mother … she …" Ganer never finished. His head fell into his chest.

"No!" Taking a back street, Tristan tried to run, but couldn't manage much more than a searing hobble. He limped over corpses, rubble heaps, and random flames. Finally, he was home; hesitating, held captive in the cold grip of shock. The building was engulfed in orange and gray. He burst through the front door, wanting to scream out in pain, barely avoiding a torrent of powerful flames. Through dense smoke, he saw his mother, motionless. He crawled, throat burning and back cramping in violent protest. She was pinned under a fallen beam as thick as his waist. "Mother!" he cried even before reaching her side. "I'm so sorry; I should have listened to you!" He wedged a foot against the wall. Each tug weaker than the one before; the timber wouldn't budge.

"Tristan, I … love … you …"

"Mom. Hold on. I *will* get you out!"

"He's here! Run!"

"What? No. I won't leave you!"

"He'll kill us both! Get out!"

"I won't!"

"Tristan. He's here! He's here! Run! Now!"

"No!" Her fearful eyes seared into his consciousness more than the lapping flames. Turning, he glimpsed a group outside, and Viktor sauntering toward them. Surrounded by farmland, he was working his way to the mountain. "I will stop him!"

"Tristan! Please. Listen to me …. You must …" Her grip slowly released. Her head tilted into the crook of his arm.

"Mother!" He scanned the room, frantic. The back doorway. Flames roiled across the ceiling, illuminating his father's saber. He felt helpless as he scurried under the surging inferno, grabbing a wooden chair and smashing the case. The sword teetered, and then toppled. He grabbed it and ran out the back door. Viktor was in his sights. Tristan slowed under the pain, clinging to a picket fence. He ignored the first few steps, but the pain became too great. It felt like a sword pierced his backside and drove his breath away. Nigel, kneeling before Viktor, became his goal.

Viktor, sword held high, towered in the same royal blue uniform he had worn the first day. His chest was exposed, sweaty, darkened by soot and blood. Smoky, blue hair was knotted in the back.

"Please! Stop this! What are you doing? You built all of this! Why?" Nigel, as white as milk, cried out.

"Because it's my destiny." Viktor swung the razor sharp sword, instantly severing Nigel's head. Its mouth quivered as it rolled away. The still-beating heart caused the now-headless body to spray blood everywhere.

"No!" Tristan's frustration fell flat, but he didn't care. No one had the right to commit such barbarism.

Viktor spun around. Unscathed, flames danced from behind and on either side. "Still alive? I'm impressed. You're resilient, but foolish for coming back for more. Stupid child."

"You've taken everything!" Tristan clung to the fence. The heat was punishing, even across the road.

"Everything but your life. Let's remedy that, shall we?" spit Viktor, glaring.

"Does all this thrill you? Is this a god's behavior?" demanded Tristan.

Viktor gleamed. "Yes, and yes. Now, I must destroy the repository."

Tristan's heart pounded. It turned frail; he feared it so brittle that it would shatter.

"Zyn is the planet's lifeblood, the same essence being confiscated by the Federation to satisfy an insatiable hunger! They seek Ebonfall's re-creation, but I won't allow it. Ebonfall is mine and mine alone! I will defy their every effort. Let the race begin!" Viktor threw back his head, appearing crazed in a burst of glee. He raised his hand.

Tristan knew that another assault would shatter his body. He stumbled, wincing, cursing his immobility. He was unnerved, unable to draw any inner strength. An icicle formed in Viktor's hand, frosted, spiked, craggy and as long as his forearm. With a flick of his wrist, it sailed at Tristan's stomach. The impact flung Tristan back, tossing him like a ragdoll, forcing him to suffocate. At first, it was painless, but he could taste blood. He grabbed for the icy object, but his hands burned and slipped. He tried again; he couldn't grasp it. He coughed; the taste was salty; he was choking. Then the pain began, dull at first, and then all-encompassing. He fell, banging his knees, unable to cry out.

The reverberations were unmistakable—pulsing and beating—the likes of which only Federation or Amstynian airships generated. If they hadn't been so loud, he probably never would have heard them, but he did. He tried to turn but collapsed on an outstretched arm. They must have somehow been alerted. The racket quieted, and then disappeared altogether.

His thoughts churned, panicked. Voices. If only he could survive until someone found him. Darkness. Men shouting. Was he dead? Was Viktor still trying to kill him? No more humming, but there was a muffled voice. It seemed somewhat close and slowly grew louder. His stomach burned like fire. The pressure was too great. He wanted an end to the constant painful pressure. Someone was sitting on him. What was happening? The voice droned on, but he couldn't understand. He peered through sticky slits; thick, black armor appeared. A Federation soldier knelt over a medical sandbag atop Tristan's stomach. He understood ... the bleeding …. The ground shook; the soldier teetered. The repository exploded, as Viktor had promised. Tristan's head fell into the dirt; the voices diminished, the pain disappeared.

✕✕✕✕✕✕

"That's it," said Tristan. "I was taken to a Federation Infirmary, treated, questioned and released. They kept it hush-hush. They said I was crazy, hallucinating. The entire town had been destroyed by the explosion. It was reduced to a field of smoldering rubble. They said there was no "Subject Six." After a week or so, they threw me out of the tent and into the streets. Southaven was no more and I was its only survivor. They left me completely alone, acted like I was deranged or psychotic or something. Abandoned and exhausted, I was utterly wasted. A few hungry nights and nowhere to go happened me upon Mawson. At first, he was just another strange face. I didn't know if he was Federation or what. I didn't care. Like the others before, I told him my story. He actually seemed to believe me. I didn't trust him, or anybody else for that matter, but he wouldn't let it go. Said he was enlisting "vengeful recruits," whatever they are. I still wasn't sure at the time if he believed me, but I had nowhere else to turn and nothing to lose."

"Tristan ... I'm sorry ...." Eliza gently patted his arm.

He shrugged. "Actually, I not sure if you even believe me, but I really don't care anymore. That's what happened."

A faint click; Bailey switched the small black slider to the off position. "I know it was hard for you to relive that experience. I'm grateful."

The others sat pensively, staring.

He nodded.

"And he hasn't been heard from since? That's kind of odd, don't you think?" asked Cole.

"Even if they did hear from him, or find him, the Federation would kill any rumors. I'm sure they think they can still control him," said Tristan.

"Ebonfall?" queried Eliza. "That's the manifesto Xander designed to implement the New World Order. Equality for all; or is there something more to it?"

"I wouldn't doubt it," answered Tristan. "The Federation doesn't share its secrets. And we all know that they have plenty of them." He was emotionally drained, but Jase was still on duty in the cockpit, probably exhausted.

Jase's tinny voice crackled over the onboard communication system. "Tristan? Get your ass up here and take over. It's your shift, dammit!"

"Uh, oh. That's my cue." He pushed back, walked over to a plate of egg sandwiches, grabbed one, and disappeared toward the cockpit.

CHAPTER

25

URSA 18, 1870 O.C.
COUNTRY: AMSTYE
CITY: NEOPOLIS, BORDER CITY
EN ROUTE TO NEOPOLIS

Sprawled beneath an imperceptible Marne—Amstye's most populated border city, Neopolis, a bustling metropolis, seemed favored; inland, a natural ridge formed along sheer, white cliffs, overflowing with lush greenery. Tristan tweaked the throttle and like a pancake, the runway flattened. An orange windsock, fully extended in the prevailing wind, snapped from occasional fierce gusts. Across the Everlin River, Oxium's Scoria displayed a contrasting atmosphere of interconnecting bridges, rows of rounded roofs topped with spirals, *all sitting empty, barren and uninviting*; adjoining cities, highly contrasted. Shadowed beneath sibylline clouds, Oxian troops lined Scoria's riverbank. Threatening a violent rebuke to caustic rhetoric from across the river, their daily movements constantly threatened an assault. War seemed imminent.

The thrill of the descent, blurred ground, was quickly replaced by glaring reality. Land-based Amstynian soldiers, clad in goggles and tan field uniforms, bore stubby rifles. Across the water, daunting Federation-equipped troops patrolled in full armor, black helmets with silver masks. Like gleaming ants scurrying about, their automatic rifles appeared like black appendages. The unsettling aura dissolved when Tristan stoked the engines and pitched up the nose; the abrupt power bleed created a floating sensation. Moist palms clung tightly, the yoke trembling under the load. Amstynian tanks, beige and heavily armored, surrounded the airfield. Black RP Defenders tanks guarded the neighboring city—Amstye had supplied both factions; only their colors were different. The Marne settled behind concrete barricades, tires screeching.

Tristan eyed his chrono; the Strategic Command meeting was scheduled to begin in two minutes—he'd probably be late. He dropped the checklist, cut the engines and waited for a runway crew to connect auxiliary power. Eliza gazed out a window, nervously picking at her fingernails under flickering lights. She followed Tristan to the exit.

"General Braxton has been expecting you," announced an awaiting soldier. A floppy gray beret hung low over blue eyes and thick, black hair. He motioned, almost curtly. "This way, please." The man gripped a rifle while inspecting barricade gaps. He turned to Tristan, possibly as an afterthought. "The Acrolyte and Paputa haven't been cleared. Please ensure they remain in the ship."

"How rude," quipped Jo in a high-pitched voice. He had just stepped onto the ramp.

"It's okay," said Tristan. "We'll not be troubling anyone and we'll be back right after the meeting."

Towering and bulky, Atlas snarled.

"Something I've always dreamed of; stuck in close quarters with a stinking, savage animal," razzed Jo as he edged around Atlas's legs and up the ramp.

Atlas turned and gestured menacingly with his hands at the little creature, as if grabbing and strangling him. His restraint was admirable, given his irritation with the Paputa.

"Tristan's right," said Bailey. "Let's just do as they say."

The air stank of burnt exhaust. Soldiers bustled about the heavily fortified base; manning heavy artillery, and hustling from tent to tent. The group drew intense stares as they moved along the only road. Through intermittent gaps in the barricade, Tristan glimpsed shadowy Oxium troops and tanks at the ready. Glimmers of sunlight glinted off the water and their polished helmets; their clanking tank treads split pavement, their vehicles coughed black exhaust. A perception of imminent war permeated Tristan's consciousness. In the distant sky, he spotted a small formation of fighter craft; dots just above the horizon.

Their destination, a nondescript, beige tent, was situated adjacent a cinderblock building marked "Quarters". They hustled through more guards and barricades and into the tent.

Fabric on all sides was certainly frail as command centers go, as queer a forward-posted control function as he'd ever seen. Tristan shrugged it off; all the while eyeing flopping canvas; one hit from some well-aimed ordinance would render this command center, and their asses, smoked. The far wall was lined with myriads of electronic devices and flashing lights. Soldiers sat before clustered monitors illuminating phosphorus-colored satellite images. The room took him back to his early training—sparse furniture, bare tables, hard wooden chairs, puke greens and puke tans everywhere.

Tristan spotted a heavily starched, dark green uniform with gold leafed shoulder pads, gauntlets, white silk scarf, knee-length overcoat and crisp, billed aviator hat; General Braxton. Across, a white-haired Azdahri in black jacket and trousers had just cleared a tent flap. He paused, dusting shoulders and sleeves. Tristan tried to place the man. He would've remembered bulging, round spectacles and a goofy top hat.

Eliza gasped. "Senator Galik!"

Her excited tone was new to him. Tristan's concern escalated; the setting unsettled him. Overhead, canvas loudly rustled. And now this.

The Azdahri politician sauntered past a row of tables. "Dear Eliza! I'm so glad you're safe!" He reached stiffly and pulled her close. His hat slid back, nearly toppling from his head.

"It's been quite an adventure!" said Eliza ecstatically. "If it weren't for these good people, I wouldn't be here." Her voice didn't usually falter. This time, it did.

Tristan scrutinized Galik, looking for any indication of deceitfulness. Their embrace seemed awkward; the man's gestures were strained.

Galik lowered himself into a graceful bow. "Then, on behalf of Azdahri who still maintain a degree of common sense, I thank you all."

The green-uniformed officer tossed a clipboard of yellow paper onto the table. In the clatter, some pages dislodged. "What delayed you?" he asked. "I'm glad my worrying was unwarranted."

"I'll need hours to tell you everything," replied Eliza, squelching her enthusiasm a little.

"At the moment, we lack such a luxury, but I'll rest in anticipation of hearing your every word. Security breakdowns between Neopolis and Scoria have spawned ugly rumors— in the next few days, we will be at war." He sighed, weary eyes moistened. "Earlier today, I spoke with Mr. Edde. He's scheduled to arrive tomorrow to escort you to Reyna. I'll travel separately. We'll convene at the World Council where you'll testify. I must depart soon thereafter but listen well; Reyna's involvement is utterly essential," said Braxton emphatically. "They are our only hope to gain any advantage against the Federation. Evidence supports that Oxium and Feria have surrendered themselves into subjugation to the Federation."

"The World Council is the perfect congress at which to expose the Federation's atrocities. We have no greater resource at our disposal." She turned to Galik. "Senator, your trip here must have been tiring. I can't believe I'm the only reason you came."

"Not quite, my dear. You know me. I did my best to stall Xander's efforts, but he had already gifted Oxium the resources to blockade Amstye. If rumors are fueled by truth and the Federation accelerates its encroachment, Amstye will be crippled in days. Hours ago, Institute VI sorties flew over Scoria."

"Surely they wouldn't dare? How could Xander consent? He's not even Sovereign! What factions tolerate this precedence?" demanded Eliza.

"His Valkyrie Militia, as well as Institute VI, report directly to him. With the election right around the corner, his victory would ensure Federation dominion over our beautiful country. Why? Because Amstynians refuse to surrender. Thankfully, some pockets of resistance haven't accepted our loving president Clexor's bullshit! Oh, please excuse the language."

"Shouldn't you be campaigning in Atomia?" Her smile cast a nervous tint. The room dimmed under a passing cloud, and then again illuminated with its departure.

"Only where I can," he stated rather proudly. "I've come to understand that my speech-making no longer carries much weight. People's opinions seem already set in stone. In preparation for the inevitable Xander regime, I promote allied troop buildup. Under his leadership, the Federation will likely become the world's most potent military force. Every resource, culture and people not already allied will be forced to submit." He paused in methodical calculation. "But come, Eliza. We have personal matters to attend to."

"Yes, of course," she replied, somewhat reluctantly.

Galik studied the others, his gaze resting on Tristan. He bowed. "I thank you from the bottom of my heart. By ensuring Eliza's safety, you've directly enhance our global initiative."

Eliza briefly caught Tristan's eye, hesitating with a flicker of desire.

Her momentary gaze spurred uneasiness. Galik wasn't as loathsome as Tristan's previous calculation, but he still wasn't convinced of Eliza's safety. The new surroundings, faces and heady conversations only furthered his unrest. If he could have, he would have trailed along behind.

The general's voice boomed. "Corporal Ashbury? I'm glad you survived the USC Headquarters' attack."

The man's unexpected candor caught Tristan off guard and put him on edge. He didn't like being pulled in two, or even three, directions against his will. But, they *were* in the middle of a warzone.

Cole snapped to attention, saluting sharply. "Thank you, sir."

"You're just too hard to get rid of, aren't you? Forgive me. I haven't even introduced myself. I'm General Braxton of the Amstynian Strategic Command, one of the fearless few challenging our feeble president. I've warded off his politicians; for how long, who knows. Already, thanks to indisputably treasonous political decisions, Amstye has been essentially stripped of most of its military."

"From across the river, RP Defender turrets are aimed this way," interjected Tristan. Sleek, black armored fighting vehicles tearing up the roadways came to mind. "They look like they're itching for a fight. How did that ever happen?"

"Oh, another great mystery. Actually, I haven't a clue."

His answer startled Tristan, subdued by another response.

"That exemplifies our "gracious, most-revered" president. For years, under the pretext of peace, he's supplied weapons to Oxium. Now doesn't that just beat all? He's downsized our military by over a third, just insane, eviscerating our country and now it's nothing more than a feeding ground for his ambition. That bastard demanded we throw down our arms, join forces with Oxium, and allow unrestricted Federation access. I put that right up there with pissing yourself. Some ambassadors and senators have gone up against him, but leave groveling. I only pray for adequate defenses. The last thing I want to do is pull down my pants and bend over for those radical Oxites."

"Sounds like the bloody bastard's drawing and quartering our country." retorted Cole.

"It does at that. We all know that Amstye is no longer a contender, since toleration became the norm around here. When the Federation engages the world, and it will, it will plough through Amstye like shit through a goose. It's a grand plan orchestrated by invisible puppet-masters. It sickens me beyond words. Oh, enough already! I don't want to talk about President Ass-Cracker anymore. Let me update you on our latest strategy. Mr. Edde has spoken highly of you all. If you understand our fragile predicament, I'd like to think that you'll join our cause." His eyes dropped as he shuffled the papers on the table.

"You'd actually take me back?" questioned a hopeful Cole.

"Corporal," replied Braxton, bloodshot eyes snapping into place. "I'd take a skinned cat if it'd help. Clearly, the Deity requires self preservation. And if that leaves only a fledgling remnant—even criminals and renegades—so be it. I'll fight to the death. Before you lost your mind, corporal, you carried a weighty resume. Yes, we desperately need experienced ground command. You in?"

Cole nodded excitedly. "I'll do what I can, sir."

"Good. Aviator Lieutenant Foard. Unless you forged them, you and Hart here also have impressive experience. We're desperate for advanced piloting skills. Deity knows we need them."

Jase pushed past Cole. "I'm in. Finally, some real action, sir."

"Good to hear, Lieutenant. And what of you?" Braxton eyed Tristan. "I hope your loyalties are no longer with Institute VI."

Tristan flushed abruptly. "No, sir. Ready for service."

"Good. I'd hate to have to hang you by your balls just to give the firing squad more target practice. You can handle a Sky Wing? It has similar characteristics to the ZX-6000. It's our most advanced Amstynian fighter."

Tristan's eagerness to soar in such a craft erupted. He lived to control cutting edge technology. He hadn't felt this ecstatic since signing on at the USC. "Yes, sir. I've logged over a hundred simulator hours in that type craft—about 40 actual."

"Excellent. And Miss Scovlin. Feel free to wander about. But I warn you. I generally hate journalists and so do my men. Don't interrupt their duties. Those concrete barricades are the front line. An attack is imminent."

"I won't be a problem," she replied.

"Jenson!"

Across the room, canvas flapped, stirring the ceiling and unsettling a musty odor. A smartly uniformed soldier, wearing an outfit similar to Braxton's, stepped in and snapped to attention. "Yes, sir?"

"Escort Corporal Ashbury to the Enlistment Center and reinstate him. He's top drawer and will benefit us greatly. But, before you do, escort Lt.'s Foard and Hart to the hangar. Present them to Titan Squadron Commander Barkley for their aircraft. Provide Barkley with Oxium battalion coordinates—on Scoria's north side. Have Miss Scovlin report to the Recreation Center where, I'm sure, she'll appreciate a less hostile environment. And for Deity's sake, don't let Ms. Nyvala or Senator Galik out of your sight! What's taking you so long? Get going!"

"Yes sir! Follow me!" The man cracked a salute, turned a quarter turn, and lifted the flap. He stared straight ahead.

Cole and Jase saluted and stepped outside. Bailey timidly glanced Braxton's way one last time before following Jase.

Tristan, envisioning a famous air strike his father had often described, held back. The thickness of aged canvas weighed heavily while a fighter screamed overhead.

"Is there a problem?" asked Braxton.

"No, sir. Just never thought I'd be taking orders from an Amstynian general."

"I won't be a general for long. But I don't give a damn. Titled or not, I'll still lead, even if only my grandkids."

Tristan appreciated the man's demeanor. He seemed in touch with the others, a welcome trait. Mr. Edde was the opposite, elusive, difficult to pin down.

"I could use you," continued Braxton. "As I mentioned, our scouts reported fighter skirmishes above Oxium. Seems your former Institute VI was involved. A few stray dogfights—nothing that's made the news. Clexor wants it kept quiet—for now. I'm reserving my best pilots for high priority attacks. This will seriously be dangerous work, son, and I have to be frank, you are expendable, but I think you know that. If you join us, I'll compensate you well."

"Whatever is required to protect Eliza," replied Tristan, viewing this as a get-acquainted session more than an opportunity. The man's offer wasn't unexpected, and his timing wasn't very appropriate. In a Federation world, his credits probably wouldn't matter much anyway. Eliza's vulnerability unnerved him. He hadn't known Braxton long enough to develop trust, placing Mr. Edde's directives front and center.

"That'd be a good start. I'll have Lt. Foard and a few others accompany you."

"I don't want to fly with him," said Tristan. He generally refrained from speaking his mind, but things didn't usually move this quickly.

"If I'm paying you, you'll fly with whom I say. Now, if you don't mind, or even if you do, this little meeting put me a week behind. The hangar's in the southernmost corner, straight down the main road. You can't miss it."

Well, that was that, indeed.

Tristan stepped out into noisy combat milieu, mulling over Braxton's lack of empathy. He breathed in the faint scent of salt air, a strange sensation, and squinted under another fracture of sunlight. Anxious to distance himself from the bustling activity, he stuck to the side of the roadway and pondered a single thought--where was Eliza?

URSA 19, 1870 O.C.
COUNTRY: AMSTYE
CITY: NEOPOLIS, BORDER CITY

Tristan awoke abruptly; the sheets stuck to him like a second layer of skin. The Quarter's environmental control system wasn't putting out any cool air, and the fans did little more than blast hot air. The Marne would have been more comfortable, but it sat on the tarmac like a blind duck. Dead tired, he checked his chrono for the umpteenth time. A greenish glow hung under a street light; he rubbed his eyes but couldn't wipe away the exhaustion. If only he could manage a couple more hours—not going to happen. He threw back the sheets, dressed and checked the charge on his bladed Droth.

Clouds hung low and seemed alive with flashes of light from cloud-to-cloud lightning. The thunder from the light show sounded distant and attributed to the great height at which the flashes were occurring above ground level. Tristan paused in the shadows, mulling over metallic echoes from across the river. Double sentries could be seen throughout; a team of soldiers surveyed the road abutting the Command Center—lights and voices trickled into the street. The air felt foreign, cool and moist; refreshing if not for his lack of sleep.

An earlier shower's remnants glistened on sagging canvas. He hung outside but could hear Braxton talking with Eliza and Senator Galik. The scent of coffee wafted past.

"That doesn't sound like a good idea," said Braxton. "General Nyvala has never indicated contempt for the Federation! Nothing! Why all of a sudden now?" His voice rang unchecked.

"I don't know," replied Galik. "But with his support and influence, the Atomians might just listen! He could take Xander down with just a sentence or two!"

"You send Eliza to him—we might never see her again! I don't believe in instant conversions. He can't be trusted!" continued the agitated Braxton.

That's what Tristan was afraid of. These men harbored his fear as well, or at least one of them from what he had heard so far. He'd worked every conceivable angle. No matter how he came at it, her life was always in danger. He caught another whiff of coffee. With each passing minute, its appeal grew stronger. He should go in.

"Perhaps my father has seen reason?" said Eliza resolutely. "He's not a bad man. He's made mistakes, but he usually responds to common sense if it's paraded in front of him. Senator Galik and I have enough evidence to convict the Federation in a world court. I would like the senator and my father with me if I'm to present to the World Council. With my father's influence, we might even convince Reyna to arbitrate! He's one of the most schooled individuals on the Federation's diplomatic and not-so-diplomatic strategies, having studied them throughout most of his career."

"I have a bad feeling about this." Braxton eased his tone, but still sounded troubled.

"Her father has agreed to meet with me. If I sense any foul play, she's not going anywhere with him. She'll be safe with Mr. Edde." The tension between the two men stiffened. "Dammit, General," bartered Galik. "We don't have time to dally in decision-making. Oxium is gearing up for an attack. If your President Clexor orders surrender beforehand, it'll be game over! The elections are in a bloody week and, if Xander is elected, Vuton and Atomia will both be under the same flag! We're out of time! Mr. Edde can transport Eliza safely to Reyna. He'll arrive today from Aurelia. His ship's cloaking device can fly under Federation radar. We need her in Reyna! If there's evidence of the world peace discussions falling apart, they can request election postponement."

"Negotiating with her father will endanger us all!" retorted Braxton sharply.

Tristan's heart slumped, but he agreed. No one could be trusted; any advantages they had were evaporating like a puddle in the desert at noon. If his reading of the situation was correct, no matter the choice, Eliza was a pawn in a global chess game. They were clearly consumed with their own political goals.

"I'll not divulge confidential information. I just want to see which side he's really on. Surely he'll listen to his own daughter," said Galik.

"Eliza. Is this really the choice you would make?" asked Braxton.

"Yes, I think so," replied Eliza cautiously.

Tristan shook his head. This wasn't her decision to make. He reached for the tent flap.

"I'll advise you and Mr. Edde if your father has changed his position. Otherwise, you'll be off to Reyna alone. I'll meet you there," said Galik.

"Thank you, Senator," replied Braxton.

"I must take my leave," said Galik. "Mr. Edde will be here in a few hours."

From the shadows, Tristan heard men approaching. A tall, gaunt officer ducked under the flap, leaving his small party outside. A finger of chilly air ran down Tristan's back, sending a shiver. He really needed that hot coffee.

"Captain Tervin?" exclaimed Braxton. "You're 15 minutes early."

"General," replied Tervin. "I must speak with you, alone."

"I was just leaving," said Galik. "Come, Eliza."

Tristan ducked behind a parked ATV, crouching as they passed. His heart rate jumped when he thought Eliza had seen him. He clung to the shadows as best he could.

After about a minute, they stopped. Galik stood a head taller than Eliza, casting his silhouette over her. She hugged herself, rubbing her arms briskly.

"Well, this is it. Is there anything else I can do for you?" asked Galik.

"No, Senator. Your support has been exceptional and most appreciated. Thank you a thousand times over. I pray that we'll be blessed with a miracle and that you'll be elected sovereign. Atomia can't survive without a leader like you."

"Thank you; but in all honesty, Atomia doesn't need another sovereign. The Senate, as a whole, should be the sole authority deciding the country's direction. It's been that way for decades. Xander has pushed for absolute power and, shockingly, the powers that be are eating out of his hand." Galik's smile was feeble. "Now our country will be ruled by one man, alone. This conspiracy of his is coming to fruition and soon, with virtually no opposition, his absolute ambition and influence will come down on all of us. If I were elected sovereign, the very first day, I would relinquish power to the Senate, and then resign!"

"How can people be so blind?" Her words trailed.

"Xander's clever. He employed crude, subtle trickery, instilling fear. He steers the country by blustering over irresolvable issues such as terrorism, war, famine. He makes people believe they need him. It didn't take long before they succumbed to his terror tactics. They'll see him for what he truly is—a long-winded fear monger that commingles fear and hate—but then it'll be too late. His kind should never have political power."

"Is delivering our allegations to Reyna even the right thing to do?" asked Eliza, her voice uneven. "What if they *can't* intercede? The entire world could become engaged in war. Millions will die. Everything we love will cease to exist."

"Yes," responded Galik. "Most territories will not avoid the conflict. But, Eliza, you need to choose. Can you really fight for those you love and hopefully prevent their subjugation? In the end, they could be taken from you, but it's what you do while this is happening that matters. Many will be taken; many. Save one."

"I understand," replied Eliza in a strained whisper.

Through the shadows, seeing her downcast gaze, Tristan detected her growing despair. He felt bonded to her and wanted to help.

"I know you think everything is riding on your decision. I won't deny that much of what will come to pass will depend on your decision, but no one truly grasps what has been set in motion or how any of this may turn out. Know this, Eliza: you're an extraordinary human being. You can handle these pressures *because* you are extraordinary. You have great fortitude, a rare trait. Never forget that." Galik embraced her dotingly. "The world needs inspiration and encouragement, someone who will sacrifice when no others will. I'll contact you soon." Galik released his hold, squeezing her arms before he turned to go.

Eliza stood quietly and sobbed. He yearned to comfort her, but she couldn't know he'd been eavesdropping. He stepped out from behind the ATV and abruptly halted, spotting the Amstynian airman.

"Are you all right?"

"Jase?" Eliza sounding confused, angered.

He had been holding back under the shadow of a street lamp pole. "Why are you up so early?"

"I was saying goodbye to the senator. Is that all right with you?"

Tristan's blood boiled. What did *he* want with her?

"Oh. Am I interrupting something?" asked Jase, glancing around. He frowned; his head seemed to shrink out of proportion.

"No. I'm fine. Later today, I'm leaving with Mr. Edde for Reyna."

"How about a drink? Looks like you could use one."

"Jase." Eliza chuckled nervously. "A drink? The sun is coming up and you offer me a drink?"

"I know it's early. Just one! Okay? I hear one calling your name. How about it?" tried Jase again.

"How about *no!*" replied Eliza pointedly.

"All righty, then. Well. You look like you haven't slept in a while. I'll walk you to your room."

"Thank you."

The shaken girl stood there for a moment, arms tightly crossed. Jase reached for her and looked over his shoulder, sending Tristan a nod and a wink.

URSA 19, 1870 O.C.
COUNTRY: AMSTYE
CITY: NEOPOLIS, BORDER CITY

If Eliza failed to reach Reyna, unthinkable global chaos was guaranteed, her greatest fear. Against seemingly impossible odds, she felt so small and insignificant. Surely, the World Council would take action. From across the river, grinding treads and roaring engines grated against her nerves. Blackened zyn exhaust hung just below swollen cumulus above. Institute VI fighters circled overhead, evidenced only by shrill roars. They could be seen only if moving toward or away, just above the horizon; directly overhead they were virtually invisible; so incredibly fast that their engines were only momentarily dwarfed by deafening sonic booms. Continual troop movements along fortified embankments were all the proof she needed—war was coming. She was rattled, and except for Tristan and the Reynan sunrise from Jo's picture, peace was a distant memory. If only ….

An Oxium fighter screamed, breaking through the clouds and screaming toward the Command Center. At the last second, it veered upward and disappeared into obscurity; harassment. If Reyna held the solution for world peace, she'd have to hear it from Mr. Edde. She didn't want to depend on him, but she was out of options. Her wrist chrono chimed; General Braxton's meeting. She didn't want to attend, but Galik had insisted. She was restless, wary and exhausted.

Most of the base had already packed into the open-air compound. Adjacent to the Command Center, it offered a reasonable view of the hanger. She strained on tip toes, eventually spotting Atlas; Jo straddled his shoulders. *"They must be getting along, I guess."* Their arrival surprised her—a pleasant one all the same. She smiled when she finally found Tristan, along with Cole. Their presence was unexpectedly calming, a novel sensation since landing. Bailey sat at a long table, busily typing. Jase stood adjacent, fussing with a small satchel. The wait turned from rife with anticipation to boring; her legs ached and the humid air reeked of mildew. She wondered if Bailey had enjoyed the Recreation Center.

"Eliza!" Jase waved, quickly giving up his prime spot. "Just in time! I was thinking you were going to ditch us. Mr. Edde is on final approach. Listen for his engines. You're almost outta here, girl," he exclaimed.

"Yes. Thank you," quipped Eliza. He seemed a little too happy about her departure. She wanted more time with Tristan, and, by the looks of it, wouldn't get any. He made her pulse quicken. She wanted to talk to him about Mr. Edde.

"Are you ready?" asked Jase. He sounded disappointed.

"As ready as I'll ever be," she replied, eyeing Tristan and Braxton in front.

Jase followed her stare.

"All right, lady and gentlemen. If I may have your attention," began Braxton. "It has come to my attention that Clexor has declared a truce, and we've been ordered to stand down. Oxium demanded that the Right of Passage Agreement be formalized into an international and irrevocable treaty. Why? Because they want bridge access right where we stand. The Oxium base Commander personally drafted this demand." He waved a beige certificate in the air. "Would you like to know my incredibly verbose reply?"

The crowd chuckled in a wave, beginning in front, and moving to the rear.

"'Up yours!'"

Laughter erupted.

"Needless to say, he wasn't happy and neither was our precious Clexor. In Amstye, I'm now considered a fugitive. Therefore, as long as I maintain this command position, expect offensives on all fronts. In fact, I'm sure they've already deployed forces to apprehend me. But, I stand before you unafraid! I will not move from this post unless I'm carried out in a body bag! If any man wishes to leave, he may do so now without fear of reprisal. Make no mistake; if you remain, you'll be labeled a traitor to your own country. The choice is yours and yours alone."

Hush descended. Eventually, a few grumbling men pushed through the silent gathering. Many eyes roved, quietly, nervously. A soldier with a ragged beard and grungy uniform bumped into Eliza. No one from her group left, filling her with certain pride.

Braxton stayed patiently, and eventually, his tired voice broke the quiet. "Now that we've gotten rid of the ass-jabbers, let's roll up our sleeves and get to work."

Screaming turbines momentarily drowned out Braxton's voice. On final approach, a sleek, dark green craft cast a spherical shadow over the gathering. Cockpit windows, illuminated in dull green, appeared ominous. Eliza had been expecting something more inauspicious, adding to her unease. The craft was nearly as long as the Quarters building and once past, it settled out of sight. Within minutes, the high-pitched whining had faded, returning a semblance of quiet to the crowded assembly. The lumbering craft turned at the far end of the runway, and then began the slow crawl back. Several crewman stood by to assist.

His speech was over as quickly as it had begun. He wasn't much for words, but he had made his point.

Braxton, scrutinizing the vessel, pushed through the crowd and over to Eliza. "Good. He's an hour early. The sooner we get you on that ship, the better." He tucked an arm through hers and escorted her across the access road. Her friends followed.

She was suddenly overcome with an unexpected sense of insecurity and aloneness. Her stomach knotted under a tightening chest; a premonition? She wrung her hands, clammy with perspiration. She glanced behind, seeking a familiar face; Tristan seemed so calm and reassuring. *Why can't he come with me?*

Activity picked up on the runway. Several armed USC soldiers, oddly familiar, disembarked. Their presence helped her refocus—somewhat—but only briefly. One of them hastily approached. "Mr. Edde is expecting you."

This was happening too fast. Eliza wanted to turn and leave, but nodded complacently. Her gaze met Tristan's. He had to be worried too.

"Thank you," she whispered.

He seemed focused on the activity near the newly-parked craft.

"Take care of yourself, Eliza," said Braxton. "Make us proud. Reyna will feel like home."

She smiled. Even then, a queasy feeling rushed from her gut to her fingertips. She became immobile, fighting with everything she had to accept her fate. The thought of boarding without her friends, without Tristan, conflicted her. She felt helpless and isolated, reluctant. She forced a smile on an otherwise expressionless face. "Thank you for escorting me. I couldn't have made it without you." She was sure her words slurred. She could barely remember what she had just said.

Bailey satcheled her journal and extended a hand. "We'll see each other again."

Atlas snarled, raising a chuckle from the others.

"I'll miss you too, Atlas," said Eliza. She didn't want to let go of Bailey's hand, so reassuring.

Cole tucked his hands in his back pockets. "Good luck!"

"We'll see you soon. I'm sure of it." Jase winked.

A soldier approached, breathing heavily. "General! Oxium forces are moving toward the main bridge!"

"Dammit," Braxton exclaimed. "Could be that time. Now, everyone to the Command Center!"

The setting forced a mental wedge that severed freedom and slavery and everything she had grown to appreciate. Her life hung in a balance as they fell in line behind Braxton. This wasn't her idea of goodbye. Was this the last she'd see of them? "Tristan!" she shouted, devastated. Her eyes pooled.

He stopped and turned, his wiry hair gusting softly.

It looked so pretty, but she couldn't tell him that. "I … . If I don't ever see you again … , I want you to know that you have been a tremendous inspiration," said Eliza, faltering. "Thanks to you, I'll be able to face the World Council." But would she?

"You're welcome, Eliza."Tristan blushed as he searched her eyes.

She wanted to feel him against her; it may never happen. She wanted to run her hands through that mop of hair. His searching, dark orbs cited a dozen stories. She dreaded leaving his side. His dark locks had fallen into his face. His chiseled jaw line was so beautiful. She couldn't believe that she had to tear herself away. "Will you remember me?" she whispered.

A loaded pallet clattering up the aircraft's rear ramp wasn't enough to remove the awkwardness. Through their gazes, it seemed the first time they actually connected. "Always," he replied softly.

A lump the size of winter squash clogged her throat. "Goodbye, Tristan." If only she could freeze this moment in time.

"Goodbye."

Cole shouted from across the parking ramp. "Tristan!"

He took one last look at Eliza before sprinting away, narrowly avoiding a refueling vehicle.

She was forced to accept that some things weren't meant to be. In a final act of defiance, she screamed within.

With swollen eyes, she faced the USC men.

"Come! We have to go," one quipped dispassionately.

His demeanor was insensitive, but she tried to lose herself in the last memories of her friends. How else could she get through the worst moment of her life? There was no going back, no way to contact anyone, and no Tristan. Eliza numbly walked the distance and jumped up onto a low hung ramp leading into the craft's swollen belly. The unrelenting racket of spinning turbines, clacking pallets, and shouting men dulled her senses, disoriented her. The USC soldiers guided her; the ramp began to retract. The high pitched whine of the engines triggered a flash of anxiety, something that she really didn't need right now. Normally, she felt in control, but this experience detached her. In seconds, her only escape route had been sealed off. She was weakened, and scared. One of the men nudged her with the butt of his pistol, motioning toward the forward bulkhead. The idea of jabbing her like that caused a surge of fear. She faced a wall painted a military grade yellow with one dark brown door. *Conference Room* was inscribed across the top panel. Something told her this was going to be a difficult journey. As she pushed it open, the engines revved and caused a resonant vibration through the floor that would have numbed her feet if it persisted. Before she stepped in, she ran her fingers through her dark hair, sending it down her back. A moment later, she faced Mr. Edde, seated alone on the far side of an empty table.

"Hello, Ms. Nyvala. Please have a seat." He motioned.

She didn't appreciate his gruff tone. "Mr. Edde! I wish you could have come outside to see everyone. They were disappointed you didn't."

"Forgive me. I had other matters to attend to. My schedule gave me no choice. As of late, I do prefer remaining out of sight. There are many people looking for me that I would rather avoid. We can't trust anyone."

Complacency permeated his reply, sounding more impatient than anything else. What was she in store for? She tried to mask her vulnerability, blaming her discomfort to the hasty departure. "I understand," although she did not. She managed a smile.

"You're so lovable. It seems that everyone wants a piece of you."

"Excuse me!" she snapped, startled; perhaps somewhat angered by his choice of words. He seemed to be toying with her emotions. Women shouldn't be addressed in such a manner.

"Well, the USC, Senator Galik, the Federation, Headmaster Mawson, Lord Commander Seryth—all seem to need you. And they each believe that their individual needs or priorities supersede the others. You have become quite 'popular,' if I can use that word, much more rapidly than anyone I know. Or should I say, more useful?"

Her skin crawled. "Mr. Edde?" She tried to manage a stern voice but felt suddenly vulnerable. He sounded perverted. But she couldn't trust her perceptions, now so awry and misguided.

"I arranged to have you captured at the Ball. Little did I know that you were the informant." He leaned back and chuckled. "I tried to have you kidnapped at the USC HQ, but you evaded my Institute VI people. You even escaped Sullivan Byrd—in his own lair! Impressive! Well, your luck just ran out. Now, I can wage war or possibly jumpstart a New World Order! As always, I'm in control."

"You ..." Her energy vanished. What kind of pit had she been thrown into? Was it possible that he was kidding? She doubted it. Her fingers started to tingle again and the sensation moved up her arms. She was panicking, knowing there wasn't anyone to help her. Why did Tristan desert her? She felt like she was floating on water, worrying her even more.

"Ah! You're trying to put it all together, but your limited intellect cannot grasp its enormity. From the beginning, I guided the Federation to its zenith! I did, me! I formed the USC, nothing but a bogus organization designed to spark fear in Azdahri citizens. They'll have no choice but to look to the Federation, for protection from… nothing! Now, because of Azdahri hatred of the USC, Vuton's and Atomia's fates are virtually sealed; with Senator Xander at the fore, they'll unite! My fingerprints are on every known national entity! I am omniscient. I am omnipresent. Soon I will be omnipotent! Oh, forgive me for seeming so arrogant, but the look on your face is absolutely priceless!"

"No!" She tried to block him out. He was a crime lord, nothing more. His words were terrifying, but not so much as his hollow eyes. Her skin crawled, imagining his cold-bloodedness. What could she do to escape? The rumbling below the metal deck answered that question, nothing. When an armed guard barged into the room, she recognized a stupid-looking mohawk. It was Tye, one of the assholes from the Ball attack, the same character who had led her onto the ship. This couldn't be. She'd been played.

Mr. Edde motioned to a chair. "Sit down. No one's coming to save you. Elimination of the final opposing Federation general is already in motion."

"General Braxton? Tristan?"

"Momentarily, Institute VI and Oxium will launch attacks. They're waiting for my signal. Would you like to watch?"

"You … No!" Tye's pistol slammed into her back. She fell against the table, and then onto the floor, knowing that a black and blue bruise would soon follow. The pain dulled, but not the overwhelming pangs of fear. They cut deeper than any knife. Mr. Edde couldn't get away with this.

"Yes … . Change of plans. Instead of Reyna, let's head to Atomia, shall we?" He reached behind and barked an order into a wall-mounted communicator.

"You …." She struggled to form the words. "You're the 'Enlightened One'!"

CHAPTER

28

Tristan crouched under the vibrant hues reflecting off Mr. Edde's departing vessel. The air thrummed—war cries from myriad pounding drums. Tristan's every nerve pulsated, then recoiled. The explosion's aftermath enveloped his body in searing heat, like unavoidably standing too close to a house fire; his eyes reflected unavoidable dread. His father had described bombing strafes, or carpet bombing; their effects could be felt a half mile away, but he hadn't believed it until today. Transition, from single-focused missions, safeguarding Eliza, and Federation adversarial run-ins couldn't compare to this immersion. Tristan stared across the waves' orange-ish glimmers, dangerously close—war's reality. To think, only hours before he had been soaring high in the atmosphere, untouchable, invulnerable. There would be no return. He dropped, wanting to escape reality just the other side of some wooden crates.

After Southaven, anger slowly enveloped Tristan like a spider wrapping its prey. Mr. Edde now had Eliza, but he still felt obligated somehow. It hadn't gone his way, like a lot of things, creating a sense of restlessness. She stabilized him somehow—reduced his ever-present fury. He would not forget her, no doubt; Jo's painting made sure of that.

Braxton's voice carried over blaring air raid sirens. His adrenalin surged; Oxium must be moving on the bridges. Braxton stood in the Command Center, impatiently delaying through the racket. "Here we go! Everyone! Listen up! They're launching the offensive! Report to assigned stations! Squadrons two and three—get those fighters airborne, *yesterday*! Air support is crucial!!" He scanned ashen faces. "Corporal Ashbury!"

"Yes, sir?" replied Cole.

"I need you to target Scoria's RP Defenders! They're lined up across the river and ready to jump! You're elected! How 'bout it?"

Cole snapped to attention. "Ready and able sir."

"That's what I wanted to hear. Assign Battalion Four to the bridge!"

A stout man with a crew cut and bearded stubble edged forward. "Sir?"

"Get Squadrons Four and Five airborne. Provide Corporal Ashbury and Commander Hendrix necessary logistics! Do I have to draw you a picture?"

Ear-shattering explosions activated wailing sirens. The group ducked in unison. Coughing and watering eyes consumed everyone as dust covered their faces.

"Hope you're ready!" said Jase, sounding off his usual, cocky self to no one in particular. He wiped his eyes, two angry black orbs darting about. "You're not pissing in your pants already now, are ya?"

"You standing there talking? Get airborne!" interrupted Braxton. "Don't waste any more time. Ashbury and Hendrix, check forward ground defenses. Hold them off as long as possible, no excuses. They outnumber us three to one and have to cross that river. We don't. I want sharpshooters up front."

Under roaring thrusters, Tristan dashed into the road. That sound meant only one thing—Institute VI fighters. A glance through broken clouds confirmed his suspicions—SB87's, Silver Banshees. Nothing compared to their firepower and speed; sleek, folded wing design, tight against angular bodies, and triple, high-caliber Gatling turrets poised to rip a target to shreds, or pierce armor. Their speed was unnerving to the ground spectator; one minute visible on the horizon, perhaps; the next, exploding rounds all about, then just a scream overhead.

Braxton boomed. "Get going, for God's sake!"

"What about her?" said Tristan, nodding toward Bailey. He feared for her life and wanted her safe.

"Not your problem! I'll take care of her!" replied Braxton. "Get going, dammit!"

"This way!" shouted Jase into the din. He and Tristan sprinted toward a mammoth, Quonset-style hangar.

The Banshees dropped another payload; explosions hammered the ground beneath their feet and splashed fire toward them. Tristan again felt white hot heat against his face. Body parts and shredded canisters from an exploding weapons cache fountained in a mass of flames. Another Banshee missile. "Look out!" He shoved Jase into a roadside ditch. Crates splintered, hurling inches above their heads. Tristan eyed the area, latched onto Jase's sleeve and bolted. Another hundred paces. The ground rocked; a foot bridge just steps away vaporized and spewed muddied water all over them.

"How are we gettin' across?" shouted Jase.

Back in the ditch, Tristan eyed the hangar and two emerging Sky Wings. Army green paint distinguished them from the silver flashes of Oxium's Banshees. They were a sight to behold, highly maneuverable, split arrowhead design, aft cockpit on two jutting protrusions. They were also fitted with their own contingent of twin Gatlings, capable of 6,000 RPM (rounds per minute). They zipped through the space, lofted slowly higher, and then shot up vertically. Afterburners ignited; they became only a memory. Adrenalin surged through Tristan's tense frame. This was taking too long. The other Sky Wings were just beyond the hangar doors. He just wanted to get to them.

"Keep moving!" shouted Tristan, diving face first into another ditch. They sloshed through mud and crawled on all fours. The sour dark brown mixture wrinkled his nose. Three more Sky Wings taxied into view, raising a smug grin on Tristan's mud-streaked face.

The Banshees, diving, threatened another fusillade above the host of silver-headed ants.

Tristan heard Institute VI rifles blasting away, from the hangar.

"Impossible!" They'd been breached already?

Pilots bolted across the parkway. One fell in a shower of his own blood, gunned down by black-uniformed soldiers.

Tristan dropped and fired, shredding the black haunts, creating a needed path. They bolted to the hangar. The place was huge. Pilots were pinned down just feet from pealing fighters. Catwalks crawled with black uniforms. Their rifles blazed three volleys at a time.

A scream. Another pilot down.

"Can't get to the fucking ships!" hissed Jase. "How'd those bastards get in here?"

"I don't know. Someone must have … ," said Tristan.

"Ah! Don't say it! You think one of our people let them in? It was probably that captain who showed up early last night, Clexor sympathizing prick!"

"Shut up and pay attention!" returned Tristan, crouched and ready to run. "Cover me! I'll get up there and deliver a nice surprise! Just keep them busy!" He pointed toward the catwalk.

Jase grabbed at Tristan's black-sleeved jacket. "You'll get yourself killed! You're a prick, but only a little one."

"Smart ass. You have a better idea?" asked Tristan before sprinting to a wall of crates, hoping that Jase would do what he had been told.

"Over here, you candied nuts!" Jase's gun erupted.

On the catwalk, fire rained down from smoking muzzles.

Tristan climbed a flimsy ladder and lunged for cover behind a red tool chest, undetected. He glanced through the metal grid beneath his mud-caked boots. A company of Oxium soldiers were firing from above; and more from below. If he didn't stop them, the pilots were hooved and hooked. He steadied himself and opened fire, halving two overhead intruders. Jase worked his way behind the crates to a Sky Wing, a perfect vantage point. Jase was trapped behind a metal bulkhead and couldn't fire from his position.

"Hold your fire!"

The familiar voice stunned Tristan. Sickened from the recognition, he glanced below at Erik Gabrio, clad in a dark trench coat. His bladed Droth hung idly at his side. "Now, now. We don't have time for charades!" said Gabrio, blond hair tightly drawn. His voice boomed, competing with exploding ordinance. "Surrender and live. Don't, and croak like a frog wedged on an ass stick!"

Jase remained crouched. "Screw you, you son of a whore!" he shouted. "Take your best shot, asshole!"

A yellow fuel tank beside an airship screamed at Tristan. The fighter would explode, but it was his only option. The catwalk would collapse and force him out into the open, a risk, but one worth taking.

"Have it your way!" shouted Erik as he fired into the adjacent crates; wooden shards sprayed everywhere.

From above, shots ricocheted off metal partitions behind Jase. A grenade tumbled toward him, end-over-end. It angled toward a crouched pilot and detonated. The man died instantly. Tristan couldn't wait any longer. Those planes had to fly. He lunged forward, exposing himself.

"Tristan!" Erik's tone was incredulous.

Tristan saw red and hated the man outlined in the smoke. He fired at the fuel cells.

Erik rushed for cover behind an electric panel. High above, metal sheets across a curved arched ceiling ruptured, severing the panel's main feed. Thick cables writhed like angry snakes, sparking and snapping. Erik ducked under a shower of burning sparks. Spanning catwalks, ablaze, twisted and groaned before finally snapping. Unwary Institute VI men screamed under falling debris. Tristan clung to the railing; his feet floated upward. The rigid surface bounced off the lower railing. The footbridge suddenly went into a freefall, crashing into the concrete floor and snapping apart at its riveted joints. Tristan lost his hold and flew, dreading what was sure to follow. He barely cleared a heap of warped railing, ducking, when a bar hurtled toward him from the twisted mass above. It hit him in the abdomen, like the icicle, but didn't pierce, and drove his wind into the open. His vision blurred. He struggled to see, gasping for air, and dove behind a heap of smoldering wreckage.

Oblivious to Tristan's predicament, Jase shouted. "Woohoo! Take that, you sons of bitches!"

They seemed to have eliminated most of their adversaries.

Tristan's energy vanished; his scared skin flexed under rippling pain. He slowly regained his composure and checked for broken bones. He'd suffer tomorrow if even he lived, but was relieved to still be in one piece.

"Back from the dead, I see!" yelled Erik from behind the panel. "I heard you were blown to shit at the Gaustead Power Plant. What a shame—still alive!"

"Sorry to disappoint!" said Tristan, breathing heavily.

"Hardly a disappointment! This time, I *will* kill you!" Erik's laugh echoed through flames, smoke and creaking metal.

"Let's see about that!" retorted Tristan.

"Ha! Look around you! You've already lost! In another twenty minutes, this entire fucking base will be sucking flames!"

"Such confidence. You should run for office; unless you govern like you fight!"

"Shut up, you hired whore! I always thought you were stupid, but this proves it. Siding with Amstye? Ha! Loser siding with a loser!"

Tristan had gotten under Erik's skin, and dug in deeper. "The only loser here is you. You're nobody, and when Mawson finishes with you, you'll be spreading your cheeks to the highest bidder, like your mom! Be sure to tell her 'thanks' from the guys."

"You think you're inside my head?" Erik laughed again. "Braxton's toast!"

Jase shouted. "Tristan! Enough with the drama! Shoot the bastard!"

"Stay out of it, Jase!" demanded Tristan, calculating his shot. He only needed one.

"He's right, you know. What petty drama. Let's settle it the right way—unless you've shit your pants. Knowing that you're going to die, why not choose honor. Let's duel the Institute VI way."

Was Tristan's distraction enough to give Jase time to board a fighter? That was critical. He glimpsed through the contorted, smoking metal. Jase, his back wedged against the wall, clutched his Droth. Tristan motioned to the closest ship. Jase nodded. Good. He understood.

"A duel? Are you sure?" asked Tristan. "I wouldn't want to embarrass you in front of your men; oh wait, they're in pieces."

"You're stalling! What, you planning on negotiating your way out of this?" chided Erik.

Smarting from an aching torso, Tristan, his black hair spread in a hundred directions, slowly rose, exposed and in direct line with Erik. Erik's chiseled jaw line was rigid, causing his grin to merge into a scowl. If Tristan could distract him, Jase would have enough time. Cole needed air support *now*. He moved toward Erik, risking his life, one step at a time. Every second counted.

The blades on Erik's Droth locked into position.

Tristan's blades clicked. He wondered how he'd fare; they'd both had the same training and were evenly matched. He gripped firmly; his body tensed like hardened steel.

Droth twirling, Erik's coordination surprised Tristan.

"It'll bring great favor on me once Mawson learns how easily you fell," taunted Erik. "Perhaps another promotion, ya think?"

The distance between them shrank; Tristan slammed his blade against Erik's, nearly dislodging it. The man teetered. His face glistened while he thrust his gleaming skewer forward.

CHAPTER

29

Erik was good, but not that good. A warrior poised to strike a crazed man, Tristan couldn't risk overconfidence. He probably appeared absurd; mud-streaked, hair matted, tattered pants. Erik's hand-to-hand style had changed—more aggressive, unlike conventional Institute VI techniques. His queer stance and bearing revealed internal struggles; Erik seemed conflicted, off kilter—glassy eyes, perspiring, jittery.

Mere distractions these; Tristan intensified his focus and summoned whatever inner strength remained. Braxton's command echoed hauntingly; he should already be airborne. His blade's glinting blue steel gave clarity to this threat. To kill Erik, he had to keep his composure. Nearly six years of combat experience compressed into a few ticks of a clock. Rigid hands are sewn to rigid corpses—let it not be him. This battle would bring Erik's demise.

Tristan came to life, his blade, death defined. Bright lights sputtered. *Clash!* Erik stumbled.

The reverberations stung like shock therapy, but Tristan had felt worse. Erik recoiled and then lunged; the weapons grated. Tristan wrenched his wrist, wincing every move, reaction, sensation was amplified. Their blades locked together, hung in time. Tristan dropped away, twisted, and slashed. Wide-eyed, Erik deflected, knocking Tristan back. Erik lunged, his face reddened. Tristan, pulse pounding, staggered back. Angered, his ears warmed from his increased blood pressure. *"Take the offensive,"* repeated in his mind.

He waited, deliberately; also departing from the convention of his training. The perfect moment came. He backed beside a yellow fuel cart, its hose dangling. He sliced through it; zyn gushed, splattering the deck like cascading water at the bottom of a long waterfall. He grabbed the whipping hose and doused Erik, sending him backward, spitting, gasping, arms flailing desperately.

"I should have known you'd cheat!" he yelled and fell backward, coughing and swiping at toxic green. It soaked his clothing. He twisted frantically, trying to avoid further immersion.

"Cheat!" Tristan wanted to laugh.

"A blonde drama queen! Just because I thought of it first!" said Tristan, Droth outstretched. He dropped the hose and thrust his blade. He pictured him dead, covered in green slimy liquid just before a raging flame engulfed him.

Erik slipped in the flood of iridescent green, his legs sliding apart in a bone-snapping split. "You're not as tough as you think!" Erik coughed and shouted furiously, his voice hoarse.

Tristan crouched, lunging upward. Erik slipped and spun, kicking Tristan and sending him sprawling. He pushed off, recoiling under Erik's steel. His jacket slackened, dangling from a glancing gash. Tristan slipped, thudding onto his backside into the foul-smelling fuel. He was now where Erik had been. Furious, he sprang upright, wanting to rid his hands of the slime. His Droth, slippery from zyn, was slipping in his grip.

"That was close, Tristan! One more inch and your guts would be everywhere!" mocked Erik, though gasping. "How much longer do you think you can last? You never were good at hand-to-hand. You cheat at everything! What did Mawson see in you anyway?"

Tristan charged, blindly, pondering if Erik would actually ask him to apologize for cheating. *"People who fight fair wake up in Hell."*

Erik's deftness was unanticipated. Their blades clashed again. Tristan bore down. He had to uncover some weakness, any weakness. Every fighter had one—just find it. Tristan's confidence transformed, along with Erik's. Erik leaped, squinting; forcing Tristan down. Sprawled, Tristan angled his weapon. Zyn dripped from Erik's overarching arms.

The deck shook; a shock wave struck as if another grenade had exploded. Erik shielded himself from a wall of searing heat. The hangar had split open to reveal a massive display of pyrotechnics across the river. Erik, holding the side of his face, was involuntarily catapulted over Tristan into a stack of crates. Jase's Sky Wing roared. As if on cue, Institute VI soldiers bolted into the hangar. Blue flame shot rearward, sending tool chests, fuel barrels, tool carts, and a few people, flying. Jase smiled and shot a thumbs up as he secured the cockpit's canopy. Tristan beamed and ran for cover.

Erik's neck filled with explosive rage. His eyes bulged. His skin ashen before the screaming craft. He faltered, and then vanished behind an idle Sky Wing.

Ripping off his stinking jacket, Tristan slipped and slid across the zyn-shimmering deck to a fighter. Supporting Cole was the priority; vengeance had to wait.

Jase shook atop 20mm rapid fire flashes from the aircraft's Gatling and lashed the black uniformed arrivals with streaking tracers. Their broken body parts flew through the giant rupture in the wall onto the blacktop, spewing their blood in all directions. Those avoiding the withering gunfire turned and ran.

Tristan leaped up two rungs and threw himself into the cockpit. He activated the power lever; in every imaginable color, a hundred enlivened LEDs danced across the console. He clipped his harness, slammed down the cockpit canopy, and exhaled a burst of air and zyn. The craft wakened from its slumber; the console rattled, instrument glass mirroring bursts of fiery orange from across the river.

Exhaust blasting from Jase's fighter sent loose metal siding and remaining Federation soldiers flying—just enough time to reach fully operational temperature. The radio crackled with a slew of jumbled voices. "This is Titan Nine—cleared hangar doors! Air support en route!" He exited from relative safety, a fiery graveyard of flaming, twisted metal and dense smoke.

Tristan's every nerve tingled from the deafening vibrations. He was next. Drifting roof sections bounced off the deck—certain death; he pushed the throttle; the stealthy cocoon pulsed, shook and edged forward.

Captain Barkley shouted. "Titan Nine. This is Titan leader. They're tearing us to shreds! Air support, *now!*"

Titan Three replied. "Get out of the hangar! It's collapsing!"

Tristan scanned the console. "This is Titan Seven! Almost at full heat!" Talking and flying didn't mix. He pressed the vertical plunger. Titan Seven shook violently, still not properly warmed up, then lurched, barely clearing a yellow fuel tank. A few more seconds passed. The craft sounded like it was drawing in great gasps of air. It was.

Technology's limitations couldn't be hastened. Once outside, engines screamed while he hovered aloft a swell of shimmering blue. Engine indicator LEDs turned green. He tilted the stick and swung right, aiming a jutting nose at a sky-bound swath of silver and army green. He shouted a single voice command, "Launch!" His head flew back and he shot skyward.

"Titan 13! I'm out!" followed Tristan.

There was still one more pilot to be accounted for. Where was the pilot's report? They needed every fighter airborne.

"I can't make it! It's coming down! Aaargh . . . !" The transmission broke abruptly.

The hangar exploded just as Tristan reached the river, incinerating aircraft, and pilot.

"Four bogies locked onto Titan Three! Titan Nine, do you read?" shouted Barkley.

"I'm on it! Tristan, cover me!" Jase shouted, his voice distorting in the earpiece.

"Right behind you!" Tristan climbed, scanning radar and the smoke filled sky. Oxian tanks were converging on all three bridges; silver craft teemed in the sparse clouds.

"Now! Now! Air support now! Tanks are killing us! Already lost four—down to our last three!" reported Cole frantically.

Tristan redlined the throttle, screaming abreast Jase. He eyed his fuel gauge—three-quarter tank. Four black dots flashed onto his screen, four silver slivers bearing down on Titan Three.

Barkley shouted. "Avoid a lock! You've got two on your six!"

Jase returned. "Pull them off me! Another second ... almost there!"

Tristan eyed the Banshees, dots like flies that morphed into menacing twin-silver threats.

"Hurry! They've locked onto me!"

Jase's turrets shattered his transmission. "Firing!" A Banshee exploded, flipping end over end above the river. "Right up his ass! Yes!"

Tristan shouted. "I'm breaking formation! Help Titan Three! I'll be a decoy!" Tristan shoved the stick forward, diving head-on into a skirmish; two silver flashes, like slivers of magnetized metal, locked onto Tristan. "Cole! Nail these ass wipes! Take 'em out!" He blazed across his path.

"Negative, Titan Three! We're getting eaten alive down here!"

"The sooner they're are out of the picture, the sooner I can help!" shouted Tristan.

"Shit, Tristan!" replied Cole.

"I'm at your three o'clock! These two are wiping my ass! Take 'em out! Just do it, damn it!" shouted Tristan. He strafed advancing silver-faced, black uniformed soldiers behind a tank formation. The tanks repositioned, oversized barrels slowly rotating skyward, shooting and hitting - nothing. Fire streaked on either side, forcing him to engage burners and practically yank the stick out of its socket. He shot vertically but couldn't shake them. Black pops of antiaircraft fire, courtesy of Cole, shook the air. A Banshee wing exploded on his starboard side, flipping it into its wingman. Two explosions spun into Oxian troops below.

"Damn! Nice shot!" Cole yelled.

"Thanks, Cole!" replied Tristan, not sparing a broad smile. His nose wrinkled at the stench of zyn and he activated the vent switch.

"Don't mention it!" laughed Cole. "Good ol' surface to air!"

Tristan lined up three Banshees trailing Titan Three. He centered the closest bogie. A shrill beeping made his ears ring. He squeezed the trigger and waited. The explosion couldn't come fast enough. He pulled up, just clipping the perimeter of fiery debris.

Barkley howled. "Titan Three! Over here, above the cliffs! I'm waiting!"

"From the south—four inbound!"

"We'll get them! Help Titan Three. Break away!" shouted Barkley.

"I'm at your twelve!" retorted Tristan excitedly.

Barkley snaked behind Titan Three's attackers and blasted. A silver tail section ruptured into twisted aluminum and smoking debris; the fighter entered a death spiral, too low to let the pilot eject. The canopy popped only a nanosecond before obliteration.

Titan 13 shouted. "What's taking you? Five have me boxed in! Now!"

"Titan Seven ....." shouted Barkley.

"I'm on it!" He banked hard to port while Titan 13 cut into Amstynian base airspace. Fire trailed out of five wing-mounted Gatling turrets. Titan 13 banked opposite, unable to shake them. A brilliant flash illuminated the early morning sky. Another Banshee down. A missile sped into Titan 13's blackened wake.

"Mayday! Mayday!" shouted Titan 13.

Titan 13's Sky Wing erupted. The inferno was almost hypnotizing as it tail spun over the Quarters building. Flames from the zyn tank created a widening ball of fire, showering tents and troops.

Tristan stared in disbelief and dove into the four remaining Banshees. They banked left and dropped out of sight.

"I got him!" shouted Jase.

Tristan glimpsed, but he was already gone.

It was now four against four. The balance had finally shifted. Four radar blips betrayed the elusive Banshees. Gray trails streaked past the brittle cockpit acrylic. That was too close. The four split in two and engaged Jase, Barkley and Titan Three. The other pair disappeared above. They'd reappear any moment. Tristan slammed his throttle forward, exhilarated from the surge of power; leaded fingers struggled home.

Titan Three shouted. "We're taking heavy ground fire!"

Barkley shouted. "Pull up!"

Titan Three screamed. "Negative! Too late!"

Tristan watched little black pops go off near Titan Three. A ragged line of jagged pocks appeared along the fuselage; burning spirals of flaming green and gray formed a smoky wake. His heart was torn when gravity clawed at the fighter and pulled it down. It could have been him.

"Titan Nine. Go around!" commanded Barkley.

"Gotcha!" Jase, his voice faltering, banked hard right. Barkley dove at the tanks.

Tristan couldn't reach the two Banshees tailing Jase and Barkley; they had dropped off to either side. "Bogies splitting up!" advised Tristan. "I'm taking the one at my twelve!"

With Tristan in hot pursuit, the Banshee banked hard left, mimicking the other. "All right!" shouted Tristan. "So, is this how you want to play?" Tristan climbed, then looped, and came up under its belly. Perfect. Tristan was in the lead. But seconds were quickly passing. He couldn't avoid missile lock. The piercing warning tensed his nerves and moistened his skin. Tristan dove at the lead Banshee, then at the last moment, he pulled up. The missile screamed past, lost its guidance, and streaked into the enemy fighter; its pilot wide-eyed, for a nanosecond. The collision of missile ordinance with the Banshee's half-tank of zyn created an immense ball of fire. Tristan looped, one of his favorite maneuvers, settling in behind the unsuspecting Banshee. He fired both guns, blasting right through the fighter's tail; no tailspin, no roll, just fluttering like a supersonic leaf, on fire.

Barkley applauded. "Good job, Titan Seven!"

Tristan double keyed his mic just as another Banshee tumbled groundward.

Jase bragged again. "Another shithead in the sewer! One left! Where is it?"

Tristan scanned. "I can't see him!"

Barkley shouted. "Titan Nine! At your six!"

Tristan glanced toward the rising sun. He spotted a growing fleck bearing down on Jase, only seconds away. "Jase! I'm coming!"

"They're breaking through! Too many tanks! I need you, Tristan, *now*!" Cole's voice was lost in a myriad of shouts and explosions.

"Tristan!" Jase yelled.

Cole shouted again. "I repeat. They've broken through! I need fire up their asses, *now*!"

Tristan leveled out. Which one was the most vulnerable? Jase was more maneuverable. If the tanks crossed the bridges, the entire base would fall. He scanned the console; river and sky flashed—three bridges and two sky-bound bleeps. He slammed the throttle forward, his head pressing into hardened foam, a giant's foot slammed into his chest.

"Tristan! Help me!" Jase managed to key his mic; his voice sounded hollow, like he was in a cave.

Tristan was instantly conflicted; he was only one man. Jase's transmission drowned out Cole's pleading.

Barkley protested. "Dammit. I don't have a clear shot!"

For a moment, Tristan felt alone, but reason prevailed. The dilemma tested fortitude unlike any other. Barkley might intervene, he'd hoped, but Jase wasn't pacified.

"They're shredding us! Air support! We can't last much longer!" Cole's petition wrangled Tristan like a mad bull.

Tristan could barely distinguish Jase, a dancing dot. Cole's tank blocked the middle bridge; nearly a dozen black tanks in opposition.

It had to be Jase.

"Jase!" shouted Tristan. "Dive to the middle bridge—on my count! I'm going vertical!"

"You're crazy! They'll blow me to bits!"

"That won't happen!" countered Tristan. "Trust me!" If it worked, he would kill two birds with one stone. Tristan jammed the stick back and shoved the throttle forward. The thrust indicator immediately glared red. His eyes blurred from a surge of adrenalin, or possibly oxygen deprivation.

"Shit!" exclaimed Jase.

Off his port side, Jase dove. The next seconds would determine victory or defeat. Tristan planned to ignite afterburners and climb as high as he dared. With enough altitude, he could outmaneuver anti-aircraft fire. He swept his wings back in prep for the massive acceleration soon to come. A heartbeat later, he melted into the padding. His head was pinned; he wondered if his helmet would crack. He climbed as a blur, crossing into the stratosphere, deep blue, almost black. He left the clouds at around 15,000 feet. Surrounded by spacious blues and golden rays, he marveled at near weightlessness. Cloud streaks etched the distance. Zyn burned his nostrils.

Cole cried out; as clear as if he sat beside him. Tristan wanted to reply, somehow comfort him, but couldn't think of anything meaningful; he was only moments away. Timing had to be perfect. The roar of power thrilled him, drove through him; he loved the sensation, how it shook him, hurled him away from everything evil and good and bespoke purity of courage and might. The stick shuddered; time to throttle back and start the free fall. He eyed the airspeed indicator as the nose hung motionless, and then slowly fell forward; if he stalled, he couldn't recover.

Soon, metal skin screamed as the stealthy fighter seared the speed of sound. He nudged the throttle; his cheeks hollowed against his jaws. No one could catch him; *or elude him.* Goosebumps surged along his arms and back. His chin was frozen in place. This was a far cry from Southaven and he loved every minute of it. The stick shook; would it dislodge? He pulled the throttle back. Two cities quickly filled his vision; he spotted blackened stick figures and tanks on the bridges. If Tristan could take out that last Banshee, the other three Sky Wings could destroy their ground forces. "Jase! Go now!" shouted Tristan.

"Right!" He banked hard right, nose down. "Make it quick, Tristan! I can't lose them forever!"

"Almost there!"

Barkley's voice crackled again. "Jase. Watch your six!"

"Where's the damn air support? They've broken through!" Cole was nearly drowned out by the chatter.

"Where are you, Tristan?" Jase shouted again.

"Hang on. I see you!" Tristan eased out of the dive; the surface pancaked before him as he aimed for Jase's silver threat.

"He has missile lock, Tristan!" Jase banked left, then right, flickers in the wind, and continued toward the middle bridge, just as Tristan wanted. Tristan fired—the Banshee lurched—a direct hit. Flaming debris showered the crowded bridge. The explosion should have been greater. The fuselage lobbed end-over-end and smashed into now-immobile black tanks. Fire spread from spewing zyn, igniting loaded ordinance. Attached ammo cans exploded furiously. Hatch covers flew open; black uniforms aflame, men fell off the bridge and into the river.

"Yeeeahhh! Take that!" Jase hurtled skyward.

Tristan's adrenalin rushed as he took Jase's six.

This was better than sex, almost.

His head buzzed from the excitement.

"Battalion One. I'm on my way!" said Barkley excitedly.

"Woohoo! The cavalry has arrived, boys!" shouted Jase, arcing into a barrel roll. Seconds later, he buzzed the deck, strafing fleeing troops.

Tristan screamed along behind, firing on anything in his path. Nothing evaded the near constant bursts of ordinance; men, tanks, and vehicles vaporized. Ammo was down to twenty percent. They had gained the upper hand. Enough ammo left for one more run.

Cole's shouts were distorted and broken up. "Damn, that w … clos …… They've pull …. back! Well d … , Titans!

"Special thanks to Titan Seven. Good work, Tristan," exclaimed Barkley.

"Thanks." Cheering was heard scattered in the transmission; Tristan felt born again. This was the best flight experience of his life.

"We'll stay up here a bit longer; smoke any stragglers!" commanded Barkley. "Then, back to base! Don't park near to that sorry excuse for a hangar. The open area to the south should be clear. Inform General Braxton—mission accomplished."

"You got it, Captain," responded Cole.

✕✕✕✕✕✕

Tristan, Jase and Barkley strafed one last time. The Defender tanks were motionless, with or without smoke coming from them, a welcome sign. The once beautiful riverside had been trashed by Federation mementoes, symbolic of things to come. The road running along the river was impassable. Entire sections of upturned pavement, and scattered debris from smoldering tanks, anti-aircraft guns, personal vehicles, and bodies transformed it into an environmental wasteland.

Black puffs of smoke spewed randomly; anti-aircraft guns were twisted and silent. He wanted to blitz again, but it would have been a waste of time and ammo. There were some visible skirmishes, but without armor and air support, enemy forces were no longer a threat. Oxium had lost its first major battle against Amstye, but more troops would surely be coming, especially if the Federation is involved. It wouldn't be long before this was a daily experience. The Titans landed, avoiding the damaged hangar taxiway.

Bailey ran up and threw her arms around Tristan, nearly knocking him down. "You had us worried sick!" she said, sounding gleeful.

"I did what I had to," he replied, the loss of adrenaline making him quite weary.

"I know." Any enthusiasm in her tone dissolved. "I'm so glad you're safe."

Atlas sauntered through the parting crowd and growled.

Cole shouted from across the taxiway. "Tristan!" After a dizzying sprint, he grabbed for Tristan's hand and pulled him close. "I owe you one, Ace. You're a damn good pilot! Amstye needs a thousand more like you!"

"In my twenty years in the Air Force," started Barkley, "I've never fought beside two better pilots. Insane potential. Magnificent! Where did you learn to fly like that, son?"

Tristan's bashfulness overcame him. Son? He was immediately displaced to Southaven and consumed by thoughts of Viktor, the closest role model he'd had since his father. Not enjoying being the center of attention, he searched for a reply. "My father once served in the Amstynian forces. First Class Captain Mitchell Hart. He taught me a few tricks."

"By the Deity himself, I knew your father!"

"Really?" replied Tristan.

Suddenly, the world seemed so small. He found himself thinking about his father. *"A victory a day."* His father would whisper that in his ear during a challenging ordeal. *"Just one victory."* Those words carried him for years, and still did.

"We should get together so I can tell you more about your father. Your flying skills were over the top, just like his. Before you disappear, we need to promote you to a position worthy of your skills."

"It's a natural gift, ya know," said Jase, beaming. "Some people are just born with it. Thank the Deity I was, too."

Atlas grunted again as the group took to the main road.

Jo brushed against Tristan's leg. "Can we leave now? That was the most dreadful experience I have ever endured! So much death! So much violence! Dear me!" He touched the back of his hand to his forehead.

Tristan couldn't help but chuckle. Jo's demeanor was always welcomed, and while his presence was novel and amusing, there was still unfinished business: "What's next on the agenda?"

Braxton stepped forward. "If he hasn't already, Clexor will soon hear about our victory. It'll really piss him off. It's time to regroup to Verdia in northern Amstye. Commander Hendrix and his division will remain behind. Corporal?" said Braxton. "Will your team provide transport?"

Cole stiffened, respectfully. "It would be an honor, sir."

"Excellent," exclaimed Barkley. "Let's get moving. Tristan, since there's no question that you can handle her, I want you to ferry Titan Seven to Verdia. Lt. Foard can pilot the Marne."

"Yes, sir, but what about Eliza and Mr. Edde, sir?" asked Tristan nervously. It seemed that they had disappeared from their minds.

"I'll contact Mr. Edde. Don't worry, son. Eliza is in the safest of hands. I promise." Braxton glanced around the group. "Get some chow and rest. Then we move out! Take care around the Quarters. There's not much left. We've set up temporary housing next to the Rec. Center."

"Stay safe out there, Tristan," said Barkley. "I hope we can fly again sometime."

Tristan shot the unshaven Barkley a quick smile. "I'll hold you to it—as well as meeting up again." The two men shook hands, allowing Barkley to close in with a whisper. "The General respects you, son; an achievement considered impossible. You should be honored."

Tristan relished the company and would have continued, but the captain had other ideas. The small group headed toward the Rec. Center, leaving Tristan to inspect his craft and prep for tomorrow's flight. In relative quiet, he felt the tug of weariness in every joint, but nothing shouted as loudly as his gnawing stomach. He refueled Titan Seven and wondered what these war-torn cities would endure tomorrow.

URSA 19, 1870 O.C.
COUNTRY: AMSTYE
ENROUTE TO NAVALASTA

Three vibrant images of the Neopolis Scoria battles uplifted Eliza—Oxium forces were losing. Freedom was mere days away. This ordeal would end; she could feel it in her bones, but was it true?

Fiery explosions, fleeing reporters, billowing smoke, a fighter spinning out of control, black uniformed men drowning in the river—tears welled, her heart was conflicted—in the grip of both hope and despair. Tye's glare darted between her and the monitors. While his companions shuffled cards, formidable black tanks lined three bridges, but they weren't moving. A silver flash clipped the screen, its roar lingering long after the image disappeared. Statistics streamed along a blue bar at the bottom of the screen—weapons production, numbers of tanks, version numbers, anti-aircraft systems. A white-haired Federation reporter cited Silver Banshee features—dual engines, upgraded technology and capabilities.

Thanks were given to President Clexor for gifting Oxium RP Defenders as a peace offering. The reporter spoke as if the gifts had actually been his to give, his voice jumping in time to a series of explosions.

She thought of Tristan and Jase. Maybe they were battling those enemies? A voice inside cried, 'please keep them safe.' She held on because of them. She wrenched her wrist straps. Somehow, she had to warn her friends; her father. A moment of clarity exposed her fear—a starved animal, fangs bared—but she subdued it. Reyna seemed elusive, yet still possible, even high in the atmosphere among these intolerable brutes; the one in pigtails dealing cards seemed to smell the worst; the rest close seconds. She couldn't give up hope.

"What you looking at? Pissed off, are ya?" hissed Tye.

She locked onto his threatening glare. Her thoughts churned like an overworked keyboard. He was stupid, and dangerously unstable.

The ship shuddered, tossed a bit and settled. How long would they keep her in this stinking room, nothing more than a foul-smelling cargo hold? The elapsed time since any of these animals had bathed could probably be measured in weeks. Surely, the rest of the ship was more pleasantly furnished than this empty, green, grungy space. She tried to lose herself in past memories, her mother's strength—a marvel in the midst of overwhelming odds. Some of that courage coursed through her blood; she needed it now more than ever.

"You got something to say, bitch?" he demanded, flicking three cards indiscriminately and kicking back his chair. He bound at her; his foot caught a table leg, sending cards flying. The others angrily threw up their hands and cursed him as he yanked her up from her seat and began groping her breasts from behind. She squirmed, her only defense a shoulder into his chest. Anything to not feel his pelvis against hers. His breath was sour like vinegar; his scruffy face prickled her neck. Disdain morphed into dizziness. Her reeling mind froze when a dagger pricked her throat. "You're in my house now, sweetheart, and I can do anything I want."

Breathless, he spun her, dirty fingertips fumbling at her buttons. His hand stunk worse than his breath, a likely indicator of where it had been recently. Perhaps they were out of toilet paper.

She hung between heartbeats, ever so still while the knife traced a menacing path over her chest. She dared to breathe, yearning for him and the stench to vanish.

"You best change your attitude," he fumed, his tone even more seething. "You're all alone now except for me and my boys. And they're not gonna save you."

She heard a chuckle, but didn't move. In her periphery, pony tails wiggled like loose ropes.

"Come here and give me a kiss," hissed Tye, his voice clearly sarcastic. He dragged a chalky tongue across her cheek.

She wiggled, but he was too strong. Steel stung her skin. Blade and tongue spawned pangs of dread. Escape was impossible. It was difficult to believe that so many tumultuous years had led to this ignoble state of affairs. A world needed saving. There was no one else. If Mr. Edde had snapped, and by all appearances he might have, she might not last the night. She'd jumped into ice water before, on a dare. The frigid water had caused shuddering, close to convulsing. She was shaking like that again, almost violently.

"That's enough! She's off limits!" demanded Mr. Edde. The door swung wide and he ducked into the room through the hatch. He slammed it shut and threw down the locking lever. *"Clang."*

Fortune had sided with her, at least for now.

Tye shoved; she sprawled, unable to catch herself against the table. The other two jumped up and backed away, letting her fall. Tye's glare spit fire.

"Keep these freaks away from me!" gasped Eliza as if coming up out of the water after a frozen dive. "Is this behavior indicative of your 'glorious' vision for the world? Is one of these assholes in line to be your 'glorious' vice-chairman?"

"My invaluable existence is interwoven into the lives of many great people, whether stately ...," he paused, clearly relishing his own affectations, "... or salty. Of the former, your father would be exemplary," provoked Mr. Edde, smiling wirily.

"You associate with sewage. When my father hears of this ..." Eliza's voice broke, forcing her to stop. Crying would be construed as weakness, forcing a straight face.

"Your father doesn't care one iota about you. If you think otherwise, you're misled. Some people want you dead because of the Federation secrets stuck inside your pretty little mind. We can't let them out just now, can we? Senator Xander, or soon to be 'Sovereign Xander', must be globally seen in a positive light. How dare you sneak off to the World Council; not that they would listen to a spoiled brat. You can thank me later for sparing you the humiliation you would have endured if you had managed to arrive there."

Humiliation? The World Council would welcome her with open arms. "You won't win!" she fired, still struggling for a clear breath. "General Braxton will hear of this! Senator Galik, too! And when they do, you'll be appropriately renounced, if they even let you live!"

Oh, how she yearned for Tristan. If only they hadn't been so trusting. This Mr. Edde was insane.

"On the contrary, General Braxton will meet with a fitting end, as will your precious senator. One day, you'll understand. Anyone who stands against our New World Order will be silenced! The future has already been planned and is in motion."

"Your delusion is boundless!" retorted Eliza. To escape from this nightmare, to vanish from his presence, was her only focus. She scanned the far wall, as if searching for an escape door.

"*My* delusion? A multitude of supporters stand ready to applaud my divine accomplishments! From inception to the fore, these very hands have guided Ebonfall's esteemed destiny! I will reign alongside the rest."

"Ebonfall is a curse! The people will see you for the pus bag you are!" shouted Eliza.

Tye seemed closer than a minute ago, knuckles as white as snow.

"Oh, oh! So, you know about it! I was afraid you did. Until the time is right, Ebonfall's growth and progress will remain clandestine. Thank you, dear." Twisted lips creased his face.

She now realized his true motive. Evil almost always exercises ulterior activities. How foolish of her; his were no different.

She shouldn't have opened her big mouth. Mr. Edde was clever, too clever. Until now, she had not had a true understanding of this "Ebonfall," remembering Galik's warnings, one of the only decent men in her life. Ebonfall should sound alarms like tolling belfries, and she might be the world's only chance to prevent global domination.

Through slits, he eyed her like a fox. "Now, if you'll excuse me, I must host conference calls; three in fact. Oh, yes, you're invited. I need a witness and who better than you. Hopefully, you'll get a taste of genuine solidarity." He chuckled and activated a communications display. The darkened screen snapped to life, unmasking Erik Gabrio's wary gaze.

Responsible for the USC HQ destruction, he was one of the most ruthless men she'd ever encountered. His image shocked her—they were connected.

"Mr. Gabrio! Pleasure to see you. From the latest news broadcast, I take it that our plans were disrupted?"

Erik's downcast voice was clipped, tinny and distorted. "They were more ... resilient... than expected. The ambush was a failure."

Tight fisted, Mr. Edde's gaze wandered to nowhere in particular. He didn't even respond. An awkward silence permeated the room; the shuffle of cards ceased.

Gabrio continued. "You there ...?"

"You see me, don't you?!" shot back Edde, not kindly. The silence continued while he collected his thoughts. "That's a shame, Mr. Gabrio. You told me you had the necessary forces to destroy that sorry excuse for an Amstynian fortification. For deity's sake, they were working out of tents! Next time, I shall not be so hasty to listen to your noise."

"You could have told me that Tristan was still alive," said Gabrio pointedly.

Eliza's thoughts instantly sharpened. Tristan. Alive? Her emotions spun like a child's top, tightly at first, then wider, drawing in any possibility of a rescue. She had every right to scream. He'd save her—it was his job.

Mr. Edde snapped back. "Why would that matter? Would you have asked to have someone not so inept to execute the mission? My order was to exterminate *everyone* on that miserable excuse of a base. I would have expected you to follow it even if your mother was there. Instead, you seem to have focused on Mr. Hart, an irrelevant nobody. You allowed a fool's vengeance to guide you and lost a pivotal battle because of some childish rivalry. Surely, you're not that stupid. Oh, wait, yes you are."

"No! No! It wasn't like that! Their piloting skills were astonishing. We lost the advantage, but we almost had them."

"Almost…, almost! Damn it! Do they give out medals for that? You know, I never had much faith in Institute VI or Oxium, and you have certainly confirmed that lack of faith. Perhaps Lord Commander Seryth was right. The Valkyrie should have been awarded the assignment."

"That's not true. It doesn't matter, anyway. President Clexor still controls Amstye. General Braxton is a rebel, nothing more. His own countrymen will hunt him down." Erik's screen flashed—a burst of white static.

"So, according to you, we should have left them all alone and let his people do your job! You were supposed to kill him and you failed. You couldn't even eliminate Hart. This rebellion should have already been squelched and yet, here we are chatting!"

Erik lowered a wagging head in shame and embarrassment.

"I don't have time for this walk down 'Memory Lane'! Meet us in Navalasta, fool. Your Headmaster will deal with you accordingly. And do bring some nice clothes, if Tristan hasn't scorched them already. Elections are just around the corner."

Mr. Edde abruptly turned a knob, causing a silver-haired Lord Commander Seryth to appear.

"Is she with you?" asked Seryth, pointedly.

"Straight to business, I see." said Mr. Edde, annoyed.

"It's pointless to have it any other way. Is she with you?" demanded Seryth.

Mr. Edde motioned, somewhat grudgingly.

Tye unfastened the wrist straps. He grabbed her arms and shoved her before a camera mounted on a table tripod, holding his dagger just out of view.

She eyed Seryth, wondering how involved *he* was.

"Eliza! Are you hurt?" asked Seryth, sounding genuinely empathetic.

"Don't feign concern, Lord Commander. You're no better than this green-haired sewer rat holding a dagger to my back!"

Mr. Edde chuckled. "And you still want this vermin to live?" he asked.

"She's not vermin!" shouted Seryth. "You'll not refer to her as that ever again; understood?"

"Of course," replied Mr. Edde indifferently. "I hope your personal feelings for this ... traitor... won't interfere with our business."

"She's not a traitor! Once she understands the majesty of our divine efforts, she'll become ... enlightened, as you so aptly say."

"She endangers the entire undertaking and could abscond with our secrets and apprise the World Council of our intentions! She assumed that was the purpose of this flight. She was going to inform them of our Reynan weapon strategy. I don't know about you, but I'd hate for that information to surface prematurely."

"I'll handle her in Navalasta on Election Day. Keep her alive no matter the cost."

"I can't promise that, Lord Commander. In fact, if she becomes a threat, I'll personally slit her throat."

"I'm paying you! You keep your hands off her. That's what it's all about, isn't it; who pays whom?"

"Hmmm .... Most of the time. But I have to keep our future in mind; something you might want to think about as well."

"Don't act so high and mighty. You might be the "Enlightened One," but remember; making an enemy of the Federation could quickly end your rise to power; and you as well. Don't play with fire, Mr. Edde."

"The only fires I play with are ones I control. Have a good day, Lord Commander. I'll see you soon."

Seryth's screen darkened.

"Tye? If you would—please."

Tye yanked at Eliza's arm and dragged her to a corner stool.

"Thank you. If she makes one sound, kill her." Mr. Edde pressed a button and a tight shot of General Braxton's face burst into view.

Eliza gasped. She was so close. If only she could let him know. She flinched against cold steel. Her arms ached from Tye's powerful grip.

"General! So good to see you alive. I heard about the ambush."

She watched Mr. Edde's lips twist into a wide smile.

"It's a good thing you left when you did. Those bastards almost finished us! But we took it to them. We have some damn good pilots!" said Braxton confidently.

"Oh?"

"I owe it all to you," lauded Braxton. "Assigning Foard and Hart to my division was nothing short of providential. And Ashbury, just reinstated to corporal, led the ground forces. You formed quite the team."

"Well, I do what I can," replied Mr. Edde, modestly; his fingers dug into his armrests. "I'm just glad you're safe, dear friend."

Dear friend? That's the last thing Mr. Edde was—a friend. He was incredibly deceptive; completely duping Braxton. How naive was Braxton? Eliza watched dejectedly, as any possibility of hope vaporized.

Braxton's forehead wrinkled. "We're heading north where we'll remain out of sight until this thing blows over. How's Eliza?"

Fear gripped her as the dagger prodded her tender skin. Her stomach tightened.

Mr. Edde softly chuckled. "She's exhausted. Poor thing has done nothing but sleep. But, I assure you, she'll be prepared to deliver her testimony to the World Council."

"Good news. I just hope she can reach Reyna in time to influence election results!"

"We're redlining our engines."

Braxton gleamed. "I'll do my best to keep you updated."

"Yes. Please do." Mr. Edde nodded and tapped his temple.

"Braxton out." The monitor flashed to black.

Mr. Edde's eyebrows lowered; dark lines forming across his brow. A sinister shadow fell over Eliza and Tye. "Transmit that our craft was shot down and that there were no survivors."

Eliza twisted violently. "No!"

"Yes, sir!" replied Tye.

Mr. Edde's mouth twisted. "No one will look for you. You see, dear child, you're already dead."

CHAPTER

32

It was Tristan's first northern Amstynian assignment; he'd always wanted to explore the region, but not during a war. Today, Verdia beckoned. The Sky Wing wasn't an aircraft known for a silky ride; it transferred every bump straight into the pilot's seat; its performance easily compensated for any discomfort. To help keep him sharp, he'd circle the Marne, but generally kept the much larger ship off his port side. Solo flight was a small sacrifice to make in exchange for the thrill of advanced engineering.

Coastal terrain varied considerably. They'd been following it for several hours since it provided the most direct route to Verdia, home to Amstye's fishing industry. The shoreline far below seemed a different world, tan ribbons unfolding, some long and smooth, some craggy, detectable even from this height. Every once in a while, craggy shoals extended into barely discernible white caps. On the increase, white cliffs bordered rich blue waters; the view was breathtaking. Vibrant greens, a painter's dream, reached inland like fingers of a swimming giant as they blanketed northern mountain foothills.

Tristan had seen vacation clips and yearned to discover Amstye's geographical secrets but doubted that he'd have the time. Maybe in another life? The shoreline sped eastward about the same time his navigation system chirped, alerting him of the approaching landing zone's far outer marker and prompting him to begin a steep ascent required to access the high altitude, mountain cleft city of Verdia.

Built on a high plateau, Verdia's outer walls rose from solid stone. If they were gods, the engineers couldn't have created any more space. Between a sheer, outer wall drop-off and an inner mountain barrier were countless pinkish structures. Several smaller ridges had been carved into the ascending mountainside, each populated with more pink buildings. A majestic, red turreted castle straddled a reservoir at the base of an enormous waterfall and marked the inner perimeter's center. Just past, the sheer cliff rose to dizzying heights, its top obscured by clouds. The lake beneath the castle proper released its overflow into a creek winding through the city and outward toward the perimeter. It then cascaded down a sheer precipice, mostly obscured by clouds, and tumbled to the ocean far below. More waterfalls dotted that steep facade and poured their contents, disappearing into wispy clouds caressing the cliff. Clouds and mist softened nature's stark handi-work, synergizing a majestic union with man.

A navigation beacon soon pulled Tristan from his reverie and directed him to the approaching undetectable landing strip. His trained eye located the adobe-colored runway nestled along the northern mountain barrier. He circled while the Marne lumbered downward, out of airspace. Within minutes, both ships were reclaimed by gravity, and Tristan joined his companions. Absent the steady drum of power, the silence seemed deafening.

The main hanger was within walking distance. Braxton led the way, pointing out various aircraft—an SP57; a sleek, swept back fighter/trainer that couldn't hold much ammo, and an Archoy troop carrier; long, wide and boxy. Nearly two dozen assorted vessels were tied down along the hangar's fringes. "This is Amstye's final safe haven. The local government supports Clexor's impeachment. Gotta love 'em. You'll be safe here."

"I'm sad to admit that trust is no longer a plentiful commodity," complained Tristan. "I've been backstabbed more times in the last month than in my entire life." He didn't want to cloud the air with negatives, but he was still troubled over Eliza's situation.

"Get over it," admonished Braxton as they strolled between two huge Amstynian tanks and into the main terminal. "It's how the world works. You'll adapt soon enough. There are still some good people left.

Finding them might be challenging, but what would life be without obstacles? Look behind you." Braxton gestured to Cole, Bailey, and the others.

Tristan paused, eyeing his friends thoughtfully. They had been trailing, not saying much, just staring at rifled-equipped soldiers scattered around the lobby. He reflected on Braxton's harshness, slowly grasping the Amstynian way of life.

"You trust them, don't ya?"

"I do," replied Tristan.

"As long as you have one trusted person … ," he paused for a moment and held up a single, slightly crooked finger, "… you're never alone. Remember that."

Tristan promised himself; it made sense. He had never thought of himself as a victim—that was the loser's way out.

"And here he comes." Braxton motioned ahead.

An officer, a soft billed hat underarm and a tuft of moppy, red hair approached with more guards.

"Don't look at his nose," cautioned Braxton. "It'll distract the shit out of ya."

Too late—it rose like a mountain. An enormously huge knob, with a growth on it as thick as a finger, was impossible to avoid.

The redheaded man's every word flexed his nose perfectly. "General! It's good to see that you're safe. You had us worried!"

"Yeah, yeah. I'm fine. It'll take more than Oxite whores and I6 bitches to knock me off course."

Tristan's suspicions were confirmed. Amstynian soldiers seemed well suited to gruffness. He reflected on Cole, Jase, and Braxton; their mannerisms were strikingly similar. Atlas and Jo's presence were more of a pleasure than he had realized.

The man's nose twitched again. "Yes, sir. Of course, sir. I didn't mean ..."

"The underground Command Center, level four please. Take us! My companions included."

Braxton's sternness highlighted the fact that his request for accompaniment was the exception rather than the rule. What was underground? He remembered caves spouting massive waterfalls;

perhaps there were more mysteries here than first impressions would lead one to believe.

"Sir ... ," stuttered the crimson-headed soldier.

"You see these stars on my jacket?" Braxton jabbed his finger at his padded shoulder. "I have three. How many do you have? Hmmm. Oh, damn, not a one. So do as I say. No more questions. I trust these folks with my life."

A shadow instantly shrouded his facial animation. "Follow me," he mumbled. Ruby strands blew in the cool breeze.

"I know the Neopolis situation seemed dire, but Amstye is far better prepared than you might think. Come. We're wasting precious time." Braxton spun smartly and led the procession onto the tarmac.

Tristan felt nervous and excited, wondering what the underground Command Center held in store. He felt like he belonged here. Their destination sounded enigmatic, definitely displaced from its southern counterparts—nearly impossible access among barren mountains— inhospitable, yet strangely agreeable.

"This is such a beautiful location," said Bailey. "I had no idea. I could write here all day. I mean, the waterfalls, the pure air; it's as close to paradise as I've ever been!"

Atlas sauntered beside Bailey, grunting as she spoke, sniffing the air.

"I could paint another landscape here!" said Jo, running and skipping to keep up, almost out of breath. "Tristan, are we planning to stay awhile? I feel I have procured a cold. The good, clear air will surely bring me back to my healthy self."

"Don't get too comfortable," chuckled Tristan, almost muttering. "Who knows what the general has planned."

"Let's just hope Eliza convinces the World Council," said Cole. "Right now, she's our primary concern. Her efforts could prevent a war."

"What was on that man's nose?" asked Jase.

Tristan glanced the other way, more interested in the sprawling buildings and flurry of activity around him.

✕✕✕✕✕✕

Before long, they had reached the southern airport entry, a small transportation hub lined with several awaiting coaches. Braxton motioned toward a blue streamlined, twelve-seat coach powered by a zyn-fueled engine. It looked more like an ocean yacht than a surface vehicle. After they stowed their gear in the rear compartment, they each took a seat. The craft hummed, rose, and glided effortlessly down the thoroughfare. Tristan settled back and took in the pervasive military atmosphere, mostly low-lying buildings painted a drab, olive green. They stood out against pink everywhere else. Except around main entry doors, there was a noticeable lack of windows.

He enjoyed the shuttle's smoothness, something that only he might notice; it triggered sensations of safety and comfort. There was no lack of personnel walking between buildings; many loitering outside the mess hall. That was one place he'd have to visit, soon. The pilotless coach floated down a nearly vacant side street and edged closer to the mountainside. Tristan pictured it as he had seen it from the air; he recognized most markings—brown and sheer, tall and foreboding, sparkling, pink stone. The road led directly to a heavily fortified entrance—a cave marked with "Entry Prohibited" signs, red circles crossed through with black X's. Three sides, left, right and above, were heavily reinforced concrete fortifications; the actual entrance was a wall of metal, a sliding door, currently open. Beige uniformed guards lined barricaded walkways approaching a security checkpoint. Each held high-caliber Serythrifles.

The shuttle subtly jolted before a drab gray warehouse, slowly settling onto smooth pink pavement. Faint zyn exhaust mixed with fresh mountain air. The side door hissed just as four guards approached, obviously intent on validating the group; Braxton fished for his wallet and flashed a military ID. The guards immediately lowered their weapons and stepped aside so they could pass. The team, unified and in high spirits, headed through the open doors, almost jogging, and into unsuspected coolness. The air felt moist and tasted a tinge salty. There was no sign of water anywhere.

It took a moment for Tristan to adjust to hazy, blue lighting; he tried to imagine what was housed in such a daunting structure. The initial sensation, overwhelming; supported by an extended view that continued so far, he quit straining to detect the end. On a lower level, on both sides, stairs led to lengthy platforms; parallel tracks ran down the middle; a moving platform loaded with green crates crept alongside. Openings were situated between the tracks, beneath which were rooms filled with racks of flashing lights and nearly indistinguishable monitoring personnel. He couldn't focus past that. Above, just shy of a vaulted ceiling, glass enclosed control rooms, like enormous silver eyes, commanded the entire operation. A crane system, like ones used in shipyards to carry cargo containers onto ocean-going vessels, transported crates onto a middle platform.

The surroundings were awash with a dizzying array of activity and sounds. Braxton seemed like a teacher leading his class as they worked their way across platform tracks and down awaiting stairs. They walked for what seemed like forever until arriving at a triple-door elevator. A handful of guards observed from a far wall. Braxton entered several coded strings and waited. When several red lights flashed green, he pressed the open button. They followed him like a brood of ducks; no one seemed anxious, but no one was talking either. The label on the wall read 'Maximum Capacity 30'. Tristan eyed it skeptically.

The slow ride down provided Braxton with plenty of time to indoctrinate the group. "In the strictest confidence, prepare yourselves for what you're about to witness. Not even Mr. Edde has seen these sights—and he never will." He perused their expressions, allowing a moment for his words to sink in. "This covert base was constructed nearly fifty years ago. That means no one, not our allies, including Reyna, and no one outside of the highest echelon of Amstynian officials has a working knowledge."

"President Clexor's never been briefed on its existence. His Jadorian blood renders him untrustworthy, and since I don't tolerate Jadori, I made my men swear to secrecy—he'll never find out. That's a good thing, too. He probably would have stripped the entire facility and sent the scraps to Jador to furnish his palaces. I'm breaking plenty of rules by allowing a Paputa, an Acrolyte, and a Ferian born Institute VI vagabond into our confidence."

A wry grin flashed across his otherwise serious composure—he obviously didn't care. "Fortunately, I can alter regulations when necessary," said Braxton, winking. "Top-dog perks." He chuckled and cleared his throat. "Get ready for the most spectacular sight of your lives."

Tristan's heart pounded. The elevator shaft, initially clad in shimmering aluminum, took on a more rustic feel, exposed dirt and rock. Just when "4" lit, the glass-enclosed room's limited vista exploded into the largest underground cavern Tristan had ever seen. Everyone except Braxton gasped, Jo the loudest. The unfolding sight was mesmerizing. They stood, dazzled and mute. The elevator shuddered, the doors slid open, and Braxton stepped off. No one followed.

Braxton turned and smiled, motioning as if he'd seen this before. The intimidating display of advanced technology made his eyes water.

Airships flew through hazy, bluish-green air. A veritable underground ocean spread as far as Tristan could see, upon which floated hundreds of naval vessels of every shape and size. Piers along land's edge bustled with activity.

In the distance, enormous, sporadically positioned stalactites hung from the endless ceiling. Bridges supporting high speed trams connected the tops of myriad stalagmites jutting out of the sea. Two Sky Wings flew loops above what appeared to be a central transportation depot where three bridges converged. White hot exhaust exited aft. Spellbound, he stared through the mist at an enormously captivating, dark gray craft—a long, cylindrical ship, fitted with innumerable weapon turrets; flashing blue lights encircled the hull—mid, fore and aft—hovering in space and gradually closing in on the central depot.

A long tractor beam, lined with pulsating red lights and an assortment of dangling hoses and pipes, stood ready to receive the technological marvel. Two smaller vessels queued patiently. The sight engulfed his every emotion. He'd never witnessed such advanced, and formidable, technology. He felt like he had been transported to paradise. "Somebody please pinch me!"

Braxton led them high above the waterline, not letting them pass until a fountain of spray had subsided. It had erupted in sync with a high-pitched hum of powerful turbines. The raw energy seized Tristan, giving him pause, drawing him deeper. He couldn't see the cause of the turbulence. Frothy water swirled and churned, and slowly unveiled its mystery. Pungent salt air stung his nostrils. Declegon's Subtrons were familiar enough, long and fat, much like the cigars his father used to smoke. But they paled in comparison to this. The flattened, sleek gray skin of the largest submergible he'd ever seen lurked just at waterline, like an alligator waiting to strike. Rows of yellow lighting, iridescent and eerie, glared through ebbing water. It seemed alive. A long line of observation windows revealed occupants stirring about. Double-winged platforms housing submerged turbines extended fore and aft. The main body of the ship, stretching aft like a tail, was large enough to house hundreds of personnel. When the vessel breeched the surface, aft, vertical turbine-powered thrusters were exposed. Lower level observation ports dotted the foreboding hull.

Cole breathed down Tristan's neck. "I don't believe this!"

Tristan couldn't answer him.

"Yes. She's a beauty," admired Braxton. "Unique only to our military, an underwater carrier. It can carry 25 fighters with full crews. We built it about ten years ago, but she's never been formally introduced to battle. Now that the world's falling to shit, her time has come."

"Incredible," mused Tristan, unable to steady his breathing.

"As far as weapons go, she's the only one of her kind. I don't believe the Federation has ever developed such technology. They've stolen their designs from ocean-going carriers, but nothing underwater. No way. It's an advantage we hope to soon employ. She's called 'DS'."

"What does DS stand for?" asked Bailey.

"Delivery Service." Braxton chuckled under his breath.

"Makes sense," said Jase, grinning wryly.

"We'll hunker down here until further notice. But we have over four hundred aircraft fighters, 32 subtrons, thirteen naval carriers, and one big DS. Too bad we have to keep it all a secret from our own country. But, in the end, this base could very well be our salvation. At any rate, we'll be able to beat the hell out of the Federation."

Tristan was lost in the dream sparked by these marvels. "This is unbelievable. I've never witnessed such ingenuity." He wanted to know everything. He imagined what it would be like flying a Sky Wing through this natural obstacle course. His heart churned with each roll.

"I feel safer outside," said Jo, scrunching his shoulders and peering up at the ceiling.

"What's next?" asked Bailey, smiling at the knee-high creature sporting a wrinkled forehead.

"Well, that depends on ...," started Braxton.

A stubby, red-faced officer approached, shouting and shaking an electronic tablet. "Sir! I have grave news!"

"Calm down, son. No need to scare the children. What's the matter?"

"Sir, we received a USC transmission. Sir, Mr. Edde's ship ... . It was ....."

Tristan's heart fell to the ground. He forgot the DS, the Sky Wings, the cavern, the underwater armada, everything—but Eliza.

"What? Spit it out, man!"

Tristan didn't want the man to spit it out. He wanted to seal his ears and run away. But, like the others, curiosity overcame.

"Federation forces shot it down. No one survived, sir."

Braxton glanced across the water and closed his eyes.

"Dammit!" Cole slammed his fist against a damp cold rail.

"No ... . Not ... ." Bailey's voice quivered.

Jo dropped to the ground beside Bailey, chin in hands. "Eliza? Mr. Edde? But ..."

Jase turned away, putting his hand over his eyes.

Tristan turned back to the open elevator doors.

"Tristan!" Bailey's pointed tone was barely audible above shrill turbine din.

Cole pulled on Bailey's shoulder. "Leave him. Give him his space."

Tristan rushed off, slowing at the landing. Far below, water lapped against the rocks. He fought to compose himself. This was worse than horrible. Eliza? So innocent, so loving, and this was her fate? If only he had been kinder, hugged her when she asked, friendlier, or ... . No, his job had been to protect her. He promised that he would, but failed. He squeezed his eyes shut. What he would give to hear her voice, proving that all of this was a lie—to hear her laugh, to see her smile.

"I know I can be a bit harsh," continued Braxton as he faced the others. "But these are hard times. Our friends will be missed. Pray for vengeance, but remember: the enemy will not stop. We can fully mourn our loved ones when our enemies are dead. I'll be down below. Please join me when you're ready. I'm sorry; so very sorry."

"In the event that Xander is elected, we must be prepared. It's time to switch to Plan 'B'." He turned sharply and continued with the officer across the lengthy bridge.

Cole reached for Tristan's shoulder. "I know you're thinking it's your fault. It's not!"

Tristan trembled. "I was … supposed to protect her … , keep her safe." He couldn't prevent his mother's death, and now this. He didn't know if he could survive another devastating failure. The last time had been nearly impossible to overcome. If it hadn't been for Mawson, he certainly wouldn't have survived, and there would never be another Mawson.

"You did everything in your power. No blame falls on you. If anything, blame the Federation. Braxton said 'vengeance.' They're the ones at fault; the ones we are going to kill. Mr. Edde was at my core; his loss is insurmountable, to both of us." Then Cole turned away.

Jase joined Jo still seated with his face cupped in his tiny hands.

"I'm sorry, Tristan." Bailey's eyes were swollen and misting. "I want to say something helpful."

"There's nothing you can do. I failed her just as I failed my mother and all of Southaven. The Federation has truly stripped me of everything dear. For the pain they've caused us, I'll make them suffer and die, slowly. I swear it." Tristan's shoulders slumped as he fell in behind Braxton.

CHAPTER

33

URSA 24, 1870 O.C.
COUNTRY: AMSTYE
CITY: VERDIA

Guilt engulfed Tristan like a flood. It was his fault that Eliza had died, his firm belief. He could have interceded; should have found another route to Reyna. Of all people, she was so innocent. Passiveness piloted him; his thoughts stagnated into oblivion. Nothing seemed right. This had happened before, but he had beaten it back with youthful optimism and wantonness. Before, clarity would surface after months of pain. Grief, an unwanted companion, relentlessly assailed him.

The tavern proved to be a temporary, but minor, stopgap between the end, and a new beginning that was as elusive as grasping smoke. Soldiers came and went, occupying barstools or tables in dark corners, drinking too much. Pink stone walls sparkled. Bathing sunlight never lasted long enough to be appreciated. A neon sign promoted local brewage. Only one man tended bar, minding his own business unless buttonholed by a chatty drunk. Steaming rolls, meat and casseroles spilled out of the kitchen, but he refused to yield, even though his stomach growled incessantly.

Over and over, he replayed his mother's death, Southaven's destruction, raging fires and Viktor's transformation. Eliza had vanished, but not from his dreams. Any viable reason to continue hoping for her survival no longer existed. He sank deeper still; psychological torment morphing into physical pain. His head throbbed, his joints ached. Pain long forgotten, a childhood shoulder injury and a torn rotator cuff, resurfaced. His hip hurt so badly that he took on a limp. Day after day, he reclaimed his barstool. His tumbler was nearly always full; he frequently lost count. It was the only way to dull his senses. He felt no shame and cared not whether stygian intruders carried him away to some obscure and distant shore. Alcohol dulled him; some days better than others.

A door swung wide; scraping metal against concrete. A world he had been trying to forget charged at him, a light too bright to comprehend. He winced from the glare in the doorway, seeing Bailey's and Cole's outlines.

"Tristan? For Deity's sake, enough is enough! You're going to drink yourself stupid!" said Bailey, planting herself beside him.

"Ah'll do what I wanna do," said Tristan, slurring words. Who did she think she was? There wasn't a soul alive that could relate to his torment, he thought. He reached for his glass.

"Oh, because you're a big boy, right?" demanded Bailey. "This is no way to mourn. You're better than that."

They spoke the same language, but that was it. A journalist, a woman—the last person he wanted to talk to.

"Come and tal' to me when ya lose everyone close to ya, alrigh'?" growled Tristan, drowsily. "You don' know what isslike. Be thankful you don't. But leave us who *do* know... alone." Tristan fished for more words, coming up with none. "Got it?"

Cole discretely motioned. "Leave him be, Bailey. A man has a right to mourn in his own way." He nodded at the bartender. "Give me a cold one. You know what I like. She'll have the same."

Two empty glasses appeared along with two dark brown bottles and slices of lemon stuffed in a tumbler.

Cole emptied his before Bailey touched the liquid to her lips. "The general's planning a supply run to Tibur," said Cole. "You remember that place?" with some sarcasm.

The general? Tristan didn't want to talk business; he didn't want to talk anything. A fuzzy recollection surfaced—rain-soaked streets and Sullivan Byrd's dance hall. Eliza was hot in that dancer's outfit. "How could I forget?" The memory forced clarity, but only for a moment. It felt so good to do nothing but sulk.

"General Braxton assigned Captain Barkley to a weapons acquisition convoy, and put him in charge of transporting military personnel back here," reported Cole. "Our Intel got Amstynian vulnerability documentation that the Federation better not see. Clexor knows all too well that, after the elections, a Federation invasion will be coming. But, true to form, his open diplomacy has compromised his military's secrets. It's like the bastard wanted them stolen. Either way, we'll need some damn good pilots. You in?"

"No." Tristan gripped his glass, wondering what Cole's face would look like soaked in bitter ale.

Clexor was a fool. Rumors of ruinous political undertakings implicated him in untold deaths. The president won't come to Amstye's defense; he's promoting global equality and doing everything in his power to degrade his country's economic and social status to that of neighboring countries. The man's rhetoric infuriated him. How could others support such stupid actions? In less than six years, Clexor had stripped Amstye of its glory, reducing it into generalized poverty and complacency. Tristan slugged down the rest of his drink, and tapped the glass.

"What? What do you mean, 'no'? Ah, I get it. Should have known. I thought I heard thumps—your balls bouncing out the door?"

Tristan slammed down the empty glass. "You serious?"

"Damn right, I'm serious! You planning to give up after the Neopolis' victory? Damn, man. You gotta believe we can do this!"

He wished that Cole and Bailey would vanish—leave him alone. "Eliza and Mr. Edde are dead, Cole! You're a fool! We've already lost!" shouted Tristan.

"Tristan," said Bailey, hushed, hesitating.

A soldier stepped up to the bar and laid down a crumpled fistful of greenish-blue credits.

"Bailey! Don't cover for this dumbass! Eliza and Mr. Edde meant just as much to us as they did to him! I wish we could have done things differently! I never would have left on Mr. Edde's ship! But how was I to know? I can't predict the future. How was anybody supposed to know? You think you're the only one who's lost someone? If that's the case, you're the same selfish prick I met when we blew up that first zyn repository—total victim! The Federation has taken something from each of us! Don't think you're the only one hurting just cuz we ain't crying about it like you! Don't let their deaths be for nothing! Honor them and fight for the freedom *they* stood for!" he shouted, and threw Bailey's glass against the wall, sending shards everywhere, ending the tirade with a frothy exclamation mark.

Jumping from one twisted emotion to another in an effort to untangle Tristan's perilous mental web, Cole's little speech sunk home. Tristan refused to twitch a single facial muscle, but Cole was right.

The angular man, tight white sleeves straining against swollen biceps, slowly revealed a semblance of acceptance, a friend. "The elections are underway. I need to find out what my enemy is saying."

Bailey rested her hand on Tristan's shoulder as he hung over a full glass. The golden liquid shimmered—a reflection of light from the swinging door and wall mirror. "I know he was hard on you, but that's the Amstynian way," she said. "Don't take it personally. He respects you and can't brag enough about your piloting skills. He's right, though. The Federation has robbed each of us. Isn't that why we followed Braxton to this waterfall mecca?"

He couldn't deny that. Her words stung only a little less than Cole's, making it clear that the bite came from their veracity and not their harshness.

"Come on. Let's watch the world vote itself into the toilet," she said.

Words failed him; sanity tugged at the chains of grief holding him to his stool.

Cole's outburst frustrated him; he'd never witnessed that side of him. Friend? Yes, he was. Combat experience had proven him worthy. That was all that really mattered. Bailey's pleas commanded attention. He didn't want to make the same mistake twice. As he swirled his glass, the urge to rise took over.

Enough. Get up and go.

It felt like he had been dragging around ball and chain. The drink's lure was powerful, but he tired of its sway. Bailey gently slipped her hand under his arm and tugged; he followed obediently, squinting into a sunlit, almost blinding, world.

Leaded steps told him that he was more fatigued than he had realized. Sleep usually came easily while on the Marne; maybe tonight? They walked; he stumbled several times while navigating pink stone now crowded with Mess Hall patrons. He kept his face down as they skirted the crowd on the way to the Administration Building's Conference Room. Sky Wings flew practice approaches; the end of the runway was a stone throw's away. The stink of exhaust filled his nostrils and the shrill of screaming engines made his head throb.

All the seats were taken; hundreds of pairs of eager eyes were glued to screens hanging from low ceilings. Tristan spotted Braxton in the fore. He didn't want to be seen this way: unshaven, unkempt, bloodshot, and stinking of neglect. It was awful. He wasn't as lazy as he appeared. He steered Bailey toward Atlas and Jase, the latter nodding as they approached. Jo sat atop Atlas's shoulders, small red hat bobbing, his gaze fixed on Tristan, holding his nose but not saying a word of criticism. Atlas wrinkled his nose. The sound system crackled; at least ten images flashed overhead. A blanketed hush turned the air tense.

The televised crowd began shouting Xander's name. It sounded like the microphones had been stuffed down their throats. In a stiff black uniform, the self-appointed dictator appeared in control as he approached the podium. Glaring lights exposed gaunt cheeks, firm smile and flowing white hair. The satellite signal was being broadcast to every country within range. How would Reyna respond?

Declegon? All of Eshen? Would Xander lie through his teeth, again? The camera panned, capturing General Nyvala's sterile gaze. Tristan's head pounded. The two men shared center stage.

Had the gray-haired Nyvala heard of his daughter's death? Would he even acknowledge that his own men were murderers?

President Drakkar's ghastly visage took center screen. Numbers scrolled on the right—over 150K in attendance—the number continued to climb. The view switched when the crowd roared; the camera slowly scanned a united mass, with right arms extended. Tristan hated that salute. It was a sign of things to come; terrible things. As far as he was concerned, if they elected him, they deserved the ensuing pain. The shot shifted to Xander before white-columned walls covered in Atomian flags—long, red banners and centered, flaming black suns.

The roar faded and Xander began. "My dear Azdahri and most notable allies, today is the grandest of days ... ," Xander was forced to pause; the response was deafening. "... a day to be remembered for centuries to come, inauguration of the Ebonfall Manifesto! It will flourish because of the safety and security secured by Federation might! Today, as promised, Vuton and Atomia will become united!" He paused again. "Let those foolish enough to stand against freedom's might tremble before this imposing alliance!" He pointed, behind and above.

Tristan studied Drakkar; his skin crawled, as when he'd first seen him at the Ball. Ghost-white hair, snowy eyebrows, stoic expression and hollow cheeks created the appearance of a dead man walking. His rigid lips quivered during the applause.

Xander paused, walked over and graciously shook a limp, pale hand. Their eyes locked before Xander reassumed the podium. "President Drakkar has entrusted me to unite all Azdahri and lead the great nation that he worked so hard to create! For his selflessness and undaunted efforts promoting our planet's greater good, honor him!"

Thunder rattled the speakers—hands flashed frenziedly. The camera swept over the crowd and recorded every aspect of the crazed enthusiasm.

"Now, let us begin. I'm sorry, but I should never be regarded as a king. I don't want to rule anyone or anything. I want us, each of us, to work together. People are like that. We should desire collaborative accord in which we enjoy one another's contributions. We must shun discord. In this new realm, there's room for each of us, and for each person's unique contributions to this magnificent future! Our good planet is rich and fertile! Couple that with my revelations and we have the recipe for a utopia—lives free, safe and beautiful. But there are those who would disagree.

"Unfortunately, my fellow freedom seekers, some have lost their way. Self-indulgence has yielded disillusionment in an attempt to spread hate into the outermost reaches of our territories. We have gleaned generations of precious insight from our history and will apply these insights to become great again.

"Be forewarned—this same insight offers a darker side, harboring the potential for absolute anarchy. While we press forward, it forsakes empathy, patience and goodness. Without such virtues, we risk kneeling at hatred's profane altar—with countless others.

"To you, my astute attendees, I warn you—do not surrender to our adversaries' greed. This darkness will pass from this time and from our enemy's sorry countenance. We must bitterly oppose the animosity from those who fear humanity's inevitable advancement. Even now, my voice is reaching the desperate, perhaps millions—men, women, and children—sufferers, under a cruel system responsible for imprisoning precious innocents.

"Eshen, our home, now harbors barbarism! Amstynians defy their own president and intend to destroy dreams clung to by guiltless citizens. They flail with deliberation! And what of their ally, Reyna? Are they not the ones who seek to thwart providential advancement? Do not fear a dying society's remaining death throes.

Again, the crowd's adulation was deafening, slowly subsiding.

"Good people. Close your ears to slavers' promises! This foul trade will only enfeeble us and has no place among us. I have defended you against USC terror and fortified Amstynian borders, but we must forever be vigilant! Absolute power promises national encroachment inconceivable! Anyone who would dare stand against us *will be destroyed*!

"Can you now embrace as I do, love for country, freedom, and future?

"Join me! We have the power to embark on a breathtaking voyage to liberation…and glory!

"May the World Council see the Ebonfall Manifesto as divinely inspired, a floodgate into a new world! No matter the cost, we will deliver to our youth a bright future, complete in enduring freedom and security. Let us enhance humanity by revering scientific reason! Let us progress ever further into the Promised Land! In the name of liberty… UNITE!"

This set off a tumult rivaling any other speech's applause, thunderous.

Tristan, burdened by his grief, was lulled into the agony of despair. He couldn't forget Eliza, but at least she wouldn't be forced to witness this process of global unraveling. This was the beginning. The others present surely sensed war's foreboding specter.

What a sorry excuse for a leader. And yet he leads.

Braxton grabbed a microphone; the speakers banged loudly. "Let that bastard try to come here with his New World Order! We'll be ready!"

Despair rolled over Bailey's face like dark clouds. "It's started," she mumbled. "I can't believe it's actually happening. World war is inevitable—no escape."

He strained to hear her, wanted to say something. "It started a long time ago," replied Tristan, doubting. "People are just now being exposed to this pseudo-reality."

Would they comprehend this folly in time? What about Reyna? They stood against the Federation, but how long could they defy this power-hungry soon-to-be tyrant? Why weren't more attempts made to block Xander's rise to power? Too many unanswered questions. Tristan craved a role in Xander's defeat, but an even greater battle loomed, his own personal firestorm. He needed to sit down.

On the center stage, Xander and the others shook hands. The crowd's roaring drove toward a deafening crescendo.

The soundman disconnected the satellite feed, instantly filling the room with silence.

Tristan scanned the room, now in complete stillness. It was somber, quiet; yet the reality of potential war and world domination had taken root. Bewildered minds watched, unmoving, waiting perhaps for better news, or a leader, or maybe some kind of 'out'? But whatever they sought, hundreds of pale faces now endured a new kind of pain—servitude's inevitability.

CHAPTER
34

Eliza watched guardedly, just waiting for the glass to shatter. Window glass flexed, deformed, and this one looked like it was ready to go. Across the room, plate glass contracted like it was a breathing membrane; outside, invisible assailants pounded, scraping and clawing to reach her, howling like dejected pups when refused. She could just imagine wild beasts, demons from her past, hunting her down and finishing her off.

The first day had been the most frightening; she skirted them with a deliberate arch on the way to the bathroom. After a week, she worried less and less, eventually venturing closer for a better look down. She was on the 85th floor of the Valkyrie Tower, an unsettling height for someone who preferred to have her feet planted firmly on the ground. She remembered the name, an important government building that housed questionable branches of military and civilian deviants. It was impossible to feel happy as a prisoner. In fact, she was convinced she was going batty—solitude tended to do that, especially with no idea how long this confinement would last. She'd give anything for a clue as to what to expect, and a satellite phone.

Bleary beige walls, beige carpeting with little brown specks, and no entertainment only added to her frustration. Meals were delivered three times a day, boring grains and overcooked meat, never any sauce, and always cold, and no plants. Breakfast was the worst, two eggs that chewed like rubber, and a piece of crunchy toast. Funny how she craved something sweet.

A single cot, dark green military style, two chairs and a pale green table furnished the room, more like a prison cell. At least she had a pillow and a private bathroom. This building was supposed to be the tallest in the city, an astounding mass of swaying concrete and shimmering glass. The second day, it vibrated terribly; she thought it was coming apart. Navalasta, Atomia's second largest city, was overpopulated. Flying vehicles of all shapes and sizes sped along invisible skyways—dagger-shaped, circular and flat, rectangular, gray with flashing red lights; countless double-seated pods crowded the skies like aimless flocks of birds. Where were they going? At least the view, cheap amusement, broke the monotony.

Navalasta's buildings were ceaseless reminders of Xander's Atomian ideals. Yesterday's speech, his most disturbing yet, still rang loudly. Were the world's masses really that ignorant? He seemed unstoppable. The World Council members certainly had tuned in, but she couldn't reach them anyway. As far as she was concerned, she had failed. Mr. Edde was the real traitor, though—eyes and ears everywhere—and had successfully secreted her to this remote sky-cave. Tristan would never find her here. Senator Galik was her only hope; but, as far as the world was concerned or knew, she was dead. A small radio droned on, no music, one political talking head after another.

Hallway footsteps keyed her, not unlike at mealtime, but it was too early for that. The lock clicked, the latch lifted; she eyed the door warily. Her pulse jumped, only somewhat surprised when Seryth entered. His presence frayed what was left of her constitution; her skin chilled and kept her planted, cross-legged, under the window. "Seryth," she said, her voice numb and complacent.

He pulled at the sides of his platinum hair, not discretely. "Please, dear."

She hated when he said that.

"I believe first names are more appropriate, don't you? I've known you since you were a child."

She would never trust that deep voice again, the antithesis of comfort and hope. If only there was something she could throw at him. The chair was too awkward, but it would have made a point.

"How could I forget?" she retorted. "I see that nothing's changed!" Her gaze dragged along the carpet, listless and unwilling to interact.

"My dear Eliza. Please! Let's remain civil. Perhaps I come bearing good news?" He spread his hands wide—a gesture of peace, and kicked the door shut.

His nails were perfectly manicured, oddly in character. "There's nothing civilized about you or your convoluted aspirations! You're no less transparent than Sovereign Xander. Don't think that I can't figure out your contemptible intentions."

"Calm down, Eliza. He's *your* sovereign too."

"*Your* sovereign; not mine, never mine."

Shouting back would have felt so good, but what lasting benefit would it bring? Already worn down, smugness seemed prudent. She might need her energy later.

"I thought you were a staunch freedom advocate. From whence cometh such venom?" he chided, a hint of mockery under shaded regard. "Sounds like you've been negatively influenced. At any rate, I miss your more docile days."

"I've been enlightened." A dour reply prompted by the latest run-in with Mr. Edde.

"By what?"

She forgot how much he enjoyed worthless banter. "By knowing that the Ebonfall Manifesto exists for one, and only one, reason, to empower the Sovereign to control the Azdahri future," she replied. "It ultimately empowers extreme appropriation ideals; theft of livelihoods and freedoms, need I remind you, globally. Just exactly where does that leave the rest of us?"

"So, you are aware of Ebonfall," he stated candidly. "Very few are privy to the details. Consequently, you are mindful of something far beyond what most could hope to understand. But you don't grasp Ebonfall's exhaustive scope.

My sweet Eliza, only I stand between you and death. The Atomian Supreme Authority views you a threat capable of crippling the new order. I have attempted to dissuade some, but will be unable to stop the inevitable. Even so …," he lightly sighed, "… I do bear good news; we've reached a compromise. In one week, you'll be extended, let's say, an opportunity for validation. Are you open to … a station within Ebonfall's ranks?" He pressed his fingertips together, piously, and folded his hands before his chest. "If you aren't, you'll be exterminated. That would be dreadful, wouldn't it, especially considering how intelligent, and … beautiful, you are?"

His suggestive manner crawled on her skin like an onslaught of marching ants. On one hand, death; on the other, him. Death beamed like a lighthouse against a blackened sky. His perverted infatuation was covertly esoteric even though it had been a constant haunt throughout childhood. Twelve years her senior, he had transformed into one of the most ruthless men she'd ever known. Even Galik was frightened of him.

"Why just me? Why not include the rest of the world? Why just Azdahri? If people *were* privy to the truth, such barbarism would be obvious to any casual observer."

He continued. "Have you ever truly studied an Azdahri, in depth? Take me, for instance. I stand tall and represent an expression of victory, not because I choose to, but because of my natural facial structure. Azdahri have glowing skin richly supplied with blood, pristine hair as white as snow, and lightly shaded eyes set ever so strongly in their sockets. They are flawless, a perfect complement to a perfect body. We are humanity's esteemed race. You, Eliza, have been half-blessed—some Azdahri blood flows in your veins."

Burnished eyes and paled skin transformed him into a sculptor's dream.

She'd never seen him in such a …, she couldn't quite uncover the sense, … calloused state. And to think he was Atomia ruling class. His heart was cold, frozen. She wasn't half-blooded by choice; at least she didn't look like *them*. She treasured her mother's contributions, hazel eyes and soft, bouncy, *dark* hair. Not a day passed that she wouldn't glean at least one awkward Azdahri stare. Even the room steward had stared crassly over the food tray.

"And you believe Xander can solve the world's problems?" she asked rhetorically, accepting the folly of her compromise.

"Show proper respect. He's sovereign and you'll refer to him as such. However, that title is so lacking; in the near future, we'll bestow one far more meaningful. To answer your question, yes. I fully embrace his revolution. I serve him selflessly—service for a majestic ideal. Do you not comprehend how disassociated we are from our ancestors? He's researched their coded intellect like no other. Our people were once regarded as deities when they ruled the entire planet! They maintained complete rule and authority! Sadly, we yielded; first to other nations' cultures, and then to their ideals—civilization's poison! Over time, these subversions wrought havoc. Oh, how great and pure our ancestors were. You must understand that I want to help you." He held out a worn, red book, cracked and stained.

She hesitated, wanting no part of his offering. He waited with hand outstretched, eventually compelling her.

"Within these few pages lies untold wisdom, intelligence vital to our way of life," said Seryth, monotone. "It will comfort you." His voice flattened. "Books like these enlighten me, soothe me. But, I've said enough. I'm a chatter box and, you know me," he said coyly. "Sometimes I overstep my boundaries—shamefully immature thoughtlessness. Trust me. This book will answer your questions." He paused to brush at some lint on his trousers. "I do beg you to try to delve into its depths." His skin glowed even whiter, ghostly; his hair seemed covered in frost.

"My mother told me to avoid dirty magazines. I bet the only way you got through it was by 'delving' into a lot of nasty pictures. You have all the intellect of a speed bump. Thanks but no thanks."

"You are quite insolent, eh?"

"How can there be any room for me in this Ebonfall?" she asked, shifting quickly from the red cover to Seryth. She'd never seen his features transform so abruptly. "I'm a half-breed." A spark of passion jumped within, which she quickly subdued.

"You've been blessed with some perfect blood. This means everything. For you, childbearing is strictly forbidden, of course. For propagation, we require pure blooded, Azdahri women. But there are men who would agree to take you for their own. See, you *do* have a role! My offer is simple—power and wealth. Never again be self-conscious.

Children are not in my future; my only desire is to share what I have built for our great people…, with the woman of my dreams."

A personal strumpet? Aghast, she flinched at a hammer pounding away at a coffin's nails; hers. The window was sealed; guards lined the hallway. Her heart raced; she cried within, to be free of this leering tyranny.

"Our lives together would be so lovely and marvelous. We'd enjoy pure, unadulterated love of body and soul. Filth would not exist."

"You are delusional! You speak of love, yet you arranged my kidnapping, at knife point, no less! The Enlightened One! Is that his definition of love? 'Love me or I'll cut your throat?'"

"The Enlightened One is expendable. It was the only way I could rescue you. You must understand …."

"Rescue me! No! I understand completely! You're a criminal—one of many!"

"Lower your voice," hissed Seryth.

"I'll not lower my voice or appease you in any way!"

Eliza sprang up, her agility garnering a stroke of confidence and a touch of lightheadedness. "My father and the entire world may be blind; but I'm not!" she shouted defiantly, straining her desire for Tristan's presence. Her heart ached in her throat. She felt doomed. "I'm well aware of what you're trying to pull off."

"Shut up!" he yelled angrily.

Convinced of his ulterior motives, Eliza shielded her ears. Muffled dread intensified as she slowly collapsed on the carpet. She wrapped her arms around her knees, pulling them tightly to her chest.

"I'm the *only* reason you're still alive!" he hissed.

Maybe no one else was on the 85th floor. He'd never expose such malice otherwise. His words struck at her like frozen rain. "My Federation obligations are to campaign for the Sovereign's message. I'll return in a week; and by then, I'll expect you will have come to your senses. If not, be prepared to face the consequences." His jaw tightened as he turned away.

At the lock's click, Eliza sprang from the floor. There was no longer a good reason to hold it together. She pounded the door for as long as her strength allowed. In time, she had no idea how much, she finally collapsed, wrenching knees to chest, rocking and weeping.

Tristan would never find her. He likely wasn't even looking for her. She'd never acquiesce to Seryth's stupid little red book or his crazed rhetoric, which meant only one thing—she'd be dead in a week.

CHAPTER

35

His past would covertly rise into his consciousness, thriving on his guilt and feelings of helplessness. Tristan fought back, one drink at a time. An easy decision; he didn't care what others thought and had learned to manage an ideal prescription, 15 minutes from the moment the elixir touched his lips, mind numbing forgetfulness was flowing through his veins. Tormenting flashbacks held him prisoner, maintaining their own debilitating schedule, worming into everything; soiling thoughts, decisions, and dreams.

On a practice flight, in his mind as a helpless spectator, he witnessed Viktor destroy his home town like it was the first time. Flames, smoke and the stench of death seemed so real that Barkley had to cite him for a near-miss midair collision. The incident shook him so badly that his flight suit was drenched, causing him to shiver during the walk to the tavern. He surveyed the clubhouse, musty from years of spilt sorrows and stifled ambitions. The bartender was courteous—his bar clean and well stocked—and knew the importance of topping off patrons' glasses. Pink walls and an empty bar seemed duller than usual. The neon sign hung silent and dark. Cole's little fling had probably broken it. Amstynian whiskey worked almost as well as pain meds and was far more effective than a string of beers but didn't filter out nearby flight deck commotion.

The tavern windows had become Tristan's reality portals. Brakes screeched, spewing smoke. Men shouted; ground vehicles scuttled precariously between pallets and fuel tankers. Tibur's supply convoy, a fleet of twelve craft, performed their run-ups at the far end of the taxiway. Strangely, he was lured outside, a sensation he associated to a priest breaking sacred vows.

Xander's speech had upset him but wasn't entirely provoking. He couldn't deny that the Federation was more formidable than he initially thought. What could Amstye accomplish on its own? Then it hit him. Letting his friends down would only make him more miserable. He couldn't sulk forever.

He skirted parked shuttles and made his way to a cluster of Sky Wings. Jase, his spiked blond hair easy to spot, knelt on a wing; refueling hose in hand. He slowed, wondering if he'd made the right decision, still bruised from Cole's confrontation.

"We could really use your help," said Jase. "In fact, I'm in need of a high-caliber wingman." He eyed him with doubt; his lips gaped as if to free another comment.

Cole, burley and silent, eyed him from an adjacent fighter.

"Your commitment seems overdone," replied Tristan, squinting at the sunlit sky. If he allowed his decisions to be based on feelings, he'd never leave the tavern. "I thought you had enough sense to recognize the inevitable."

"We're not *all* cowards," said Jase, retraining the fuel nozzle.

That smarted. He'd just as soon return to lifeless pink and neon than face this, but he wasn't a coward; Jase didn't understand. Flying into a senseless battle was paramount to suicide. "I didn't think making an intelligent decision was cowardly."

"Dammit, Tristan! Get over yourself. Don't you dare say that these selfless men are foolhardy! Their loyalty demands respect!"

"You're right. I'm sorry," apologized Tristan, feigning humility and caught off-guard by the impromptu response. "I don't know what's gotten into me."

"Alcohol, a shit ton of it too. Anyway, you're useless like this. Don't know why I'm even bothering." He sighed. "Take care of yourself, Tristan. I hope you find purpose in your deity-forsaken life."

He was right, but was it too late? "Jase ..." stammered Tristan.

Jase glanced up, appearing more interested in the fueling operation.

Tristan wavered, struggling to come up with a response. "Be careful out there." He wanted to feel important, needed, but tumbled down the slippery slope of rejection.

Jase dropped down the ladder and attached the nozzle. He seemed so confident. Desperation returned as Jase re-positioned the cart. Tristan loathed defeat; it clung like a wet robe.

Braxton, ducking under the dagger-shaped nose, suddenly appeared. "No point worrying. You could join them and ensure their safety," he remarked, gently tracing his finger along the fuselage.

Tristan flushed. "I failed Eliza and couldn't bear one more. I need to say my 'goodbyes.'"

A Sky Wing screamed past on a go-round, drowning him out.

"What plans have you made?" asked Braxton.

The query surprised Tristan. Was this a question he should have expected from someone who could probably see right through him?

"None, really. I don't know what I'll do but I'll figure out something. I always do."

"It's not my style to harbor bad feelings. I'm thankful for the support you provided at Neopolis. You're a damn good fighter and everyone knows it." Braxton extended his hand. "Please take care of yourself, Tristan."

He wondered if he should return the shake—or salute. "Thank you, General," he replied, his voice lost under another flyby.

XXXXXX

Refueled Sky Wings were being lowered into the top-secret cavern via a descending flight deck large enough to manage two at a time. Tristan jumped onto the platform just as distant aircraft concluded their warm-ups. "Deafening" silence gave way to the pleasant sound of cascading water against huge boulders.

Tristan had seen it from the air. He didn't want to take part in the looming war, but wasn't sure what to do or where to go; perhaps Aurelia? No, too religious and antiquated. Declegon? No, too cold and fabled. Reyna was the closest and best choice, but the Federation would probably target it first. To hide was cowardly and confining—none of these choices would work.

Moving up a maze of gray-painted stairs lit by bright fluorescent lights, he made his way to the communications level. Commandeering the Marne seemed the best option, but he had to say goodbye to his friends. Bailey and Atlas had been good companions, and he wasn't really keen on leaving them hanging. The radio room just around the corner was her favorite hangout. She said it helped her feel more in touch with the outside world.

Her voice rose above the clatter. "You're the most illustrious fool I've ever met!" An argument between Bailey and Jo, painfully tense, was underway. "How could you possibly think of traveling alone? And by what means? You can't fly; you're not a pilot!"

"I'm not a coward either! I'm sensitive!" pleaded Jo. "That's because of the artist in me. I'm not as weak as you believe! You know better than anyone that I've managed myself out of more than a few scuffles."

"Jo! Listen to yourself!" barked Bailey, nervously. "We don't even know who's responsible for this transmission! It reeks of entrapment!"

"The commander said it was intercepted!" replied Jo. "We weren't meant to know! Maybe that's a blessing in disguise?"

"It's not a blessing at all. It's pure madness. Even with your usual begging, you'd never enlist any sane pilot."

Tristan listened with some degree of ambition, wrestling curiosity and scheming enough to break a sweat. What transmission was Jo referring to? *He* could fly Jo wherever he wanted to go.

"I'll bribe someone!" continued Jo. "Maybe, Tristan?"

"No! He's leaving! Remember? Plus, with as much as he's been drinking, I don't think you'd want him flying you anywhere."

"I'll take a drunken pilot! I must secure passage somehow! With the right incentive, surely, he won't refuse. All he has to do is sober up."

Staring at the dull paint, alone and restless, his moodiness resisted quelling; haze clung like morning fog, sure signs of imminent defeat—but he would not abandon his favorite friends.

"No, and don't you dare ask!" demanded Bailey. "He's been through enough and your request would only make it worse!"

"He's a grown man," said Jo, with furrowed brow, "… and can fend for himself."

"Urgh! You've been sucked into the Amstynian attitude more than I realized."

Jo sounded so tall. Tristan chuckled when the knee-high creature asserted himself. Jo made him feel differently, somewhat agreeable, if not quite ready to face the unknown.

"My people need me!" yelled Jo.

"You don't …."

Tristan lifted his head and choked down his pride. "Uh, hello," he stammered meekly, managing to sound somewhat innocent as he entered. "Why are you arguing?"

"Tristan?" said Bailey, eyebrow raised.

Jo jumped up and down, waving his arms. "Tristan! Please help me," he shouted. His ears twitched excitedly. "You arrived in the nick of time! The Comms team intercepted a coded Federation broadcast and I find myself completely compelled to act!"

"You're reading too much into this, Jo!" said Bailey, rolling her eyes impatiently.

"An intercepted broadcast is generally not trustworthy," cautioned Tristan. "The intended sender and receiver are unknown—highly suspicious. If it were me, Jo, I'd blow it off."

"Subject Six!" Jo panted.

"What?" exclaimed Tristan, his pulse quickening. "That's Viktor's code name."

Jo gleamed as if he'd hooked a huge fish. "I know where you can find him!" he said, reeling in the line.

"Jo! That's enough!" snapped Bailey, not lightly. "Tristan, don't take anything he says seriously. He doesn't think clearly when he's upset."

"Wait," said Tristan, holding up his hand. "Let him continue."

Jo promptly expounded. "The intercepted broadcast described an abandoned scientific facility in Feria. A remote outpost until recently; it was converted into an experimentation complex. Paputas are confined in immense test tubes as subjects of ghastly experiments! Scientists, intent on discovering our magical properties, dissect them and analyze their organs! They are desperate to discover our Grand Master's secrets; they want his portraits and think that they'll learn the art of time travel! But his location is secret! If they could have, the Federation would have already found him. Can you imagine them controlling the most powerful military the world has ever seen *and* time travel? You must help me, Tristan! Save my race!" Tears pooled along Jo's tiny eyelids, spilling onto his red vest.

"And what about Viktor?" asked Tristan. "I mean, Subject Six?" He was enraptured by the thought. What an unexpected turn of events. Finally, something was going his way. The furry being before him was the most potent lure to a new life he could have hoped for. Tristan would fly him wherever he wanted to go.

"The Federation found him, Tristan. Subject Six is in a coma and confined to that abandoned complex. I know that you want to learn the truth about the man who destroyed Southaven. Please, help me save my people! Think about it!"

Tristan glanced at Bailey. "I'm in," he said.

"Tristan … ," said Bailey, alarmed, sounding like a mother scolding a child.

Tristan kept his focus on Jo, drinking from the bottomless well of vengeance. If his gaze reached Bailey's, she'd power him down. This was his chance to bring closure to an old and ruinous story.

Jo was elated. "Excellent! Thank you so much! If I owned a fortune, I'd cede it to you! I must gather warmer apparel." He jumped to the shiny, gray floor and skipped into the hall; his tiny red hat bobbing uncontrollably.

"You don't know what you're getting into," warned Bailey. "We don't know if the transmission was contrived!"

"What do we have to lose? Think about it," said Tristan. His confidence had returned. Plus, he'd already committed to the most creative being he'd ever met.

"Tristan! How can you talk like that?" chided Bailey. "You're not only endangering yourself, but Jo too! Paputas are nearing extinction!"

"What if his race *is* in trouble?" asked Tristan.

"You don't really care about them, do you? You just want Viktor. You know I'm right. Don't pretend to care for others when your ultimate goal is killing Viktor."

"You want to give me a hard time? Go ahead! Everyone else does!"

"I just don't understand why …"

Tristan leaned in closer, able to catch a faint whiff of her perfume. "You're right; you don't get it! Quit pretending that you do! Viktor ruined my life. He robbed me of everything I valued! I'm where I'm at today because of him—a ruthless mercenary, a killer. Those are the only things I know! My future is ruined. If I could have saved Eliza, things could have changed. Since Southaven, maybe for once I finally could have done some great things. But that failed too.

If Viktor is unconscious and in one of those tubes, ending his life would be delightfully uncomplicated. Nothing would make me happier than seeing him dead!" His ceaseless anger had finally found an outlet. He'd questioned the rage before, but never really understood it. Now, he did.

He hated Viktor. No one should be allowed to cause such devastation and live to gloat. Thoughts of possible relief surfaced as he imagined delivering the killing blow to the man who had destroyed his life and family.

After a deliberate pause, Bailey searched his eyes but continued to resist. "… It won't free you, Tristan. You'll be driven deeper! You're blind if you think otherwise."

"You'll never understand," replied Tristan, buoyed by self-discovery and confidence as he turned to leave. Leaving on such a sour note saddened him.

"Wait!" said Bailey. "If you're actually going to do this, I'm coming too. And, so is Atlas."

"That's ridiculous," replied Tristan. His heart raced again. They would only get in the way, or would they? He could imagine them helping, doing something, anything. It seemed right but he didn't want to admit it. "I don't need your help."

"We're not going there to help you. We're going there to help Jo. I know your priority will be Viktor. Someone has to look after that defenseless Paputa."

There was nothing more to say. She had him. He couldn't look after everyone. Consuming thoughts formed his purpose—Viktor's trail of destruction would come to an end.

CHAPTER 36

Tristan left Bailey, Jo and Atlas and the clatter of dishes and food prep, in the captain's galley, narrow and definitely not roomy enough for four souls, and poured himself into the pilot's seat. Someone could bring him a snack later.

It felt good to be back, but, at best, tolerably confining. Autopilot allowed only minor corrections; nothing was perfect. Like pouting children, aches and pains demanded attention, but sleep would have to wait. Droning engines were his magic carpet most of the time; but today, familiar sensations ventured into uncharted territory. Viktor and Southaven's destruction played in Tristan's mind vividly, like an endless video loop. Revenge simmered, captivating or bewitching, depending on the moment. Whether good fortune, or doom, he planned to end his night horrors and Viktor's rampages. Eliza's death proved more potent than refined zyn; he wouldn't yield, no matter the obstacles. Waiting was as intolerable as the senseless devastation; each required compensation. The real question was which one would win.

The area chart showed that they were nearly on top of the facility. Relief would be swift. Be smart, careful; stay determined. He had to look to himself for support, approval, and, of course, the obvious element, courage. Busying himself would keep him distracted, so he reached for the landing checklist.

Marne's transponder system falsely announced to the world that the vessel was a recreational shuttle. No one paid attention to those, as long as they couldn't see them. Security was supposed to be lax, so the set-up seemed ideal. He scanned panels of flashing lights, switches and digital readouts, and listened for customary sounds. No disruptions—everything appeared in order; he trusted his senses as much or more than any computer. Subtle floor vibrations indicated engine health. Smooth glass and metal skin whisked through the atmosphere, jettisoning faint reminders, a negligible rush of power and presence. They had stowed enough weaponry and munitions to arm a large squad of well-armed troops. He double-checked the transponder settings over the sparsely-populated forest region. Enormous pines tucked the facility away like a giant holiday wreath; small rivers its ribbons. Overcast skies muted their arrival somewhat, but nothing could completely conceal Marne's screams.

He and Bailey donned protection—reinforced mesh for torsos paired with half sleeved, olive drab, fiber-impregnated shirts and trousers, black gloves and caps. Not perfect, but more than adequate for a team of nerdy scientists. Atlas went for a high-powered rifle with scope, hefty and best suited for long range firing, still looking rather small in his clawed hands. It might be a little too much for inside work; Tristan doubted they'd need that much power, but, hey, just in case, what the hell. Better to have it and not need it than need it and not have it. The lion-headed sphinx sprouted a toothy grin and worked through the bolt actions; he appeared unstoppable. Lions frightened people, especially ones with tremendous manes and fangs standing on two feet. They mirrored the sun, both in splendor and awe-inspiration. Tristan's confidence swelled.

The autopilot began chirping frantically; Tristan scanned the displays—nothing suspicious. Radio broadcasts, mostly fragmented transmissions from local flights, weren't uncommon. Nonetheless, he ran through the abort protocols. Better safe than sorry; he could always come back around. A cloudy mist fell like moon dust, delicately blanketing the landing area and facility. Gray skies affected his mood just like when he was a child and made him feel a bit lethargic above the lifeless outpost.

The Marne slowly nestled between two horizontal, tube-shaped silver structures. In a former life, they might have been troop shuttles. Turbines' housings, jutting from the ends and tarnished black, were smattered with dark green ivy. So much vegetation made the area appear like a rain forest. Trees towered, too many species to identify, a stone's throw from the intruding campus. When spray from superheated water dissipated, he radioed that they were delivering another Paputa. Rain began to fall, splattering against the windshield. So dreary. Jo was to be used as "bait," an idea concocted by Bailey. Tristan didn't want anything to do with it. The main facility door parted, discharging two black-uniformed guards. Tristan eyed their rifles warily from the aft ramp.

"You must be Gango Consway," quizzed the forward guard. His portable radio blurted something unintelligible; he adjusted the volume.

"I am," replied Tristan tersely, unwilling to relinquish any semblance of control.

"Where's the Paputa?"

"Behind me," replied Tristan, disturbed by the man's insensitivity. "Just get inside."

Jo's forehead crumpled as he silently approached with cuffed wrists.

"Follow me," barked the guard, motioning behind him. "Professor Godwin has been expecting you. He'll approve your reward, but then you depart…immediately."

"Thank you," replied Tristan, glancing at Bailey, hoping that the rest of their tenuous plan would transpire so smoothly. Jo seemed so small and helpless; his wrists were no bigger than Tristan's thumbs.

One of the guards clipped a collar to Jo's neck and turned toward the entrance. The thin tether hung limply, dragging on the ground when Jo ran to keep up.

The building's interior was anything but abandoned, furnished with state-of-the-art lighting and chromed furniture so sterile it appeared ultra-modern and out-of-place. Tristan whiffed fresh glues and plastoids, and death's fetor. The latter reeked of vinegar; pungent, sour. Someone had dumped a lot of credits into this place. He soon realized the reality of what lay before them while staring at a spherical grid loaded with hoses, small tubes and such, connected to large cylinders containing Paputas suspended in some thick solution. They didn't move and there were no air bubbles coming from the hapless beings in the dense liquid. Blue lights, evenly spaced, ran down the wall, causing the room to shimmer like water in a sunlit lagoon.

He blocked Jo's view, fearing his reaction. They passed a huddled collection of unarmed scientists scrutinizing piles of ringed binders; their gray-edged, white coats creating the air of anonymity. With only one guard posted down the long hallway, it seemed that the minimum-security assumption had been correct. No one eyed them with suspicion except the silent guard beside Jo. Atlas signaled, a hasty nod aimed down the hall, when they turned into the blue room. Closer observation revealed obscure shadows, more than Paputas, but the tangles were perplexing in the obscurity. The room embodied death.

A scientist with dark splotches under his eyes extended a hand. "I'm so glad you've arrived! I apologize, but I doubt that I'll be able to conceal my excitement for this new specimen." He knelt and scrutinized Jo. "Thank you, kind …" He tried to stroke Jo's arm, but Jo growled and jerked back.

His enthusiasm absolutely contradicted his demeanor.

The time had arrived.

Tristan hefted his Droth and blasted the two escorts. Blood and bullets sprayed the wall and their bodies dropped like rag dolls. That was fast.

Atlas covered the room's back entrance, firing down the hall, dropping the lone guard before he had time to turn. The gun blast was deafening. He activated a door pad—a powerful hiss ruptured overhead—and sealed them in the blue room.

The scientist's brushed back white-hair exposed a high forehead. He shouted and jumped, stumbling from a listless leg. "What's the meaning of this?" he shouted nervously, grabbing counter's edge.

Bailey steadied her gun. "Oswald Godwin! How nice to finally meet you. You've gained tremendous popularity with the Federation. I see that you're still conducting grisly unethical experiments," she said, slowly tipping the barrel between his now saucer-sized eyes.

"Who are you?" demanded Godwin. "What do you want?"

From behind Atlas, Jo meekly asked, "You … . What have you done to my people?" It was higher pitched than usual. He ran over to the outsized, rotating grid filled with crowded tubes and whirled around, wagging a defiant finger. "What atrocities have you committed—my people?"

"Listen, I don't know what you want, but … ," began the scientist obstinately.

Tristan released the safety. "You'll provide everything we ask. Refuse and kiss your legacy goodbye!"

"You're with the Amstynians!" shouted Godwin, seething in the quickly developing predicament. You'll never leave here alive!"

"And neither will you if you don't shut up!" retorted Tristan, scanning the far wall and wondering where they had hidden Viktor. He had to be close. "What are you doing to the Paputas?" He was more interested in how he'd destroy that nightmare of a man than the Paputas, but still needed to get his bearings.

"You can't do this! Who do you think you are, barging in here and … ," demanded Godwin, ignorant cockiness flaring with reddened vengeance.

Bailey wheeled her gun against his skull. The impact cracked loudly, sending a stream of blood down his face.

"Owh!" groaned Godwin, gripping his head and staggering forward. "How dare you!" His lips moved again but no words followed when he sunk to his knees.

Tristan grabbed Bailey's arm. "Easy. Not yet. Make sure he stays conscious."

"I have a more effective method of extracting information," said Bailey, eyeing him slyly. "Access the central server. I want to know every secret your silly-assed team is hiding!" She jammed the muzzle into his jaw; loose facial skin wobbled. "… and I don't have all day… tick, tick, tick."

"All right! All right! Please don't hit me again," pleaded Godwin, wincing and recoiling.

"Good," said Bailey.

Godwin scrambled to his feet, confused, and dawdled with a keyboard. He typed, glanced around and waited. Eventually, dual displays began streaming, pausing every few seconds.

"Excellent. Thank you, my good professor. I'm in, guys," exclaimed Bailey enthusiastically, eyeing the screen dump. "I can upload this data to Braxton's server." She quipped. "We'll soon know all of your dirty little secrets. Atlas! If he tries to escape, rip his heart out, after you tear off his balls."

The lion man growled and leveled his rifle. As he shuffled closer; Godwin flinched, threw one hand over his heart and the other over his crotch.

"What are they doing to my people?" asked Jo frantically.

"Hold on, Jo. This file might have the answer," said Bailey.

Tristan, rather pleased by Bailey's digression, suddenly had more respect for reporters. He grabbed the professor's sweat-stained shirt and breathed harshly. "Where's Viktor? Where's Subject Six?"

Godwin's brows arched. "Subject Six? What do you know of him?"

"I'm asking the questions, professor!" retorted Tristan. He glanced past the morbid collection of fluid-filled caskets, wondering if Viktor had met with the same fate. He ached to face him; he could taste the beginnings of sweet revenge. No one would stop him now. "Answer me!"

Godwin pointed. "Over there!" he said.

Tristan eyed barely discernible lines etching a wall behind shimmering tubes. Adrenaline burned in his veins, stoking a next move.

"I'll show you, but please, don't hurt me!" entreated Godwin timidly.

Tristan shoved the professor at the keyboard, nervously checking his chrono. This was taking too long. The Marne sat, unprotected. He pictured the man sprawled and bloodied, unable to beg for mercy. The professor, his fingers trembling, typed again, glancing between monitors, Atlas and closed doors.

Bailey exclaimed. "These documents … are clearly confidential … and revealing. The Federation has its mitts into almost everything imaginable."

"Anything stand out?" questioned Tristan, his gaze riveted on the professor.

"Where should I start?" she replied. "Mutants, Reyna, Atma Stones, weapons that can level entire metropolises …?"

Jo piped in. "What about the Paputas?"

"Still nothing. I'm looking."

The professor was obviously stalling. "Speed it up!" yelled Tristan, and jabbed Godwin's back.

"Professor. What have you done?" demanded Bailey incredulously. "What … are … these … mutants?"

"You couldn't possibly understand," rebutted Godwin, still typing.

Bailey interrupted, a mix of passion stirred with agitation.

"Thracian mutants discovered. Two beasts, similar appearances in nearly every regard. Height- 12 feet. Beasts that eat human flesh. Non-intelligent, magically inclined.

Antegonians—lizard-like creatures, highly intelligent and formidable, evolved language, dwell in underground caverns. Unable to infiltrate. Mutants in Aurelia. Other-worldly … folklored as Man Burners (initiating immolation). Display heightened perception and awareness. Propel fire from limbs and face/mouth."

Bailey's voice crackled in disbelief. "When did the Federation begin believing in magic?"

The professor faltered and rubbed his head. "As the superior race, we must understand everything our realm has to offer," Godwin replied indifferently. "… We must exercise complete control and prohibit any display of weakness. Magic, or the like, threatens the Federation's cause simply because it has yet to be understood. But that will soon change. That's why Paputas are so precious. They create illusions, but there's one in particular, able to transform illusions into reality—the Grand Master!" Feigned empathy quickly transformed when his gaze dropped to Jo.

Jo reacted like he'd been shot, speaking with authority much greater than his size. "No! You'll never find him! No matter how much you persecute us, we'll never disclose his location."

"No one can hide from the Federation, you imbecile! We're aware of Paputas' chronophantasm magic, and we know of the Grand Master's association with the time traveler."

Jo retorted. "How could you possibly know that?"

"Your race's secrets are not as well guarded as you believe." A grim smile twisted across Godwin's face, exposing rows of teeth, brown from excessive smoking and neglect.

"What have you done to them?" cried Jo.

"The same that I will do to you when I get my hands around your neck." With writhing fingers outstretched, Godwin fearlessly advanced.

Jo, eyes bloodshot and bulging, squealed and cowered between Atlas's furry legs.

Tristan slammed the stock into Godwin's face. "You want to act cocky now? Who's holding a gun on whom?" he screamed, releasing an exaggerated amount of anger and impatience. "You will …finish what you started! Viktor! *Now!*" demanded Tristan, raging. He couldn't do anything for the Paputas; Atlas would protect Jo.

Godwin stumbled to the keyboard and fumbled, grimacing and gritting.

Bailey continued reading. "They even have spies in Reyna! It says that their princess plans to take a small entourage to speak with Thracia's King Veeken! They assigned High Marshal Eston to silence her! She's been forcing World Council favors by speaking out against the Federation." She turned on Godwin. "You Azdahri are animals! Do you intend to silence all those who disagree?"

Godwin sneered. "We do what must be done!" he replied tauntingly, his white hair smattered across his blood-stained forehead. "With the overall populace controlled, I have freedom to experiment on anything I deem necessary to advance our cause! World Council ethics will become obsolete!"

"Enough!" barked Tristan. He pressed cold, hard steel against Godwin's temple. A ring of reddened fat squeezed around the muzzle. He fought a violent urge to finish the task.

Godwin's lips curled. His eyes darkened. "As you wish."

His hand fell onto a sliding lever. The wall behind Tristan slowly slid upward. Not until it was half way was Tristan sure that he'd reached his goal. Hanging motionless in dense blue liquid was a chiseled, half naked body clad in shredded dark trousers. Bubbles rose haphazardly, popping when colliding with the membrane surface . Viktor's indigo hair, awry, drifted gracefully and stoked horrible memories; the breathing mask seemed to render Viktor helpless, but he was gifted at ruses. If it weren't for the bubbles, Tristan would have given him up for dead.

The professor snarled through clinched teeth. "There's your prize!" He glared and pointed dramatically.

Tristan could end the nightmare. Viktor's fate rested in the power of a well-aimed projectile, but how many people would he really save? He had no idea. In vengeance's clutches, he slowly lifted the Droth. A familiar rush of adrenaline heralded trembling hands and pounding heart. Was this the reason he had survived Southaven? Would Mawson want Viktor dead? The high-powered scope, cross-hairs seized Viktor's forehead, spoke to him. It seemed so right, yet so wrong. His fingers tingled.

Godwin stayed Tristan's pondering. "What do you think you're doing? Stop this!" he babbled, gasping.

"I'm finishing what I should have finished years ago," countered Tristan, not removing a gaping scowl from the blue-haired man. The fat of his forefinger spread against a cold, hard trigger.

"Tristan!" thundered Bailey.

His finger twitched when he tilted his head.

"She's alive!" shouted Bailey. "Eliza's alive!" She continued to peel the data feed.

Tristan's heart raced. His mind clouded; his eyes fogged—Viktor blurred. The Droth became too taxing to bear; he stared into a slew of streaming bubbles. "What?" His incredulity united with hers.

"She's being held in Navalasta on the 85th floor of the Valkyrie Headquarters' Tower!"

Navalasta? That was one of Atomia's densest cities. How did she end up there? His mind reeled like a spinning disk as he calculated flight time. "Eliza …." He'd save her, but not before dealing with Viktor.

"This is great news!" said Bailey excitedly, still racing through the data flood.

Tristan stammered. Talking seemed so foreign. "I don't understand …. Mr. Edde …. The report affirmed their deaths …. Was that just some perverted scam?"

Metal clanged. Tristan flinched at steel against steel; his weapon sagged.

"You always were pretty slow," said a familiar and despised voice.

He spun around, dreading what he was forced to face; at least a dozen Institute VI assault rifles. Erik Gabrio with a Droth and in a dark trench coat and wearing slicked down, blond hair, faced him from across the circular room. Tristan had to think fast. Otherwise, Viktor would survive and Eliza would die.

"Never was good at putting the pieces together, were you, Tristan?" questioned Erik. "Surprise!" with his palms up and extending his fingers in mocked expulsion.

Atlas growled, low and deep.

Jo winced.

How did Erik know that Tristan was here? He was furious.

"Intruders!" shouted Erik. "Drop your weapons! I won't hesitate to order my men to blast you into the next life."

It was a trap; a fake transmission. Bailey had been right—Tristan's lure, not Jo's. Tristan's Droth bounced once and submitted. Bailey motioned to Atlas; two more weapons clattered at their feet.

"It took you long enough!" roared Godwin. "He's insane. He almost pulled the trigger—my precious specimen—we worked so hard!"

"I knew what I was doing," replied Erik, glaring.

"Dammit ...," seethed Tristan.

"I see your wheels turning, Tristan," said Erik. "Can't solve the puzzle? Here, allow me. You've been duped from the very beginning. Mr. Edde played you like a cheap harps-a-chord. He arranged for you to conduct Eliza!" Erik burst into laughter. "Brilliant! You've been on the wrong side the entire time. Poor ... little ... boy. How does being a laughing stock feel?" Erik slowly maneuvered between tubes, ducking under low hanging cables and hoses. "And now, you're in my hands and you'll play by my rules." His face darkened.

"This is horrible!" cried Jo.

"And it's only going to get worse. Paputa screams are etched into these very walls and I can't wait to hear yours."

Jo's tiny body began to quiver. His eyes widened as he cowered behind Atlas.

"Eliza ... . What happened to Eliza?" demanded Bailey.

"I'm sure she'll meet a similar fate as yours."

Tristan charged forward. "No!"

Erik swung his Droth; it cracked loudly against Tristan's chest; he crumpled to the floor.

"No! Wait! I need him!" Godwin threw up his arms in a rage, waving wildly.

Erik hesitated, not lowering his weapon.

"Calm down, professor. I'm just softening him up. We'll be fine as long as his mouth still works."

Tristan glared. "Need me? For what?" Somehow, he had to change the odds. Erik had never been that smart. He thought back to the hanger when he was looking for Erik's vulnerabilities.

"Subject Six won't wake up. I saw this as an opportunity to lure you here since I know how preoccupied you are with him. The professor believes that, because of your previous association with Viktor, you could reach him. Since you're the sole Southaven survivor, you fit the profile as a perfect candidate. How exciting!"

Erik yanked Tristan upright, dragging him before Viktor's glass prison. "There you go. Now talk!" He smashed Tristan's face against the chilled surface and his Droth into Tristan's side.

"What am I supposed to say?" This was a most preposterous situation; his cheek-bone ground against plastic. Tristan couldn't have been prepared. How could he have readied himself for a run-in with his personal nightmare? Viktor's mind came out of another realm. He wished that he had pulled the trigger when he'd had the chance.

"Talk!" demanded Erik belligerently.

"Viktor!" cried Tristan, strained. The bubbles popped steadily.

Erik stole a probing glance of the professor and Tristan.

"Viktor! It's me, Tristan!"

Erik tapped his foot impatiently and then kicked at the back of Tristan's knee. "Focus!" demanded Erik.

"Remind him of a shared event!" encouraged Godwin. "Was there anything he liked about you?"

Seething and wanting to smash Erik's face, Tristan stiffened and drew in the silent form. His mind churned. He wanted to kill him. "Viktor. I remember when you came to Southaven. You fooled everyone. I saw you as a mentor, an inspiration when you were nothing but a murderous apparition. You massacred every person that was important to me and stole my life! I discovered your true cowardice as you hid behind your so-called magic. In the end, you knew that you were nothing more than an experiment gone awry! A mad scientist created you, but you were *and still …* are nothing!"

"Stop this!" demanded Godwin emphatically. "You'll upset him!"

Erik's rifle cracked into Tristan's back, forcing him down.

Bailey screamed. "Tristan!"

Erik checked the chamber and slid the bolt forward. "He's of no use to you!" erupted Erik. "I'm going to end his misery."

"Wait! I said I needed him!" coaxed the professor. "Viktor hasn't stirred; Tristan's our only hope."

"How could he possibly benefit you?" demanded Erik. "He's a danger to everyone and will escape if we don't kill him now …"

"Lock him in the cellar. Put all of them down there so we can deal with them later, but give me my Paputa. I'm wasting precious time and need to continue interrogations."

Jo cried out, hugging tightly onto Atlas's leg. "No! Please! I beg you!" he pleaded.

Erik stomped angrily, like a child. "Fuck! Fine! If you don't use him by first light, I'll personally kill him, and I won't ask for your permission."

Godwin eyed Jo, gleaming. "So be it."

Erik motioned toward the dozen-man army staring silently and bathed in shimmering blue light. "Take them away!"

A flurry of black uniforms and ready rifles hastened past Erik, commandeering Atlas and Bailey. It took three of them to manage Atlas. They encircled the group and moved them between the tubes and through the doorway.

Tristan's head throbbed; he thought he'd collapse at any moment. Glancing back at Jo, he dreaded parting with the tiny creature. He glanced once more at Viktor. Bubbles escaped, maybe a few more? Viktor's mask was secured firmly and his head hung low, swaying silently in the thick liquid. A rush of bubbles joined the steady stream just as Tristan reached the landing. He tried to stop, but another rifle butted his back and shoved him forward.

Did Viktor's fingers twitch?

Tristan had only ever seen jail cells from the outside. He had prided himself with his personal associations and generally avoided people whose influence would have changed that view. Black bars, green-tiled walls, and glaring white lights made him feel like a criminal. His freedom had been robbed. The transition from subsonic flight to stool pigeon was worse than jumping out of a perfectly good airship. Atlas, caught up in his own silent frustrations and spurred by a nature not so tame, paced and growled—a voiceless beast. He'd leer at the wall separating him from Bailey, making Tristan really nervous.

Erik's crazed manner proved as unpredictable as a rabid dog. Crazy people are disadvantaged because, well, they're *crazy.*

His weakness simply had to surface.

They had about five hours to devise an escape plan … or die. The oversized lion-brute, fierce and protective, would be a key player.

Tristan loathed the separation from Bailey. He stared into the hall as if waiting for his luck to change. "You all right?" he whispered but couldn't see her.

Bailey didn't reply. He plopped down with his back against the damp wall, stained with something unknown.

Someone had stepped into the hall but didn't speak. Bailey finally replied, a low whisper. "I'm fine. We really got in over our heads this time."

Her reply encouraged him; he grinned. He expected her to sound sad, not chipper. "It's my fault," he answered woefully. "I'm … sorry. I should have seen it coming."

"You didn't twist anyone's arm," she replied. "We wanted to help just as badly as you, and don't forget Jo's determination."

Tristan pictured the professor dropping Jo into thick, green gel; Jo was gasping for air, stopping and starting several times, and then twitching twice.

Atlas stood and towered, his stench overbearing while he pounded the wall. The metal floor resonated like a drum.

"With what we've uncovered, we can wreck the Federation—but now this? Get us out of here!" exclaimed Bailey. She started again when Atlas stopped his pounding. "It'll follow us to the grave."

"Don't talk like that," said Tristan. But she was right—they had to connect with General Braxton, anyone, but who could they trust? He should have shot Viktor, then Erik showed up with his dozen goons. "As long as we're alive, there's hope." He thought of Eliza. Hopefully, she would still be in that tower, such a long shot. "The Federation will pay," said Tristan. I'll see to that if it's the last thing I do." He wondered if it was wistful thinking. Why else would this strange set of occurrences have brought him to this point?

"Too little, too late. Why weren't you motivated like this before?" chided Bailey, cresting a well-honed undertone. "You could have put your ambitions to good use in Amstye."

"Hell, I was probably drunk. Anyway, Mr. Edde played me like a cheap banjo …, again. How the hell was I to know?" said Tristan.

Atlas grabbed the bars and yanked. Metal ground against mortar; the food tray hatch dropped. Another surge from Atlas brought it back into place, clanging when the lock hit. "I trusted him, and Eliza is trapped and maybe dead because of my ignorance. If only …"

Atlas yanked again. The little door swung freely, but his hand wouldn't fit through the opening.

Tristan hugged his knees. The metal floor hurt his backside; he tried to ignore the pain. He seemed to spend a lot of time ignoring pain. Atlas dropped down beside him, grunting in frustration. Both sat with their backs against cool tile, silently staring at dirty, gray grout lines. Except for Atlas's raspy breathing, it became deathly still. The air soured from his pungent breath, or B.O., or both.

Tristan rubbed his wrists and could only guess what time it was. His impatience was snowballing. Sitting like this sucked. Atlas seemed even angrier. He wouldn't sit still and was soon on his feet pounding the wall again. Glaring white lighting added to the *appropriate* sense of imprisonment, because it was … a prison after all.

Without warning, Tristan's instinct to steady himself kicked in. The floor shifted and floor grates dislodged. On his feet and wide eyed, he pushed his face against the bars. Nothing but cells and an empty corridor. Atlas roared, glanced at Tristan and threw himself into the bars. Tristan barely got out of the way.

Stupid move. They didn't budge.

The floor wavered like it was sliding, quaking every few seconds. Dust clouded the air and settled on the bars. He didn't want to breathe that crap. Suddenly, the corridor heaved; a giant crack appeared along the outside edge. These bars would be their death.

Atlas looked strong …, but not strong enough; a giant of pure muscle, stranded and helpless.

"Tristan?" yelled Bailey.

Her tone quickly got his attention. "I'm right here!" he hollered back. He was desperate; if only Atlas could …?

"… What was that?" asked Bailey.

The dust thickened. "I don't know," replied Tristan, grabbing his ears and coughing.

"Tristan!" shouted Bailey. "I think my door just moved!"

"What? How?"

"I don't know—the explosion. Hang on, let me …!" Metal scraped against metal.

The dust swirled; Tristan squinted into obscurity. What was she doing? Sweet deity, he hated this. Then, a trembling apparition appeared. Her face was pasty, her eyes streaked, like a ghost.

"What?" asked Tristan, thrilled to see her.

Atlas growled; then yelped like a pup.

"Dead …, a dead man," she whispered. She glanced behind her and trolled with a listless hand.

"Who?" He couldn't see past her hand.

"Atlas. Stop wasting time," she said. "We'll die without our weapons! A locker fell—I saw rifles."

Atlas roared and shoved; hinges snapped; he held the massive barred door and flung it down the hall. Bailey ran to the storage locker and grabbed Tristan's Droth.

Tristan stared at the space, ducked under the mass of golden fur and lunged. In a moment, he was sliding a fresh clip into his Droth.

Bailey followed suit and motioned for Atlas to do the same.

He found his long rifle, and all three stared when an enormous roar echoed down the stairs. That had to be Viktor.

Bailey panicked. "This place is a death trap!" she shouted. "The building's going to crush us!"

"Come on!" shouted Tristan, running toward the stairs. He was probably carelessly running too fast, but he didn't care--until another explosion knocked him on his ass. He was afraid Jo was drowning; he might already be dead. Once up the stairs, he sprinted toward a slatted glass window and peered through dirty panes. Institute VI soldiers were all around the Marne, at least a dozen, black-clad idiots.

"Not going that way," he hissed.

"The hangar! It has to be under this building." said Bailey. "Maybe they have Federation hovercrafts? All we need is one."

"Then you and Atlas go check it out. The technical people probably took 'em, but maybe there's one left. I have to look for Baby Jo."

"What! Are you nuts?" she exclaimed. "I can't fly one of those things!"

"I can," grumbled Atlas.

Tristan stared at the once mute beast.

"You … you can talk? Good god, I've seen everything."

Atlas's nostrils flared. "Only if I have to."

"Okay … ," replied Tristan, his speech dragging. No time to guess. Did Bailey know?

"You … two … ," Tristan stuttered. "… Go ahead! I'll be right behind. If you find one, get it to the launch platform!"

All three bolted up the stairwell.

"Be careful, Tristan!" said Bailey.

"Shit, I was born careful."

Atlas ducked under the door frame; the dust and shadows enveloped him.

In the hallway, Tristan almost puked in disgust. A scientist had been pinned to the wall by a metal rod. His mouth gaped wide and his eyes were sunken. That had to be Viktor's work. He looked like he had been screaming—at nothing. Tristan was too exposed; Viktor could be anywhere, watching. Given the chance, Viktor wouldn't hesitate to kill him. An explosion had destroyed the cylinder room doorway and a few of the cylinders. A blue haze filled the corridor; the floor was slick with green slime. Viktor, with most of his tube, was gone. Tristan heard a cry, but otherwise, the room stayed silent, except for the noise outside. A flicker off to the side; Jo was completely submerged, hitting at a cylinder wall. His red hat had slipped around his neck. Another movement beyond Jo—Tristan froze—Viktor stood over a keyboard, typing frantically. Tristan raised his Droth.

Without turning, Viktor started talking. "Here we are again, Tristan. You really should just give up."

Tristan's mind sped back in time; he had never left *that day* and felt trapped, again.

Jo struck at the glass, muffled bursts. Bubbles floated past his tiny, furrowed brow.

"It seems," continued Viktor, "that once again, destiny has brought us together. Perhaps I'm not appreciating your greater purpose? You want to hurt me? Oh, Tristan, my boy, I'm so far beyond you. Your anger blinds you. Careful, boy. It'll be your undoing."

Tristan steadied his Droth. "I want you dead."

Viktor's blue hair glimmered. Green goo pooled around him. "You think you can cap me with that silly Droth? I guess you forgot the extent of my power. You've learned nothing."

Tristan wasn't sure what to say.

"Your passion to pull that trigger is evident, but you ignore a greater one, one for her …."

"Eliza … how …?"

"You never were good at hiding your emotions. You can't think through the pain. Emotions and logic—a human dilemma and its downfall. Your kind is pathetically weak. Yet, they persist, always claiming what isn't theirs. We're bound together, Tristan. I don't know if you realize that. I should desperately want to kill you—I should—but, I'll wait for a more fitting time. One day, you'll no longer be of use to me or the rest of the world. Allow me to gift you your life so that you can run after that woman, even learn to appreciate her. Those precious moments may never come again."

Had he heard him correctly? Was Viktor giving him a pass? He didn't want it, but if he was, he had to go. Viktor was right about Eliza. "Humanity is more resilient than you'll ever know," replied Tristan. "Love takes us into places you'll never see or even know about."

"Your type only wants to destroy other lives. You worry about situations beyond your control. You insist on striving to achieve the impossible simply because it's impossible. But your most fatal flaw is forcing your beliefs on others. The Federation does the same and it will destroy them, yet they're blind and still driven to dominate the world."

"And what about you? You destroy others—you're flawed too. You force others to submit, die!"

Viktor motioned to the opened broken wall. "I tire of this banter; we've no more time. Leave me. The launch pad—it's your only escape."

"What are you going to do?" asked Tristan, feeling relieved and stunned. He didn't trust Viktor, but now he had to.

"There's someone else gifted, like me. Her name is Subject Thirteen and she was my tube-sister."

Tube sister? "Yes," Tristan mused, and then he remembered. "In Southaven, you told me you were going to destroy her."

"Godwin tried to protect her, but I just found her." Viktor slowly turned to Tristan, blue hair, appearing almost black, raking down a piercing scowl.

Ice crept down Tristan's back. Viktor's eyes were sunken, his features not prominent and strong, like in Southaven. He expected a more handsome man. Their eyes locked. Tristan had intended to kill him and Viktor knew it, but Tristan felt powerless and wanted to run.

Jo! A stooped doll of a being; he was dying. Tristan fired his Droth low and away from the Paputa. The glass shattered in shards as thick as his palm, and a gurgling Paputa sprang to life.

"You could have shot me!" his trembling voice cried. His red hat sped past on a river of green slime.

Tristan didn't know if he should pick Jo up, and shouted, ignoring Viktor and turning to the hole in the wall. "Come on, Jo."

"Are you done debating that deranged animal? I thought for sure you were going to leave me to this intolerable fate!" said Jo hysterically, gasping, madly wiping green goo from his eyes.

Viktor retreated into the blue shadows. His gape, under a lowered brow, began to blaze. Even in his disheveled state, he seemed to manage considerable clarity. "Before you leave," he paused, "determine your own destiny. It will benefit us both."

Tristan hesitated. The warning confused him even more.

"Enjoy your humanity, Tristan. It won't last forever."

The slime from Jo's shattered coffin drenched the floor.

Tristan grabbed Jo's hand, cold and slippery, and guided him toward the gaping hole. Viktor would surely continue the destruction—it was in his heart, his *soulless* heart. If Atlas and Bailey had located a craft, hopefully they had raised it to the launch pad. Hopefully.

Tristan glanced at Jo, such a tiny thing, so frail, and scooped him up. He could feel his pounding heart and wondered what churned through his other-worldly thoughts. Stained with goo, they walked through the genocide of charred little bodies; the facility smelled like an embalming-fluid filled morgue.

No wonder Jo complained so much. Tristan wanted to understand Paputas more than ever. He wanted to know their magic. What would a city of Paputas look like? Did that even exist? Could they all paint like Jo? Tristan glanced behind him, wondering if Viktor had followed. He could have destroyed Tristan with the flick of a finger. He wondered if Viktor's capture had been staged somehow. Eliza had unwittingly been kidnapped. Who had done that? He wouldn't sleep until he found her and destroyed her captor. He'd been tricked and had lost so much time. He had to think harder, be more vigilant, calculating, and thorough.

Erik seemed to be the only constant in this maze of confusion. He had a habit of showing up no matter where Tristan went. That had to stop.

"Put me down!" demanded Jo, his voice shrill. "These legs will do just fine!"

He expected more reticence; so much for that. Tristan bounded up the stairs, two at a time, while Jo squirmed in his arms, turning at the landing and sprinting up another. Whining engines, unnerving; reverberating corrugated metal, deafening. A hundred thoughts struck him at once. Bailey, an escape craft, Erik, Eliza …he had to try to focus.

"Where's my guardian, and Atlas?" demanded Jo, without a tinge of reserve.

"Stealing a getaway ship. You're welcome, by the way." The little guy might be magical and all that, but he was acting the ingrate.

Tristan forged ahead. One small light swayed benignly, flickering sporadically. The landing pad should be just above.

"Should we help them? She can't fly a ship! And that oversized furball won't be much help either!"

"You'd be surprised." They were halted at the next landing by a concrete wall streaming water that pooled into a bed of moldy green. Orange misted upon them like colored moon dust. He lifted Jo onto a rung and quickly scaled up behind. The manhole cover clanged loudly, and Tristan stared across the pad through an obscuring haze. Overgrown ivy draped from surrounding trees, a few rats scurried frantically with pups in tow, appearing alien bathed in orange. Like the face of a clock, a throbbing orange ring kept time around the pad. Its hue glimmered off the skin of a stealthy, black Trident, an awaiting ghost. The motionless craft defied gravity—rigid stabilizers, triple medial tail fins, vertical thrusters—sleek and angular. It was faster than the Marne, but could they reach it? Atlas and Bailey were nowhere to be seen; Tristan wished he'd been the one gone looking.

Four men sauntered through swirling mist, black uniforms, walking shadows, approaching the Trident's gangway. Erik led them, cocky and confident, his black trench coat flapping. Tristan wanted to ignore him and flee, but contempt ruled like a crown prince. It seemed he'd never be rid of that asshole. Professor Godwin, in a white gown, was sandwiched between the soldiers like an oversized white-cream filling, held up on each side by a burly arm.

Jo yanked at Tristan's pant leg. "Looks like we took a wrong turn!" A trembling finger pointed at the advancing delegation. "Let's go back down!" said Jo, "before they see us." He eyed them warily.

"Uh-uh. We're right where we should be." Tristan crouched low, and clung to him, maybe a bit too tightly. A certain sense of protective parent prevailed, doting and undeniable. Maybe this was how a father loved a son. A son that looks like a prairie dog.

Jo pinned his hands onto his hips. "I was afraid you were going to say that! We're outnumbered!" Large, round eyes, too wise for his comedic body, pleaded desperately.

Jo was so small yet so defiant. Inspired, Tristan rose from their heart-pounding huddle. He unclipped his Droth and aimed. *Bang! Bang!* Two orangeish shadows tumbled from the ramp; a fleeting ghost in the night, the professor bolted into the mist. Erik, alone and isolated, spun, Droth raised, and bore down on Tristan.

"Urgh!" moaned Tristan a little too loudly, acutely aware of an almost-empty clip.

"I knew I should have killed you when I had the chance!" seethed Erik in ignorance.

Godwin, glowing like an oversized tangerine, threw his hands high. "Now wait a minute, Tristan," he yelled, Trident engines heightening the spat. "Don't do anything rash! Let's think about your choices."

Tristan gave up the wall and motioned for Jo to stay put. "And what's there to think about, Professor? Unethical experiments or Subject Six—an out-of-control monster? Some choice." He wondered if his rebuttal had been lost in the turbulence. The professor was only a distraction; he kept his gaze fixed on Erik.

Erik's hand shifted forward.

"Don't even think about it!" shouted Tristan, straining through auburn haze. Wind spit from low, pregnant clouds, rattling a grove of false banana trees and diffusing rain's residue from their wide green leaves. The stench of Zyn made Tristan cough.

Godwin raged. "You idiot! There's no time to argue! Subject Six is going to destroy the entire base! We're next! If this shuttle isn't airborne soon, we'll all be dead!"

Tristan grinned slyly, keyed by the man's sudden awareness of what was happening.

It had been planned.

"Good! Then maybe you'll understand the horror of your ways!" His throat ached from yelling and inhaling the orange mist; a soreness that would linger for days. Neck hair bristled and then he learned why. A glass cockpit appeared just over the edge, shimmering tail fins and then cockpit dash lights, an ear-shattering din roiled through his torso like a jack hammer.

"Thank the deity, they made it." Tristan thought.

"It's Bailey and Atlas! We're saved, saved!" screamed Jo, clapping his hands, poised to dash.

"No!" shouted Tristan.

On one knee, Erik trained his Droth. Tristan dropped, rolled, and fired. The deck buckled, slapping him with invisible whips. Erik flew sideways; Tristan sighted in his pale, drawn glower. Erik, blond hair and scattered gaze, scanned Tristan's way.

The rising shuttle collided with twisting metal; fire shot out the exhaust.

"Tristan! I can't breathe!" whispered Jo frantically. "Smoke is burning my lungs, and it stinks! We have to reach the shuttle! That stupid cat will wreck our only hope to get out of here. Cats can't fly. Why won't he come get us? Doesn't he see that we're ... ?"

"Stop!" barked Tristan, throwing a quick glance at the boxy shuttle. He wished that they'd found something fleeter.

Another explosion threw Tristan against the wall; lightning slammed into the deck, breaking masts and showering sparks like glimmering stars. Somehow, they had even angered the heavens. Viktor had wasted no time; they needed to go.

Was Erik too daft to realize he was knee-deep in shit?

Godwin sprinted back to the craft, more a frenzied hobble, Erik nearly running up his back. Tristan fired a single shot; fire flashed from the barrel; Erik froze.

"You're not going anywhere!" shouted Tristan.

Erik glared across the shadowy flat, struggling to regain what little composure remained. "You're more trouble than you're worth. You're fucking toxic!" derided Erik as his arms leveled.

Tristan reflected on Viktor's words: *"Before you leave, determine your own destiny. It will benefit us both."*

Atlas engaged the throttle; the thundering craft's intake breathed in the misty orange, its exhaust spewed clouds of blue, indicating poor fuel consumption for lack of good oxygen.

"We'll all die, you idiot! The structure's disintegrating!" shouted Erik, pounding the air at the smirking lion, who, by all rights, knew exactly what he was doing.

Jo watched him too, cupping his hands over his ears.

Tristan opened his clip; it was empty. He thought if he couldn't shoot, he could play Erik for a fool. "You frightened?" chided Tristan. His blade clicked into position.

Atlas circled back, bringing rivets and black skin so close Tristan could spit on them.

Erik laughed. It sounded weak, strained, and arguably effeminate. "You want to play that card on me?" He leveled his weapon, poised after a set of clicks. "You don't frighten me."

Tristan's head numbed; he wanted Atlas to back away; the blare was throbbing in his aching head; hopefully, Erik's as well.

Erik charged. He braced and blocked, parried a blow, deftly sidestepping. Erik countered, struggling for footing. Their blades collided; sparks flew. Tristan lunged, hoping to rip through Erik's white shirt, but Erik spun, slicing downward. Tristan ducked, parried again, nicking Erik's sleeve. The garment, saturated red, became a moving target. Tristan lashed out, gashing deeper. Their blades scraped and locked. Their energies collided like opposite poles of magnets.

Erik came around, wrenching his Droth to freedom. Tristan battered back and sent Erik's Droth flying. He pivoted and rammed his elbow into Erik's jaw. It cracked loudly and he went sprawling. Erik staggered, swept his leg under Tristan and dropped him to the deck.

Tristan, stunned, felt out of body as Erik raised his blade. Tristan extended his reach and slashed into Erik's gut. Erik croaked, loudly over the din, staring straight at Tristan. Another explosion sent the deck reeling. The descent made Tristan's neck crack, the deck jarring abruptly when it caught. Tristan scrambled beneath the shuttle's bow, avoiding the screaming vertical thrusters. His skin burned; his trousers felt like burning silk.

A woman screamed. "Tristan! The building is coming down!" Bailey pointed frantically.

Tristan eyed Erik's orange silhouette. Atlas's furry head strained behind cockpit glass, pointed ears flattened on either side of his thick mane. Tristan scooped up Jo and turned back—the distance seemingly infinite. He slung Jo at Bailey with all his might. The creature shrieked, arms flailing. Tristan would have to answer for that later. He glanced back; Erik was a blood-darkened mound.

The pad erupted; Tristan stumbled; Erik tumbled. Metal grids heaved and roared. Concrete fractured, frays of cables sparked everywhere.

Erik pawed the deck, an arm jutting high; the deck fissured, paused and transformed into a cauldron of warped metal and flaming smoke.

Tristan ran from the flame wall and leaped, the widening fissure snapping and growling. His fingers held, tiny splinters on mighty boughs; his arms seared like they'd been stabbed with red-hot pokers— he couldn't hold; he braced for death. Suddenly, "fingers from heaven" dug into his skin; Bailey clamped down just as the dual thrusters roared to life. He coughed, better than dying, and gripped the ramp's edge like a vice.

They rose; he flailed through fountaining smoke and fire so searing that he felt the hair on his ass singe. He scanned blackened flames, even though it hurt to turn back—barren except for four corpses and a crippled craft. He winced when its wings exploded and bathed the deck in flaming zyn; the bodies exploding after they came to rest under the inferno's blanket. Tristan's knees slammed into the ramp as he was lofted by the powerful updraft; he wondered if his legs were broken. A realization shot through him, infusing him with both dread and relief—he'd never see Erik again.

A padded headrest was the closest thing to a pillow as Tristan could find; he closed his eyes and pushed back into the semi-rigid bolster. The engines vibrated through the hardened foam, but that didn't bother him. He knew a good fight would make him sore, but not as much as this. He hadn't been training like he should have been either; his knees smarted with every move. Oddly, a tingle of despondency prodded him when he pictured Erik, in flames. He was unprepared for remorse. He supposed that eventually he'd feel something. Erik had been dependable; they'd sparred quite often, long ago. They weren't exactly friends, but ..../fear/ had been yarned into his memories—the devouring orange mist, Viktor's rampage, brutalized Paputas, Bailey's desperate grip … .

Jo commanded the narrow aisle, double seats on either side, taut like a tightrope walker high above a circus, training a sharpened gaze on an untidy, golden mane.

Tristan gradually sifted through jumbled thoughts; not even a Reynan sunrise could help. Cold air streamed through the vents; little blue ribbons danced above their heads. After the battle, breathing actually seemed a simple pleasure. Atlas's form appeared comical, enormously furry, overflowing the modular pilot's seat, maybe somewhat majestic. His shaggy torso spilled into the aisle just enough to keep Jo at a distance.

Tristan wondered if Atlas's stealthy piloting maneuvers adjacent the platform had distracted Erik. Deafening thrusters had nearly ruptured his ears. His energy had all but vanished. He tried to raise his arm; he couldn't imagine piloting. He followed Jo's decelerating pace and slumped shoulders. The sight filled him with remorse; so many Paputas had died.

Bailey approached from the rear, soot-streaked and frazzled, gripping his seatback to steady herself. His eyes met a brief reminder of unbridled courage. He wasn't sure how to thank her. They were battle-worn and seemed to relish the steady hum of the engines. He so wanted his mind to settle.

"How you doing?" asked Bailey, cheery, yet reserved.

Tristan twitched and managed a flick of a grin, but was more interested in watching the backs of his eyelids.

She wanted something.

"I've seen better days." He moved to reposition himself but thought better.

"Watching your friend die must've been difficult."

That's all it took to realize how little he wanted to entertain. He didn't want to be rude, but the onslaught of images and emotions had embittered him. He'd probably never erase that groaning structure and mass of shooting flames—Viktor's work. Dried blood, brown and crusted, covered his sleeves; his favorite jacket was ruined. "He never was my friend," replied Tristan indifferently. "Honestly, I had no friends until I met you, Eliza, and the rest. Friends are trustworthy and have your best interests at heart."

"Everybody needs saving sometimes," replied Bailey. She pressed on her shoulder, pursing her lips, revealing a non-journalist aspect of her personality.

"Yes, they do and Eliza's next." Tristan had been given another chance to redeem himself and he saw it as exactly that. He would ride in upon a flood of adrenalin and emotion, weather any storm, and save her.

"It's not that simple," replied Bailey.

"Has it ever been?"

"No."

"Once in Tibur, we'll need to debrief the Officer of the Day," said Tristan. "General Braxton has been compromised and the mission could very well be toast already."

Bailey took a moment before she replied. "What do you mean?"

"If we infiltrate Valkyrie Headquarters, Xander will no doubt leverage that against Amstye; probably launch a full-scale attack. At a minimum, the border towns will be the first to go."

"If that's the case, why would he do it?" asked Bailey.

"He probably sees it as sacrificial, maybe religious, and certainly tactical. If the Federation attacks Amstye, Reyna will likely counterattack, and that would mark the beginning of Xander's global conflagration."

Bailey nodded, fumbling with a strap and looking nowhere in particular. "You've changed." Suddenly, she beamed. "A little more talk like that and you might convince me that you actually care."

She didn't see him as Eliza's only hope.

"As a mercenary, I was non-committal, a combatant without allies or enemies," defended Tristan. "My focus comprised targeted objectives and flight into another day. I was paid to execute missions, and that's exactly what I did. I changed because I finally recognized Xander as the enemy. I want to be one of the 'good guys', as funny as that sounds. Changes in the geopolitical landscape affect us all and have forced me to see the varying levels of gray in what used to be so black and white."

"So, you're really going to save her?" asked Bailey.

"Yes," he replied. "Alone if I have to."

No one could talk him out of it.

She dug through a dusty satchel and retrieved her tablet. Her wavy blonde hair, damp and matted, fell over her eyes.

Tristan cringed, trying to savor even a moment of quiet. His leg spasmed, forcing him against the opposite armrest.

"I know this might seem inappropriate … ," she said.

He couldn't have said it better. He glanced out a narrow window and waited, wishing he was already in Tibur.

"Your outlook is strangely unique and you did promise me … ," her voice trailed.

The shuttle lurched—an air pocket—tossing them unexpectedly. She plopped down and buckled in next to him.

He didn't have the energy to avert another confrontation. "Okay, okay," rolling his eyes, then nodding, sounding more cynical than supportive. "You're excited to see how my story ends. Or, better yet, how I would meet my death. You must think me suicidal. Tell the truth."

"Well, you're a one-man army planning to infiltrate enemy lines, not to mention Lord Commander Seryth's personal command center. Surely you realize that under all that platinum hair, he nurses heartlessness in a way that redefines cruelty?"

Tristan snickered. "Heartlessness? My, such a big word. Well, at least I'll go out in style… heartlessly," dripping in sarcasm.

She crossed her legs, repositioned her tablet and glanced at Jo. "I would hope not. May I please ask you a few questions?" As if asking even mattered.

"Go for it. Hell, I'm dead tired, pissed off and ready to kill someone, but go right ahead and ask away. Never been more focused in all my life," answered Tristan. He tucked an extra shirt around Jo and smiled when he didn't wake up.

"Since you betrayed Institute VI and the Federation, I'm sure you're filled with doubt. Are you?"

"Doubt? Doubt? How long you been doing this?" replied Tristan, puzzled by a seemingly unsophisticated triple pounding coming from someone who should be better at this than an 8th grade cub reporter. Had she no empathy for what had so recently transpired? "Firsthand accounts of Federation atrocities have eliminated uncertainty … or 'doubt'. Their *new world* is a glorified slave camp. I can understand why Eliza, General Braxton and Senator Galik maintain such determined resistance. A free world is one where all nations decide their own beliefs, laws and politics. But what betters one over another? The Federation attempts control only because it has positioned itself as the ultimate arbiter of righteousness. What about Reyna and the World Council? Declegon— they have a vote, right? Must we adhere to a single persuasion; and if so, whose? The Federation is a careless oppressor. I should have seen this coming. I was stupid." He turned to the window, momentarily captured by streaking, moonlit clouds.

The cockpit radio crackled; Atlas leaned forward and adjusted a knob.

"Was there a particular turning point that molded this new view of our habitat?"

"… Not just one. I've learned a lot from the best. It's true that I've been privileged to rub shoulders with many great people whose ideas I've selectively adopted. But … , Eliza Nyvala—she's the one who inspired me most of all."

Bailey's resentment surfaced like a sand bar at low tide. Her face became drawn and drained of life. She reached for the power button, but then pulled back.

"She's an 18-year-old girl struggling to enter womanhood, and she shared a forgotten slice of life. Her courage fosters tranquility more elusive than a cold breeze on a hot day. Bailey, do you realize that she abandoned family and friends to champion her cause? That's a scarcity in my books."

"So … would you say that your choices and resulting actions were out of love?" she asked, rather daringly.

Tristan felt clumsy and out of his element, like trying to put on a shoe while standing on one leg—too much emotion and too little time for a clever response—but his exposed feelings prompted truth. Their eyes met. "Love?"

"It's obvious you are smitten by Eliza. She lit a fire in you. Before, you didn't seem to care about anything, but when she popped into your life, she got your attention, quickly, it seems. I watched you lose control when she died and gain it again on her survival. Did justice's champion come about from that love?"

Her candid interrogation made him feel worse than awkward. She was jealous; his disdain was so thick he could taste its salt. He'd never learned how to escape the cell of a woman's sentiment.

"Well?" she demanded.

"What are you getting at?" he replied, his sharpness honing hers.

"Just answer the question."

"You're taking liberties you haven't earned."

"What are you afraid of?"

"I'm not afraid."

"Then answer it. Are you fighting out of love?"

"Is there anything else worth fighting for?" He rearranged Jo's covers and slid into the aisle. At least a lion man wouldn't ask him stupid questions.

CHAPTER

40

URSA 30, 1870 O.C.
COUNTRY: AMSTYE
CITY: TIBUR

The annoying, high-pitched monotone of an Air Traffic Controller's voice jolted Tristan; Atlas needed it that loud. He sat up, groggy, and listened. Atlas grunted into the mic and eased the speeding shuttle into the narrow confines of final approach. Jo squirmed, curled in a ball, resting head and shoulder on a wad of Tristan's shirt. Brief thruster bursts resonated throughout, interposing the skyway's familiar gyration-inducing commands. The descent steepened, nose down, decelerating, craft shuddering. The ATC scolded Atlas; they had veered out of the flight path and were too hot. Tibur unfolded beneath, an immense urban sprawl. Light rain-and-snow along the portals smeared and vanished. After a few minutes of bumps and yaws, and Tristan's hasty check list read, the shuttle settled onto the pad. Cabin lights flickered when external auxiliary power was connected; everyone squinted under the suddenly intense lighting of the main cabin. The turbines wound down and brought with them a bustle of arrival preparation. Bailey gathered her satchel and Jo and unlocked and pulled down the cabin door's lever. A snowy blast greeted her, instantly forming droplets on the metal floor in the warmer confines. She carried a sleepy Jo down a frozen ramp, followed by Atlas and Tristan.

"By the way, great job flying," said Tristan.

Atlas was more intent on Bailey; not even a nod. Snow morphed into droplets on his broad back and matted the fur on his face. Like most felines, Atlas avoided water, or *any* form of moisture on his person. He growled quietly in complaint.

"Don't want to talk anymore, eh?" prodded Tristan, getting no response. Atlas had played a key role in their escape, so Tristan wasn't offended. He'd grown friendly toward the golden-haired creature, even though he knew practically nothing about him. His stealth commanded respect; quiet people usually did, at least until they opened up. Learning more about the magnificent creature would certainly prompt an interesting conversation … someday.

He imagined an entire nation of lion men. It did exist. He could be sitting in a café, drinking coffee with someone quite literally twice his size. Did Acrolytes drink coffee? That would be quite the sight; a massive furry beast with crossed legs, holding the cup with pinky extended, brushing some lint off a pinstriped three-piece gray suit, complemented with silver cufflinks and a blue paisley necktie.

"Consider yourself blessed," boasted Bailey. "He's spoken with me only on the rarest of occasions." She snugged her collar and reached down to straighten Jo's red hat. It was stained with green goo.

"Ha!" chirped Jo excitedly, freeing himself and jumping just out of reach. "What's this, some game? Everyone knows cats don't talk."

Atlas growled half-heartedly. He glanced down, at Jo first, then Tristan, and seemed almost to smile.

Jo obviously didn't get that impression. When an Acrolyte smiles, it bears its pointed teeth. Jo screamed and clutched Tristan's leg.

The four lingered under a stubby trident tail, as much out of the weather as possible, shivering and waiting on approaching linemen. Jase popped out from behind them, waving dramatically.

"Didn't expect you all back here," said Jase, giving Tristan a once-over, unable to conceal a sporty grin. "Changed your mind?"

"Long story," replied Tristan; glad to see him, even with his overly-friendly flair.

Jase ignored Tristan's veiled indifference, seeming more interested in the tow cart's activity.

The shuttle moved quickly, surprisingly, once the linemen leaned into it.

"I got the time," returned Jase with a cheesy smile as he ran his hand around the pitot tube's dent . Water beaded and dripped down his arm.

"Maybe later," said Tristan, turning to the open hanger harboring two fighters and a boxy troop carrier. The bustling militaristic surroundings helped him to unwind—it felt good to be on an active airfield again—like he was home. "We uncovered highly sensitive Federation Intel and are going to debrief General Braxton."

Cole popped out from between a pair of Sky Wings, wearing a drooping, dark blue rain hat dripping at the edges. "Don't think you can just show up and start barking orders," he said bluntly. "I thought you'd quit." Cole's animosity seemed deliberate, but bearable, considering Tristan's previous emotional state. They had left in a rush under Jo's theatrical auspices. Tristan had gotten caught up in it, too.

"I did. Now I'm back."

"It's not quite that easy, pal," Cole's tone sharpened.

"C'mon, Cole," implored Jase. "We're low on decent pilots and you know it. For deity's sake, we're not in a position to refuse."

"Okay, I screwed up," admitted Tristan. "Don't try to stop the debriefing. Let the general decide my fate. I think I earned my wings."

Cole tightened his arms across his burley chest. "... All right ... ," he replied. "It had better be worth it." He jogged back between the two craft, tucking dark hair under the brim of his hat, his raincoat gusting behind. Jase, light of step, led the group along crisscrossed yellow stripes, passing closely beside the enormously imposing parked carrier. Two women in gray-green fatigues, their hair tightly pulled back and tied off with black bands, sat inside, oblivious to the giant lion-man and his companions.

The Command Center was located at the far end of the walkway. Beyond the fighters and troop carrier, the lobby was occupied by a half dozen men facing a drop-down screen displaying rough terrain. An officer gestured with a laser pointer along a depicted mountain range and river. Security checked badges and stepped aside.

They walked past, their goal a door at the far wall. Through a small window in the door, Tristan glimpsed Barkley and some officers leaning over a table, talking. General Braxton had joined them via vid-conference. Tristan pushed past the door; only one of the men glanced over.

General Braxton took note. Tristan was surprised he could spot them before they reached the table. The connection was remarkably clear—no hesitation and heavily laden with authority. Braxton included him right away, motioning him over. Two men turned. Tristan didn't want to waste any time—the Professor, Subject Six, Eliza, Mr. Edde, and a mountain of top secret Intel Barkley had uncovered. He was the most important person there, at least as far as Tristan was concerned. With a sweeping gesture and smile, Barkley finally acknowledged him. Tristan started recounting the Facility experience; it took about ten minutes. He wrapped up and waited, trying to read their reactions. Deer in headlights; not including Barkley.

Braxton could only exclaim, caught completely off-guard. "I'm sick, sick to my guts!" he shouted, rummaging nervously through some papers just out of sight. "We've been strung along like jackasses following a damn carrot; spoon-fed cow shit and then asking for seconds."

The others nodded, their expressions unified.

"Mr. Edde's conned us from the start," brooded Tristan.

"I want him to be the first to go—I'll gladly do the honors!" snapped Cole. "Scum! No, less than scum! Screw him! I vote that we smoke his sorry ass … yesterday! He knows way too much!"

"Let's not be hasty," countered Braxton crisply. "The Federation's probably already aware of his secret activities, and we don't know how far-reaching his influence is."

"I agree—and advise a lower profile," added Barkley. "Let's use this Intel against the Federation, especially on our western front. The western front is severely under manned! Oxium is better equipped than we realized and could quickly compromise that border; send reinforcements."

"But if we do, our southern front would suffer," cautioned Braxton, leaning into the camera, a firm eye catching Barkley.

Barkley continued, growing restless. Oversized green fatigues made him look sloppier than he really was. "But if the west falls, Oxium military can clean sweep directly into the capital!"

Braxton tightened his gaze. His remoteness didn't temper his intensity. "The Federation, *not Oxium*, is our greatest threat!" he exclaimed.

Tristan grew antsy from their jousting and stared hard into the prism. The long flight was catching up with him. "We have to rescue Eliza!"

A hush immediately descended. Outside, engines wound down, filling the room with a high-pitched scream.

"That's ridiculous," exclaimed Braxton, after the air calmed. "What could we possibly do? She's holed up in *Valkyrie Headquarters*. Do you have a death wish?"

Tristan was prepared for that. "Excuse me, sir..." he tried to counter.

"We can't afford to waste valuable resources," interrupted Barkley. "Our air fleet needs to be in Verdia *yesterday*. The northern region isn't supported at all. We're all painfully aware that the west is in the worst shape—and that's where we go."

"Enough on the bullshit Oxium defensive!" snapped Braxton, pushing a white scarf to one side. His face reddened and suddenly blurted. "It's not happening!"

"General, if I may." Tristan tried for the group's attention. "I can infiltrate the Valkyrie Tower, destroy it and cripple their command structure," countered Tristan.

"Offer up one good reason why we should divert valuable resources." demanded Braxton. He seemed interested, surprisingly so after how he had been nudged by Tristan.

Every eye descended on Tristan.

"It's a golden, first-strike opportunity. They'll never see us coming," said Tristan, exposed and wishing for some indication of support. He glanced at Cole, tight crew cut and sleeveless arms, for some semblance of support. "We could strategize. Cole, you have tons of experience. What's your take?"

"I don't have a damn thing to add," retorted Cole, preceding an awkward four-second pause in the discussion.

"Okay ... okay," answered Tristan, visibly annoyed. "This is not just about Eliza. It's a first-strike opportunity. If we take out that tower, we cut off the snake's head. The place is lousy with intelligence personnel and sophisticated surveillance and communications equipment. It stands to reason every command decision and logistical command has filtered through that building. I'll tell you that as formidable and impressive the place is, all the intelligence and communication eggs in the Federation basket are in that tower just waiting for the fox."

"And why would we want to do that?" asked Barkley, tight-lipped. "That would be an act of war! There'd be swift Federation fury on Amstye. Thirty days and we'd be fodder."

"That's right," said Tristan. "We wouldn't have a chance—*before* an attack on the tower. But if we destroy that tower, Xander's Federation will lose virtually all communication capabilities, giving us enough time to regroup—and they won't be able to counterattack without communication or logistical support."

"Engaging the Federation like that is suicide, Tristan," said Braxton.

"It's suicide if they expect us, but they won't. They're overconfident and full of their own bullshit. We're *already* at war, dammit! And if we don't strike soon and decisively, the Federation will be scraping us off the bottom of its boots like the dumb shits we are for not seizing this opportunity—we might not have another chance. They think we're afraid. They won't expect an offensive strategy! If the Federation actually *does* attack Amstye, President Clexor will *have* to fight."

"If Oxium and Feria side against us," rebutted Barkley, "we'll lose for sure."

Tristan pondered. "Maybe a necessary sacrifice? Reyna will help, especially after Eliza speaks to the Council, which can only happen if we rescue her ... Reyna's allies will help, too. We probably can't avoid total war, but they've forced our hand—sitting on our defensive asses isn't an option!"

Braxton tapped his tablet and continued. "Dammit! Tristan is right. Let's force Clexor's hand and make him piss his pants. It'll be good for him." His eyes sparkled with new vigor.

"What of an airborne convoy to Reyna?" inquired Barkley.

Tristan rebutted. "First, we extract Eliza, then rendezvous in Tibur on our way to Verdia. I need time to fly her to Reyna."

"I assume you have a plan to infiltrate the tower?" asked Jase.

"I'll need help, but, just like those zyn repositories, we'll know when the time's right."

Tristan wanted feedback from Cole; none forthcoming. "Only this time, we'll have no traitors." He thought back to Lathe and Voleta playing them as fools. *It won't happen again.*

"In order to compromise the main entrance, we'll need at least two RP Defenders," started Cole, excitedly. "Those tanks'll blow the shit out of ground security. We'll do the bomb trick in the underground, too; business as usual."

"Don't be stupid," retorted Jase. "Our best chance is a surprise air-offensive. Eliza's on the 85th floor, ten floors from the top; it would be fast—hit-and-run."

"And your exit?" asked Bailey, surprisingly knowledgeable. "Radar will ping you the second you hit their air space!"

Jase nodded slyly. "I have stealth, sweetheart; plus access to a few abandoned shuttle craft, thanks to Neopolis. Trust me, I'm already in."

Bailey answered the condescending remark. "Call me 'sweetheart' again, reach out to hold my hand, and draw back a stump, asshole."

That lightened the mood, at Jase's expense. There were more than a few chuckles.

Tristan appreciated their suggestions but had other ideas. "We'll need both air *and* ground," he said. "We'll penetrate security and commandeer a service elevator to the 85th floor, but from the roof." He waited for their expressions to return to normal.

"They're recruiting," said Bailey seriously. "The confusion from so many people there could provide great cover."

"Consult the expert in this field and the problem resolves itself," said Braxton, grinning on the vid-monitor.

"You want to add to the plan, General?" asked Barkley.

"How many reserve fighters do we have, Captain?" queried Braxton.

"Eighteen, sir."

"Hmmm ..."

"Did you have something in mind, sir?" hesitated Barkley.

"Like I said, consult the experts ...."

Bailey opined. "Ground maneuvers are too risky, probably impossible. Air is more viable. I've personally visited this Navalasta Valkyrie Tower.

You cannot access ground entry, period. Redundant measures at ground entry points make an attempt there just plain stupid."

Barkley nodded in approval. "Okay, I'll authorize a pair of shuttles. Penetrate their defenses, rescue Eliza, plant the bomb, and run like hell; real simple, eh? Rescuing that girl is our second priority, though."

"What?" Tristan was indignant.

"You rescue the girl and fail to blow the tower, we're all dead; just later rather than sooner."

"Each shuttle can carry five men," cited Barkley. "The first shuttle holds the bomb squad; the second—top floor air cover. And General, those lovely aircraft you spoke of—they'll provide plenty of distraction. They'll be decoys, enabling us to distract Valkyrie air defenses. We'll program the shuttles to transmit SOS alerts that they're under attack. The Valkyrie will dispatch intercept fighters, giving our shuttles enough of a window to breach defenses and survive the assault. Plan accordingly so that there's enough time to land, set the explosives, acquire Ms. Nyvala, and retreat. It'll happen fast; be prepared!"

Tristan liked the plan overall. A few more details, but Barkley had done his job.

Braxton flashed a thumbs-up. "I like it. Let this be the start of their great war, except they're not the ones starting it. I pray that our Reynan alliance holds fast. Who's going to be squadron leader?"

Barkley continued. "Tristan. You and Lt. Delmont command the lead shuttle; Lt. Foard and Corporal Ashbury the second."

"I wish to go with Tristan," said Atlas, quietly and unassuming.

Barkley's mouth dropped. The other officers froze.

"Did that big ass cat just talk, Captain?" challenged Braxton.

Barkley stuttered. "Y-Yes …, sir. I believe it did."

"If you would allow me, may I join you, please?" reiterated Atlas calmly. His moist nose flinched; long, black whiskers briskly wavering.

Speechless, Barkley's mouth remained wide open like a stimulated Venus fly trap.

Tristan beamed. "I can't think of anyone else's company I'd rather have."

"Atlas?" said Bailey.

"I may not be human, but I understand many of your ways. My people hate the Federation as much you, probably more."

Jo eyed Atlas warily and adjusted his red hat.

Bailey nodded admiringly. "Acolyte respect is difficult to attain, Tristan. You should be honored."

"I am, deeply."

"Then I'll lead the squadron," said Barkley. "After the initial attack, the plan is to provide a twenty-minute window; there'll be more blood in that turnip. This is a suicide mission if I've ever seen one."

Tristan shrugged and crossed his arms. "That's not exactly a stamp of approval. Hmm, let's follow that line of optimism. All we have to lose is our lives." He lost himself in thoughts of racing down an 85th floor corridor and crashing through Eliza's door. "Failure will *not* be an option. If you think this is suicide, we'll let you stay behind and go out in a blaze of glory when the place goes off."

Braxton clapped. "Ha! That's the spirit! Fearless. I wish you all well. Captain, make the necessary arrangements. I expect this mission to be underway by 18:00 hours tomorrow! He glanced at Bailey and smiled—that's 6pm for you. Understood?"

"Clearly, sir." Barkley snapped a salute, somewhat reserved.

"Braxton out." The monitor went black.

"All right. You heard the general," remarked Barkley, taking a moment to tuck in his shirt. "Let's get to work!" He led the way to a computer table and began planning.

Tristan glanced through a row of windows at a screeching fighter.

Bailey approached Tristan. "Are you sure you want to do this? You heard the captain. It's suicide."

Tristan replied, "I hope the captain doesn't tell you to shit your pants ... suicide. Maybe? But some things are worth dying for."

"Eliza?" she asked.

Tristan masked his irritation at her jealousy.

"Foard and Hart on another whirlwind adventure!" Jase could barely contain himself. "You're damn lucky to fly with me again. Expect to learn a lot." He chuckled quietly, listening for a response.

"Stop laughing and get off your shit-stained ass," quipped Cole. "No time for being stupid, Jase. Tristan, there's only one reason good enough for me to want to come along!"

"What's that?"

"Hey, I want to witness the shitstorm! This is the first time I've seen you give a damn about another person. Maybe I can take a snapshot; you and Eliza posing, and behind you, I'm blowing the shit out of Valkyrie Tower. Hell, we could sell the rights to the movie."

Tristan laughed, for the first time in ages. "That's a great idea." If only it would be that simple.

"Forgive me, Tristan," said Jo as he yanked on Tristan's sleeve. "I wish I could join your endeavor, but I'll be occupied in my own important matters." He gathered the stained folds of his red jacket and stood tall, his head reaching Tristan's knee.

"Like what?" chided Cole. "You going to paint a nude Paputa?"

Jo's forehead suddenly wrinkled. "Like I started to say before that unnaturally perverse and juvenile comment," replied Jo. "I must locate the Grand Master. I do hope you'll understand."

Tristan dropped to one knee, not excited about Jo's change of plans. "I understand," he said quietly. He thought of the paintings and hoped that they'd be reunited soon. "And I thank you for all that you've done. I hope to see you again, very soon, my little friend."

"Me too. You're a good man, Tristan. Bring Eliza back. And I'm not little. You're big."

Cole rolled his eyes.

Bailey adjusted her satchel and joined Atlas. "I wish I could go, but I'm no good with rifles. I'd be better off in the convoy. I'll be waiting to hear of your success."

"Plan on it," replied Tristan. He had no idea what to expect; the prospect of finding Eliza was remote. To reach her, he had to face the world's greatest power in a foreign country and then breech the tightest security they had to offer. It would be the fight of his life.

APUS 1, 1870 O.C.
COUNTRY: ATOMIA
CITY: NAVALASTA

Tristan was right where he wanted to be, sitting beside Atlas piloting his team of five through hostile Atomian territory. Nothing like a dangerous day. The Acrolyte mostly kept to himself. Bailey still couldn't figure out why Tristan was pissed off at her. He had better things to think about; flying did that to him—a highly angular craft screaming through the atmosphere, true to its sleek, cutting edge contours, was better than a doctor's prescription. Speed thrilled him, but not turbulence. Their path traced the leading edge of a cold front, bucking along like an unbroken horse. Even his iron-clad stomach churned. Aft, three solders, Tibur-based Lieutenants' Kelvin, Boaz, and Clark, complexions a mix of beige and green, kept to themselves. Boaz fumbled with his rifle, while Clark and Kelvin, heads bobbing, dozed restlessly.

Captain Barkley led the Sky Wings' team, trailing Tristan a thousand feet above. Their radios were tuned and active, scanning constantly. They knew that they were flying into the unknown that may very well be on a one-way trip. None of them had ever faced the Federation. Troubling rumors abounded. In the not-too-distant, clouds intermittently obscured an opaque but glowing urban ring surrounding Navalasta. To cast such brilliancy, the city had to be enormous. The Valkyrie Tower lit the night sky; spots of light through gaps in the clouds declared its massive height. Navalasta's dazzling cityscape was a concrete jungle abuzz with nighttime activity. At horizon's edge, the sun was creeping upward. The view was streaked with cirrus clouds, appearing dark between the ship and the gradually growing glowing orb. Beneath their cover, at least a dozen buildings shot out powerful lasers—whites, greens, and purples. Swirling haze, stained with darkened hues, painted a circling fighter squadron. Just past the city, ominous clouds brooded, threatening the captive city with unseen fury contained within. Tristan wondered if Eliza was gazing upon them as well.

Over the radio, Jase requested clearance from Valkyrie Air Traffic Control. Tristan's heart tripped over itself in anticipation. Under pressure, Jase had proven himself, but this might be different; Atlas displayed a nervous edge; serrated but pensive.

"If ATC doesn't go for this, Atlas, we might be kissing our asses goodbye," said Tristan.

A grunt.

ATC's response triggered dancing green lights along the bottom edge of the transponder. "We have you on our scope. Please identify."

Tristan's shirt was immediately drenched.

The man's tone was pleasant enough, but non-visual assumptions killed many an unsuspecting pilot. Jase peered out the starboard window and keyed his mic. "Shuttle Volkon and Shuttle Spyria. Code red. Amstynian Sky Wings in pursuit! Permission to land on Valkyrie Tower! They're closing on our six!" shouted Jase.

They waited and held their breath, all eyes on the radio, seemingly another human face. The plan had commenced; no turning back now.

ATC's delayed reply was edgy, but the curtain hadn't dropped. "Shuttle Volkon and Spyria. Unable to identify; repeat clearance sequence."

His hand shook as he fingered four nubby transponder dials.

"Check again!" Jase yelled frantically. "Their stealth must be operational! We need air support now!"

"Shuttle Volkon. We still don't ... wait, we see them. Nine fighters incoming!" The controller's peal blew one of the small, panel speakers.

Jase banked left toward the world's tallest tower. Thick purple lasers penetrated murky ether, marking their destination.

The radio crackled again. "Air support—inbound! Expect visual on your ten o'clock at southern outer marker. Clearance approved." A host of commands were issued, prompting as many frantic replies. Most of the voices were younger, yet all were toned with discipline.

"Roger!" replied Jase.

Tristan smiled smugly. The plan was working. He switched off the console lights, instantly calming the occupants of the cockpit. Tristan activated his private comm link.

Jase immediately broke through. "It worked! I told ya it would! Ha!"

"Don't get too excited! There could be a shitstorm waiting. Titan leader. Are you ready?" queried Tristan. No premature celebrations. He hoped that ATC didn't have the technology to monitor their private channel.

"Bring on the bastards! Prepare for battle, Titans!" ordered Barkley in his own DNA. No one sounded like he did under pressure.

The nine-fighter group, circling just past the city's southern border, was abuzz with excitement. Tristan listened blindly, intent on Jase.

"Twenty minutes, shuttle team," transmitted Barkley. "That's all I can guarantee—and I hope it ain't a lie."

"That's all we'll need! We'll be outta there in ten!" replied Jase.

Tristan scanned the dawn, locking onto a T-57 formation about to pass overhead. The lead fighter had landing lights on, making the craft appear like a Heavy. Zyn thunder rattled the shuttle, jostling him and the others like dice on a card table. Tristan cinched his straps. Dozens of the formidable fighters converged in the twilight sky; three turret configurations hanging from leading edges and triangular stubbed noses, appeared darkly sinister—swarming wasps ready to assault a hapless gopher. Shrill turbines screamed, piercing the shuttle's hull like it was paper. Mere seconds marked the moment they had been dreading.

"Damn, they're fast!" shouted Jase.

Tristan keyed his communicator. "Titans, prepare!"

"All right men. Attack strategy "Delta! Execute!" commanded Barkley.

The battle commenced; turrets pounded. The Sky Wings activated rapid fire mode, hammering out three-burst volleys while the T-57s returned single-fire salvoes. The sky was filled with showers of detonations. It appeared strangely symbolic against multi-colored laser markers. Fire arched from an incendiary explosion, curving high and fizzling out over Navalasta's far reaches. Looked like a T-57 crashed. Tristan wondered what the people below must think. They probably had never been in a war.

Without pilot stealth, the odds were against the Sky Wings.

"You ready to land, Tristan?" Every time Jase's voice crackled, Tristan felt massive nearby discharges. The sensations shook his confidence. He thought of Eliza, her image merging into his fears.

The Tower was dead ahead. Tristan needed and craved success, wishing that the battle would be over and Eliza would be in his arms. He vowed to stop at nothing, Seryth included, if he showed himself. His heart throbbed like a jack hammer. Trying to will himself into calm proved useless. "Let's do this," he shouted, wiping moist palms on smooth, black leather pants. Nervously, he pushed back his dark hair, but it fell right back into piercing, blue eyes. He grabbed at his waist-length jacket, caught the zipper and tugged.

"Expect escorts once inside," said Jase. "We'll cover you while our men approach the entrance. I'll bring Cole around. Once inside, you're our only eyes and ears. We'll do our best to cover you from the air—but we'll need constant updates—and don't think I'm some kind of a miracle worker."

The instructions offered Tristan fleeting assurance. "Right," he replied in the face of Federation soldiers guarding the roof hatch. One held a portable radio and pointed at them. "Atlas," shouted Tristan. "Light 'em up!"

With surprising agility, Atlas sprang out of his chair and slammed a magazine into a floor mounted gun. He released the port side door and blasted away. Ear-piercing discharges echoed harshly in the confines; smoking casings descended like sparks from a lathe.

The soldiers spewed their own blood and landed in pieces.

"Area cleared!" shouted Tristan, catching a faint whiff of settling gun smoke as he dropped the shuttle to the roof. He skipped the landing checklist, activated the aft ramp and cut main power. Once extended, he could hear eruptions from nearby turret bombardments. The sky flashed with each onslaught, like beige lightning, lighting up everything, but the thunder in this case did not follow the flash, it preceded it. His twenty-minute allocation was slipping away faster than he wanted; he flew off the ramp and ran for the hatch. He was most vulnerable now but couldn't run any faster. *Just get off the roof.*

Jase hovered close enough to blanket the roof with zyn exhaust. Its side-door retracted; stubby arms extended, claw-like, awaiting a payload. Motors whined, rappel lines fired and soon dangled within reach. "Nice shooting, Atlas! Volkon team on approach!" said Jase. The lines lolled and then whipped like angry snakes while riders clipped on and silently dropped.

Tristan adjusted his earpiece. The air reeked with pungent exhaust. His breathing shallow, he was anxious to sidestep the downdraft.

Atlas crouched just ahead, waiting for Tristan to catch up.

"You stay with the ship," ordered Tristan. "Do you understand? If we're not back in twenty, say a prayer and fly your furry ass outta here!" Tristan shoved a radio into Atlas's massive paw.

Atlas nodded and fumbled with the toy.

Jase's men were nearly down.

Tristan counted eight black uniforms. He wished there were more—so few. As soon as the last one landed, he waved his Droth and the ropes recoiled. "Let's go!" he shouted.

Like water through a spigot, the men fell in behind Tristan. The third man jumped ahead, motioning with closed fist. He ran forward, wedged a digital timer into a clump of gray explosives and molded the matter into place. Seconds later, the metal disk blew into the morning sky. At once, the men and their oversized packs spilled into the smoky shaft. Tristan waited at the bottom, keeping his eyes on the largest pack. It carried the explosives.

"Guide us, Tristan," Jase asked.

Tristan replied, "On it!"

It was now or never as Tristan trailed the others. Two Federation guards were dead. The plan was working; ten floors to go. Even so, the 85th floor seemed another continent away. Like a pack of yipping dogs, high-pitched sirens began to chirp all around. The din was ear-piercing, worse than fire alarms. Tristan wanted to scream. Building security was probably on its way. Jase's cover was key to their success. Tristan adjusted his transceiver's volume under the mind-crushing chirping.

"You all right, Titan Leader?" queried Jase.

"We've lost Titan Seven! Dammit!" said Barkley, his voice faltering. "They're tougher than we realized. Titan Three. Two bogies just straddled your six! Fire 'em up, now!"

Once the volume was set, Tristan focused on a constant stream of updates. He envisioned Barkley's plain drawn face, downcast eyes and mouth cupped with wrinkles. A scream burst through his speaker. With each step into the building's belly, twenty minutes would pass like shit through a goose. The view through the 94th floor's stairwell door caught Tristan by surprise. He stared into an enormous chamber—a massive open area three stories tall—with elegant, circular staircases on either end. Red and black Atomian flags hung along the long wall, draping the floor. The facing wall was the longest stretch of plate glass he'd ever seen. Had Jase discovered this advantage? It would make his job much easier; the occupants were completely exposed. Maybe the staircases could be used for cover? Life-size portraits of Valkyrie officers were strategically interspersed between flags along the lower sections. If they could place the explosives on the 85th floor, the cavern would crumble and the upper supports would fail. A chain reaction would demolish the entire structure. The 93rd floor stairwell signage gleamed brightly; in the adjacent hall leading from the stairwell, a dozen or so Valkyrie guards fired sporadically and hunkered down behind a row of desks. One of Jase's men was hit. He flew back against the stair railing, arched his back and fell over it. He hadn't reached out to catch the railing. He was dead. The rest of his men crouched along alternating steps. One yanked open the door and two others returned fire. "Jase!" shouted Tristan. "93rd floor, southeast corner! Just the other side of the stairwell." The squeal of power thrusters under the enormous strain of a banking vessel immediately answered.

An entire section of plate glass exploded, spraying bullets and shards like water from a fire hose. In fluid motion, Cole slid open the side door and fired. As if suspended by an invisible cable, Jase swiveled the craft; Cole emptied his over-sized magazine into the vacant office space. Desks, chairs, and cabinets splintered a thousand ways. Valkyrie guards, pinned helplessly, cowered. Cole gunned them down in a dazzling display of firepower. Cole's flurry of rounds went through anything the guards were using for cover. It was akin to spraying leaves off a driveway with a garden hose; furniture and men flying backward, blood spraying in the same direction.

Tristan shook from the excitement, the burst of adrenalin as tasty as coffee. "Got 'em! Thanks! We lost one man!"

"Dammit," shouted Jase. "Don't lose anymore! See you on the next floor! We'll clear out the Valkyrie before you arrive!"

"Affirmative." Tristan didn't want to lose any more headcount, but what could he do? Federation troops were apparently well trained and more numerous than expected. The vast cavern echoed Jase's turbines while Tristan's group descended. Cole damned another group of guards caught rushing from an elevator, but not before they opened fire into the 92nd floor stairwell, killing Boaz and Clark outright. Tristan used the commotion to scramble down two more levels to the 90th. They were ambushed by concealed guards. Tristan returned fire, connected with two. Kelvin jumped before Tristan, took cover behind the open door, and leveled his high-powered rifle, knocking two more down. One of Jase's men lobbed a fragmentation grenade; it rolled under a desk and took out three more. The excitement from close combat sent Tristan into overdrive. If Jase hadn't covered them …. Five floors to Eliza. Was she still there? No one knew. She had to know he was coming by now.

"Titan Six! Behind you!" radioed Barkley.

Another explosion and another dreadful scream. The stairwell felt like it was blowing in the wind. A Sky Wing fell from the sky in a circular pattern angling slowly downward from its forward momentum, flames and black smoke trailing.

He had to hurry. The 88th floor exit door burst open and the landing flooded with office workers. Screaming and shouting, they poured from the "concrete dam", never looking back, evaporating like steam as soon as they had emerged.

"Twelve minutes!" warned Jase.

"Okay!" replied Tristan, his features flushed with urgency as he scanned his men. "Let's do this!" He'd never felt so keyed and constrained at the same time—so galvanized. Lives depended on him.

Cole covered Tristan's descent, his presence galvanizing, shattering glass and mortar while Jase descended. The explosions ended abruptly; one moment he was there, and the next, daybreak's ghost.

Tristan froze. Where did Jase go? Without him, Eliza was lost. It would be like throwing rocks at heavy machine guns.

Tristan's headset came to life. "Tristan, there's a fucking whole battalion holed up on the 70th floor. They're shooting up at us, and they have the firepower to take us out. They're backed up to the elevators! Hurry up, man! They're coming!"

"Hold them off as long as you can! We can't do this without you!" Tristan's thoughts were swimming. 86th Floor. He motioned to two behind him to back up. "Androids!" shouted Tristan. Five battle-ready androids, silver, polished, and deadly, dropped out of the ceiling. Sweet deity—the ceiling? What next? Their brows flashed red, beating in time to mechanical hearts. *Stay calm.* They were no different than any other. They could make short work of them if they stayed calm. Droids were attracted to noise; he needed a diversion. As if by magic, an adjacent wall exploded. This was his chance; the droids stopped firing and turned away. He lunged through the strewn concrete and dropped behind a desk. The droids faced open air. Another of Jase's men fell in a heap. Tristan returned fire, ducking under a shower of flying glass. "Jase! We need you. 86th floor, North side! DROIDS!"

"I can't get close enough!" screamed Jase. "We're under heavy fire! They're not letting up!"

"Do *something*!" pleaded Tristan.

Cole's heavy machine gun blared.

"We're stuck!" shouted Tristan. Eliza was under his feet. He couldn't fail, but advancing seemed impossible. Anger seethed, blurred his thinking. He refused to crumble.

"We can't do a damn thing, Tristan!" shouted Jase. "I'm telling you. If we keep moving in this direction, we'll lose any possibility of cover!"

Furiously, Tristan and his smoking Droth dove at one of the robots. He shattered the android's head with a triple blast. Kelvin tossed a grenade. *BAM*! Four synthetics wobbled and sparked, fountained in a blaze of energy, and then fizzled, falling face first into twisted heaps. Two of them toppled out into space. Tristan's chest hammered as he retreated into the stairwell. Just below, Jase's engines' roar worked its way up his neck and into his head. Leaping over piles of fragmented mortar and gnarled metal, he calculated his chances, slimmer with each passing second. Seconds were all that he had left. He read the door—85th floor. He ran to the guard station and grabbed for an electronic tablet, struggling to locate Eliza.

"Tristan! We only have eight minutes to blow this joint!" Kelvin planted himself and faced the door.

"Then set the damn thing! I'll find Eliza!" snapped Tristan. He hadn't noticed Kelvin behind him. He didn't care about the bomb; he cared only about Eliza—she was so close he could smell her, he thought.

"Tristan!" Kelvin fired back.

"Go! Set it to detonate in fifteen minutes! We'll need that much time!"

"We don't have that much time!" shouted Kelvin.

"We're not going to make it back in eight minutes! Barkley has to fend off those T-57s. It's our only hope!"

"Son of a bitch!" Kelvin motioned wildly, and he and his partner ran down the hallway.

"Where are you, Eliza?" muttered Tristan as he raced through screen after screen of floor plans. 85th floor link—he tapped. 'Detention Center' blossomed onto the screen. "Found it!" Room 5B. Tristan tapped "unlock" and sprinted past security.

Kelvin's rifle blasts echoed—more Valkyrie. "Tristan!" blared in his earpiece. "They're coming up the elevator! You're out of time!"

42

The tension of the moment seized Tristan as rigidly as his grip on the Droth. Only Kelvin stood between him and advancing Federation troops. Volley after volley echoed down the brightly lit hall. Room 5B, strangely still not visible, played on Tristan's mind. As long as Kelvin could contain the advance, she was within reach. Tumbling granules in time's hourglass now assailed like a sandstorm. Even after reaching her, they would have to fight their way back to the roof. And then there was the question of the bomb. He feared for Kelvin's life, but he did have a chance. 1B ... 2B ... 3B ... 4B .... 5B.

Numbness doused him like ice water. His ears rang, leaving him detached, unnerved and feeling absolutely impotent. She had to be on the other side. Chills raced down his spine as if on a high speed track. He hadn't rehearsed what he'd say. Had she been tortured, or worse? Could she walk?

"Move!"

His fingers came to life. He pressed the buzzer; nothing. He pushed down on the latch; it caught and then gave way. Taking one last deep breath, he cracked open the door, expecting the worst, wondering what would come next.

Morning's rays were vexing. He squinted and shielded his eyes. A gleam later, her silhouette—thin and fragile—spilled onto the carpet mere feet away. He ached for her touch. Only that would relieve the torment. She drew her hands frightfully through her dark hair, no longer full and soft. The sun's glare obscured her skin. Did it still have a radiant glow? Would she remember him? Surely, she would.

The bomb. He had to hurry. Her silence was like a flashing yellow warning light. And then, she arose, standing awkwardly, as beautiful as when they had first met. Golden hues shimmered against her hair. Shadowed, her piercing gaze drew him further in. He stared back. She must have spent most of her time sitting on the floor in the sparsely furnished room. She had been through so much, alone. A smile slowly formed.

Suddenly, she bolted toward him, face frozen in amazement. "Tristan .... You ... remembered me," she sighed quietly, years of suffering, moist tears on every word.

"Always." His throat seized.

She collided with such force that they flew back in a tight embrace. Tristan half expected the enthusiasm but hadn't planted himself quite well enough. Her hair pleasantly tickled his stubble—its scent was intoxicating, nothing special—just her. She didn't seem to notice Jase's roar, just outside. Without a care in the world, they clung feverishly, her moist cheeks nuzzling his neck.

Tristan savored every second, but Father Time was banging against his head. His heavy burden began to lift. Eliza was in his arms. Tristan gathered her chin and drew her face in. "We have to go, now!" he said, fully aware of what that really meant.

That's when her eyes swelled.

He led her to the door, out of reunion's elation and into a tightening maw. She had no idea, or maybe she did. Kelvin's rifle hailed; three short bursts of relief. Her safety was his concern. He absolutely desired Kelvin's success and fought to reign in fear, but his senses were already awry. As they raced back to the guard station, his feet didn't seem to hit the ground. His radio clattered.

"Tristan ...!" yelled Kelvin.

"What's your status?" asked Tristan, hushed, reaching for the stairwell door. He pictured their return flight, a trail of destruction.

"We set the bomb, but are under heavy fire!"

"Dammit," retorted Tristan. "I'm coming for you!" A perplexing situation, he didn't know which way to turn.

"No! I repeat, No! Too many!" shouted Kelvin. "Get her out of here! I'll hold them off as long as I can! Take your fifteen minutes and go!"

Wincing, a fiery exchange bursting through his headpiece forced his choice. Eliza clung desperately; Kelvin's life hung precariously a few seconds away. "Kelvin!" Tristan shouted.

"Go!" Gunfire distorted the transmission, determining his choice.

He pulled Eliza into the unknown. On the next landing, two waiting Valkyrie lie prone. The defenders, ignorant of the purpose of this raid, were looking in every direction, not knowing from where their fate would be dealt. Tristan forced her back and quickly fired. Perfect head shots, the Droth leaving no flesh above their gaping mouths. Landing after landing, they ran, battling every step. With guns blazing, five Valkyrie burst through. Tristan fired, dropping one. Outnumbered, he retraced their steps and lost track of what floor they were on. He crouched adjacent a glass wall and waited. The glass shattered; powerful gusts whipped through, cold and unexpected, but an adjacent balcony was now within reach. Hand in hand, they lunged across the breach, landing just feet from the railing. The height was staggering. Buildings, like treetops, reached skyward—and open space; it felt like flying at 50,000 feet. No one would attack from here, a false sense of security. Gusting wind landed them against the wall. He pulled Eliza down, stalling for a lull. They were trapped.

"Tristan!" shouted Eliza, barely audible over the sounds of the conflict.

Gun fire approached; she must have noticed it too. Tristan pulled her around and fired through the rift. He needed Jase, but the radio had gone silent. He could barely distinguish his own thoughts. His eyes stung. Crouched, he keyed his mic. "Jase! I need back up now! I have Eliza!" He eyed the far door. "We're outside on the balcony—88, I think! Hell, I don't know!" When he realized how little they had moved, his knees turned to butter.

"I see you! Stay down!" replied Jase.

Tristan tensed and shoved Eliza beneath him. Jase hovered alongside and Cole opened up. Triple volleys terminated the guards' advance. Tristan waved and keyed his mic. "Thanks!"

"It's what we do!" replied Jase. "Now get her to the roof! Atlas is waiting! We don't have much time! My chrono gives the bomb twelve minutes! Hustle!"

Barkley broke through. "We can't hold them any longer! I've lost five ships! Repeat! We can't hold them any longer! We are breaking off."

"Shit. Tristan," said Jase. "Get you asses out of there!"

Tristan gathered Eliza and headed through the breach.

Jase shouted. "Find the maintenance ladder—rungs on your right! Climb to the 92nd floor! Then enter the stairwell through the access shaft. After that, just three more to go! It's almost over! Don't look down!" A sorry attempt at humor.

Angry for wasting precious seconds, Tristan scrambled. Gaping at a 90-floor fall, his arms and legs were already numb. But it was safer than the stairwell. *Grip those rungs with everything you have.* He hoisted Eliza's small frame; she eyed the sheer drop, went completely colorless, and reached above her head. One by one, they advanced, flattening themselves with each wind surge. More aircraft approached; would they have enough time?

Each rung brought more bad news through the earpiece. "Federation reinforcements have been spotted! Get the hell out of there! We're out of time!" shouted Barkley.

He reached a hinged, metal door and yanked the lever, and was immediately faced with eight Valkyrie. Bullets zinged past, forcing them to teeter precariously. Cold metal dug into his skin. Gloves would have made this so much easier. He lobbed a grenade inside, catching a glimpse of it tumbling down the duct. The explosion blew past and destroyed the far wall. He helped Eliza through, dropping onto a debris-strewn landing, catching his breath. They crouched below a glass wall. "I'm going to get us out of here!" pledged Tristan. "I promise!"

"I know!" she said, keeping low.

Tristan struggled; could he really save her? He watched her tremble and blamed himself. She had to survive. Four guards fired. He tossed another grenade, his last; the devastating blast was more effective than he had expected, but now he couldn't hear a thing. He peered over the wall—clear. "Go!" He yelled, hearing his own voice reverberate through his skull, as his ears were now useless as he directed her forward.

He turned a corner into a flying concussion projectile from a grenade launcher. Blazing white blinded his eyes and bloodied his ears. The blast catapulted him into the wall. White plaster and glass shards showered down, drawing blood from a dozen slices. Tristan stared blindly and heard nothing but temple bells ringing between his ears, waiting for white to fade into gray, then something familiar. He lunged, groping, finally feeling her hand and pulling her close. Blood trickled down his face and burned his eyes. His side hurt terribly, he couldn't move without the pain seizing him.

"Tristan!" cried Eliza. She pointed at his blood-soaked shirt.

He couldn't look down; she was the only thing that mattered. "Go! I'm all right!" He gathered all his stamina and slowly rose into the haze, teetering like a towering pine in a storm, ready to snap, stumbling toward a shattered opening. The haze in his vision thickened. "Eliza!" He crouched; broken glass crunching underfoot. He slunk over jagged edges into the stairwell. *Bam*! Another small piece of mortar came down on his back, rendering him prostrate. Fear blinded reasoning as he retrained onto a dusty vision.

A dreadful image formed; Eliza, a hand grasping her neck, and a pistol planted against her temple. He narrowed a painful squint to recognize the shadow looming over her.

Platinum-haired Seryth, like an aged monolith, glared through the haze.

Pallid hair wavered in Seryth's wake, transforming a sedentary politician into a mad scientist on the run as he hustled Eliza through the 92nd stairwell doorway. He yanked, roughly, negotiating glass and marble debris like a child dragging a ragdoll. He paused, eyeing the disaster zone strewn with riddled desks, chairs and electronics; calculating and clinging menacingly to a dazed Eliza.

"I suggest you give up, whoever you are!" he shouted, pushing her behind. "I'm in control. Your Amstynian forces duped us once, but I promise—not gonna happen again! I am owed and payment is due. Listen to me! For every soldier you've killed, I'll personally slaughter a hundred of yours. That's my promise."

Still crouched, Tristan tried to follow Seryth's image on the reflective surface of an overturned desk. Eliza hung limp, frighteningly lifeless in his grasp. He could chance it, but if he died, she would vanish, probably forever.

"Based on what you've already invested into this failed exploit, you must care quite a lot for this little whore," continued Seryth, driving his taunts down an unnerving, low-pitched road. "Is she that valuable; worth dying for?" A gust of exhaust unsettled his locks; he tossed back his head and continued to search the wreckage that was once a finely furnished laboratory.

Tristan inched forward, halting apprehensively before a mangled heap of what had been desks.

"Humph . . . no reply?" bullied Seryth, his voice piercing, still unable to find him. "Okay then, let's play a game. I'll count to five. You don't toss your weapon onto the marble; I blow her pretty little head off her neck. Do you understand the rules?"

He couldn't be serious. An Atomian leader? Vengeance was driving him like an unrelenting master drives a beast of burden.

Seryth jammed his barrel into the base of her skull. Her cheeks flashed, burnished from sweat and tears.

Whatever Tristan chose to do, he had to do it now.

"One ... two ..." Seryth counted. His tone flexed with exhilaration.

Tristan, reluctant to leave his cover, stayed low. He was not cowering. Somehow, six more Valkyrie materialized behind Seryth. They must have come from the elevator. He gave himself no more than five or six minutes before Kelvin's handiwork bore fruit. Then, this magnificent structure would be blown straight to hell.

Barkley blared in Tristan's earpiece. "We can't hold them any longer! We're pulling out! I repeat. We're gone!" Tristan pictured his Droth spinning away on the marble. He could pick off Seryth, but not without the risk of hitting Eliza. Another decision; no choice a good choice.

"Three ..." continued Seryth.

"Tristan!" shouted Jase. "We can't wait forever! We've got to go, now! Do you copy? Tristan!"

An earpiece *"click"* isolated Tristan from any semblance of hope. Either Seryth would kill him and Eliza, or the explosives would. No one would ever know.

"Four ..." shouted Seryth.

 "Don't do it!" yelled Eliza. "Don't do it!"

She came alive. She sounded alert; he could leverage that—somehow. But he had to toss the weapon. *Do it.* It clattered end over end, and fell silent.

"Sir! That's an Institute VI weapon!" quipped a voice from the side.

"Come out...*now!*" demanded Seryth, his voice almost lost in the wind and exhaust.

Tristan, greeted by a blast of chilled air, six menacing rifles and seven frozen stares, raised his hands and stepped forward.

Eliza weakened at the sight.

Seryth lost his hold.

"*YOU!* I remember you, you pig!" yelled Seryth, distorted and strained. "The fucking traitor! You've been a thousand lifetimes of grief to me!" Seryth seemed to forget Eliza and shifted his attention to Tristan.

Eliza's eyes darted; her knees starting to buckle.

"You fool!" shrieked Seryth. "You would *die* for this half breed!" He grabbed her hair; her knees immediately gave way. She cried out and fell to all fours. Seryth almost lost his balance.

It was more than Tristan could bear. He lunged. A shot rang out, freezing him in mid-stride. Marble shards flaked his skin. He recoiled, desperately missing his Droth.

"Don't even think about it!" seethed Seryth.

Eliza struggled to her feet, twisting, seizing Seryth's wrist.

Tristan couldn't stand seeing her like this. That man, no more than an animal, was treating *her* like an animal. It was intolerable.

Seryth pinned the pistol against Eliza's neck, wrenching her around to face him. He seemed consumed with anger. "You prefer this stupid boy over me? You abandoned my world, a brand-new life filled with more greatness than you could hope to imagine! He's no better than a slave! You offend me, bitch! Perhaps our sovereign was right! Half-breeds can't be trusted!"

Seryth clutched Eliza's arm and leveled his pistol at Tristan. "And you! You think that you've beaten me? Maybe you've won this half-breed's love, but you're stupid! She'll sleep in your bed till she's finished with you. She's scum, blight on the Azdahri people! By joining her, you're humanity's blight!"

"Seryth! Stop!" shouted Eliza, twisting violently. "Why?"

"I'm showing what you showed me by rejecting my love! I would have given you everything. You will be punished! Let's just say, love for love—I demand his life! You'll learn soon enough that he is nothing!" Seryth dropped Eliza's arm and aimed his pistol toward Tristan.

"Seryth!" screamed Eliza. She thrust into him.

Tristan immediately lunged. The entire scene became an orgy of flailing limbs, groans and roaring exhaust.

Seryth toppled backward to the floor as his pistol fired into the air hitting his head hard on the floor.

Eliza fell to the floor, shouting in pain from the stray bullet.

Tristan charged, desperately trying to cushion her fall, but not even coming close. Then he lay still, dazed and groggy, veiled under Seryth's shadow as he regained his footing. He tried to move closer, reaching out, wincing at the sting of pierced skin. He touched her neck, careless and indifferent to the madman's gaze; her heart growing fainter with each pulse. He gathered her neck with one hand, dreading the sense of impending death, cloaking him like morning fog. He wiped the corner of her mouth the same way he had his mother's.

"Eliza!" His voice jarred both him and her. It seemed strange to attempt to be protective in circumstances where life was wavering like a dying flame in a wind tunnel. She began to choke, softly at first, then gut-wrenching. "Eliza!" He glanced at Seryth with an attitude of deliberative respect gone awry. Tristan's hand was covered in Eliza's blood.

Seryth, ashen and trying to fight the concussion from the fall, fought to breathe a grating whisper. "What …. You stupid … stupid bitch!" His mouth looked like a gaping fish before his fury exploded. "You did this to her!" He brazenly struck out his hand. "You made her believe some foolhardy ideal and you will pay!" he screamed. "You did this! I hold you and no other responsible!" He raised his pistol and centered his aim on Tristan's frown.

In that instant, Cole unleashed a maelstrom from rapid-fire undercarriage Gatlings. Papers, debris and anything not tied down crested in its fury. Tristan whirled around and threw himself over Eliza. Four flaming barrels hung from the shuttle, moving in unison. Three Valkyrie turned to run, but exploded into pieces, like they had ingested explosives. Seryth, astonished and utterly stupefied, spun and ran, blasting haphazardly into his wake. Tristan yanked Eliza, frightened, convinced that he was too late—bullets flew into desktops and file cabinets, thudding or clunking mercilessly, intended for anything in motion. He lowered his mouth to a petite ear. "What were you thinking?" he asked as he stroked her damp hair. He felt so weak, so helpless, but sensed the passing of immediate danger—except for the explosives set which would rival Armageddon. If she stopped breathing, he couldn't begin to think of how to react. "Why did you risk your life?"

"Tristan ...," she replied faintly. What flush remained paled in her next breath.

"Eliza .... Why?"

"—You ... needed me ...." Her eyelids fluttered and her head slipped to the side.

Tristan pressed his lips to her ear. He cried. The warmth of fragile cartilage demanded his passion. "Hang on, Eliza! Don't you dare give up! Fight!"

Seryth, the white-haired reaper, was nowhere to be seen. Tristan cradled his baby and raced for the stairs, pausing only to grab his Droth. He couldn't feel her weight for the first few steps. He imagined the rooftop shuttle— probably gone. He switched his earpiece on. "Jase! Do you copy?" All the speed in the world couldn't fix what he dreaded.

"... Have to go now! Tristan, answer me." Jase replied frantically. "I'm sorry but we're out ... time!"

"Jase!" yelled Tristan. His emotions peaked, focusing away from distractions and fueling his fury. "Wait!"

"I'm sorry! It's taking everything I have to maintain altitude! My craft's shot up and Federation fighters are inbound!"

Sweet deity. He's gotta wait! "Atlas!" shouted Tristan. "Do you read me? ... Atlas! Come on, answer me! Do you read? Dammit! No! Help— she's injured!" Gasping, fire burned in his lungs. "We're almost there. Don't do this! Atlas!"

His life was linked to hers, ebbing and flowing in unison. He refused to surrender. The fleet's presence was too concentrated, too near, too present. But they *had* to wait.

"I won't leave you," cried Tristan. "I promised I wouldn't give up and I won't." His arms drooped; he plodded, one step at a time, hoping that Seryth was still running. Short rifle bursts echoed from somewhere, above or below. His only mission was to save her. She stirred, gasping, her chest faintly rising and falling; her skin burning like she'd been caught in a summer wildfire.

The last few steps were impossible, but the end was in sight. Suddenly, sunbeams came to him through a cracked door. He glimpsed Atlas, glorious and golden, the most beautiful sight in the world, dancing a victory prance. He shook his rifle over a heap of five dead Valkyrie and roared in victory, if somewhat premature.

"Atlas!" shouted Tristan, overcome with emotion. Though his vision blurred; his strength returned, almost. Atlas pounced forward, effortlessly hoisting Eliza into his arms. In a moment, she was aboard and strapped in. Tristan followed blindly into the surreal surroundings, fending off an onset of resignation. He now understood blind faith. He struggled to buckle in as the engines revved and slammed him into his seat. Familiar sounds comforted him, telling him everything was going to be okay. Barely turning, he glanced about—Atlas's back, flashing console lights, his hand holding a wad of cloth against Eliza's abdomen—continuing, hoping for a glimpse of Kelvin before a raging inferno.

Tristan slipped off his jacket, worn and stained with Eliza's blood. His favorite shirt, displaying a surprising number of new rips, would have to be retired. Wincing from a stabbing side pain, he folded the jacket and wedged it under Eliza's head. Dizziness and a warm trickle down his side forced him to consider his own issues, but there wasn't much he could do without proper supplies.

More than pain settled in; it was not lost on Tristan that death had almost denied their narrow escape; he would add it to a growing list of chancy adventures—his lot in life, yet not quite a source of pride or something he looked forward to. He firmly believed Viktor had everything to do with his fate. Before his interjection into their lives, life was reasonably tolerable, if not pleasant, until his father died. He didn't spend any appreciable time dwelling on that, though. Pressing concerns usually garnered far more attention, including his concern for Eliza. He yearned, not only for her recovery, but also her peace of mind. She was young and should easily recover.

Powerful sensations—vibrations, hydraulic machination, manufactured ozone, and artificial lighting—gradually worked their way into the calming center of his brain. Sometimes it took a while, but they would eventually worm their way in. Droning engines, g-forces, and barely distinguishable creaks and groans created a forceful surrealism. Some uncontrollable subconscious notion had him on the verge of believing that they actually hadn't made it, but he would come back to reality. Yes, they had.

He was so very gratified Atlas could pilot. Radar pings echoing from the cockpit, audible warning tones, confirmed they weren't alone. Valkyrie craft were crowding their flight path; several fighters crisscrossed at their 10 o'clock, sparking fresh concerns. Thank the deity that their craft was transmitting the proper clearance code. He reached for a leather satchel and slid it under Eliza's pillow, then gently stroked her hair. Tibur, an hour's flight to the nearest infirmary, seemed a world away.

Eliza struggled to meet Tristan's gaze. "Tristan …. I'm scared." Her words sounded cold, clammy like her skin.

"It's okay. I'm here. You're safe with me."

Her voice faltered, unnerving to Tristan. Her eyes dulled. He wasn't sure of her medical condition beyond what he could see; her life seemed to be hanging by a thread.

"I'm in so much pain," she sobbed. A faint tear streamed down one cheek.

Hearing her say that mildly panicked him. He'd give his life for hers any day. "It'll stop," he whispered, continuing to stroke her hair. "We're Tibur-bound. Try and rest. Don't be afraid to sleep; we'll arrive soon and you'll be patched up and back on your feet in no time."

"Promise?" The soft reply instantly transported him back to the Ball where she had been so free and alive.

"Yes," he answered, hoping that she wouldn't sense his distress.

"I knew you'd come for me …." Her voice quivered. "I didn't know how, but deep down …." Her eyelids fluttered and she stopped.

"I thought you were dead," he confided, not sure if he should say anything at all. Could she understand; would she remember? "After that last transmission, I thought you were dead. I … thought I had lost everything." He wanted to continue.

"Tristan." Her voice could barely be heard over the engines.

"Shh. Don't talk. Save your strength." He found himself comforted by the soothing tone of her voice. "I remember when we first met, when you approached me at the Castalia Ball. You were fearless. When we danced …," he managed an awkward, reflective chuckle, "... you made me discover who I really was. You completed me. I doubt you can hear a word I'm saying, and maybe it's better that way, but I have to get this off my chest. If I don't, I'll forever regret it. Wherever I am and whatever I'm doing, our first dance will always be on my mind. That was the happiest moment of my life, not just because of the dance, but because it was the day that we met. I wish I could re-live it a thousand times." He caressed her cheek with the back of his hand; her skin was cool and moist to the touch. He leaned forward, through a searing stab, and softly kissed her forehead.

XXXXXX

Tibur finally came into view and proved an uneventful landing except for a distressing number of Amstynian soldiers milling about the flight deck. The increase in force was significant. Two or three-person squads had been replaced by droves of armed men and white-gowned medics. Within minutes, Eliza was whisked into an awaiting ambulance—a large, white van with flashing blue lights. Tristan wanted to accompany her, but he'd serve no real purpose. He watched them load her and lingered while Atlas secured the craft. "Atlas, thanks for not leaving us," said Tristan.

"To not abandon a comrade is in my peoples' blood. I would have stayed until the end."

"I owe you one, or perhaps two," said Tristan. They were bonded forever as far as he was concerned. He hoped he'd be able to return the favor. "Eliza would still be in the tower without your courage."

"You owe me nothing, never will." Atlas's curt rebuttal surprised Tristan as he turned toward the hanger.

"Tristan!" Jase shouted, running at his usual full speed. He grabbed Tristan's hand, unable to stop, practically dislocating it. "I expected the worst. I'm totally jazzed you made it out in one piece."

Tristan drew him close, surprised by the impulsive affection. "Thanks, Jase."

"How's Eliza?" asked Jase, showing his concern.

"I don't know," replied Tristan. His gaze fell slightly. "Seryth shot her. Since then, she's been in and out of consciousness."

Jase nodded a firm scowl, which quickly vanished.

Cole emerged from a crowd of flight deck personnel. "What happened?" he asked. "Why didn't the explosives go off?"

"We don't know, but Kelvin did set them," answered Tristan.

"Dammit," exclaimed Cole. "So, it was all for nothing? We were so close!"

"It wasn't all for nothing," retorted Tristan. "Eliza's here, isn't she?"

"Yeah. Yeah. You're right," returned Cole, quickly skirting the issue. "First thing tomorrow," he paused in deliberate fashion, "we're outta here. We anticipate that a Federation advance will strike Tibur within the next few days. If we can consolidate our forces, we'll have a better chance. Let's just hope that Tibur can hold out until we return."

"What are the chances that the Federation's attack will happen that soon?" asked Jase.

"Fairly high, I think. For Tibur's sake, though, I hope not, but they have developed some serious defenses," replied Cole.

Jase shrugged. "Then we should start getting ready. Come on, Tristan. Let's move like we have a purpose. If you're able, you can assist with loading the ships. Who knows? That might keep your mind off Eliza for a while. She needs her rest anyway."

"I intend to be there when she wakes up," countered Tristan, wincing as he turned to follow. Kelvin didn't make it, but Eliza had, a bittersweet reunion he knew he would never forget.

APUS 2, 1870 O.C.
COUNTRY: AMSTYE
ENROUTE TO VERDIA

Casting a silhouette far greater than a numeration of a thousand starlings, Command Ship Galacia harbored above northern Tibur's frigid terrain. It could be seen from miles away. A heavenly spectacle, enormous and unwieldy like a massive airborne submarine, keeping a watchful eye. Strings of shuttles, replicas of the freedom flight from Navalasta, filled with Tibur's residents, traversed the invisible skyway. The unparalleled undertaking, an engineering marvel born out of fear and preservation, ran flawlessly, or so it seemed, like dual conveyer belts, ascending and descending. The ascent afforded Tristan a closer look at the looming vessel; closing in, it transformed into a weaponized fish—an enormous underbelly dorsal, flexing orange wings, top fins like a sailfish, four double turrets fore and aft, and more along the fuselage. With Sky Wing support, swarming gnats, it seemed impregnable. Bulbous siblings hovered fore and aft like offspring. None retained Galacia's grandeur; most didn't appear armed or have a bottom dorsal. Two distinct ranks of Mech shuttles ferrying anxious payloads streamed from ground to sky.

Amongst the ever-swelling ranks, Tristan gained his bearings, traversing Galacia's many levels. Most corridors appeared identical; white walls and floors gleaming like operating rooms. He'd been issued an updated chrono fitted with a wireless port that provided status updates, and unlimited clearance. Ports were located along corridor walls; a few feet of proximity was all that were needed to hear the muted beep. At a glance, he would be apprised of defensive and offensive movements. The masses, occupying every public area, awaited lodging. Most were patient; an occasional argument surfaced but would quickly be quelled. The giant ship had already made two southern stops. Without its presence, Tibur's residents were fated to Federation chaos.

Even now, he wondered how Amstye had organized such a feat. The giant sky-whale, tethered to a high altitude docking station through a maze of cabling, hoses and rigid devices, brought back images of an underground ocean stocked with countless arrays of military-grade craft. Advanced technology fascinated him; his father had spoiled him, early years stippled with super-speed flights and handling the controls that made them possible. Next generation discoveries, covert power and stealth, harvested his respect above fine women and wine. But—Galacia stunned him—anticipation robbed him of sleep—he'd only heard about it the other day. Knowledge had surely increased.

The onboard Command Center, a central communications hub responsible for disseminating fleet orders, housed a handful of high-ranking officials. The remainder, over a hundred strong, had been scattered throughout the convoy. Rumor had it that nearly half had taken flight earlier in the week. Tristan's orders were to familiarize himself with the ship. He found it difficult, though. Most of the crew was busy quelling anxious passengers and outfitting stores. About three thousand civilians were forecasted; it seemed that as many were already on board. Many wandered the corridors, sat in cramped waiting areas, or were holed up on other levels of which there were at least ten. He had already visited the cafeteria, infirmary and training room, and was impressed with the ship's offerings—a virtual self-sufficient metropolis boasting a fantastic assortment of modern conveniences. Numbed by the constant bustle, he tried to concentrate on the Federation's advances. Viewing portals lined most hallways through which he could observe the fleet's daunting size, still dwarfed by Federation resources. He wandered back to the infirmary to visit Eliza and to have his dressings changed.

Eliza's doctor motioned him aside. "She'll be fine. The bullet passed through; entry and exit points were clean. We patched her up nicely.

She'll be up and around before you know it, but she does require rest. How's your side feeling after I patched you up?"

"It was a scratch. Not a problem." said Tristan. His heart burned while he gazed upon her restful features. She looked like a princess awaiting Prince Charming. "Thank you, that's the best news you could have given me."

"The nurses told me that you slept by her side last night. If that's the case, I suggest you throw down some chow and find yourself a real bed. She won't be awake for several more hours."

Tristan tensed. "I promised she'd never be alone again. I intend to keep it."

"I assure you, she's quite safe on Galacia, and especially under our care."

Tristan found himself doubting the doctor's lofty remarks. He'd failed before, but never again. Her safety warranted every sacrifice. "No, she's not. Once he discovers she's still alive, the Enlightened One will not stop searching. I'm gonna protect her at all costs."

The doctor scribbled on a pad, and then glanced up. "She's lucky to have you. Most people never come close to showing such love."

"Love?" He was right; a dawning reality refreshed him like a light spring shower.

"Yes. Love. I'm a doctor. I'm well aware of the telltale signs. I guarantee her safety under my care." He smiled coyly. "No one can enter this ward without access codes and my express permission." He pointed to the guards, four stout men bearing rifles and positioned alongside polished steel doors. The doctor handed Tristan a prescription and set down the pen.

"Thank you, Doctor." Tristan shook his hand and tucked the paper away. For the first time since he awoke, hunger pangs stirred. The cafeteria was two levels down. Biscuits and gravy sounded great, some sort of salad too.

As Tristan worked his way through the crowded hall, Jase's bustle of excitement broke through, and almost collided with him. "Tristan! Come quick!" he shouted.

"What is it?" asked Tristan, instantly curious. His chrono beeped. *"Some things never change,"* he thought.

"The Federation! They're attacking Tibur! Follow me aft!"

"Already?" exclaimed Tristan, cringing.

"They're annihilating the southern outskirts."

"What!" exclaimed Tristan. Was the Federation that merciless? Murdering civilians? It couldn't be. The World Council would have no choice but to declare war. He forgot about hunger and followed Jase two levels down, continuing further aft. As they cut through the cafeteria, Tristan could sense the crowd's tension. Jase punched in a code and pushed open an unmarked door behind the salad bar and led him to an exterior door leading to an outer balcony. Tristan squinted in the sun's first rays. A quick survey displayed their convoy repositioning toward Tibur. Vessels of every size and shape surrounded them; fighters, stealthy falcons on the hunt, swarmed, screening the cigar-shaped shuttles under fleeting wings. Galacia's aft was covered by two Sky Wing squads, triggering memories of recent encounters. He spotted military personnel on other balconies; they, too, stared in the direction of the southern horizon. Tristan pushed through to the outer railing. Cole, Bailey, and Atlas opened a space, allowing full view of the skyline. He had wondered where they were. Tibur melted into the horizon, yet its mass was unmistakable. Angry orange and yellow torrents clearly identified the unfolding attack. Flashes, creating thick blue columns of smoke as they hit their targets, too many to count, beamed from ships to the surface. Each hit generated a giant mushroom cloud, like a giant kick into the dirt, but with humans dying in its wake.

Cole's mouth was agape. "Deity be with us ...."

"They're leveling the entire city!" exclaimed Jase. "Those beams are frying everything they hit!"

"Will they reach us?" asked Bailey.

"Their priority is single-minded, to strike fear into people's hearts," responded Atlas. He reached behind his neck and scratched. "Used since the beginning of time, an old and reliable tactic. There isn't enough defensive military presence or capability to warrant this level of destruction. They're trying to weaken our resolve."

"It's working," replied Jase.

"President Clexor will have to retaliate," said Tristan as he examined a swath of vessels speeding past four enormous mooring stations. The collection of such powerful technology had caught him completely off guard. "Their ships …. Where did they acquire these technological advances? And how did we not see it coming?"

"What could we have done?" demanded Cole. The desperation in his tone didn't match his stature. "We shouldn't have attacked Valkyrie Tower! This is our fault!"

Now was not the time to lose perspective. What good would it do? "This was inevitable," replied Tristan. "No-one can blame us for that. It was just a matter of time. Attacking civilians is criminal. Right now, we need the World Council's involvement!"

Bailey interjected rather pointedly. "With this amount of evidence, Eliza won't even need to present her case."

"So, it really has started," said Cole hopelessly. "There's no going back. We'll have to live with our choices. We've just introduced the world to an all-out war."

Tristan continued to study swirling columns of multicolored smoke. Through it all, he could only imagine the horror. With nowhere to hide, the city's inhabitants would be immersed in rubble. If left alive, by nightfall …. Cole's words haunted him. A chill shook him from head to toe as he witnessed the beginning of a massacre that seemed would inevitably overwhelm every aspect of life.

APUS 2, 1870 O.C.
COUNTRY: ATOMIA
CITY: EMPYREA

The capital city of Empyrea, Atomia's largest city, had been voted the most unique Federation cityscape. Atomian architects had sculpted especially tall and narrow towers, like blowing reeds, almost too frail to stand. Salvador Seryth, 200 floors above solid ground, examined the gangly monoliths like a doting father would admire his own children. The Federation Command Center, situated on the top five floors of prime real estate, served as the center of societal order and national strength—directing the nation under its self-assuming authority. The expanse of jutting steel, glass and concrete offered a sense of stability amidst a most definite sway in the wind. Wind currents whipped up a frenzy, raging like brawling beasts in the summer's heat. He peered through high-powered quadraviewers at a handful of wide-eyed observation deck tourists. This height rendered summer's warmth void. Most faced the invisible gusts in heavy coats and hats.

Far below, black and red Federation flags fluttered along main thoroughfares, giving rise to heightened expectations of Sovereign Xander's upcoming speech. If the weather would allow, Seryth, General Nyvala, and President Drakkar planned to meet Xander on the leeward balcony where he would declare war against the Amstynians. Viewing monitors, strategically placed, stood poised for the most brazen event of all time.

Seryth mused over his power, pleased that so many followed without question. This could only happen in Atomia. He was annoyed that today's celebration was about to be marred by a meeting with General Nyvala. If he could have, he'd have re-scheduled it, but that might have drawn unwanted attention, from the wrong people. He assumed the subject of the meeting was Eliza; they really had nothing else to discuss. He'd covered every detail; no one could possibly suspect him. He was awkwardly anxious to shift the general's wrath to a more worthy cause—Amstye's annihilation.

An abrupt knock turned him about in the richly adorned office strung with black suns against fire-red backgrounds. He stepped across lush, red carpeting, readying himself. His personal secretary, smartly dressed in the uniform of the day, snapped to attention and saluted. Seryth preferred the crisper black uniform, but shale gray piped with aqua blue stripes on sleeves and pants had been selected instead.

"Lord Commander. General Nyvala has arrived."

Seryth brushed back his platinum hair and casually motioned. "See him in." He did his best to ignore mounting unease in anticipation of the upcoming conversation.

"Yes, Lord Commander." The assistant turned and exited.

A moment later, General Nyvala burst through the door in a blaze of either exultation or rage; it always seemed the same, regardless of the blaring opposition of these emotional states.

Attempting valiantly to second-guess the man, Seryth chose his words carefully. "I've been anticipating your arrival and am thrilled to meet on this most auspicious day, General."

"Get to the point, Lord Commander. You know why I'm here."

Unable to quell the iterations of images pinging his brain, he could still sense Eliza's perfume. He walked to a small bar and lifted a hot water canister. "May I offer you some refreshment?" With his back to the room, Seryth effused a tea bag with steamy water.

"No trivial formalities. What happened to Eliza? Where is my daughter?"

He stirred and returned a silver spoon, making sure to allow an exaggerated *clink* before responding. The image of Eliza laying helplessly, her blood spilling on the floor, rose before him larger than life. The bullet had been meant for Tristan; strength ebbed from his core. He wasn't weak like Nyvala. "I don't know …," he said, a forced mumble. "You've seen the Tower reports. Had our bomb unit not detected the device, the Tower would have been demolished." He forced more stamina.

"She was in your custody! You assured me of her safety!"

Seryth's lips smarted on the steamy porcelain. "The building was nearly razed!" he rebutted angrily, more from the tea cup than rage. "They used Federation shuttles, a well-executed maneuver."

"What happened to her?" demanded Nyvala.

Seryth set his cup down and spread the warmth over his hands. "They killed her." He paused with baited breath. *"Will he believe the lie?"*

"What!" Nyvala's ghost sprang to life.

"After they captured her, they attempted to transport her to the roof. My squadron and I pursued, but they used her as a human shield, and then," he bowed his head, "… shot her—right before my eyes. I'm haunted by the recollection." With his hand on his forehead, he forced a practiced sob. "I did everything I could to thwart those barbarians, but they were ruthless; utterly senseless murderers." His voice broke. "Eliza was a helpless victim."

"Why wasn't her body returned for proper burial? We have our customs! Now, we cannot bid farewell!"

"Must you press me so? An explosion devastated the entire area. The bodies were unrecognizable. It was something your eyes should not see!"

Visibly shaken, Nyvala struggled to breathe. "Who's at fault? General Braxton?"

"Yes. But there's another, an Institute VI renegade—Tristan Hart. His files are on the server. He's a genuine hothead who needs to die. He's devious, a terrorist, and must be rendered powerless and without breath. He killed Eliza. He threw the grenade that took out several of my trusted guards."

The general patted his forehead with a crisp handkerchief. "I never wanted her life to end like that. Sure, we had our disagreements, but she was my daughter. I wanted her protected and feared for her every time she would run off on one of those exploits. In a way, I admired her for that, something I never had the freedom to do; she was fearless. I never told her, but I loved her as much as I did her mother. If only I had told her. How will I break the news to my son? It will destroy him. They were so close."

Time stood still; horror and disbelief a shared bond, however fleeting.

"It was a tragedy."

"What action have you taken against this 'Hart' bastard?" Nyvala reddened, his eyes narrowing.

"I've ordered that he be hunted like the animal he is—a war criminal. I want him drawn and quartered. He'll be punished for crimes against the state."

With the ruse almost complete, Hart's fate would be perfectly sealed and he could then move on to more global concerns.

"Good." The general sighed, drawn and turning indolent. "I want him to endure the worst fate imaginable. He deserves nothing less than death by a thousand cuts." Monotones had transformed into vibrant bursts of passion. "All of Amstye must pay—my daughter will be avenged! Tibur was only the beginning. I will push north and force civil war upon them. Amstye will gift us Braxton and Hart's heads! Every delay will bring them unthinkable devastation! Like Tibur, Amstye will be turned into a white hot skating rink! And anyone foolish enough to join their cause, including Reyna, will suffer the same."

"Revenge *is* justice!" Slowly, creases aside Seryth's broadening smile took form.

"I swear on Sovereign Xander's name that there will be no draft-dodgers or rebellions. A master race is obliged to eliminate all forms of dissention from the lower castes." Nyvala's fists clinched tightly.

"Given your military skill, Braxton and Hart had better soon face Federation justice. Their deaths will destroy Amstye's military morale."

"Come. Our leader awaits."

"Yes, General." Seryth's smile had fully matured. He basked in his ability to control others; he felt fearsome and absolutely willing to unleash his persuasive skills on any and all Federation opposition.

The two strutted onto the main balcony where the sovereign was waiting. Handshakes were exchanged, a formality that bored Seryth.

He wanted the day over with, especially his proximity to Nyvala. The earthbound crowd's roaring, barely discernible so far below, drifted skyward. It sounded like a ferociously blowing wind. Seryth eyed broadcast monitors, viewing tens of thousands lining the streets. The crowd saluted—extended arms raised high. Xander appeared, a Federation flag wind block his backdrop, and took his place between the men. Applause erupted from a cluster of speakers.

"My dear Azdahri! Soldiers, sailors, aviators, Valkyrie, Institute VI and Federation Legions! Men and women of Atomia and Vuton. Hear me! The sands in destiny's hourglass have shifted. The time for a just war is upon us." Another eruption forced a pause. An audio technician quickly dashed over and lowered the volume. "And so, war has been declared!"

The cheers continued with chants of "war, war, war."

Xander continued. "To the President of Amstye who would, and does, harbor the terrorists who attacked Navalasta's Headquarters Tower: As each moment passes, these barbarians have fêted hindrance on Azdahri advancement and endangered our very existence. With the entire world as our witness, the Federation has exhausted any and all peaceful alternatives to avoid the torment now being ushered into Eshen. Amstynian terrorists are attempting to destroy our dreams, our ideals, our culture, *our people*! But, with our military strength, we will destroy such cancerous, such audacious, ambitions. It's clear now that political power should never be relinquished to Amstye. They would be wild brutes at the helm."

"Support us! Support your military! Gather behind us as we seek to destroy this enemy, this cancer, before it spreads! My father once said, 'Let not the world decide your destiny; rather, decide the destiny of the world'."

"We have chosen our path, a path to eternal freedom! We have crafted our own destiny! Our fight will be relentless; death our only reprieve. Eloquent oratory did not provide me this office; strength, candor and character did. Let me prove myself as your Sovereign, my people. Arise!"

Deafening applause garbled the speakers, sending the audio technician back to the amplifier. Xander's repetitive name carried into the room like a religious chant.

When he turned to Nyvala, Seryth was quaking from chills racing down his back. How he loved the sensation. He wondered how impressed Nyvala really had been. Drakkar stood, clapping. He caught Seryth's eyes and casually strolled his way. "Isn't he great? He's the savior of the human race."

Seryth nodded eagerly. "Yes. Yes he is." He fully believed in Xander's abilities as the Federation leader, thrilled to be part of the greatest global movement ever known.

"Doesn't it fill you with a sense of imminent justice?"

Seryth's smile dissolved. "I do not maintain any sense of justice. My task is simple—the destruction of all Federation enemies." Drakkar's stunned reaction fanned his passions. "You will learn to appreciate these qualities. Enjoy the rest of your day."

Seryth strolled back to the quiet of his office, relishing the fact that Amstye would soon fall and Eshen would be Federation-controlled. He stopped at a full length mirror, dusting his shoulders and tucking his hair. Perhaps the gray uniform did look better. Perhaps an even greater prize, Aurelia, would finally meet its demise. He reached for the cup of tea, still warm, and gazed out at a hundred engineering marvels, baffled how they remained upright. Then, and only then, would Reyna and its World Council be destroyed.

CHAPTER

47

Countless infirmary visits bored Tristan beyond words. He craved alone-time with Eliza, but with so many injured being cared for, that was certainly out of the question. Even though Tibur's devastation was now beyond the horizon, the horror he witnessed continued to inflame his dreams. Imprisoned in the massive, airborne ferry, his life was on hold. Surely he'd be given an opportunity for retribution. Gusts of cool wind blew across the balcony as the Galacia continued the passage. He loved watching the world pass by, so far below. From this lofty height, he found himself not wanting to return. It felt so liberating, and yet so dangerous, but isolated enough to allow him to gather his thoughts. Xander's speech demanded a forceful response. Morale among the passengers had changed for the worse; downcast gazes and hushed conversations told him more than a slew of military reports ever could. He had grown tired of assumptions, couched in ignorance, about the Valkyrie Tower. How narrow-minded those ignoramuses were if they blamed Tibur's downfall on that single event. His courageous group had saved one of the most important people in the free world and had nearly succeeded in toppling the massive tower. Kelvin's sacrifice was not in vain; words couldn't convey the man's courage. He had to have known that he would be killed in the attack.

He gazed at the Amstynian countryside; lush green spots intermingled with towering cliffs; he pondered the great nation's fate at the hands of the Feds. He could only imagine Seryth's deceitfulness, working to turn those willing to guard freedom's cause into vicious unwitting beasts. Braxton's demise had been assured. Tristan languished in these reflections. He glanced into clear sky and allowed the nighttime's star-filled canopy to captivate him. Was someone or something up there so far removed guiding, controlling these atrocities? Whoever that power was, was it now powerless against today's events—the bloodshed, the hatred, and the destruction. Were world events being played like a chess game? And if so, who was playing white and who controlled the black pieces? What kind of satisfaction could possibly be derived? Tristan was no philosopher, but he would have appreciated some answers.

"I kind of figured you'd be out here all alone." Eliza stood at the door, wrapped in dressing and wearing a thin, green infirmary gown.

How did she traverse two levels, through all those people and then onto the balcony? Her resolve, in and of itself, was inspiring. "What are you doing?" asked Tristan. "Shouldn't you be resting?"

She shifted slightly, repositioning her cane. "Yeah, but I've never liked being told what to do."

Her rebellious attitude lifted him somewhat, raising a chuckle. He scanned her features, trying to discern any weakness. "It's one of your finer qualities that I've actually come to appreciate."

She moved deliberately, approaching the railing, her gaze fixed on the darkness of night. "It's so lovely, isn't it? I was worried I would never see it again, so serene and peaceful."

"You had us worried." He was pained from the repeated realization of how close death had come.

"I must have. I never properly thanked you for rescuing me." She ran her fingers along the smooth metal railing and relinquished her outward gaze.

"And you'll never have to," replied Tristan thinking of Atlas's commitment.

Eliza turned. Pallid cheeks had turned rosy. "This beauty makes me want to dance with you. Maybe after my wounds heal?"

"I wouldn't miss it." A familiar chest throb returned. He wanted to hold her, speak tender words, draw her close.

"Perhaps ... now?" she suggested coyly.

"I thought you said …."

"Just a slow dance—please?"

Their eyes locked, followed by their hearts. He reached out and she laid slender hands into his strength. He brought her close, slowly, gingerly, afraid of hurting her. His arms encircled her back while she rested hers around his neck. The upward movement forced a wince. They swayed slowly to the rhythm of the wind in their hair. His heart thumped wildly, spurring an ever-increasing tempo. "So, what are you planning to do now?"

Her voice dropped to a whisper. "My brother Leo should be arriving soon. I need to tell him what I know now."

"Isn't that dangerous?"

"Yes. I'll be cautious," replied Eliza confidently. "He's the only family member that can be saved. Tristan, I have to try. But I also have to support Braxton any way that I can. We both know that he's our first and only line of defense. I pray that Reyna will get involved. If they sit on the sidelines, we're toast. What do you think?"

"If it means you'll still be in my sights, then I welcome your idea." Stubbornness had built a wall. He strained to peer over it.

"Aren't you afraid?" she asked as they worked their way down the curved deck.

They turned in each other's arms, quietly unified.

She tried again. "You can tell me."

"Yes." He didn't want to tell her, but their closeness moved him on.

"What are you afraid of?"

"Lots of things, I suppose. Perhaps I'm afraid of making wrong choices and having to deal with the consequences: or worse, an innocent someone else having to deal with them. I've lost so much in my life. And I keep hearing a gnawing voice asking what the point is in living when everything seems lost. Why fight when, in the end, I could just be taken and not enjoy the benefits of victory? Is what I'm sacrificing really worth it?" He felt he had flooded her with a lifetime of burdens.

"Tristan. We have so much to live for. We have … each other." They stopped dancing. "And what we have *is* worth fighting for. We fight so others may experience what we're now feeling." She placed her hand on his broad chest. "Your heart's racing. These are the wonderful moments that give life deeper meaning. I want to share all of them with you and I want others to experience the same. Let's fight for them, together …."

Tristan couldn't help but grin. "You certainly have a way with words."

Their gazes locked; starlight glinted in their eyes.

"What are you thinking?" asked Tristan. He wanted to know everything he could about this mesmerizing woman.

"When I'm with you, I can never be close enough …." She stopped and reached for the railing.

He touched her flushed cheek and was taken by her tenderness, pressing his lips fully against hers. The cool breeze continued to push against them as they sped toward the unattainable horizon.

EPILOGUE

APUS 5, 1870 O.C.
COUNTRY: ATOMIA
CITY: CIECYN

Leomaris, Eliza's brother, anticipated Ciecyn, his Atomian home and birthplace, almost as much as last year's whirlwind adventures. Thirty minutes crawled like a three-legged turtle, especially if he thought too much about his father, probably adorned in golden general boards and eagerly awaiting his return. At least, he hoped he was. The Nyvala family had claimed Ciecyn as their home for four generations and he hoped to continue so, savoring each beautiful memory. Marked by clear, blue canals and red and white buoys, their ship angled into the approach path. He could sense home more than ever. Rich blue water, teeming with colorful schools of fish, made him tingle with anticipation. He wanted to dive into its splendor and lose himself. He loved sailing and the technology that made it possible. Once a childhood fantasy, he forever longed for vast oceans and exotic destinations. With a foot in either, he could escape, discover new freedoms, and fulfill his now-insatiable cravings. It'd only be a matter of time before he'd depart on another adventure and fulfill his father's New World Order aspirations under Sovereign Xander. The reflection gave him chills.

Thrusters resonated loudly, their vibrations thumping like wide paddles mercilessly beating the water. His heart joined in the excitement. He hoped Eliza would also be waiting. His sister's arrival seemed to consummate any gathering; maybe it was because she was so much like her mother? Sentiments welled, more intense than ever;

he couldn't wait to bolt across the ramp into their embraces. Atomia represented civilization at its peak, a far cry from the varied backwaters he'd recently left. Aurelia had been the worst, completely devoid of any technology. He never seen so few flush toilets. If countries were people, Aurelia would be a pauper. Even worse, its social structure was archaic, religious, and their stubbornness to maintain slavery only widened the void between them and other progressive societies. He, Waldar, with pipe in hand, and Karla patiently watched the docking tube extend. Out of habit, he brushed through his ear-length white hair. The tubing took forever. How would his father receive a Darshan slave? Would her freedom anger him? He had thought it through as best he could; she was as old as he, a robust 16, the perfect Xander Youth League age. Never mind that he was ready to enter the famed Valkyrie training program. His father would burst with pride.

Waldar glanced out a port-side window and stroked his medium length, graying beard. He chewed nervously on the gnawed edge of a pipe and added a subtle tilt to his felt hat. While the ship's engines quieted, deck vibrations almost vanished and Leo caught himself keenly observing Karla's many changing expressions. He couldn't get enough of her dark hair and long sweeping bangs. Dark eyes and hair were non-existent in Atomia as far as he could remember. Everyone had white hair, or some minor variant. He'd have to get used to that all over again. It'd probably seem nonsensical at first. It usually did—bobbing seas of snowy heads milling about.

She wore a beige dress, his arrival gift, nothing fancy, yet closely fitted and appealing. As if a newborn, she excitedly took in the new sights and sounds. He could only imagine what was whirling through her thoughts. She had never been exposed to these technological wonders. She particularly enjoyed airships, often telling him she wanted to fly. He had all but lost the thrills she seemed to discover time and time again. Her animations were a bit disturbing, reminders of childhood gone by. It must be so special for her. He knew he was destined for all things great; there was no going back. They had spent hours going over the family's history; Karla remembered everything. He could only hope that a Darshan in the Xander Youth League would be accepted as a universal beacon of hope, proving anyone could become a player in the New World Order.

After Customs, they were soon walking across the harbor plaza; Karla craned to study a forest of buildings and colorful ships. White-uniformed sailors hurried in different directions, handling mooring lines, directing traffic, and cargo. Near the entrance to the enormous Arrival Terminal, Leo spotted Federation guards milling about, a clear indication that his father was in the vicinity. He took the cue and ran ahead, decidedly pleased with his choice; his father stood waiting. Guards were never present in large numbers unless a high-ranking official was nearby. That was how it had always been.

"Father!" Arms open, Leo collided into the elderly man, knocking him back a few steps, requiring an adjustment to his shoulder boards, oblivious to the gaping mouths of his personal guards. Today, he wore corded epaulets—it was truly a special occasion.

They laughed like old friends, awkwardly readjusting their clothing and regaining composure. Leo swelled with pride. One day, he'd be just like him. He'd have to be more careful, though. He didn't want to hurt him. The notion raised a knowing smile.

"Leo!" said his father, embracing him as if he hadn't seen him for years. "How are you, Son?"

"Couldn't be better. I have so many stories, Father. I've traveled the world and discovered technological innovations that would greatly advance our cause." It was as if he'd never left.

His father slapped Leo on the back. "That's my boy."

Out of breath with his felt hat askew, Waldar trotted up, white-knuckled grip straining to hold his pipe. "Hello, Sire."

"Waldar!" The general extended his hand. "It's good to see you, old friend. The journey wasn't too severe, I hope?" A cool grin followed.

"Not at all, Sire." Waldar poked at his pipe and struck a match. He motioned to a man struggling with an overloaded baggage cart.

Eyeing him questioningly, Nyvala couldn't conceal his pleasure. "I hope Leo behaved himself."

"No more than you did when you were his age," said Waldar with all confidence, sucking a deep draw from the fragrant cherry pipe.

"That's disturbing." Seeming comforted, Nyvala turned to Karla, scanning her up and down as if inspecting a side of beef. "And who might this be?"

"Father, this is Karla. She's of Darshani descent. I recruited her into the Xander Youth League. She'll be a global example, proving that no matter one's origin, we can better the world. Plus, it'll instill reminders that ..." Leo beamed while he wondered what his father was thinking, desperate to clue him in on the particulars. He so wanted to please him; would he receive Karla the same way?

"That's fine, Leo. I watched yesterday's video transmission. We'll discuss it once we're safely home." Nyvala nodded approvingly at Karla. "You must be exhausted, young lady."

Karla timidly returned the greeting.

Leo could sense Karla's duress, eager to ease her stress. It was nowhere nearly like when he found her in that field, starved and abused. "Where's Eliza? She always considered these reunions a priority. Is she at home?"

His father swallowed hard, shifting a clumsy glance. "When we can speak privately, we'll discuss your sister, Son. Now's not the time."

"Something vexes you, Father? I hate when you're troubled. Is she still ranting on about an anti-Federation platform?" He was unable to restrain his curiosity; he missed her more than he had realized. He glanced at Karla. Surely, she could sense his desire? "My sister has a good heart, she truly does. But she's never fully embraced Azdahri beliefs. She will soon, won't she, Father?"

"Come, Son. Another time. Our transport is snarling traffic. The boat was late; let's go home where we can relax." With an impatient wave, his father turned General. "Guards. Their bags, if you will."

Something was amiss. What was his father hiding?

Waldar followed the general. "Come. He has much on his mind."

Karla tugged on Leo's arm. "Oh, Leo! It surpasses my wildest dreams! I've never seen such structures—they're so high! And machines that fly? It's unbelievable!"

"You haven't seen anything yet. I hope you're prepared. There're many lessons you'll have to experience, above all, discipline and Federation loyalty." For the first time since they'd met, he felt detached, and not a little disturbed about his father and Eliza. Maturity magnified awareness. He was older now. Of course, this was how it was supposed to feel. He'd conceal his true feelings until they were reunited—it wouldn't be long. "You'll have meaning, genuine purpose—for most, an impossible dream." He studied her, aloof and distracted by a troop of soldiers clad in dark gray marching uniforms—black hats, boots, and gloves, the latter appearing as fitted end pieces to precision weapons—snapping across cobblestones with exacting precision. Their presence was oddly troublesome. Did his father require that much protection? Another troop, just down the street and some 50 or 60 strong, marched in an intense and echoing cadence. Pedestrians parted, timidly, warily, their white hair in striking contrast to the soldiers' dress uniforms. Some rushed into side streets. Others stood proudly, extending a Federation salute.

"I'm prepared," replied Karla, her glance darting between friend and fortitude. The sparkle in her eyes dimmed. "I want the Federation to grow into Sovereign Xander's dream. Leo, I want the entire world free and I'm excited to help in any way. Words cannot describe my feelings." She continued to glance across the plaza, carefully following the blur of precision movements.

APUS 5, 1870 O.C.
COUNTRY: VUTON
INSTITUTE VI

Headmaster Mawson, safely sequestered behind Institute VI walls, sat sullenly at a polished mahogany desk contemplating a ream of paper labeled "Status Updates: E. Nyvala; T. Hart". A sandstorm raged just beyond; pocked glass blurred the view. The situation couldn't have soured more, and, for the failures, he blamed Seryth. By all accounts, Eliza was dead, but he needed proof. It could mark a major juncture in his quest to control the outcome of the global uprising he yearned to perfect. He had caught wind of Seryth's lies, craftiness delivered to Nyvala out of fear of reprisal. Most Atomian leaders feared Nyvala, and rightly so. The highly-decorated man traced Xander's footsteps.

If Eliza were alive, she would be slated for immediate liquidation. Too many people esteemed her far too highly—especially the Reynan World Council—the catalyst in an already explosive situation; they expected her report. The reaction had heretofore been triggered, however, and now that the Federation had gained the upper hand, it was time to initiate the next stage of his grand plan: eliminate opposing elements. Braxton, Hart, and their renegade operations at a minimum, in short, anyone standing against the great Atomian nation would be crushed. That meant his private mercenary army would have their hands full.

Startled by hissing air from a sliding door, he glanced up to discover Loci Talbot, his trusted second. Nearly always groomed to perfection with flowing brunette hair smoothly brushed, the visage caused his heart to stir. Too much eye makeup for his liking, but she preferred a more intimidating look. "The Lord Commander has arrived," she announced. She rarely minced words.

Lately, in Seryth's presence, Mawson felt slightly ill, like a cold that he couldn't shake, mainly because of the man's ineptness. There was no excuse for the recent Valkyrie Tower disappointment. How could he not answer to Eliza's condition? "Excellent. Show him in."

Almost immediately, a tall, silver-haired man blew past Loci. He pushed longer than usual locks over his shoulders.

"My dear Lord Commander," said Mawson, grimacing internally. "If perceptions serve me well, you became quite carried away at the Tower. You must agree that your choices defied better judgment and have deposited you ..., well, us, as strange bedfellows, eh?"

Seryth immediately raged. "Shut up, you fool."

The angry voice wore at Mawson's fragile bearing. He clinched his fists, deliberately, hidden from view. It took everything to contain a response in kind. *No one* addressed him like that—ever—especially not a power-hungry white-haired freak.

"Has the Enlightened One contacted you?" demanded Seryth.

"No. He's waiting on us." There wasn't a hint of emotion in Mawson's candid reply.

Seryth steamed. "Well, come on! Raise him on the commlink!"

Irate at the man's lack of couth, Mawson unhurriedly used one finger to peck slowly at the keyboard. The slower, the better. A ceiling speaker clicked dully.

Triple monitors radiated Mr. Edde's image into the room. "Good morning, gentlemen." His voice, a deep timbre, synced with the trident view.

Mawson, preferring the center monitor, stared into profoundly blue eyes. "Mr. Edde. You look quite peachy this morning."

"Juicy tidings never fail to serve up a cheery mood." Mr. Edde pushed back dark brown and gray streaked hair and adjusted his glasses. He seemed more tense than usual.

"What information do you have on Eliza?" demanded Seryth, somewhat less heated.

Mr. Edde's eyes flattened when he leaned toward the camera. "So, curious are we now, Lord Commander? Was it not you who sanctioned her escape?"

"I put a bullet through the bitch. I did all that I could."

Mr. Edde hastily challenged. "And I thought you were a natural-born killer. Tsk tsk. Either you've lost your edge, or I was dead wrong, or both. Pardon the pun."

Mawson's smirk twisted in morbid retribution, elated that the man had put Seryth in his place. Less work after the call.

"Can we continue?" said Seryth edgily.

"Eliza is still alive," shouted Mr. Edde, pounding his fist. "She's alive!"

Cannons exploded in Mawson's head, the kind that left a splitting headache. Finally, the truth. Seryth *had* failed.

Seryth was indignant. "How do you know this?"

"You've forgotten who I am. I'm incredibly disappointed with you. Her very close friend supplied this information. Don't worry. I'll keep you posted with timely updates, but for now, I expect the highest confidentiality."

"What did you do to achieve such heightened betrayal?" asked Mawson.

"None of your business. Speaking of business, let's get to it! We must decommission four apostates immediately. They openly threaten our New World Order resolve. If we don't stay their illicit efforts, we risk dissolution. The first of these parasites is Princess Kiahna of Reyna, who's intent on manipulating Thracia into resisting the Federation's cause and joining her cause. She believes she can prevent a planned Aurelian massacre. Eliza Nyvala, our precious half-breed princess is second on the list. Her World Council aspirations, as well as her dangerous exploits, must cease. General Braxton, coming in at number three, is an adversary who won't tone down his terrorist organization in Amstye. I'm sending Eliza and Braxton's contracts to you. Fourth and final …," Mr. Edde hesitated and scowled heavily, taking the time to lock stares with each man. "… well, I'll handle him personally."

"What kind of game is this?" demanded Seryth.

Mr. Edde snapped back. "It's my game, Lord Commander. You've proven that you aren't as skilled a player as you led me to believe. Consider yourself demoted, immediately. Henceforth, you report to me." He gave Seryth a moment to digest. "I hope you've learned a lesson in mercy, Lord Commander."

"Mercy? Mercy can only cause demoralized dissension, an ideal in which I'm well versed." Seryth's gaze flitted downward.

"Finally—a glimmer of hope after all. Good day, gentlemen." Mr. Edde clapped once and reached forward. The room darkened.

Mawson and Seryth, opposing shadows, glared like abysmal ghosts.

"Well? What are you waiting for?" demanded Seryth. "We've definitive targets. Silence them. I expect them out of the picture, post haste!" He turned for the door.

Loci sighed. "Well? What's our next move, Headmaster?"

"The princess is not our concern—orders have already been sent to High Marshall Eston. Next move? We'll assume Ms. Nyvala and General Braxton. Patch Zeddicus Sangray through, please."

"Of course," she said. Her fingers flew across the keys; Zeddicus popped up in triplicate.

Under dull lighting, gleaming black armor glared down, dark and ominous. A metallic voice reverberated in time to flashing red along his shoulders. "Headmaster?" he quipped, expressionless.

Mawson strained through the din of blasting sand against the window, frowning more out of exasperation caused by Seryth than nature's vengeance. "Zeddicus. Loci will upload two contracts."

He nodded. The lights flashed again.

Mawson relished the next moment as if he were savoring his favorite dessert, a double serving of lemon pie. What better power play than to commission this covert operation to Institute VI's most formidable soldier. "Pay attention; I have a special request. Unfortunately, it doesn't come with a contract. The name alone should motivate you … Tristan Hart. He's been a burr in our boots for quite some time, but I believe you are just the one to afford him a grand traitor's death."

The sound of grating metal ground intensely. "It will be done."

Mawson raised a finger; a diamond sparkled, igniting unabashed conviction of absolute control. The world would be subjugated to his bidding, and, like pawns in chess, the inflexible would be repositioned or consumed. He glanced at his rook in shining black, thought of lands and knights, and pondered over castles, courts and queen. Only the astute could, would, grasp each masterful advance as he cleared unwitting opponents from his board. "Good hunting, Sangray. Let us begin! Mawson out." His pleasure caused a sigh as the knuckled digit fatefully fell; blackened screens masked destiny's incessant glow, soon to become an epic tsunami, simple surging sparks becoming a raging conflagration would storm over water and desert in unchecked madness, encompassing the world.

www.ingramcontent.com/pod-product-compliance
Lightning Source LLC
Chambersburg PA
CBHW070738190726
48292CB00002B/325